AFTERBIRTH

AFTERBIRTH

A Novel

Emma Cleary

HarperCollins*PublishersLtd*

Without limiting the exclusive rights of any author, contributor or the publisher of this publication, any unauthorized use of this publication to train generative artificial intelligence (AI) technologies is expressly prohibited. HarperCollins also exercise their rights under Article 4(3) of the Digital Single Market Directive 2019/790 and expressly reserve this publication from the text and data mining exception.

This is a work of fiction. Names, characters, places, and incidents are products of the author's imagination or are used fictitiously and are not to be construed as real. Any resemblance to actual events, locales, organizations, or persons, living or dead, is entirely coincidental.

AFTERBIRTH. Copyright © 2026 by Emma Cleary. All rights reserved. Printed in the United States of America. No part of this book may be used or reproduced in any manner whatsoever without written permission except in the case of brief quotations embodied in critical articles and reviews. For information, address HarperCollins Publishers, 195 Broadway, New York, NY 10007. In Europe, HarperCollins Publishers, Macken House, 39/40 Mayor Street Upper, Dublin 1, D01 C9W8, Ireland. In Canada, address HarperCollins Publishers Ltd, Bay Adelaide Centre, East Tower, 22 Adelaide Street West, 41st floor, Toronto, Ontario, M5H 4E3, Canada.

HarperCollins books may be purchased for educational, business, or sales promotional use. For information, please email the Special Markets Department at SPsales@harpercollins.com or in Canada at HCOrder@harpercollins.com.

hc.com

Originally published as *Our Monstrous Bodies* in the United Kingdom in 2026 by Borough Press.

Sarah Sloat, "[You could hardly have missed . . .]" from *Hotel Almighty* (2020). Used with the permission of Sarabande Books, Inc.

Typeset in Adobe Garamond Pro by HarperCollins*Publishers* India

FIRST U.S. AND CANADIAN EDITIONS

Library of Congress Cataloging-in-Publication Data has been applied for.

Library and Archives Canada Cataloguing in Publication information is available upon request.

ISBN 978-0-06-342094-6
ISBN 978-1-4434-7427-6 (Canada)

26 27 28 29 30 LBC 5 4 3 2 1

For my sisters, and yours,

and for Shane and Saoirse, always.

Part One:

All Those Strangers

1

'You'll be lonely in this city.' My sister appeared as a disembodied head on the screen of my phone. I cradled the screen in my hand before my own face, looking into hers: the lift of her thin eyebrows, dark wells beneath her eyes. 'Are you sure you want to come?'

Pallid sunlight filled the window behind her, the city she wasn't inviting me to a scant presence beyond the glass. Her head was wrapped in a stained white towel, leaching a purply dye from her hairline. It made my scalp itch just to look at it. 'You'll be bored,' she warned. 'It's not like you think. It's a long way from home, Brooke.'

Since I'd left Japan that summer, I'd been living back at Mum and Dad's, temping wherever the agency sent me and applying to arts programs with funding packages, wherever they might take me: Lancaster, Brighton, Glasgow. I was living in my childhood bedroom with a view of the other council house gardens, a little claustrophobic, my ideas of the future more or less adrift.

Mum had wallpapered the bedroom to her own taste while I was living abroad, but the walls underneath were still pockmarked from the art brut posters I'd tacked up as a teenager, and the fashion prints Izzy had pinned up before me, Parisian women sucking dainty cigarette holders. Our childhoods barely overlapped. Izzy was eleven years older and still treated me like a kid.

'I won't be lonely,' I told my sister, her face freezing for a moment and then returning to me with a curl in her upper lip, a familial expression we shared. 'I'll have you.'

I'd just got the bus home from a shift at the university library, which housed the collections for the science, technology, and engineering faculties. I shelved books, made photocopies, and answered the telephone. 'Hello, I'm a robot,' I'd say in my most professional phone voice. No one ever reacted.

What I liked about the job was that they kept us moving: workers pushed trolleys of books, hot-desked, and roved the aisles looking for lost patrons. I'd temped for the library before, and they requested me specifically from the agency whenever they needed someone. I was good at finding things the database insisted were missing – misplaced texts, jewel-cased CDs, a dissertation from 1964. 'Pray to Saint Anthony,' the other, permanent library assistants would say, nodding at me, their arms crossed. I was scared I'd made them look bad. 'Tony-Tony look-around.'

That's why I was free to go out there and be with Izzy, step out of my own life for a six-week stretch in the lead up to Christmas – because of my stopgap existence, everything in-between. Mum liked to reassure me that I was a late bloomer, which made me think she was expecting something more to happen. I was twenty-seven. I liked to joke that she'd blinked and missed me blooming, that I'd bloomed elsewhere, out of sight.

On the call, I reminded Izzy I'd lived in Japan for almost two years, all by myself. 'At least the language will be the same in Vancouver. Besides, what will you do without me? Who'll look after Sunshine?'

*

I arrived in early November, a few days before my sister's myomectomy, a procedure to remove an abnormal growth from her womb. Mum and Dad paid for my plane ticket. I was sent to Canada as a kind of proxy. Mum couldn't get the time off work – she was a school counsellor, it was midterm – and thought I'd make a good nurse, given my own recovery. While I booked the flights on her credit card, hunting for the cheapest travel dates, Mum chatted about something called a 'monthly nurse'. I think she was using the term incorrectly, as when I typed it into the search bar, the results were mainly about midwifery and postpartum confinement in the Victorian period. Monthly nurse did sound like something to do with menstruation, I supposed.

I'd been a miracle baby myself, born after a series of miscarriages once my parents had given up trying – a 'spare', Izzy called me. She had come easily, a honeymoon child from our mother's first marriage – Mum's first husband a void we never talked about. Mum treated me as if I was both blessed and terribly, temptingly precious, like I shouldn't really be here at all. A late-blooming latecomer.

I had a lot of time to think on the plane. I had to fly down to London first, so the journey was around thirteen hours. I'd dashed through the airport to make my connection, travelling between terminals on a small bus through a grey labyrinthine concourse. On the flight from Heathrow to Vancouver, the entertainment system was broken on my screen; a flight attendant tried to reset it, but quickly gave it up for more pressing concerns. With nothing to watch for the nine-hour leg, I attempted to sleep in my upright seat. But there was a baby crying, a mother pacing the aisle, shushing. I couldn't bring myself to eat airplane food; even the smell of it turned my stomach, and my head started to pound. After a while, my brain detected a pattern in the noise of the engines – or beyond the engines, a distant, strangely musical caw from the plane's underbelly, an echoing sound like a human wail as we flew over the Rockies.

I wondered about Izzy's resistance to my visit. She hated fuss, and liked to do things by herself, insisting she didn't need any help, so her reticence to accept mine hadn't surprised me – that's why I'd framed my visit the way I had, as if I was really there to look after Sunshine and not Izzy at all, not really. It was the way she'd levelled that word at me: lonely. *You'll be lonely*. Did Izzy never feel lonely, living so far from her real home, for so long? Or did she think I was especially vulnerable to loneliness, unable to make strong connections, as I had been at thirteen? But if you could unpick the shame from it, loneliness was only loneliness, no reason to stay away. It would be better to be lonely in a new place than to be lonely where I came from.

I landed in Vancouver in the dark. The plane banked as we descended from the sky, peninsula starred with lights, the ocean a black void pushing against the city's outline. As distant skyscrapers came into view, I was hit by a wave of vertigo. The descent felt endless, the plane dropping and then rising again, circling the airport, the pilot's voice an indecipherable staccato over the intercom. I folded my arms and dug my fingernails into my skin to distract myself from the lurch in my stomach.

It was after we'd landed that I felt something real: a pinch of excitement, a sick thrill of nerves. My head was swimming with fatigue, my hands shaking; I needed to swallow something sweet. Izzy had come to collect me and was waiting somewhere out there beyond the gate. It had been a long time since I'd seen my sister in the flesh – three years, come Christmas.

I dragged my suitcase along, craning my neck, when suddenly I was intercepted by another body thrown against my own. Torso pressed to mine, arms wrapped tight around me, mouth exhaling next to my ear. I squeezed the bulk of the body back before pulling away, looking into a woman's face. It took me a beat to recognize my sister.

When I thought back on this moment later, I felt foolish – who else would accost me like that at the airport? But for a moment, I'd held on to a stranger's body, searching only for the right words to extricate myself from their embrace. Neither of us were natural huggers.

'Izzy,' I said, laughing. 'I didn't recognize you.'

Izzy smiled and touched her palm to her face, as if to wipe away the scratch of my unruly hair. 'You're late. I've been waiting here for ages! What have you been doing, putting on makeup?' Despite her complaint, I could tell she was excited – she didn't get many visitors from home. She remained so uncomfortably close to me that I could see the pores in her skin. She wore no makeup at all, her hair clean-smelling and scraped back neatly from her face. 'What's that in your ear?'

My fingers went automatically to my triple helix. 'Have you just not been looking at me when we talk?' I laughed, although it was true that in person I could see changes in her that had eluded me on screen. 'I got this in Japan.'

'We don't talk often enough, I suppose. You look well.' She

squeezed my shoulder with one hand and relieved me of my suitcase with the other, steering it towards the sliding doors and escalators of the station, asking me about the journey. She wore a long wool coat that covered her whole body, from her throat to the middle of her calves, and carried a homemade sign that read: 'Party of Noone.'

'Nice little pun,' I said. Noone was our surname.

'Thanks, I was pleased with myself. Did you watch any good movies on the plane?'

'My screen was broken,' I told her. 'All I had to watch was the little plane avatar tracing lines across the map. The girl next to me kept pressing her bare feet into my leg.'

Izzy made a face to signal her disgust and sympathy. 'I'm surprised she dared with all that metal in your face,' she teased, looping her arm through mine, pulling me close to walk alongside her. 'How did you even get through security? Are you warm enough in that jacket?' She gathered me and the suitcase onto the train.

I'd landed at night, so there wasn't much to see on the SkyTrain from the airport, just points of light kaleidoscoped by the rain-streaked windows, then a tunnel under downtown. Our reflections in the glass made companions of us, and the train rocked and whined until I nodded off on Izzy's shoulder.

We climbed out of a taxi into the dark night in front of Izzy's looming apartment complex, rain pelting the pavement and dripping from the concrete slab that beetled over the glass doors of the entrance. I glanced up at the puzzle of lit windows as the driver hefted my suitcase from the car boot and Izzy paid the fare.

We were in an older part of the city than we had been driven through from the SkyTrain station – those streets flanked by tall, anonymous glass towers. The outline of Izzy's building had an austere presence, the concrete surface pitted and rough where the light touched it, with two curved columns portioning the facade into three. Black-railinged balconies jutted from the structure like ribs, and footlights illuminated the redbrick pathway from the street. The grounds seemed to have been landscaped with piles of large, jagged rocks, giving the impression that the building had emerged whole and intact from the Earth's mantle. A monolith.

We splashed inside, entering an echoey lobby space, every surface painted a dreary deep green, except for an alcove of bronze mailboxes. There was a glass-fronted manager's office just near the entrance, the desk abandoned, a coat hanging from the back of an office chair, and a bank of television screens showing black-and-white footage of the building's communal spaces.

'There's a courtyard,' Izzy said as she pressed the call button for the lift. 'I'll show you tomorrow.'

The lift deposited us in a sprawling hallway, its textured wallpaper marred here and there with a dirty handprint or black scuff lines, as though furniture had been dragged along the wall, and its carpet patterned with a swirling mass of faded orange and green leaves. Izzy's apartment was just around the corner from the lift landing, and she paused to pull her keys from her pocket at the shadowy green door. 'Oh, damn,' she said, and reached over to turn the bulb in the dusty wall sconce. It buzzed and flickered to life.

Her seventh-floor one-bed was smaller than I expected, severely neat and a little spartan, despite the chew toys scattered on the rug. Sunshine greeted me like an old friend, spinning in dizzy circles and throwing himself at my legs. Here was my future guide to the city, with a blond bearded face and dark body, a white underbelly and a woolly coat that bellbottomed around his paws. The breed was anyone's guess; he looked like he'd been crossed with a mashed potato.

'That's funny,' Izzy said as the dog rolled over to show me his belly. 'He doesn't usually like strangers. We must smell the same.' She took off her long coat and hung it in a cupboard in the hallway, then held out her hand for mine.

I'd been shocked when my clean-freak sister allowed a rescue into her home. 'Lucie kept sharing pictures of him online,' she'd said. 'He was the only one left from this lab they raided. He looked so hopeful.'

We'd had a dog when I was small, a long-haired dachshund named Maxi. Mum and Dad adopted her to keep me company, but Izzy didn't like her at first. She complained about the dog's smell and the fur it shed in dark clumps and wisps on the furniture. But I remember her crying with me when Maxi died, holding my hand and saying she was sorry, so the dog must have grown on her in the end.

Now, looking around, I wondered if Izzy had craved the company, another soul to care for. Sunshine had been so mistreated in his past ('I'll spare you the details,' Izzy said) that he required a strict regimen of medical and behavioural care. Izzy had prepared a small booklet for my reference, titled 'Looking After Sunshine' and printed in Comic Sans. It included a section on his likes and dislikes, and things to be avoided at all costs: skateboards, stairs, bridges, and tall men who walked with a limp. It was clear she loved the dog with a deep maternal efficiency.

I wheeled my suitcase into the living area, where a bookshelf sagged against the wall. A framed photograph of Mum and Izzy sat between a scented candle and a large amethyst geode, everything scrupulously dusted. 'Mum's pregnant in that,' Izzy said when she noticed me looking, though the bump was obvious, Dad's hand resting on it, the remainder of him out of frame. In the photograph, Mum and Izzy both wore their hair in two long dark plaits. 'I think it's with you. The age is about right.' Our mother was ladylike, serene, melon bellied. I took after Dad.

A pair of porcelain hands, cupped as if in supplication, held some of Izzy's white gold jewellery, small, tasteful pieces I'd seen her wear to family dinners. I recognized several cookbooks as gifts I'd sent over the years. They looked too clean to have been used.

'What's the crystal for?'

'I don't know, protection or something. It's from Lucie; she's all about that shit. She means well. Are you hungry?' Izzy stepped into the galley kitchen and started banging around inside the cupboards, while Sunshine shoved his nose inside my suitcase and ran off with a pair of balled-up socks. 'I could make you some noodles.'

'Yes, please. My stomach thinks my throat's been cut.' It was an expression Mum used. I felt its foreignness as I said it aloud in Izzy's apartment, though she herself sounded the same, just as she always had, just like us.

My last meal had been at breakfast time in the UK. My addled brain couldn't work out how many hours that had been; I'd crossed time zones between our two kitchens, an eight-hour gap. My stomach growled and clenched as I unpacked the things Mum had sent over and set them on the coffee table: Bisto gravy granules, three tubs of Maykway curry, packet of Paxo stuffing, Quality Street chocolates. My body still felt in motion, the apartment thrumming in waves around me. 'Is it okay if I take a shower?'

'Go ahead. It's the door next to the front door, on your right when we came in.' Like it was possible to lose my way. There was only the bedroom and the hall cupboard's concertina door to confuse it with.

The bathroom was windowless and dated, with a mint-green tub, toilet and sink; the linoleum had seen better days, and a large, tarnished mirror doubled the room. But Izzy's towels were bright white, freshly laundered, and her shampoo smelled of coconut.

I brushed my wet hair out with Izzy's bristle brush and then coiled it into a snake on top of my head, knotting it into itself as I couldn't find any pins. I was still growing out an undercut Cecelia had given me. I touched the shorter strands of hair in the unfamiliar mirror, remembering the tiny bathroom in Ogaki: the blades whirring in Cecelia's hand, the red woven bracelet circling her wrist, her breath on the nape of my neck.

Mum had given me a pair of new pyjamas for the trip and Izzy a matching set for the hospital. I put mine on and joined Izzy at the table, where she'd set a steaming bowl of noodles and a slice of buttered white bread. I waited for her to comment on my hair, the underside exposed, the rest in a twist of reddish curls on top of my head, but she was busy texting somebody. I could tell because she moved her lips slightly as she composed the message. It was late, so it must be someone from home. Or was it too early there? 'Is that Mum?'

Izzy placed her phone face-down on the table, its surface covered with a plastic cloth, easy to wipe. 'Just checking the weather for your first week. Lots of rain, I'm afraid. Eat your noodles and we can go to bed. You must be tired.'

The broth was salty and spicy, exactly what I needed. Izzy laughed when I placed the bread on top of the dish, to let the butter melt into the noodles. 'You used to eat them like that when you were a kid.' She ignored her phone when it pinged again, watching me twist my fork, watching me eat. For the first time I considered that her protests about my visit hadn't been for my sake or born of her own stubbornness. Maybe my presence here meant the absence of someone else.

Izzy rested her chin on her fist. 'You eat so beautifully now,' she said. 'You'd never know.'

She didn't comment on my hair at all.

2

That first night, Izzy changed into a baggy T-shirt inside her walk-in wardrobe. She'd left the door ajar, the contours of her body illuminated beneath the overhead light, her stomach swollen and rounded as if she was pregnant. She'd sent me photos of her bloated figure, but it was something else to see her struggle out of her clothes, the tenderness palpable.

She moved differently – different, at least, to the way she'd moved when I'd last seen her, at home, before I moved to Japan. She'd zip around the kitchen helping Mum with dinner, always throwing on a chic outfit to run out and meet old friends in town, and sweet-talking Dad for a lift. Dad and Izzy were close; he'd raised her since she was a tiny child. It wasn't until I was a teenager that I'd found a photograph album from my mother's first wedding, her face so young, put the dates together and realized that Izzy and I were half-sisters. When I asked Mum about it, she simply said, 'Oh, I thought you knew.'

Now Izzy was showing me her stretchy elasticated trousers, of which she owned half a dozen pairs. 'Do you remember when Mum used to make you take me clothes shopping?' I asked, folding myself neatly under the covers at the edge of the mattress. Both nightstands were clear except for a matching pair of lamps, an alarm clock on her side, a box of tissues on mine.

'She didn't *make* me.' Izzy squeezed a blob of cream into her palm from a tube, then rubbed it into her hands and elbows. 'I just couldn't bear to see you in those goth outfits of yours. God, remember that velvet hat you loved? Tragic.'

'I think that was my grunge phase, actually.'

'All that hanging around town, buying scarves and joss sticks from Quiggins with those gawky little friends of yours.'

'Well, I was gawky, too,' I said cheerfully.

On those shopping trips Izzy would turn me to face the changing-room mirror, tugging and prodding at straps and waistbands, then get fed up when I couldn't make up my mind. She was always sighing over how skinny I was, and then sucking in her own stomach, though I was still technically a child and she'd have been in her twenties.

She sank into the mattress next to me, radiating heat where our bodies touched. 'Bloody hell, Izzy,' I said. 'Aren't you warm?'

'Boiling.' She rolled away onto her side and pressed a pillow between her thighs – to support her hips, she said, apologizing for turning her back to me, and put out the light. It was only dark for a moment, then the city lights pressed at the window, casting our bodies below the covers in an eerie green glow.

We'd shared rooms and beds before. We knew each other's bodies, our humiliations and insecurities: she'd taught me how to tweeze my eyebrows and squeeze blackheads from her chin, both of us staring into the magnifying mirror on top of Mum's dresser.

Izzy had left for Canada a few weeks before my sixteenth birthday, to build a life with a man who left her shortly afterwards, Martin

Feathers. I always gave him his full name whenever I thought of him. Mum called him Marty-with-the-tattoos. After he left, Izzy stayed in the starter apartment they'd rented together – this one. It was odd to think that Martin Feathers, a person who'd become so obsolete to us, had once lived with my sister within these walls, had been the reason she'd left us in the first place. He might even have slept in the same bed we were sharing.

I was about to ask her about him when her phone buzzed against the surface of the nightstand. She swore and reached out to silence it.

'Izzy, are you seeing someone?' I asked into the room. 'Am I in the way?'

'Of course not,' she scolded me. 'Why would I keep something like that from you?'

'I can think of lots of reasons.' I spread out beneath the covers on my back. 'He could be, like, a Hells Angel. Or really hairy. Or a secret agent. I've kept my own liaisons quiet for these exact reasons.'

'Very funny. But no. I'm *alone*. Well, not quite.' She looked pointedly at Sunshine, who snored like an old grandad from the carpet, the lump of him obscuring the band of light beneath the doorway. The gap was abnormally large, the door ill-fitting in the frame. Before coming to bed, Izzy had administered an array of pills and serums to the dog, which she promised to explain to me when I was up to it.

A small plastic animal crate sat in the corner of the bedroom, its interior lined with an old plush robe Sunshine had taken a fancy to when he first arrived from the rescue centre. He'd carry all sorts of things in there: a dirty stuffed chipmunk Lucie had bought him, an odd sock, bits of old receipts. Izzy enforced a strict embargo on removing him from the crate or taking things from him in there. He needed to be afforded a space that was entirely his, free from human interference – she liked to allow him some autonomy, she said. He seemed to prefer sleeping on the carpet.

Izzy and I struggled to sleep – it was strange to be lying next to one another. She turned her whole body to face me, support pillow and all. We whispered to each other about family holidays, as if we were scared to wake someone. Maybe we imagined our parents on the other side of the wall, instead of Izzy's neighbour, whose three-year-old sang herself to sleep.

'Don't those shadows look like the Babadook?' Izzy said, pointing into the sick green dark.

'Where?' I was surprised Izzy had seen the film. *Ghost* was more her scene.

'From the curtains, on the ceiling. There, see?' Her breath brushed my ear. 'Ba-ba-dooook!' she croaked.

'Fuck off, Izzy!'

It was the last thing I said to her before we quieted down and I finally drifted off, dreaming myself back onto the SkyTrain, my head against my sister's narrow shoulder.

Izzy kept her phone by the bed each night, and checked it whenever she woke, the bright square lighting the room. She got up to use the bathroom frequently, one of her symptoms. In those first days, hunger would gnaw at my stomach at around four a.m. I'd eat a piece of toast in the dark box Izzy called a kitchen and then crawl back into bed. I always washed my hands but Izzy detected crumbs in the sheets. She swore she could smell butter.

Izzy worked the day shift at the restaurant right up to her surgery, so I had some time to kill. She'd leave in mornings black as midnight and return not long before sunset. I'd hang out with Sunshine or put him in his harness and take him for walks, alert for any signs of discomfort. Izzy made me promise not to exert the dog too much, citing a degenerative spinal condition the vet was seeking to stave off. No frisbee in the park for our happy little mutt. No tussling with animals larger. Though Izzy paid into a pet insurance plan, Sunshine's conditions were all pre-existing, so these instructions protected her financial security as well as the health of the dog. She told me that even a couple of X-rays had set her back thousands of dollars. She spoke at great length about the dog's care and not at all about her own impending procedure.

It was through these short, circular walks with Sunshine that I oriented myself to the neighbourhood traffic, its steamy coffee-shop doorways dripping with wet coats and umbrellas, green-awninged grocers with discounted pumpkins spilling onto the street. Where we'd grown up, all the houses looked the same, but here the blocks were lined with a patchwork of weathered apartment buildings, concrete towers, and bright clapboard houses split into flats. Red handprints splattered windows and a severed foot hung from a tree – leftover Halloween decorations. Sunshine kicked off at a yard scarecrow, and people laughed at him in the street.

It was possible to follow Izzy's street all the way to Stanley Park and be on the seawall in about twenty minutes, longer if I took the dog. I'd done this on my first full day while Izzy was at work, hitting the park and then turning towards ocean, the smell of pine resinous in the wet. A golden aspen, startling against the grey slate of sea, released its yellow leaves over the two of us, in the throes of a gorgeous death scene.

Pedestrians stopped in their tracks to say a kind word to Sunshine – the dog had a happy demeanour, his mouth open in the guise of a smile and his tongue lolling from his mouth as he trotted along. 'So cute!' they'd say, or 'Sweet little guy!'

The name Izzy had chosen was a big hit. 'Sunshine?' they'd repeat in near-delight. 'Hi, Mister Sunshine!' They asked a lot of the same questions, to which I had no answer: what breed is he, how old, was it difficult to train him, how big will he get? 'I think this is it,' I'd say, sheathing my hand with a poop bag, 'he's not a puppy any more,' adding, 'I'm sorry, he doesn't like strangers,' when he snubbed their advances. I encountered more skateboards and more tall men with limps than I ever had before, sending Sunshine into a spin. In these moments, he produced a guttural noise and lashed out like something from *The Exorcist*. The transformation was extreme. One man got to his knees to croon 'I love you' into Sunshine's ear outside Lucky's Donuts. I paused with bated breath for Sunshine's reaction as he weighed the man up, friend or foe? He licked sugar from the man's fingers before dismissing him.

Almost spectral with jetlag, I walked the gridded streets as if I hadn't quite arrived with my body, Sunshine pulling me along by the purple lead, having all these interactions. I'd heard Vancouver was unfriendly, but with a dog it seemed nobody would leave you alone. No matter how incorporeal you felt, they'd confront you with your own existence.

I'd wake up famished and energetic, excited to explore, but burn out quickly after cooking eggs, confused by something as simple as someone crossing my path on the street. My body temperature careened all over the place, overheating on a street corner one minute and shivering inside my jacket the next. I had to remind myself to drink water, guzzling a glass down just as Sunshine lapped from his bowl when we returned to the apartment.

These were familiar symptoms from my first days in Japan. My arrival there had felt somehow sudden and surprising, despite the fact that I'd gone through a lengthy application process that included a panel interview at the Japanese Consulate in Edinburgh. When they asked me why I wanted to work in Japan, I floundered for a way to answer the question without simply saying, *I want to be far away*. I had a dog-eared copy of Jun'ichirō Tanizaki's *The Makioka Sisters* in my bag under the plastic orange chair, and my hand reached for it automatically before my eyes fell upon a floral brooch one of the panellists had pinned to their blouse. 'I love irises,' I said, entering what I can only describe as a sort of fugue state in which I enthusiastically regurgitated the contents of a TV show about Japanese gardens that I had watched some time before with my parents, sitting between the two of them on the sofa.

I'd graduated a couple of years earlier with an English degree, was broke and still living at home, commuting to my admin job and imagining myself trapped forever in my childhood bedroom. Part of me wanted to follow in Izzy's more worldly footsteps, or even to one-up her – working abroad in Japan for a couple of years sounded a lot more exciting than emigrating to Canada with your boyfriend. Later, I found out that Cecelia's interview had been held on the same day at the Consulate, and I sifted my memory for any flash of a silver-blonde curl, half convincing myself we had brushed elbows in a doorway.

When I finally dropped my bags inside my little apartment in Ogaki – the address scrawled on a piece of paper in my purse – I felt a surge of panic. I'd poured my future into this moment, and now I was stranded in a sleepy castle town I'd never heard of, entirely alone.

I met some of my fellow English teachers at orientation. The program rep, Tanaka-san, walked us along the market street pointing out local delicacies and monuments to Bashō – the poet had ended his most important journey and resulting masterwork in Ogaki. We crowded a row of street vending machines, buying green tea and peach juice, putting our coins into the slot and laughing like children before Tanaka-san moved us along. He showed us how to use the town's spring water wells, using only the ladles provided to fill our drinking bottles, never contaminating the water with our hands. Three old men were sitting on the stone steps around the well, filling large plastic containers and encouraging us to try the water. I didn't have a bottle with me, so I cupped my hands and Tanaka-san ladled a cold splash of water into them. I brought my hands to my mouth. 'Samui ne,' said one of the old men cheerfully, an arm braced across the worn knees of his trousers.

Although I'd felt a bit abandoned in Japan at first, I didn't feel like a tourist. I'd ride my bike to the train station, thinking *I have a job, I'm really here!* My trip to Vancouver had the same sort of urgency, a visitation shaped by service and love.

I tried cooking for my sister. I thought she'd be sick of the kitchen from her long days at the restaurant, but she'd bring food home or purse her lips at my amateur attempts at tuna salad or spaghetti puttanesca; my curry tasted nothing like Mum's. Izzy invented errands to keep me busy, sending me out to pick up toiletries or library books her friends had recommended – on fertility diets and attachment styles, with titles that taught me new meanings for words like *breadcrumbing* – though she never appeared to read them. Izzy didn't believe in sitting around and made it her goal to prevent me from doing so. She circled art galleries on tourist maps, knowing I was into that sort of thing.

On Tuesday, Izzy didn't arrive home at the usual time. I started to worry – she'd looked especially tired the night before, with heavy grey shadows beneath her eyes. I'd already walked Sunshine twice and fell asleep with him on the sofa while I waited for my sister. It was almost midnight at home, and I must have slept heavily because it was a dream-soaked sleep, the contours of which fell away with the buzz of my phone from the arm of the sofa. It took me a few moments to realize where I was, the dog stretched out beside me with a battered stuffed lamb, its threaded eyes eaten away.

Staying late, Izzy had texted. *Last minute, sorry! Eat without me.*

I sighed. I needed something to keep me awake, otherwise I'd never get myself on West Coast time. I went into the bathroom, splashed water on my face and ran my fingers through my hair, then slicked on a smear of purplish lipstick. 'Sorry, Sunny,' I told the dog. I gave him a treat to keep him busy while I slipped out the front door.

Tuesday was the Vancouver Art Gallery's entry-by-donation evening; it was also discount day at the local cinema, and there was a nice-looking Italian restaurant offering a deal for fifteen-dollar pasta. I'd done my research before I came. I'd earned about twelve hundred quid in my latest stint at the library, so I had spends, but I wasn't sure how long I'd need it to last, what kind of work I might get when I returned home. I had a list of queer art spaces I wanted to check out, but most of them were on the other side of the city, east over the bridge, and I didn't have my bearings yet. There was a warehouse venue that put on drag musicals and dance parties, and I thought I might take Izzy along before the end of my trip for a gentle post-surgery celebration, if all went well with her recovery. We'd never done anything like that together before.

I'd gone to the gallery for the Giacometti exhibition, but was disappointed to find it was over. For all my careful planning, I'd mixed up the dates. In my head, I'd been expecting to see *Dog* again. We'd met before, at the Tate Liverpool, before I went to Japan. I loved it because, when I saw it, the sculpture felt like me; I had an impulse to get down on all fours in the gallery space. All sorts of words flooded my brain, like *hangdog* and *gaunt* and *lope*. The figure felt very alive, as if I'd seen myself through sheets of rain, slinking around a street corner in a busy city. I could feel the brittle cradle of the pelvis under my own skin. It felt much more like me than *Standing Woman* or *Woman with Her Throat Cut*, which I'd stared at for a long time, unmoved. The gallery label for *Dog* read: Self-Portrait, bronze, 1951.

The VAG was offering a Cindy Sherman retrospective, which took up each of the large ground-floor rooms of the gallery. I'd never seen Sherman's work before. Around that time, I'd fastened on to women artists working in their eighties and nineties. I liked to hear them talk, watch footage of them moving purposefully around their studios, lodged inside their insights and eccentricities: Louise Bourgeois building cells guarded by huge spider sculptures, calling them *existence*; Paula Rego filling her studio with costumes and mannequins, drawing chapters in the lives of childhood toys.

I picked up a thin pamphlet about Sherman's photographs and videos to read as I wandered the rooms. The first was darkened for a film rolling on the wall – an animated short, depicting the artist as a paper doll. Sherman's cut-out figure tried on dresses until she was returned to a plastic sleeve by a gargantuan hand. Opposite the film, a light shone over a book of photographs called *A Cindy Book*.

It followed Sherman through childhood and adolescence, a kind of family album. The exhibition pamphlet told me that Sherman had started to make it when she was six years old. She'd circled her face and body in green ink and written 'Thats me,' underneath every permutation of herself. The photos were numbered and glued inside what looked like a school exercise book, the pages yellow with age. *Thats me, Thats me, Thats me*, the photographs said, devoid of apostrophe, the artist's handwriting seeming to change over time – sometimes in pencil, sometimes in the green marker pen. In the pamphlet, Sherman explained her impulse behind the creation of *A Cindy Book* as a way of finding herself in the family – she was much younger than her older siblings. I looked at the book for a long time, especially the family photographs, that thick green line marking her out – *there I am*, it seemed to insist, *among the others.*

My altered state had created a kind of delay or gap, and somehow I found myself swept along inside a tour group. A guide walked us around the gallery's white rooms, describing notable moments in Sherman's career. Most ground-breaking was her *Untitled Film Stills*, a series of seventy small, mostly black-and-white glossy photographs. Sherman had made many of the images inside her own apartment, the guide told us, recruiting friends to help her shoot as she posed in wigs and costumes, the cityscape behind her a rear screen projection on her apartment wall. Though she wasn't recreating any particular film scenes, there was something familiar and uncanny about the images. These were not self-portraits, but a catalogue of female types – *pure persona*, the guide said. But the photographs felt intimate to me, the women vulnerable, lost in thought or on the precipice of crisis. There was something transfixing about seeing them hung together on the gallery wall, as if they all belonged to the same cinematic universe.

After the tour, I wandered back there, to Sherman's film stills. One of the pieces in the exhibition was worth more than three million dollars, but they couldn't tell us which one because it would cause both a security risk and a terrible crowding of the artwork. Something told me it was none of these small, modest images – the artworks grew larger in scale as I walked around the exhibit, the costumes more elaborate – but they were my favourites. I closed my eyes and tried to picture myself as a '60s film starlet with heavy kohl and backcombed hair, my skin smoothed to greyscale. After a while, I noticed the guide standing behind me. She smiled when I looked at her. 'It's the orange one,' she whispered, fingering the silver amulet around her neck. 'Over there.'

'Oh.' I laughed. 'I'm not looking for that.' The sound of stiletto heels echoed off the white walls. 'Why aren't these self-portraits, did you say? Do the costumes obscure who she really is? Can't they tell us anything?' I resisted the urge to reach out and touch the glass. Wasn't it still her, underneath? *That could be me, That could be me?*

The guide spoke for a while about Hitchcock and French New Wave cinema without seeming to answer my question; maybe I'd missed some nuance, something Cecelia could have explained to me later, in bed. I smiled and smiled as the guide talked, then I thanked her and traced my steps through the exhibition space. I wondered if Izzy would be home yet.

I bought a child's set of mixed pastels and an art card of one of the film stills in the gift shop. I chose number thirteen, because Sherman played a glamorous blonde, reaching for a book about dialogue on a high shelf. *Crimes of Horror*, one of the other spines blared. *THE MOVIES*, said another. The photograph reminded me of the stacks at the library back home, where I'd get bored doing shelf revision between the rolling bookshelves with their arcane handles and fantasize about all manner of things: Cecelia discovering me balanced on a kick stool, her face lit with forgiveness, a lusty tumble onto the green carpet.

I left the gallery and walked back to Izzy's place along Robson Street with the tourist map in my jeans pocket, rain pounding the pavement around me. I'd forgotten to take the umbrella Izzy had set aside for me, so by the time I reached the apartment I was soaking wet. I greeted Sunshine and dried my hair on one of Izzy's pristine bath towels.

I placed the art card on Izzy's shelf with the truncated family portrait – Izzy, Mum, baby bump, Dad's hand. Izzy noticed it instantly when she arrived home, full of apologies for her lateness.

'It's only nine o'clock,' I said, already on the sofa in my sweatpants.

Shrugging out of her coat, she picked up the Sherman and made a face. 'You finally made it to the VAG, then?'

'I was waiting for the cheapo night. It was good timing on your part.'

Izzy went to the hallway to hang up her coat. 'Sorry, again. We were just swamped. Did you eat? Something more than toast, I hope?'

'I'm good.' I went to the shelf to look at the film still more closely. Gelatin silver print. Almost poetry. There was an ominous air about the image, the girl looking up and over her shoulder, as if reaching for the book was somehow transgressive. I realized that of all the film stills, this one looked the most like Cecelia, with her bleached blonde hair and vampy aesthetic. I slipped the art card under Izzy's amethyst, to keep it safe.

3

The interior of Izzy's apartment building was curious, with corridors branching off all over the place, patterned wallpapers from the '70s, psychedelic carpets, and potted ficus plants lining the lobby. From the street the building looked starkly symmetrical, almost brutalist – though scarred by weather and eroding at the edges – but on the inside it seemed to sprawl according to its own internal logic, like a warren. I walked the same path each day from Izzy's apartment to the lift and out through the lobby, but I could swear I noticed changes. A mirrored surface where I expected to find an exit. A happy-face sticker smiling from the wrong door.

The building was named the Leonora, after a woman who had won a local Mother's Day contest for exemplary mothering, according to a framed, decades-old newspaper article near the bronze mailboxes in the lobby. Clutching Izzy's household bills and supermarket flyers, I skimmed the yellowed article – it was scattered with phrases like 'family values' and 'sanctity of motherhood'. The headline ran: Meet City's Monumental Mom.

Standing in front of the newspaper print felt a little like discovering a time capsule, and I had an urge to bury it on the grounds. Izzy had given me a cursory tour of the narrow interior courtyard, which was entirely hidden from the street and seemed to serve mainly as a smokers' den, judging from the butts collected beneath the gnarled, woody lavenders in the flower beds. But she hadn't shown me the basement rooms yet – for laundry, rubbish and such – and I was reticent to go down there alone, even in the middle of the day.

Sometimes I ran into an old woman roaming the halls or grounds in a housecoat rich with grime, her face pressed into a permanent scowl. I was walking Sunshine the first time I noticed her beyond the building. She appeared like a sentry on a street corner as I passed, then trailed behind me at a distance, muttering to herself and wearing the housecoat even in public, her grey hair loose. She'd looked frayed, pecked, and crumby, as though she'd been feeding the pigeons. When we reached the glass-fronted lobby of the Leonora, I held the door open for her. She snapped crossly at me to let it go. 'I can do it myself!'

'Sorry.' I turned and let the door bang shut behind me. I kept my back to the door as I waited for the lift, but she didn't come inside. I felt her eyes burning a hole in my jacket. Sunshine strained at the end of the lead towards the window, and when I turned, I caught her tapping the glass.

When she noticed me looking, her hand dropped and her face became a mask. With the scowl gone, she looked somehow absent, with large, striking features, her jaw puddled with soft jowls, her cheeks hollow. I pulled Sunshine away.

'Oh, her?' Izzy said. 'She's part of the furniture. She's rude as fuck to everyone, don't worry, it's not just you.' I sat on her bed as she packed a bag for the hospital, stuffing it with thick maxi pads. 'It's like always being on your period,' she said when she saw me looking.

'But worse.' Her symptoms had started years before with sharp cramps and unpredictable bleeding. She'd endured menstrual clots and rushes of blood that had surprised her at work and in hotel beds, sheets soaked in red, a ruined sofa. A terrible embarrassment in the restaurant kitchen, her friend Sasha mopping the tile. She used the word *flooding*.

This wasn't her first visit to the specialist about her condition – she'd been reporting her symptoms for years and had been sent for numerous exploratory scans. But over the last eighteen months or so things had grown rapidly worse. 'It feels like I'm going in to have a baby or something,' she said, a hand on her bloated stomach.

Or something. I mimicked the rapid breathing I'd seen couples do in Lamaze classes on American sitcoms. 'Breathe,' I told her. 'Breathe.'

She laughed, mirthlessly. 'We call her Medusa. Bit sad, really. I hope I never get like that.'

'Why Medusa?'

'Because of her hair? I think so anyway. I can't remember where I heard it. She's been here forever. Gets a bit curious about the new ones. Or the new ones are curious about her. I hardly see her now.'

'But she must have been here when you moved in?'

'Yeah, I'm sure she was. Come to think of it, I saw more of her after I got Sunshine. But there was this whole drama about a dog turd in the hallway. I think some of the older residents were playing detective.'

'Sunshine! You wouldn't do that, would you?' I scratched behind the dog's ears.

The dog watched Izzy closely as she packed, his head twitching back and forth, accounting for each secreted object. Every now and then he let out a strained little whine, as if he recognized that she was going away. I thought briefly of one of Sherman's film stills – a suitcase open on the bed, a woman pressing her back against the wall, her eyes squeezed shut. I could have sworn there was even a dog in the image, but my memory could have been playing tricks.

'You've got to admire the way she clearly doesn't give a fuck. I hope I give less of a fuck when I'm old.' I tilted my head. 'Fewer fucks?'

'Really? I hope I still care.' She cut the tags off her new silky pyjamas and folded them into the bag. 'A nightie would've been better. Why did Mum get me the same as you? She should know.'

Izzy had been told to pack for up to four days, *just in case, hopefully out in two*, and folded in her most matronly nighties – white cotton, calf-length and billowy – along with the pyjamas.

'The PJs can be your party clothes,' I said.

'Ha.'

It wasn't just that Izzy preferred nightdresses but that a nightdress would be easier for her after the operation. Mum should know because of the hysterectomy she'd had more than a decade earlier – those visits we made to her hospital ward, ignoring the urinary catheter bag hanging indiscreetly at the side of her bed. Izzy making a promise to do all the vacuuming when she came home.

'I'd love to draw her,' I said. 'Medusa.' There'd been something commanding about her wrinkled face, the arch of her noble nose and fleshy, broad jaw.

Izzy's phone pinged, then pinged again. She picked it up and stared into the screen.

'You should get that attached to your hand,' I said.

'Sorry. Lucie's messaging me by the minute. Wishing me luck.'

I wanted to ask Izzy if she was scared, to excavate any complicated feelings she might have about the myomectomy, the hopes she had for life after. But I was scared I might make her feel worse, violate her stoicism. I kept saying *how are you feeling about everything* instead, which at once felt too general and like some sort of salvo.

'How are you feeling about everything?' I reached out a hand and thumped her shoulder. 'Really.'

'Okay.' She smiled ruefully. 'I just want to get it over with.'

In truth I was a little jealous she kept turning to Lucie, when there I was standing right in front of her. But why would she turn to me? Serious about her role as big sister, she never had before, not really. With me, she brave-faced. I had no idea how to make a way for her to open up. We were fixed in our old, lifelong positions, like Giacometti's bronze statues.

'Imagine how you'll feel when you come out,' I tried. 'Not straight away, obviously. But in a few weeks, or months. You can go swimming again.'

She exhaled, dropping the phone onto the bed. 'I suppose that's true. Whatever happens, I'll be glad to be rid of this.' She pressed her hands over her swollen stomach, making a sort of triangle slightly to the right of her bellybutton. 'It's like carrying something knotted inside you the whole time. It's not soft, you know? It's hard. Like a big firm muscle. Feel it.'

I leaned across the bed and reached out my fingers, but hesitated, holding back. 'I'm scared I'll hurt you.'

She grabbed my fingers and prodded them into her stomach until I felt a hard, irregular lump through the fabric of her shirt. I even thought I felt a sort of bumpy ridge, like a misshapen elbow or an unripe star fruit. It shifted beneath my fingers.

'Oh,' I said, pulling my hand away. 'Sorry. It's like . . . a spare knee or something.'

Izzy snorted. 'To be honest, it's hard to remember what my body felt like before, so I'm really not sure how I'll feel after.'

'Are you scared?'

'Yes.'

'Of the pain?'

'Not really. Well, yes. It's not going to be nice, but I can't be a baby about that. It's more the outcome that . . .' She tucked several pairs of underwear into the bag's side pocket. 'But I can't wait any longer, in case it gets bigger. If it keeps growing like this, there'll be fewer options.' She pulled the zipper closed and finally met my gaze. 'That should do. Don't worry about coming in with me; I'll take a cab in the morning. You stay here with Sunshine.'

'No, of course not. I'll walk Sunshine while you shower, then come with you.'

'There's no need.'

'I'll come straight back if you really want me to. But I want to be there. Will you let me, please, Izzy?'

'If you want,' she relented, rolling her eyes, and I clapped my hands, startling the dog.

Under the covers that night, I thought I heard a soft cry. I held my breath; I felt Izzy holding hers. I turned towards her, but she kept her back to me, the shape of her body clearly outlined by the light coming in through the window. Wisps of her hair tipped in that eerie green.

I wanted to hold her, like maybe I would have done, once, when we were younger. But she was holding herself stiff as a board, braced for any attempt against her defences. I put my outstretched hand in a star against her back. She flinched. 'I'm okay,' she said. 'Honest.'

'You're upset.'

'I'm not upset,' she insisted, her voice perfectly even. I sat up and passed her a tissue from the box on my nightstand, brushing it against her bare arm. She took it.

'I'm sorry I'm not better at this,' I told her. 'I wish I knew—'

'I'm not upset.' She sniffed, crumpling the tissue. 'I'm looking forward.' She reached over and patted me awkwardly. 'I need my rest. Go to sleep. I'm not upset.'

'You are looking forward,' I agreed, trying to strike the same note of confidence. 'Night, Iz.' I turned away, but shifted a little closer to her in the bed, so I could feel her body heat, our breath rising and falling together. My body remembered the feel of the growth inside her and shuddered. With a horrid clarity, I thought: *knuckle*. That's what it had felt like. A joint of meat. I tried to put the thought out of my head, afraid that Izzy might intuit my revulsion and push me away. But the thought pressed itself against me, *knuckle, knuckle*, and my dreams were full of the abattoir, splattered with red and rich with gristle.

When I woke in the morning, her bag was gone and the bed was empty but for me.

4

When I got to the hospital, Izzy was still in theatre. *Under the knife*, I thought, and shivered. I was surprised; her surgery should have been over. 'That can't be right,' I told the nurse. 'Are you sure? It's Isobel Noone, like midday, but with an "e" on the end.'

The nurse looked at me like I was talking nonsense.

'Did something happen? I'm her sister.'

The nurse deftly ignored my concern and advised me to go home. It was a routine procedure, she said. But Izzy had had so many problems. Last year she thought she had appendicitis. When they opened her up, her pelvis was full of 'bad blood' from a burst cyst. Why did the language sound so garish and at the same time so mechanical? *Cyst. Uterine. Fibroid.* The words were probably from the moon, etymologically speaking. Or madness. Or entrails.

I wasn't sure what I should do at the hospital window, the nurse having already dismissed me. Should I demand to speak to a doctor? Buy something for Izzy from the gift shop and have it waiting for her when she came out of surgery – an oversized, overstuffed animal in the chair by her bed where her sister should be, like one of Paula Rego's studio creatures?

I traipsed back to the apartment to wait. I crossed the intersecting red bricks of the wet pathway and passed under the dripping concrete lip over the entrance, bumping into an old-timer Sunshine was fond of in the lobby. I'm not sure he recognized me without the dog. Neighbours would sometimes stop me to pet Sunshine, but they never asked my name. 'Enjoy your walk,' they'd say politely, and we'd head out into the rain.

November was all rain, even when it wasn't. Early that morning, Sunshine had been circling a scent while I stood unwashed and looking like death, swaddled in a hoodie on the street corner. I could hear rainfall all around me, dripping from the barren oaks lining the pavement and sloshing in the gutters as cars drove by. But I couldn't feel the rain, and when I went back inside, my clothes were dry. The raindrops must have missed me.

The relentless quality of the rain reminded me of tsuyu in Japan, those wet weeks as spring cleared the way for summer and the fruit ripened, baskets of yellow, red, and purple plums for sale along the market street. The rain came in gentle, insistent waves, the atmosphere humid and monotonous. Our elderly neighbour, Yamamoto-san, had warned us it was coming – she'd effortlessly recruited me to water her houseplants and overstuffed balcony garden whenever she went to stay with her son in Okayama. But still I'd been surprised at the contrast – temperate afternoons ceding to dull, wet skies and mould blooming in freshly bought loaves of bread, between the pages of books, on a jacket hung near the window.

I pushed the key into the lock and swung Izzy's green door open, kicking off my scuffed boots in the hallway. Sunshine was snuffling the living room rug intently; I must've dropped toast crumbs at breakfast. 'Sunshine, aren't you going to say "hello"?' In reply, he sneezed.

The empty rooms were fraught with suspense. I checked my phone in case I'd missed a message from the hospital. While Izzy was at work, it had been almost pleasant to have the apartment to myself. Now the place felt vacant despite the presence of my sister's well-worn belongings, a cavity full of odd furniture that didn't rhyme, like a sad waiting room.

My apartment in Ogaki had been decorated with tatami mats and sliding shoji, the translucent paper panels making the interior walls feel somehow permeable – to light and shadow, the noise of insects and traffic, and the vibration of footsteps. The apartment was inside a small four-storey building close to the river, a quick bike ride to Liquor Mountain, which sold foreign foods as well as booze. I'd inherited a green bicycle and most of my furniture from the teacher who'd lived there before me. In fact, I'd had to pay for them, though I drew the line at using the stained futon mattress and went out to buy my own. I cycled everywhere, including to the mattress shop, which had posed some difficulties on the way back, and I had to pull over to the side of the road and call Daniel, a gentle Australian I had met at Tanaka-san's orientation, to come and help me.

Three of the apartments adjacent to mine were inhabited by other teachers on the program – Daniel, Rivkah, and Audrey – and we'd knock on each other's doors whenever we felt like company. At weekends the four of us would climb onto the rooftop with the booze we'd bought at Liquor Mountain, for a view of the rice fields at the outskirts of town, their umber pools reflecting a watery sky. In those early days, Daniel would lie flat on his back and watch the clouds tracking the sky overhead, the rest of us using his body to rest our heads. We tended to a neglected juniper bush that had been abandoned up there in a plant pot, naming it, for some unknown reason, Bruce.

During term time, I'd cycle or catch the train to the village schools for work. But while the children were on summer break, we reported each day to the offices of the Board of Education. When I first arrived in Ogaki in August, that's how I'd spent my days, sharing a desk near the door with Audrey, watching the workings of a Japanese office. We were supposed to be making lesson plans, but could only do this in the most general terms, having little knowledge of the schools, teachers, or students we'd be working with. We made basic notes: 'Animal names, can you guess?' 'What things do you like/dislike?' 'Directions!' Audrey read manga and drew funny little comics for her future students, while I filled pages with hiragana, trying to memorize the sounds. I even copied the characters onto the back of a letter home to my parents, as if I was a kid again, showing off my schoolwork.

What I learned at the Board of Education was that the most important workers in the room sat farthest from the door. If you finished work before your co-workers, you had to say goodbye before you left for the day: 'osaki ni shitsureishimasu'. Excuse me for leaving before you. I loved these formal phrases and used to write them down in the pocket diary the teaching program had given us to organize our days. My favourite was 'yoroshiku onegaishimasu', which Tanaka-san had prompted me to say when I first met the Japanese teachers I would be working with. It was an expression that couldn't be captured in English, falling, in this context, somewhere between 'I'll do my best through the future' and 'please be kind to me'.

In summer, I'd arrive back at the apartment soaked in sweat, close all the windows and put on the air conditioning. It was nice to know the others were living out these same routines on the other side of the walls. Some evenings, Rivkah would lounge on my futon flipping through magazines, tearing out pages to pin to her wall, while we listened to British radio stations through my laptop. They'd be playing breakfast talk shows and retro music hours for people driving to work, punctuated with short traffic announcements and advertisements for autoglass repair. Rivkah was from London and had confessed that, like me, she'd been gripped by homesickness the moment she stepped off the plane, though I never would have guessed this from looking at her – she always looked cool and unruffled.

The program ran social events for the teachers, and that's how I met Cecelia, in a beer hall in Gifu that served cheap booze. It was full of Americans, and we lost Audrey for the evening to a group of other New Yorkers. The beer hall was long and narrow, with bench tables for social seating and a bar at the far end. An older woman issuing orders from behind the bar was the only person I ever heard speaking Japanese in the beer hall – the staff answered her in English. As I chatted awkwardly among the other foreigners, I tried to sift through their voices, the words crashing up against each other as they swore and laughed and asserted.

What I noticed first about Cecelia was her voice. Not just her accent – Glaswegian, familiar and lovely – but something else, a pitch that was inviting and challenging at the same time, as if she was lifting her chin at everyone around the table in that bar in Gifu. When she said something funny, she'd screw up her snub nose. She was already in the thrust of a conversation about horror movies, a drink in her hand, sitting next to Rivkah, who looked bored. Cecelia hadn't noticed me yet.

'There's so much period blood in that film.' Cecelia held forth about *Carrie*. 'I mean, a full-on close-up between Sissy Spacek's thighs in the changing-room shower. A gush of fake period blood. Then the gym teacher has it on her shorts and the principal can't stop staring at it with this grossed-out look on his face. Of course, the whole thing is that Carrie thinks she's *dying* – her mum's never had the talk, or whatever.' Cecelia scrunched her nose, then sipped her drink. 'The camera lingers on all these "pubescent" bodies – they cast all these skinny young-looking girls and put them in schoolgirl outfits. It's pervy as fuck.' I could tell she was enjoying herself.

'The lens is so male,' I agreed, drawn in. Cecelia looked at me for the first time. *Carrie* was one of the few horror movies I'd seen back then, intrigued because it had terrified my mother – the prayer closet stirring veiled memories from her Catholic schooling.

Under Cecelia's gaze, I pressed on: 'I mean, the way the camera pans through the girls' locker room, how they're slapping each other with towels? Sissy Spacek *massaging* her soapy boobs?'

The table fell quiet. *Soapy boobs* had swallowed all sound, and I blushed. Cecelia seemed amused by my answer; the lull it created gave her licence to go on. Her voice felt like a kindness, redirecting the attention away from me.

She told us that during the prom scene, when they turned the fire hose on Norma – wearing her red cap even with her chiffon party dress – the force of the water burst the actor's eardrum. When she cries out in pain, her reaction is genuine. 'She was only meant to have a bit part,' Cecelia elaborated. 'But the director fucking loved her red cap. She wore it to her first audition because she wanted to look like a tomboy. She didn't want to compete with all the other gorgeous actresses. He told her to keep wearing it.'

'Little Red Cap,' I said in a quieter voice than before. 'Like the fairy tale. Little Red Riding Hood?'

I felt Cecelia weighing me up across the table, something fizzing deliciously in the air. Before long, she was visiting my apartment in the heat of summer, lying down with me on the futon in her underwear to listen to the air circulate around us, her defined body close to mine, fine blonde hairs stippling her forearms. She'd sometimes bring thoughtful presents – sticker sheets, an air plant, little onigiri triangles to eat. My favourite gift was a red sandalwood stamp of my name in katakana: the characters ブルック for Brooke, or in Japanese, Burukku. The Board of Education had given us simple versions of these hanko seals, which we used whenever we had to sign a document or collect a parcel. But Cee's gift was shiny and chunky, the cherry-coloured wood so dense it felt like a stone in my hand, and it came with a tiny round pad of red ink, like lip gloss. 'It's gorgeous,' I'd said, a little guiltily – I was bad at reciprocating the gifts, overthinking what Cecelia would like. 'It might be the nicest thing anyone's ever given me.' She'd beamed, then shrugged it off as something small. I wish I'd been able to keep it.

'I'm sorry for what I said about the girls in *Carrie*,' she said one afternoon on the futon, uncharacteristically earnest, her eyes not on my face but somewhere around my solar plexus.

'What did you say?' Scary movies were far from my mind; I was lying there in a kind of afterglow, hypnotized by the rumble of the air conditioner, my heart still racing a little. I felt very alive.

'About their bodies. Like, their little girl bodies. I didn't mean to make you self-conscious.' A dubious look crossed her face, and she touched my arm. 'I'm not your first, am I?'

'Oh.' My face felt instantly aflame. 'No . . . no, you're not.' Those words hadn't come out of her mouth before, *little girl body*, not until she'd lain next to me in my flower-print underwear. 'I'm sorry if I was . . .' I searched for a word to gloss over my shame. 'Inhibited.' I was three years older than Cecelia, and this word was the opposite of what I'd felt with her: everything within me had leaned towards her without thinking.

She kissed my forehead, then my burning cheek, then my collarbone. 'I'm sorry,' she said again. 'You don't have to be so shy with me.'

I didn't know what to do with that information. I thought of Norma in her red cap, pointing and laughing at Carrie on stage, the real pain of her burst eardrum. 'Do you know what the final line of "Little Red Cap" is?' I asked, to change the subject. Bravely, I pulled her into my arms, ran a hand through her staticky hair. 'The Grimm version? "And Little Red Cap returned home happily, and no one harmed her." Isn't that just the best ending?'

She kissed my nose. 'You're cute,' she said, then got up from the mattress.

Inside Izzy's apartment, I lay on her bed looking up all the words she'd used to describe her condition, making notes in a blue spiral notebook I'd found in the kitchen drawer. Cyst: cell or cavity enclosing reproductive bodies. Uterine: related through having had the same mother. Fibroid: composed of fibres, as a tumour.

The wardrobe door hung open, showing a row of Izzy's smart shirts, neatly pressed, florals and spots and patterns. She'd told me I could borrow these, but I wasn't planning on going anywhere special. My own clothes spilled haphazardly out of my suitcase: the sight of my ripped jeans and pilled knits had offended Izzy so much, she'd pushed it all underneath the bed.

A message chimed on my phone, but it was only Mum asking

if Izzy was awake yet, how everything had gone. I video called her, and when she answered she was walking around, her phone held out before her, saying, 'One minute, love. I'm just putting the spuds in the oven.' Behind her, the kitchen at a vertiginous angle, the yellow cabinets and white tile. 'Where are you?' she said, off-screen, the camera wobbling and tilting, then cupped by her palm as she propped it up on a surface. She stepped back, still tending to something on the counter. 'Any word on Izzy?' She leaned in and squinted at me. 'Are you in bed?'

'She's still in surgery,' I said. 'I mean, she was when I tried to see her. I've left messages on her phone. I'll go back to the hospital soon.'

Mum nodded. 'Yes. Well. These things never run on schedule. Are you getting along all right? Let me know as soon as you hear anything, won't you? How was she this morning?'

'I don't know,' I confessed. 'She left before I woke up.'

'You didn't go with her?'

'I don't think she wanted me to.'

'Oh, well you know what she's like. Probably didn't want you hanging around the hospital. Horrible places. The sooner she gets home, the better. You'll look after her, won't you? Make sure she rests.'

We chatted a bit more and then I let her get back to making dinner. After Mum's face disappeared, I stared at a cartoon womb on the screen, a map of fibroid locations. The growths were sketched inside the womb like little purple clouds or brains, and I copied their shapes on the lined page of the notebook, two of them, with spiny cords reaching out from their sides like they were holding hands. *Uterine cysters*, I wrote underneath, *enclosing reproductive bodies*.

Another word for fibroids was leiomyomas, pronounced lie-o-my-O-muhs. Faintly, I heard the little girl next door singing, a wavering sound suspended in the air, disembodied. There was something familiar about the tune, but I couldn't quite catch it, and my mind kept turning the melody into the sounds I was reading, producing a songful *lie-o-my-O-muhs*. I found the word insulting, but I couldn't say why, only that the first syllable seemed solidly accusatory, the final one vague and mocking. The sounds returned me to the past – not to Japan, but back even further.

I thought of the doctor I'd seen that kept sending me away for two-week intervals, as if it and I would just go away. 'I can't eat,' I'd tried to explain as his gloved fingers probed my stomach, poked at my ribs. 'When I try to swallow, I gag. It's like something in my body rejects it. My throat closes. Something won't let it in.' He looked alarmed by my thinness and asked me if I liked chocolate biscuits, like I was a little girl. I'd had to perform self-diagnoses, then request referrals, as if it was all in my head. As if nobody could see me at all.

5

Your old trouble, Izzy sometimes called it. It was easier to think about external things like that, the doctor interrupting, scratching notes at his desk, squinting at me through his glasses. Inside was something else: something tangled in my spasming stomach, bringing me to my knees in front of the toilet, bile burning my throat. When I'd dimpled Izzy's belly with my fingers, the cyst growing in there had revealed its contours and textures to me; I felt a kind of recognition, as if I knew it, and it knew me. A familiar regurgitating pressure had taken hold. An impossibility, of course; surely it couldn't really have felt like that, like something that could reach out and grab me, clutch at my fingers.

When I finally got to see her that afternoon, Izzy was hooked up to an IV playing cards by herself. 'Are you winning?' I asked, pulling the curtain halfway closed, wanting privacy but not wanting to be rude to the row of anonymous patients in identical beds.

'I don't know what to do with myself.' Her skin was ashen, and she looked wrung out. 'The drugs aren't as exciting as I'd hoped. They just make me feel . . . elsewhere. But not in a pleasant way.'

Her speech was slower than usual, and her eyes were slightly unfocused. I put my coat over the back of the visitor's chair and leaned down to kiss Izzy on the cheek, realizing as I did so that my lips were dry and chapped. 'You tricked me,' I said. 'Creeping out of the apartment like that.'

'I didn't want the fuss,' she murmured.

A bouquet of purple chrysanthemums sat on the clinical nightstand; I was reminded briefly of the bloom of cartoon fibroids. 'That's nice,' I said, lifting the accompanying card and opening it up. Everyone from the restaurant had signed it, a picture of a cat on the front with a bandaged paw. Inside, so many scribbled signatures. I hadn't heard her talk about most of them. I only recognized one name: *love, Sasha*. None of the brief, cheery lines presented themselves as particularly intimate. Still, their flowers had made it there before me.

'You've had visitors already?' I sat in the chair.

'Yeah.' Izzy scratched absently at the tube feeding into the back of her hand, her skin blotched pink and papery, her veins stark and bulbous. It made me lightheaded whenever she did it.

'What does it feel like?' I asked, trying to ignore the tube.

'Bloody sore. Like I've been dragged through a hedge backwards.'

'That sounds like an understatement.'

My sister fiddled with a fan of cards between her fingers, not looking me in the face.

'What are you playing?'

'Nothing. They're tarot cards. Lucie brought them for me, I don't know why. Look.' She held out a picture of a dog barking at the moon, another of a heart pierced by three swords. A third card, its image obscured by the others, spelled out *temperance* in gothic script.

'That's a weird gift for hospital. I didn't think you believed in all that.'

'Lucie says it's just another way to process your feelings. Anyway, I'm only looking at the pictures. I'm sick of the walls already.'

'Who else has been to see you? I'm sorry I wasn't here earlier. I mean, I was here, when you were in surgery. I must have mixed the times up? But I was here. I'm sorry.'

'It doesn't matter.' Izzy scratched again at the tube feeding the vein in her hand. I reached out and grasped her scratching hand, gave it a squeeze.

'How did it go?' I asked, forcing a cheerful inflection into my voice. 'Has the doctor been in to see you?'

She cleared her throat. 'Can I have some water? I thought I had some here. I asked the nurse for a cup of tea, but she never came back.'

'Shall I go and find some tea for you?'

'Just the water, please.'

I found the dented plastic bottle among Izzy's belongings, loosened the top, and held it out to her. She sipped from it and then screwed the cap back on tightly.

'Well?' I said.

She shook her head. 'It didn't go the way it was supposed to.' She went on like that, matter of fact, examining her fingernails, picking at the cuticle. The ultrasound hadn't shown the doctors the full scale of things. Izzy had been carrying a mass the size of a watermelon inside her, and now they'd taken everything away.

'Everything?' I echoed. 'You mean . . . ?'

'Everything. There was . . . so much of it, the growth, and they kept finding more, cutting away, cutting it out. Until I haemorrhaged on the table.' She winced. 'Sorry, I feel odd. It's the morphine. I think I don't feel it and then I do. I'm not making sense, am I?'

'Yes,' I said. 'You're making perfect sense, Izzy.'

'They took everything. They had no choice. I could have bled out. I could have died.' She turned, lifting herself to look around the half-closed curtain at the ward doors, as if she was expecting someone else to walk in, a soft expression on her face.

'Izzy, it's okay,' I said, and she leaned back again. Her hospital gown had a polka dot pattern on it, and on the bedsheets was a tiny brown bloodstain that made me think, helplessly, of our old dog, the stains she'd leave when she was in heat.

There was a machine somewhere beyond the curtain, bleeping, and a nurse talking in the corridor, her voice rising and falling. I heard her say, 'Fresh hysterectomy.' I wished we were at home, that the cadence of the nurse's voice was like mine, like Mum's. It reinforced how far away we were, hearing the sounds pulse against the membrane of the curtain. Izzy was listening to her, too. I could tell by her face.

'Can they do that?' The question spilled from my mouth before I could evaluate it. I had nothing else. 'I mean, can they do a hysterectomy without your permission?'

She blinked, wiped at her dry face. 'I knew it was a possible outcome. One possible outcome. I had to sign a waiver. The surgery can damage the uterus.'

'You never said.'

'What was the point? It was the only way.' The drugs they'd given her made her sound spacey and detached. 'The only chance I had of getting pregnant, in the future. So.' She lifted her shoulders, the cards forgotten on the table in front of her, her eyes glazed and fixed on a spot behind me.

'I'm sorry, Izzy,' I said. 'What can I do? Do you want me to call Mum?'

'No, it's okay. I already called her, before you arrived.'

'What did she say?'

'She offered to fly out. But I told her not to be silly. Such a fuss.' Izzy sighed. 'I'm still fucking bleeding. I'm bleeding *more*.'

'That's to be expected, isn't it, at first?' My eyes flicked to the stain, so small, insignificant.

'They say it should slow soon, then they'll let me come home.' We heard the ward doors swing open, then close again, ribboning the air. 'I don't even feel different. I'll never feel different.' She was struggling now to keep her eyes open.

I reached out and stroked her hand again, the one without a tube in the vein, but she pulled it away, frowned, pulled at the bedclothes. 'Just let me sleep for a bit, then I'll tell you, at the end of the night,' she said, and smiled at me, incongruously, the smile of a child turning back to look at an adult for reassurance.

'It's okay,' I said again, but didn't touch her.

'I'm too splintered,' she whispered, closing her eyes. I don't know if even she knew what she meant.

After Izzy dozed off, I watched her sleeping, my eyes drawn repeatedly to the papery skin on the back of her hand, the bruise forming there. Her body was propped at either side with blue hospital pillows, and her gown and sheets were in a tangled mess, one black-socked foot sticking out from the folds. I noticed the catheter bag had been left there under the covers, between her legs. Her body looked desperately uncomfortable and tender, as if she had been thrown from something fast-moving and was lying where she'd fallen.

I stood and quietly wheeled the table away from her bed, the tarot cards splayed across it, wishing I'd gone to find her that cup of tea. Such a small request. Why couldn't they bring her some tea? Why was the catheter bag just slung there, on the bed? I stared at Izzy's chest rising and falling as her breath deepened – *fresh hysterectomy* – and felt a wave of something like anger, tears suddenly pricking my eyes.

I picked up the corner of the sheet and covered her foot. I didn't want to disturb my sister, but I didn't want to leave her either. Eventually, I fell asleep in the chair next to her bed, until a nurse put their hand on my shoulder and shook me awake.

I walked back to the apartment through a downpour, scurrying into the lobby, shaking off the rain. I dripped across the carpet with its dizzying pattern in my sodden trainers and pressed the button to summon the lift, trying not to think about Izzy lying on an operating table, haemorrhaging blood. The lift doors groaned open and I took a step forward, but a figure in a filthy mauve housecoat was already inside, standing in the corner and facing the wall.

I stumbled backwards, a strangled *fuh* escaping my lips. Medusa still had her back to me. A tangled mass of damp hair crawled down her housecoat, a purple shroud that seemed to be growing its own fur. She rocked from foot to foot, not turning, but huddled there in the corner. I froze in place on the lobby carpet, my eyes refusing to tear themselves away from the hulk of her body as the doors shuddered closed. I waited for the lift to carry Medusa away before I pressed the call button again.

Inside, the apartment smelled of something I couldn't place – a mixture of wet dog, leather, and parma violets, a smell I associated with the interior of old ladies' handbags, with Yamamoto-san digging through her purse to give me her keys, or offering us sweets when we bumped into her in the hallway. I opened Izzy's windows, tidied up a little, although the place seemed neater than when I'd left it. I tightened the tap to stop it dripping into the bathtub, which I noticed was ringed with pink grit. Sunshine curled in my lap as I fielded Mum's texts about Izzy for the rest of the afternoon, until finally I video called her again.

It was getting late at home, and Dad had gone to bed. Mum sat on the sofa in her dressing gown, her eyes still fixed on the TV as she lowered the volume. She knew about the emergency hysterectomy from Izzy, but wanted a rundown of everything she had said, what she'd eaten, whether she'd slept, questions I'd already answered over text message. 'Did you know she wanted a baby?' I interrupted.

'Most people want babies one day.' Mum's eyes looked glossy and tired, and she held the camera too high, so that her face only appeared in the bottom half of my screen.

'Did you?'

'Did I what?'

'Want children?'

'Your father and I tried very hard for you.'

'I know you did.' I thought of everything Mum had endured, all those miscarriages, years of her life given over to maternity. 'But why?' She'd never spoken about the pain of any of it; I had no details, only the story of trying. Mum was younger than Izzy when she'd had me, early thirties, and a young bride when she'd fallen pregnant with Izzy.

'Brooke, are you making yourself useful over there?'

'I'm just saying, I didn't realize that was what it was about, the operation. Underneath everything else; the swelling, and the blood—'

'There's no need for hysterics, love. Just be there for your sister. You're good in these situations, very sensitive. How's it going with the dog? She worries about it, you know. Does it moult? Why don't you give the place a once-over with the hoover? You'll feel better if you do something practical. Don't worry so much: God's good and the devil's not bad to his own.'

I couldn't be bothered with wrangling the vacuum cleaner out of the hall cupboard, but I did dust Izzy's shelves, pulling out the books and flipping through them, pages bookmarked with ticket stubs and torn envelopes, three addressed to Izzy Noone and one red envelope that said *mon cœur*. It was empty.

One of the jobs assigned to me at the library involved tearing old pages out of the reference ring-binders and inserting new ones, updating the information they contained. The old pages were recycled. At first, I just shredded the pages and collected the paper guts in the appropriate bag. But then I started to smuggle out the innards, planning to make something out of them. I'd been reading Sarah J. Sloat's *Hotel Almighty*, a collection of blackout poems that erased pages from Stephen King's *Misery*. I'd already read whatever I could find of hers online. Sloat made poetry out of the horror, lifting lines like 'you could hardly have missed the *Thousands of impossible flowers* trying to be born' from the typed page with a few strokes of the pen. The process of piecing the language together fascinated me, how visible it was. I was forever searching for the right words for things – emotions, desires, those other things passing between people, fraying the air around them. Language was a kind of magic; it could make things real.

The torn-out pages from the reference binders remained untouched, stacked under my bed at home, until Mum started to bug me to throw them out. 'Only lonely old people hoard like this, Brooke.'

'It's for my *art*, Mum,' I'd say in a pretentious voice, and she'd scoff. I knew she believed in me, just not in art as a viable future. I'd won a photography contest at uni and had a couple of drawings published in an online zine and a local newspaper. But Dad was most proud of my temp job at the library because I had *knuckled down* and was *earning a wage*.

I threw them out, all those juicy definitions. It made no sense, once I saw them in the bin under the eggshells and teabags, but I couldn't bear to spoil the pages. *How dare you?* The pages seemed to whisper in judgement when I'd hovered over them, marker poised.

At the library, I roved aisles of bookshelves wearing a T-shirt that said *Search Me*. As if I myself were a lexicon or compendium. One time they gave me a ring of keys and asked me to find all the locks they belonged to in the building – a library of doors and desk drawers and filing cabinets. That's kind of how I felt once I learned about Izzy's longing for a baby, the driving force behind the surgery. Like I was holding something powerful, and I didn't know where it fit, unsure whether I could find the corresponding part, what might be unlocked if I did. What did it mean to have your uterus cut out? What had been taken away from her? The idea seemed too large to hold all at once.

'Mon cœur,' I said, still grasping the empty red envelope. Mon cœur.

Four in the afternoon felt like midnight – everyone at home was asleep, and the streets outside were dark. I ate popcorn and olives and drank red wine; I went without makeup and got ID'd at the liquor store. I'd message Izzy and see the word 'delivered' under the blue box of text, but she'd take forever to message me back. I imagined her sitting in a hospital glow reading the tarot, but she was probably sleeping.

It was the dead of night at home by the time evening fell in Vancouver. It was still early in Japan, but I realized there was no one left in Ogaki I could talk to. Other people lived in our old apartments. Cecelia had gone back to Glasgow, and things hadn't ended well between us anyway. She'd called me weak as she wheeled her suitcase out the door. That there was no one to call in Ogaki felt like a failure, somehow, like I'd wasted two years. Like a buried life I couldn't access any more.

6

When I visited my sister the next morning, I found her propped up in bed with her hospital gown gathered around her hips, a bulky icepack resting on her belly. She stared towards the windows across the ward, though the view was of a blank grey wall. She couldn't even see the sky.

I'd bought her a cup of Earl Grey tea at the coffee shop on the corner, and I placed it carefully on the nightstand next to the chrysanthemums. 'Morning, Iz,' I said quietly, and she slid her eyes to look at me, her head still tilted towards the window, purple hair ruffled across the pillows.

'Oh hi, Brooke,' she said dazedly, smiling.

'How are you feeling?' I leaned in close, putting my hand on her leg through the thin hospital blanket. The catheter bag wasn't under there any more; it must have been removed. 'Does the ice help?'

She nodded, touching the icepack gently with her fingertips.

'Shall I draw the curtain?' I asked, and when she nodded again, pulled it closed around the bed.

'I'm sorry,' she said, blinking heavily, her voice sounding somehow slack. 'I'm a bit out of it. They upped my pain meds and I'm feeling . . .'

I waited for her to finish the sentence, but she just closed her eyes. Across the room, an electric fan whirred, though it was too far away to stir the closed curtain. I sat with Izzy for a while as she drifted in and out of sleep. She seemed so altered from the day before, so docile and frail, that it alarmed me – almost straight from the operating theatre and she had sounded more like herself. I missed my sister's gentle mocking, even her annoyance. Was she declining?

Whenever she opened her eyes, I took her hand, or, from my phone, I read out the messages Mum had been sending, using my most Mum-like voice, energetically musical – a voice that could pick you up, turn you around, send you on your way, and essentially right you. But Izzy remained monosyllabic. When I showed her a photo I'd taken of Sunshine with his tongue lolling at the park, she gave me a wan smile, then dragged the icepack from her belly and turned gingerly over, drifting off again.

I carried the wet icepack away and threw it in the bin. All the ice had melted, and it had dripped from one corner, great splotches left behind me across the ward floor. I searched the corridor for a nurse I recognized from the day before. 'My sister seems much worse today,' I said when I found one. 'Is this normal?'

She explained that they'd increased Izzy's dosage because it had been difficult for them to get her up and moving around, that it was important she did this, to lower the risk of blood clots. After I'd said goodbye to Izzy – soft pat over her bedclothes, whispered *see you soon* – I asked another nurse the same question on my way out. She told me brusquely that it was to help my sister sleep, that she needed more rest. Perhaps both things were true.

When I returned in the afternoon, Izzy was much the same –

drowsy and immobile, though she'd changed out of the hospital gown and into one of the nightdresses she'd packed in her overnight bag. I was surprised how much it cheered me to see her wearing something of her own, something I'd seen her wearing to butter toast in the kitchen while the radio played.

'Shall we get you up?' I asked. 'We could walk around a little?'

She looked at the ward doors, one of them still swinging behind another patient's visitor. They carried a small fleet of helium balloons. 'I actually need the bathroom,' Izzy said, scratching roughly at the swollen vein in the back of her hand again. 'Will you take me?'

'Of course I will. Be gentle with yourself, there.' I gestured to her hand, and she paused her scratching and looked at it, as if noticing the tube in her vein anew.

Izzy got herself inchmeal into a sitting position at the edge of the mattress, her supporting arm shaking with the effort, her other hand grasping my shoulder. Once she was ready, I held both of her hands, careful of the needle feeding into her vein, and she lowered herself tentatively onto her feet.

I bent to slide on her flip flops, briefly touching her calves, her fingertips pressing into my back. My hand at her elbow, she walked in a jolting fashion, stooped over and clutching her belly, as we shuffled to the bathroom with her IV stand in tow. It was as if the thing that had been cut out of her had left behind an unbearable weight, the bloody wound bending her double.

We closed ourselves inside the small tiled room with its antiseptic smell, and I stood with my back to her while she peed. She told me how, earlier, a nurse had helped her into the narrow shower cubicle, that she'd had to sit on a plastic stool under the spray, and now she was worried how she would manage at home. 'It's much better, though,' she said, her voice hoarse. I heard the tearing sound of her changing her maxi pad. 'To feel clean.'

'I'm sorry I wasn't here,' I said. 'It should have been me helping you to shower. I can help you tomorrow morning, if you like?'

'Oh, it was fine,' she said. 'It's bad enough you're seeing me like this. Can you help me up?'

I turned and helped her to stand, leaning over to flush the toilet, glimpse of blood in the water. 'You don't seem as out of it as you did this morning.' I pulled her underwear up and smoothed her nightie over her legs. 'There, is that better?'

'Oh, God,' she whispered close to my ear as we shambled back across the tile, dragging the IV stand. 'They doubled my morphine. I told them not to do it again. I couldn't feel my fingers.'

At the end of my visit, I kissed my sister on the forehead and told her to get some rest. My heart snagged on the image of her effortful climb out of bed, the way she'd squeezed my hands, her limbs trembling. I left her lying under the harsh fluorescent lighting of the ward, the cool blue air hitting my face as I stepped through the automatic doors and into the welcome bustle and clamour of the evening, hoping some sleep would do her good.

The kettle screamed on the hob. I poured myself a cup of green tea and washed the dishes while it brewed, wiping down the counter, then wringing out the sponge carefully like Izzy would do, so that it didn't grow bacteria. I'll admit that while cleaning the kitchen, I wasn't only thinking of my sister, shuffling unsteadily in her flip flops across the dirty hospital tile. I was trying to distract myself from reliving the moment of Cecelia's departure, how she'd called me weak as if levelling an accusation, and that squeaky wheel on the suitcase as it trundled over the threshold, rolled down the carpeted hallway, then bumped and scraped its way along the cobbled street beneath the apartment window, drowning out her footsteps.

At Mum and Dad's, it was almost easy to shutter the episode away, pretend my life in Japan had never happened, scratch it out. But now I felt its breath on my neck, a revenant in my sister's empty Vancouver apartment, a bluster outside, hail striking the window like the hand of Catherine Earnshaw. I knew how memory worked: every time I retrieved the moment – wheel squeaking down corridors – my mind created it anew, reproducing until her suitcase rolled across the threshold of every door I'd ever stepped through, my very concept of a door bound up in Cecelia leaving, my femme fatale flickering in the tape loop.

Cee loved horror films, and had a particular obsession with kabuki theatre. She traced its elaborate stage tricks, its trapdoors and passageways, into modern Japanese horror like *Dark Water* – which was set inside a leaking apartment building, with, she told me, a very memorable elevator scene. She was fascinated by J-horror's corporeal ghosts and doubles, how they saturated hostile domestic spaces. This passion was one of the reasons she'd joined the teaching program and wanted to live in Japan; she achieved a much better grasp of the language than I ever did.

Cecelia was disgusted I'd only seen the American remakes of *Ringu* and *Ju-On*, and that I'd only watched the latter because I had a thing for Sarah Michelle Gellar. This was sacrilegious to her. 'You'd actually love *Ringu*,' she insisted, pulling her knees to her chest, traces of classroom glitter on her bare legs.

We were at her place, which was more remote than my apartment, and I was massaging my calves after cycling there through the autumn evening. Cecelia had been assigned to a single village school, while I was travelling between four schools for one or two-day visits with different classes, the kids ranging in age between four and twelve years old. Cee already seemed more integrated than I felt, had teacher friends and favourite students.

The light shifted and I noticed a sheen of glitter on her cheekbone. '*Ringu* is a quiet film, full of gaps and clues and like, hazy images – it's almost an investigative procedural, but of feminine rage. The remake doesn't capture the same sense of the uncanny. Here,' she said. 'Let me do that.' She pressed her fingers into my calf muscles until I gasped.

She'd had me at *full of gaps and clues*. Cee held me as we approached the movie's terrifying climax, as Sadako – her hair long and black like a river, her body hidden under a dress gauzy white – climbs from a well and crosses the distance between it and the screen. Her walk is jolting and off-kilter as she approaches the camera, her face completely obscured by her hair. She emerges through the glass screen of the television head-first, one hand reaching out to drag herself into her victim's apartment, her movements so agonizing – her bones broken by the fall into the well, her nailbeds bloody and torn from her attempts to scratch her way out.

After the movie had finished, the room seemed to fill with the light of the moon, Cecelia's belongings unfamiliar and silhouetted in black, the street outside eerily silent.

'They cast a kabuki actress to play Sadako,' Cee told me as we lay in bed under the moonlit ceiling, her laptop closed and secured under a pile of clean towels, lest Sadako leak out of it. 'Rie Inō. They filmed her walking backwards, then reversed the footage. That's why her exaggerated movements are so unsettling. Our brains know something's wrong.'

It was true that her movements were jarring, that the film's big jump scare was the reveal of Sadako's eye – her gaze capable of murder. But the cursed videotape that conjured Sadako unsettled me most, with its strange hooded figure, crawling bodies and dizzying text. We, the audience, had watched the tape, too. Would Sadako come for us? Was our fate marked?

'I can't sleep,' I whispered to Cecelia, shadows of leaves playing across the walls, rain falling lightly against the window. 'I'm too scared.'

'So am I,' she whispered back.

While she'd managed to convince me to entertain a few slashers – 'You have to watch *Psycho*, at least, you boor! The birth of the genre! It's *immortal*.' – I flat-out refused to watch the zombie movies she adored: *Train to Busan*, anything with 'of the dead' in the title. My stomach turned at their fleshy appetites and undead bodies, porous with sores, so grossly carnal; Cee was convinced she'd survive the apocalypse because of the hours she'd put into studying the oeuvre. She once tricked me into watching *The Descent* by describing it as a British indie about spelunking, neglecting to mention the cave-dwelling, cannibalistic 'crawlers' the cast would meet. Deceit by omission.

'Why does the sight of blood bother you so much?' Cecelia teased as the heroine emerged from a pool of gore, her body slick and fresh-bright with Technicolor red. 'You menstruate.'

'It's not the same though, is it? How can you eat ice cream to this?' I held a hand over my face, watched the screen through the gaps between my fingers.

'I just figured you out,' she said, pointing her spoon at me, suppressing a laugh. 'You're one of those girls that always goes down into the basement. You're a "follow the strange noise in the dead of night" kind of character. Far too curious to survive. Sorry, I don't make the rules. I'd come back to avenge your death, though.' She sucked the ice cream from the spoon, melty strawberry at the corner of her lip. I held her chin and kissed the ice cream away.

'Promise?'

'Cross my heart.'

Cecelia had particular language for categorizing the films she rated. *The Descent* fell into one of her favourite categories, mommy horror, which must have been a borrowed term because she said it with a vaguely North American accent. *Ringu*, its heroine copying a cursed videotape to save her child, *Carrie* with all its menstrual terror, and *The Babadook* fell into this category, too. I watched the latter on a laptop in bed with Cecelia, who'd seen it before. We turned up the brightness of the screen because the movie was so dark, but still I saw my own face in the shadowy bedroom of the main character, played by Essie Davis, who'd lost her husband and was raising their troubled son alone. When the woman screamed, it was in response to my own frowning expression looming in the darkness, a curl of Cecelia's silver-blonde hair across my shoulder.

'The maternal body attacking the child is so fraught with the abject,' Cee said. She always talked like that.

'Creepy,' I replied, thinking not of the maternal body but of the Babadook confined to the basement with the relics of the family's grief. My sympathies lay with the monster; he seemed misunderstood. 'But the kid *is* really annoying.' The son whined and cringed, little hands crawling and clutching, elbows and knees thumping against the mother's back as she tried to sleep. A tooth rotted inside her mouth; Davis cradled her jaw with the ache, the way sometimes you had to press against a tender spot to mitigate the pain.

I'd taken to doodling my way through these movie nights in my notepad – homing in on a single image, feeling my way around it, making it safe. Sometimes a word or phrase of Cecelia's would make it to the page. That night I sketched out the imagined tooth, wrote *child of abject body* underneath.

Because she knew I'd agreed to *The Babadook* only to please her, Cecelia kept warning me about the events of the film before they happened. When she let slip that the dog was about to die, we had to stop watching. More specifically, she told me that the mother killed the dog with her bare hands. 'Why?' I asked, horrified. Cecelia couldn't remember for certain. Some transference had happened between the dog and the child, or the Babadook and the mother, a violent confusion in the family. Regardless of motive, one of them had to die, and where else would you start? I couldn't root for anyone's survival once I knew that. Cecelia was a cat person.

Cee lay down beside me in the dark, promising to protect me from the Babadook, hooking her fingers inside my underwear to stroke my hip. But she fell asleep first, leaving me with the shadows in the eerie glow of the bedroom, just as Izzy had my first night here.

When we split, Cecelia didn't only leave me – she left the country. Within the space of forty-eight hours, we were on different continents. People kept asking me what had happened, where she'd gone; I avoided their bewilderment by holing up in my apartment with my own. That's how I spent my final weeks in Japan – coming home from class to stare at the translucent membrane dividing the rooms I would soon be leaving, or watching pedestrians pass beneath my window – until Yamamoto-san came knocking with her key and her soft, kind face, asking me to water her plants, and I had to tell her that I was leaving, too.

I felt wretched, like a monster Cecelia was running away from, or some ungodly experiment she'd abandoned. But mostly, I was impressed by her ability to do that, to make it happen so quickly, evacuate her entire life. Walk out on her village school with a broken promise to return, desert her students and friends, leave empty the apartment we'd sprawled in together. She could change her mind whenever she wanted, without a care for what she was leaving behind. She really was prepared for a zombie apocalypse. Osaki ni shitsureishimasu. Excuse me for leaving before you.

Weak. I'd show her. I found *The Babadook* on Izzy's TV, watched the fictional dog-killing with one hand covering my eyes and the other buried in Sunshine's fur, the sweet thing curled in my lap. The movie was fairly bloodless, for mommy horror, but after she'd broken the dog's neck, Davis put her fingers into her own mouth and ripped the troublesome tooth from the root. A wound spilled blood inside her mouth, dripping from her chin. The extraction gave me a sick, dizzy feeling, like when Izzy scratched at the swollen vein in the back of her hand, putting me too inside my own body – my veins, my guts, my bones under a layer of yellow fat.

An alarm sounded in my pocket. I'd set it for nine p.m. each night so that I remembered to take Sunshine for his evening walk. I felt a bit guilty about taking him out as early as that, his last opportunity to pee before bed. It's not like it was any darker by eleven or midnight than it was now, but Mum had drummed it into me never to walk alone at night. Nine o'clock suggested a temporal threshold, the clock face in the kitchen so neatly quartered.

I silenced the alarm – there wasn't that long left of the movie. When it was over, the characters were mostly in the light again, burying the dog in the garden. I felt a rush of protectiveness towards Sunshine. He looked a bit like the dog in the film.

'Okay, Sunny,' I said. 'Let's go.' I put him into his harness and clipped the lead through the eyelet.

The street was quiet, with pools of yellow light for us to step through, our dog-woman silhouettes illuminated. I'd been warned to stay alert for skunks, which roamed the residential streets at night. With an intense seriousness, Izzy had cautioned me not to approach a skunk, as if she expected me to try to sell one double-glazing. She was mainly concerned about Sunshine getting sprayed. He had his own drawer of grooming products in the bathroom, including Izzy's gentle home remedy for de-skunking, one that didn't require hydrogen peroxide. I'd taken the cap off to sniff it and didn't ever want to have to use it. As I walked the dog, I made a mental list of the potential danger spots on our route where a skunk might surprise us: a vacant lot waiting to be developed; parked cars; a gap in a chain-link fence; bushes. All these in-between spaces where something might lurk.

Izzy's tree-lined neighbourhood was actually pretty pleasant at night. There were a few people out – young people in small groups, single men with their hands tucked inside their pockets, other dog walkers – and the apartment blocks glittered above me with squares of light that reflected in the tall glass towers in the distance. Cold, crisp night air, the day's traffic quieted. A neon sign buzzed over the bodega on the corner, and inside the coffee shop, all the chairs were upturned on the tables, a strip of electric light still glowing behind the counter.

I was thinking about the ending of the film. How the mother had finally commanded the Babadook back to the basement. How she'd fed the Babadook and nurtured it to keep it at bay, down the stairs, living underneath. She had acknowledged the monster, given it a place in their home, mothered it.

For Cecelia, horror films were a way of processing fear within a container – that's how she'd phrased it. She knew the movie would end, often guessing exactly how. *The Conjuring* would run for two hours, but afterwards she didn't have to live in the haunted house. But I felt differently – I was frightened the horror would follow me around, the images burrow into my brain forever, living there rent-free. I felt like, in the dead of night, under the bedclothes, or even in the fluorescent brightness of a supermarket aisle, I might go searching for the fright again. Or even if I didn't, it might find me.

After Sunshine had done his business, I bagged up the evidence and deposited it in a wheelie bin at the edge of a small park bordered by colourful clapboard houses. The park afforded a view of a patch of star-streaked sky between apartment blocks. There was something welcoming about the green square with its empty benches and silent fountain. As the lid closed with a soft cough, I heard another noise. Not quite a voice, but a human sound. It was just after ten p.m., which a sign told me was the park's closing time. Curfew.

A few dried leaves skittered along the path, and that soft human noise came again, a little closer. We weren't far from Izzy's building, but I knew women had been killed on their own doorsteps after waving off the athletic boyfriends who'd driven them safely home; every time I opened my browser a sex offender vanished from a halfway house in Vancouver. My skin crawled.

Six tall conifers edged the dark lawn; in the gap between them, a streetlight glowed, emitting a high-pitched hum, and beneath it, a void shape where all the light seemed to have sunk and collapsed in on itself like a black hole. Perhaps I imagined the sigh I heard next, but the shuffle of feet was definite, exact. The dog whined.

I turned and quickened my pace back towards Izzy's building. I splayed the spare keys between my fingers, like I'd seen people do on the internet for self-defence. Damned if I was going to be the first victim, the girl who goes to investigate the strange noise. Damned. A second set of footsteps stalked my own – distant, steady, unrushed. I passed the chain-link fence. Parked cars. A vacant lot. Bushes.

The lobby seemed flooded with light as I approached it, my feet pounding the red bricks, the key taking forever to turn in the lock under the concrete canopy, jingle of the dog lead as I hurried Sunshine inside. I hit the call button for the lift, keeping my eyes on the glass door, watching it swing shut; I'd noticed that, sometimes, the lock didn't quite catch, and anyone might wrench it open and enter the behemoth Leonora, losing themselves in its corridors. Was I praying? Yes. I prayed that Medusa wouldn't be inside the lift when it arrived, and breathed a sigh of relief when the cab was empty, the mirror reflecting my own face back to me above my black velvet choker. 'Good boy,' I told Sunshine on the ride up. He looked at me with questioning eyes. 'Don't worry.' I stroked his soft white throat. But even along the interior corridors – leaf-patterned carpet underfoot, low buzz from the lit sconces – there was something else travelling with us, something phantasmagoric, hot on our heels. As I hurtled towards the corner on my way to Izzy's door, I twisted to look behind me, and collided full-frontal with another body, hard.

I let out an involuntary cry, throwing my hands up. I was eye to eye with Medusa. Her breath in my face, a smell like rotting leaves. Her lips parted, but she said nothing, her body a soft wall against mine – breasts, belly, thighs. A substance clung at the corners of her mouth, a residue crusted over. Under the housecoat she wore a grimy woollen smock, almost monastic. We stood stock still for a moment, until Sunshine jumped wildly at her legs, spinning and jangling the lead.

'I'm sorry,' I said, stepping away, gathering myself. 'Sunshine, down!' But he persisted, pawing at her shins. I yanked the lead, too swiftly, feeling a twist of guilt.

The wall of Medusa's body still blocked our path. 'Get that mutt away from me,' she exploded. 'Or I'll kick it!'

Izzy's keys slipped from my grasp as I bent to scoop up the dog. Medusa pressed onwards, muttering a little under her breath as she passed me to reach the lift. 'I'm sorry,' I blurted at her back, my cheeks hot with shock.

She reached out a hand to press the call button and didn't say a word. Then she turned her head and looked at me until the power of her gaze moved me along the corridor, backing around the corner. Her laugh followed me, and she rasped, 'And then I'll eat it!'

I waited around the corner until the lift had come and gone before I went back to retrieve the keys.

Inside Izzy's apartment, I pressed my back against the door, my pulse thudding through my skin. I bent to kiss Sunshine's head, his body bundled in my arms. 'Mummy's little hero,' I told him, a term of endearment I'd heard Izzy use. My right hand throbbed and stung, and there was red on the dog's fur. A crescent of blood at his soft white throat. I dropped to my knees, checking him over. Had I been that rough? But then I saw it. Dripping from a small seam that had opened in the fleshy part between my thumb and forefinger – a rip. Red welts had formed on my palm where the keys had pressed. The door key was marked with red, too, and now the dog was licking at a couple of blood drops on the beige carpet. I scolded him and pushed him away, feeling a tear of pain as I stretched my hand across my face to suck at the wound.

It's just a scratch, I told myself, tasting metal and blood, *don't be such a coward.* I pushed away the thought of Izzy's operation, the surgeon's knife slitting her abdomen, opening her up, the everything scooped out of her. *The size of a watermelon*, she'd said. *Uterine cyst.* I pictured it held inside a glass jar like a wet specimen, rough with dead skin, something spiny reaching from the mass. Slumped there in the doorway, the walls of the apartment swam. I would not let myself throw up. My hand was nothing, less than nothing, even if it hurt. It was only blood, only blood, my fingers curled around my jawbone, my tongue against the tear. Just a little scratch.

7

That night, in bed with my bandaged hand, I could hear the child next door singing in Japanese. 'Tōryanse, tōryanse.' The rest was indistinct, but I'd heard the song before. It conjured a twilit Ogaki sky, crows roosting in the twisted pines, and a particular creaking sound. A shiver passed through my body.

The little girl's voice rose and fell. It seemed late for her to be awake. Maybe she was a troubled sleeper, like I was. Already, I'd lost most of my Japanese from disuse. *Let me in*, I thought the phrase meant. Or was it, *you may pass through*? I strained to listen, the next line coming to me unbidden, its rhythmic intonation imprinted on my memory: 'Koko wa doko no hosomichi ja?' *Doko* meant *where*, and *hosomichi*, I knew from Bashō, referred to the narrow path.

It was a nursery rhyme Natsui-sensei had taught the little ones to sing in the playground. There was a game for them to play, similar to the game I knew as 'London Bridge is Falling Down'. Two children would hold their hands high to make an archway, and the rest would dance their way underneath, until an interval came in the song when they would lower their arms and catch the unlucky child.

Natsui-sensei was one of the older teachers I worked with, perhaps nearing sixty. When I chatted in the staff room with Watanabe-sensei, who wasn't much older than me, he told me he hadn't been familiar with the song – not before he heard the children singing as they caught each other in the trap of their outstretched arms. 'But after some time, I realized I did recognize the tune,' he said, stirring a plastic cup of ramen from the microwave. 'Because they used to play it at pedestrian crossings.' He hummed the first couple of lines, gesturing with one hand as if keeping time.

Old Saitō-sensei was napping in a chair at the back of the room, and at this point he snored loudly, nearly waking himself up.

'No! It's so creepy,' I whispered after a pause. It made sense because of the song's refrains about pathways and passing through, but its melody was so haunting, its chanted lyrics mournful. I couldn't imagine it guiding me across a road, making the way safe.

Watanabe-sensei nodded. 'It's a scary song. I never teach it to my classes, but they hear it in the playground and sing it anyway. Sometimes I find myself singing it at home.' He wiggled his fingers at me. 'That's how it gets you,' he joked, and we laughed.

I'd tried to translate the lyrics into English when I'd first heard the children singing, thinking it would make a good exercise for class, something different from 'Head, Shoulders, Knees and Toes'. But the translations I could find felt too complicated, or else too approximate, the meaning of the lyrics shifting uncannily the more I read about the song.

Its alternating lines formed a conversation between a mother and a gatekeeper: the mother is trying to visit a sacred place with her child, and the guard is warning her about the danger of the narrow path. Some interpreted the mother's visit to the sacred place as a rite of passage – to return an offering, to thank the Gods for their protection, and to ask for continued favour for her child. Other readings were more sinister.

But that sky, the balmy autumn air around my shoulders. I can't remember where I was walking home from. Likely I'd been for a drink with Watanabe-sensei or Haruta-sensei at the izakaya after work, or maybe I had simply lost track of time exploring the streets around the shrine with my sketchpad in hand, the good weather inviting me to linger.

Dusk fell, deepening the shadows inside the sacred grounds. An arcade of red torii gates hung with banners, crows cawing overhead from their roosts. Lengths of rope called shimenawa were still distinguishable in the dwindling light, draped over some of the doorways, indicating the spaces were sacred, or inhabited by spiritual beings.

Under the soft blue sky, I took a wrong turn, even though I had been following the river towards home. The narrow, unfamiliar street I found myself in bristled with shadows and echoes, and was abruptly empty, as if I was the only one foolish enough to walk there at twilight, to risk encountering . . . what? Some malevolent yokai, perhaps, the veil thinning between this street of ordinary houses and the otherworld. Why was I alone there?

I walked further along the path, finding myself in an empty playground, a swing set creaking near the railings across the field. Something ruffled through the trees behind the swings, like a black feather. I stared at the spot. An outline of something there, yes. *Was* I alone? I opened my mouth to call hello, my voice coming out small and child-like: 'Konbanwa.' I waited for someone to call back, but the silence was punctuated only by the whine of the swing.

I turned and hurried away, cutting through a short alley overgrown with kudzu vines. I stepped out onto a broad road flooded with streetlights that illuminated a pedestrian crossing. On the other side, the cobbled riverbank. I hit the button a little frantically, though there was no traffic, the road deserted. The crossing flashed for me to walk and the song played from its speakers, tinny and mechanical, my brain filling in the words: 'Tōryanse, tōryanse. Koko wa doko no hosomichi ja?' The nursery rhyme spilled into the twilight.

I froze. The melody seemed to reverberate in the air around me. I'd never heard the song play at any of the other crossings in Ogaki. From the corner of my eye, a sensation of movement – my body anticipated the trap of outstretched arms, the terror of being caught at a break in the music. I didn't turn my head, dashing across the black and white lines, my feet and heart pounding. I ran towards home along the riverbank, slowing only when I reached the welcome pink glow and frenzied rattle of a pachinko parlour, the streets busy and friendly once more.

I wondered where the little girl had learned the nursery rhyme. Her mother? I sensed it was just the two of them on the other side of the wall. Izzy's neighbour wasn't noisy, exactly, but the wall between the bedrooms was thin, and aside from the child singing there was another kind of performance: the rasp of drawers opening and closing each night before bed. When the family moved around next door, the floor would creak near the doorway of Izzy's bedroom – always the same noise, always the same spot.

It must have taken time for my sister to grow accustomed to living like this, stacked with all these other people. We'd grown up in a terraced house on a council estate, where me and Mum and Dad still lived. That was a different sort of panoptic arrangement, but we had a garden and three bedrooms, and aunties living in nearby houses that made the surrounding streets somehow familial too, little points on the map where we were welcome to enter.

I shoved my earphones in and listened to true crime podcasts until I really freaked myself out and brought Sunshine into bed with me, something my sister had expressly forbidden. The gory content turned me off – violence and forensics – but I was sucked in by the sense of unfolding mystery, of clues waiting to be strung together. I worried I'd have nightmares, or, darkly, that I'd sleepwalk to the knife block in the kitchen. At least the heft of the dog against the back of my legs was soothing; I'd grown to love the bass notes of his snore and the frenetic twitch of his paws. When he growled or yapped in his sleep, it became clear to me that he had his own consciousness, creating an inner world I could never imagine.

Wind rattled against the glass, giving me the weirdest dreams: nurses stalked the labyrinthine corridors of Izzy's building like nuns in white habits, knocking on doors. Three raps. In another, Izzy and I occupied two separate vessels, the ocean swelling beneath us in fat bursts; each time a wave lifted me, I reached towards her, trying to catch a great silver fish she held out for me in a net. But I couldn't meet her eyes properly, and each time I bobbed up to the brim, I missed her and sank away again. I woke myself in the night mumbling something incoherent.

The weather hadn't seemed extreme, but when I woke the next morning, the power was out. I wasn't sure what to do, so I waited. The sky was dark and heavy, with a crack in the clouds like broken crockery. I kept reaching to flick the light switch by reflex. Then I'd huff and go to turn on the TV or the kettle, as if I had some sort of goldfish brain.

The lifts were defunct, so I had to tramp down six flights of stairs to walk the dog. The trees were strung with broken branches, but just a few blocks over people gathered in coffee shops charging their phones. Sunshine led me to a downed power line like some sort of bloodhound for electricity. There was no repair crew in sight, just a sign warning me to avoid loose cables.

I crossed people on the stairs carrying bags of groceries and resting against the handrail. I kept a wary eye out for Medusa. I helped Izzy's neighbour with her stroller, lugging the thing up the painted concrete steps while the toddler clutched her mother's hand and pointed a stuffed pig at me. 'Obake,' she said. She wore her hair in two short bunches. I recognized the word from all the J-horror I'd absorbed second-hand from Cecelia. An obake was a kind of shapeshifting spirit, or ghost.

'Obake,' the little girl repeated, extending the stuffed toy. It made me think of the classrooms in Japan. *Gaijin*, the kids called me at first, not directly – I was addressed as Brooke-sensei to my face. But to each other, in a friendly, excitable way, I was gaijin. Outside person. They giggled while I learned to use chopsticks, sitting at the lunch table with them. They drew me cards and pictures; I stuck silver stars to their homework.

'Oh,' I said, holding my hand out for the stuffed pig. 'Kawaii.'

She cradled the pig to her chest.

'Sorry.' The mother laughed and coaxed the child to sing her tōryanse song, the cadence of her small voice melting into the walls of the stairwell. We smiled at each other, and climbed the stairs.

I visited Izzy twice a day. On the morning of the power cut I encountered a bespectacled man with thick, beautiful eyelashes and long, elegant fingers sitting in the visitor's chair across from my sister. The room was soaked in the powerful scent of lilies; a bunch of them sat in a vase next to the chrysanths, white petals smeared with tongues of hot pink.

'Brooke, this is Sasha.' My sister sat upright, her hair clean and combed. A pinch of colour in her cheeks, the remains of a partially eaten meal on a tray in front of her. Whenever Izzy had mentioned the name before, I'd assumed Sasha was a woman, but it was somehow short for Alexandre. He was French-Canadian, from Montreal. I had to mentally reconfigure the story Izzy had told me about Sasha mopping the kitchen floor after her menstrual flood.

'This is your sister?' Sasha said, lifting his eyebrows. He rose from the seat and gestured me into it. 'Good to meet you. Well, I would not have put you in the same family.'

We laughed politely, having heard it before. He gathered his jacket in his hands, so I expected him to leave, and I turned to Izzy with news of the power cut. But Sasha hung around at the foot of Izzy's bed, asking me how long I planned to stay and how I was enjoying the city. When he left, he leaned in to touch the back of Izzy's hand tenderly and gave me a reluctant smile.

'See you at games night,' he said, and winked at Izzy.

'Bye,' I said, then, after the ward doors had swung shut, 'Games night?'

'It's a thing,' she said, shrugging it off. 'It's hard to make friends here unless you do stuff like that. Yoga and swimming clubs and stuff.'

'Do you get together and play Monopoly?'

'It's mostly charades!' Shrill, amused.

'I'm not judging.' I held up my hands.

'Have you injured yourself?' she asked, noticing the bandage. I'd found it inside Izzy's first-aid kit, which she kept in the kitchen cupboard next to a small fire extinguisher. I'd sprayed antiseptic, dabbed at the blood with cotton buds, wrapped my hand while standing at the sink, then cleaned the carpet.

'It's just a cut.' I hid my hand inside the jacket folded on my lap. I didn't want to worry her about Medusa and the dog. 'I was making a sandwich. It's only a small cut, but it hurts like mad. I keep knocking it.'

'Twins.' She lifted her left hand gently, the vein covered by gauze and tape. The IV needle had been removed. 'Yours needs changing. I can see a bloodstain.'

I nodded to the flowers gathered on her nightstand. I didn't know what the lilies meant, but I'd looked up 'purple chrysanthemums' since my last visit; they symbolized a wish for good health. Someone at the restaurant had been thoughtful in their selection. Or maybe they stocked violet mums in abundance at florists near the hospital. The internet also said that fibroids could grow back after a myomectomy, and that you should try to get pregnant as soon as your recovery is complete. It made me wonder how immediate Izzy's plans to start a family had been.

'Does he know you don't like flowers?' I asked.

'I love lilies actually. They're the only cut flower I like.'

'They stink,' I said. 'I'm surprised they're allowed on the ward. They remind me of . . .' My voice shrank away. I was going to say *funerals*.

She didn't seem to notice. 'How are you getting on with Sunshine?'

I pictured the dog as I'd left him, sprawled in the bedclothes with all four paws in the air. 'He misses you, and he hates the stairs, but we're doing all right together.'

'Hopefully the power won't stay out for long. All the power lines are above ground here, in case of earthquakes. But they can't handle a bit of wind.'

'It could be worse – you could be on the top floor. So, was that . . .' I motioned to the space Sasha had occupied moments before and wiggled my eyebrows. 'A *special* friend?'

Izzy rolled her eyes. 'No. He has a wife back in Montreal, actually.'

'That's far away, isn't it?'

'And two kids.'

'Shame. I thought he was a woman when you mentioned him before.'

'That's because you're very presumptuous and often wrong.'

I smiled. Izzy was still pale and had dark circles under her eyes, but she was much brighter than the days before. 'You seem in good spirits today.'

'I cried in front of the doctor this morning,' she replied, pushing the tray away from her. 'He screwed his whole face up and said' – her voice took on a quality of stern concern – 'does this happen often?' She gave a small laugh. 'Like it was a symptom.'

'God, is he from the fifties?'

'Or not even like it was a symptom, like it was . . . I don't know. The wrong response. I suppose I should be grateful. Apparently, I'm recovering well, and they're pleased. They just want to monitor me a bit longer because I'm bleeding so heavily.'

'Still?'

'Maybe I'll just always bleed – watching TV, going shopping, swimming laps, leaving a trail of red behind me.'

I paused. 'You can have a cry with me, if you want.'

She picked up the pot of apple sauce in front of her and licked inside the plastic wrapper. 'That's all right. Look, I have an upset stomach, so they've put me on this very special diet.'

When we were growing up, Mum was tyrannical about food waste. But this meant she'd submit easily to our preferences, like plain spaghetti instead of spaghetti Bolognese. If we took too much – a greedy portion of cake, an overflowing bowl of ice cream – Mum disapproved only if we left any, playful as she scolded, 'Eyes bigger than your belly?'

Izzy's teenage requests were all about monitoring her weight – she wanted Mum to leave butter and cheese out of her meals, or take her various dietary point systems into consideration, remember which days were red days and which were green. Rather than accommodating these requests, Mum would strike compromises with Izzy, or sometimes she'd just hide things, as if she wouldn't notice their taste and texture – fatty lardons of bacon at the bottom of Izzy's bowl. But Izzy would bribe me when Mum wasn't looking, the two of us in the living room, eating in front of the TV. For the rewards of listening to her CDs, wearing a coveted hairband, or being taken on some minor outing, I forced myself to eat whatever was on her plate: cold, sour-tasting lumps of cottage cheese, or thick, muscular beef hearts dripping in gravy. Chewing the meat took so long I was sure Mum would catch us in the deceit.

When I left Izzy's hospital bedside, she called after me, 'Be more careful with those knives – they're chef's knives, very sharp.'

By my afternoon visit, Izzy seemed to be flagging; she trembled until a nurse brought her something in a tiny paper cup. I read to her from UK editions of glossy monthlies I'd bought at the airport, but Izzy didn't know half the celebrities any more, so the gossip held no flavour for her. The editors were still circling stretchmarks and cellulite on women's bodies at the beach, and speculating about whether their bellies were baby bumps. I regretted buying it.

'Did I tell you that what they cut out of me was the size of a watermelon?' she interrupted.

'Yes, you did.'

'I'm not even forty.'

I wished we were by ourselves: in her bedroom at Mum and Dad's, where as a kid I'd watched my big sister getting ready for nights out in a fug of perfume and hairspray. Or back at the apartment with Sunshine guarding the door.

'Do you feel . . . ?'

'Empty? No.'

I slid a grape into my mouth. I'd bought them on the way here. A young girl in a green apron was giving out samples at the grocers. 'Try one,' she'd said, her gaze flicking over me in my dog-walking clothes – baggy pants, tank top, work shirt, and what they called a *toque* here. 'They'll make you pretty,' the girl said. I told Izzy about it to make her laugh.

'And then you bought them for me,' she said. 'Cheeky bitch.' It was more of a cough than a laugh, and she flinched at the same time, like something had pulled taut or snapped inside her.

8

All along my sister's block the power stayed out, even as the apartment buildings around me lit up one by one. At dusk, I lit the candles on Izzy's bookshelf, fearing they weren't actually meant to be used – the wicks had never been lit. The fat amethyst glittered in the candlelight, like a stained mouth or a vagina dentata.

I watched a woman across the street cooking dinner and watching television with a pang in my gut, feeling as though I'd been cut off from civilization. This was worse than earlier in the day, when everyone in the neighbourhood had been in it together, all looking dishevelled and charging our phones at public outlets. Now I felt distinctly alone, facing out from my lonely square of window. I wore a head torch I found in Izzy's earthquake kit and ate from little bags of baby carrots, playing Scrabble by myself. Since I had no competitor, I set myself the challenge of playing the longest words I could make. Marriage. Internet. Loneliest.

I'd found the Scrabble set inside Izzy's wardrobe, along with a board game called Mr and Mrs and an ancient Kerplunk, which I'd upset from the shelf so that a shower of marbles and plastic sticks rained down upon me. The gash in my hand made me clumsy.

I'd scrambled to collect them before Sunshine got himself into mischief, casting the beam of the head torch around the bedroom as if taking part in some sort of heist. The Mr and Mrs game had a bunch of stupid question cards: 'What would he say is your most annoying habit?' 'What item of your clothing does she hate the most?' I read the questions aloud to Sunshine, whose major annoying habit was the desperate whimper he made as he humped his stuffed giraffe.

'You're perfect as you are,' I'd assured him. I hid Mr and Mrs in the furthest reaches of the walk-in wardrobe, under a set of hand weights. It was there that I found a folded pile of pastel-coloured babygrows, and a super-soft stuffed bunny. I'd sat on the floor of the wardrobe stroking the material, then left them exactly as I'd found them, hoping they'd look undisturbed.

I shoved my hand into the Scrabble bag and pulled out a letter C, placing it on its own at the top of the board. This was tragic even for me. I got dressed in the semi-darkness, blew out the candles, and left Sunshine alone in the apartment.

I walked a few blocks to Davie Street, half hoping to feel drawn inside one of the crowded bars, for the friendly press of bodies, noise and movement that might drown out the beat of my reluctant heart or distract me from the image of my sister bleeding in her hospital bed. But I knew it would be useless. Instead, I wandered inside a cheap sushi restaurant with soft amber lighting, scratched-up booths and photos of the food on the menu. I ordered gyoza and a couple of sushi rolls, drank the strong green tea the waitress brought me. The restaurant had a cosy, familial feeling, a reprieve from the blacked-out apartment that seemed to be waiting for Izzy's return. Even so, once I'd paid the bill, I found myself hurrying back to the Leonora, where I knelt on the floor with the dog licking my chin before taking him out for his evening walk.

When we went to bed, I raked my fingers through Sunshine's fur and watched the line of ambient light seep under the bedroom door, the city pulsing at the windows. It was almost a comfort to watch the light for shadows or steps, for signs of intrusion, the neon glow keeping the total dark at bay.

The fridge started to smell – rotting veg and sour dairy – but I couldn't face the walk down to the basement, where the bins lived. I kept getting lost on the stairs, emerging from the wrong door and stepping out into the narrow courtyard, the blank windows replicating endlessly above me. Or sometimes I'd open a door from the stairwell and expect to step outside onto the redbrick pathway, only to find myself in the black expanse of the underground car park.

I decided to wait until the power came back on, so I could use the lift and take all the rubbish out in one trip. My phone didn't work properly without Izzy's wifi – I couldn't afford the roaming charges, so I tried not to use it – and before her landline died it beeped frantically to let me know it was out of juice. There was no hot water so I couldn't wash my hair. I was scared of catching cold and having to stay away from the hospital.

The windowless bathroom was pitch dark at noon. I'd leave the door open while I peed and think about that year of undergrad I'd missed when I was ill, how Mum used to hold my hand around the bathroom door to keep me company. I'd been so dizzy and sick, the walls would shift around on me. I lost the hang of rooms, of standing still. 'I'm sorry,' I used to cry, grasping Mum's hand around the doorframe as I sat on the toilet, feeling like a child. 'I'm sorry.'

One night, Mum got me out of bed and opened a bottle of champagne. Just for the hell of it. To make me feel alive. We drank it in the kitchen in our cotton nightgowns. Dad thought we were a bit loopy, but he had a glass. Another night she brought me dinner in bed with a little blue flower from the garden in a vase. Breaded chicken cutlet from the freezer, instant noodles, sharp slices of spring onion, all sweating on the plate. 'Please,' she'd said. 'A little something. Please try. You're just existing up here.' That was a lonely year. I wrote Izzy actual letters, with a purple gel pen. When I got worse, she came back.

Since Izzy had gone into hospital, I'd seen pregnant people everywhere, in singles and doubles, in blouses and overcoats. I kept thinking about how Izzy had described the hysterectomy, as a cutting out, imagining her as a body excised from a photograph with a craft knife, creating a void. I stared at the picture framed on her bookshelf, glowing in the circle of light from my head torch, of maybe-me inside our mother's womb, of Dad's hand there, resting. Mum and Izzy mirrored each other with their two dark plaits framing their faces. Was I in the picture at all? Or was it one of the other pregnancies?

I remembered the set of pastel crayons I'd bought at the gallery and rifled through my bags until I found it. I searched Izzy's kitchen drawers for some scrap paper, and sat at the table in the candlelight, the flame throwing my shadow across the wall. Most of the pastels in the set I'd chosen were deep pinks and reds, and for a while I smeared them in layers without giving it much thought, my fingers smudging goo across the stiffening page, deepening the colours, staining my fingertips with a pink viscosity. It was easier to work like that with my injured hand; I couldn't hold a pencil properly. The result was a kind of abstract silhouette of a face, or rather several faces overlapping with their shadows, like ancestors or ghosts.

I left the drawing to dry and ran my fingertips under the tap, the kitchen calendar confirming it was still November. The day I'd arrived was circled in pen and Izzy had written SIS in block capitals, then scribbled my flight number underneath. *Thats me*, I thought – just that way, without the apostrophe – and dotted the date with a pink fingertip. The calendar was illustrated with vintage botanical prints; a robust squash and yellow blossom marked the month, umbrellaed by a broad green leaf. I flipped back through October, September, August, counting the red dots that denoted, I assumed, Izzy's days of extended bleeding, and here and there a question mark or star I wasn't sure how to decipher. Sex? Ovulation? I tried to remember when my last period had finished, whether it might be due soon.

Sunshine whined and scratched at the cupboard under the sink, where Izzy organized her recycling and organics. The smell from the bins was driving him nuts; I'd picked up a small rotisserie chicken for dinner and thrown the rest of the carcass in there, to avoid opening the fridge. I'd given Sunshine all of the requisite pills and potions, syringing his liquid medications into pieces of pepperoni or a spoonful of baby food from a jar I kept cool on the balcony. But otherwise, he'd been leaving his food: a bowl of kibble sat untouched in the area designated for his eating.

'Okay, boy.' I sat on the linoleum and pulled out the organics bin from the cupboard. Sunshine practically somersaulted as I lifted the lid. I prised off a hunk of meat – I'd really wasted quite a lot of the chicken, my appetite dying suddenly away – between my finger and thumb, the grease seeping underneath my fingernails, and gave it to him, then licked my fingers. Too salty for him, really. 'No more,' I said, but too late – he'd leaned in and pinched a shard of dark bone between his teeth, running off with it towards the living area. 'Shit!' Izzy had been very clear on the dangers of chicken bones, the damage the sharp splinters could do to Sunshine's gut. I chased him and stuck my fingers in his mouth.

My fingers slipped over gristle; I clamped down on the bone and yanked it from between his teeth. The dog bit me, but not hard, then let go and looked up into my face as if to beg to take back the bone or the bite, or maybe both. It was the wishbone, snapped. As I held the mangled hook between my fingers, he lunged for it again. Instinctively, I crammed it into my own mouth and chewed it down, cracking the greasy bone between my teeth. Then I went back into the kitchen for a glass of water, clearing the shards from the inside of my mouth with my tongue, and rinsing my fingers again under the tap.

A well of panic began to rise in me. My hands trembled, and a cold sweat crept across my body. I crawled into the bathroom, crying already because I didn't want to kneel in front of the toilet bowl. I didn't want the shitty linoleum under my knees or the unforgiving ceramic near my face. I didn't want to do it, but my stomach had already begun to churn and contract in a way that felt familiar and terrifying. I pushed the door closed with my foot so that nobody would see me there, not even the dog.

The next morning, I left Sunshine in the apartment and walked several blocks to the water, my greasy hair slicked into a bun. Although I'd forced myself to stand under the shower nozzle in a blast of cold water, I felt unclean, like I'd forgotten how to be a person. I found a coffee shop facing the harbour and an available socket where I could charge my phone. My croissant flaked all over the table as I tried to eat it while scrolling through the internet, reading about Vancouver's renovictions and a furore over an expensive public art installation beneath a downtown bridge. I'd had a few cheery texts from Mum, so I typed out a message to her summarizing my latest visits with Izzy. Then I took a photo of the croissant and the coffee cup and sent her that as well.

Are you OK sweetheart? She messaged back. *Izzy says no power.*

All good! When it's back on I'll call you. Miss your face. I added three hearts.

I searched for Cecelia in the apps, something I did periodically and always regretted. She'd unfriended me across platforms when she disappeared, so I expected to find only the small round window of her profile photo, which she updated now and then. She'd changed her hair several times since we split, dyeing it turquoise and yellow, cutting it above her ears and then adding extensions, a true chameleon. To my surprise, her photo feed loaded on my screen, a grid of thumbnails, all of which I could access; she'd made her account public. I fell back in my chair and accidentally pulled the charger from the wall. My phone flashed a low battery warning, and I shoved the charger back in, my elbows making an angular shape on the table as I pored over the images.

Her most recent photos were a couple of weeks old, from Halloween: graveyard selfies, *Lady Snowblood*, the results of various experiments with makeup tutorials. I doomscrolled through months of posts, back to when we were together, to find myself edited out of her time in Japan. She'd deleted all trace of me and replaced me with other things: a close-up of sakura and off-centre sunflower fields, a depopulated Ogaki Castle, a series from the Site of Reversible

Destiny without me in them, except for one photograph where you could still see the corner of my backpack, part of my hand clutching the strap, my fingernails painted cornflower blue.

As a result of her spate of reposting, her timeline was all out of joint. Images of Cecelia at the Ogaki festival amid a parade of marionettes and dancing children, a team photo in her football kit, and with Rivkah, Daniel, and Audrey at the local izakaya we'd swiftly abandoned the beer hall for, all out of chronology. I imagined myself just outside the frame, out of time. For some of the images, I'd been behind the camera.

I'd known she was going to end things. That's why she'd come with a suitcase, that night, to collect her belongings from my apartment, accumulated over almost two years. Gathered her jumpers and tights, her boots and beauty products, even the small gifts she'd bought me, which took her ages to find. She rifled unselfconsciously through my desk for the red name stamp. Why would she take something with my name on, except out of spite? But I didn't know she was going to leave the country, cut me out of her life so ruthlessly.

I searched through her feed for my favourite photo of us, taken on our trip to the hot springs in Takayama. It used to be the image saved on my lock screen, before I'd decided to forget her. Our bodies half submerged in the milky water, the landscape almost sepia, except for rocks mossed with green and a pallid blue sky. We aren't even touching. But our bodies are in sync, as if one of us was an echo of the other. Cinematic, Cee had called it. 'Like the backdrop to *Creature from the Black Lagoon*.' In her repost, she'd cropped the image so you could only see my shadow falling over her perfect contours. Her smile is so wide, showing her small pointy incisors, like a child who is very pleased with themselves. Like a child who could tear through hearts.

I started reading the comments, looking for a reference to me, to a girlfriend, to her sudden flight from Japan. There were none. I pressed 'like' on the photo at the hot springs, my heart throbbing in my fingertips, a feeling in them similar to when I'd worked the pastels. Maybe I shouldn't have done it – she might make her account private again, decide I was some mad stalker – but I wanted her to know I'd seen it. That I was a real person, that I remembered us.

In case Cecelia should check my profile, I posted a selfie of me and Sunshine, our heads smooshed together companionably. I sprinkled a cryptic array of emojis in the caption box: mountain, dog face, anatomical heart, tentacled globe of the sun wearing a human smile, beaver, evil eye, door, maple leaf. My phone began to light up with likes from a ragtag crew of family members, uni friends who'd become acquaintances, and a couple of old gals from the library.

Once my phone was fully charged, I cleared the crumbs from the table and crossed the street to take in the views of the cloud-cloaked mountains. Determined joggers panted along the seawall, leaving soggy slipstreams in their wake. My body vibrated with an uncomfortable energy, and I fought an impulse to run after them. I was sure I'd seen this view before in a movie, or snapshots of it in several movies. It felt unreal, like a photography backdrop unfurled behind the moody cityscape. The implied proximity of the mountains pulled at me, but I could see no obvious way to reach them. The green bridge disappeared in the middle.

When Cecelia rolled her suitcase over the threshold, I waited only as long as it took her to reach the end of the street. I ran after her. *Please*, I'd said. *Please*. I took off my shirt. The street was deserted, it didn't matter. *What are you doing*, she'd yelled. *Stop. But please*, I'd said, unfastening my jeans, *you can't go. Brooke, stop it*, she'd said, picking up the shirt I'd discarded in the gutter. She came to me and grabbed my wrist, where I was unfastening, and she pulled me and the suitcase back inside, closing the door behind us. She looked furious. *You don't have to love me*, I said. *I'll just love you. I don't care*. And I continued to undress because it was all I had to give her, until she put her hand over my mouth and pushed me down onto the futon mattress. Her watch snapped the elastic of my underwear. *What is wrong with you*, she said, one hand still covering my mouth. *What the fuck is wrong with you.* Her fingers scraped as they dug into me, but I pushed myself against her, sore, moaning, and kissed the palm of her hand wetly. I wanted to kiss her lips, but she held her face away from mine, withholding. *Is this what you want?* She said, after the fact. *Is it?* I started to cry, the noise pushing from my mouth involuntarily in a 'yes' against the heel of her hand. *Please*, I said. *Please, please*. I pretended to come and her grip relaxed; I rolled away from her before she could tell the difference. She lay next to me all night with her clothes on, even her shoes, and I listened to the nocturnal beasts moving around on the other side of the wall, until the light changed and the morning traffic began to thrum the distant expressway. When she left me again, I didn't protest. I didn't even turn over to watch her leave.

Distracted, I walked the street where Sunshine had found the downed power line. It was only day three of the power cut. Part of the street had been cordoned off, and there was a white Hydro truck and three or four orange-suited workers surveying the damage. Neighbours had mustered in a loose circle beyond the perimeter of the cordon. A maple tree sagged, lifting several paving slabs and exposing its roots, and a fat cable slumped across the road like a limp body. 'What are you all watching?' one of the workers yelled. He gestured to the men in the orange suits, the truck, the sky suddenly blueing behind him in the alleyway. I felt as if I hadn't seen the colour for so long. The workers laughed at our gathering at the source of our severed power. 'There's nothing here to see.'

9

Sometimes when I arrived at the hospital, a friend of Izzy's would already be there: someone from the restaurant, Lucie the dog lover, or Talia from swimming – a new mother unhelpfully full of baby talk. If Izzy had company when I arrived, I'd usually slip off so she wouldn't have to bridge the conversation. I'd sit in the canteen and read hysterectomy pamphlets. When I came back with two paper cups of bitter coffee, her guests would usually make their excuses and leave. But that afternoon, Lucie leapt up from the visitor's chair and darted away, then pushed another over beside it. 'This is cosy,' she said, ushering me into one chair and plopping herself down at my elbow. 'Izzy tells me you and Sunshine are already the best of friends. Such a sweet baby, isn't he? You'll have to meet my guy.' She dug around inside her handbag, which had chew marks on the handle. 'Here's my Cosmos,' she said, holding out her phone. It lit up to show an image of Lucie kneeling on a woodland path, embracing a large brown dog. He looked to be some sort of shaggy mountain dog, with soulful eyes and a thick, rugged coat. I told her he was handsome.

'He's a slobbery old thing,' Lucie said, taking the phone back.

'Still full of energy. We're always out on the trails, if you ever want to come.' She told me she had to brush the dog's fur out of doors, otherwise her whole apartment would be lined with it. 'Like a nest!'

I'd brought more clothes in for Izzy and started to unpack them into her nightstand while Lucie chattered on.

'That can wait, Brooke,' Izzy interrupted, lifting a weary hand. 'Do it later.'

'You'll be hiking with us again before you know it,' Lucie said, leaning forward and squeezing Izzy's leg through the thin blanket.

Most patients were released from hospital three or four days after an abdominal hysterectomy, but it would take six to eight weeks to recover from the surgery – some of the pamphlets said as long as twelve weeks. It was Izzy's fifth day at the hospital. She seemed subdued and out of spirits, impatient with her bleeding body, impatient to leave. She muttered something about one of the nurses and shifted around in her bed.

'I never heard how you two became friends,' I said. They seemed so different on the surface that it was hard to imagine their circles overlapping.

'God, who can remember?' Izzy replied. 'It was so long ago.'

'We joined the same sewing bee.' Lucie laughed. 'We were the youngest there by about a decade, so naturally we buddied up.'

'Sewing bee?'

'It was more of a workshop,' Izzy said. 'They supplied all the equipment.'

'Izzy's a demon with a needle and thread,' Lucie said. 'I don't have the patience, I need a machine. We still get together with friends sometimes, exchange patterns and drink wine.'

'That sounds nice,' I said. 'Do you do tarot readings, as well?'

'Hm? Oh, no.' Lucie's gaze flicked to the deck left out on Izzy's nightstand. 'It's all very practical. Repair and reuse as a path to sustainability. Though that's not incompatible with . . .' She paused to consider the right word. 'Divination.'

After Lucie had left, Izzy asked me about the amethyst geode. I was meant to bring it in along with her clean clothes, but it wasn't on the bookshelf where I swore I'd seen it last. I'd hunted through the wardrobe, the bathroom cabinet, and poked around Izzy's orderly shelves. I couldn't find the Cindy Sherman art card either. I'd reached for it in the place I'd left it on the shelf, just as the girl in the photograph reached for a book, before I realized it wasn't there. The print was missing, the amethyst had disappeared, but Izzy's sourness told me she didn't believe me. The twist of her mouth accused me of dismissing the power of crystals.

'You seem a bit agitated,' I said. 'Are you tired? Do you want me to leave, too?'

'That's why I needed the amethyst. Lucie's offended I didn't bring it with me.'

'Really? She seemed fine to me.'

'She didn't *say* anything, I can just tell. She really believes in this stuff, Brooke. She called it a "womb votive".'

'A what?'

'It's some arty thing, I thought you'd know about it? She made me promise to bring it. I *know* she's been wondering where it is.'

I shrugged. 'She's your friend, I'm sure she'll understand that carting a big sparkly rock to the hospital wasn't your top priority. You didn't used to be such a people pleaser.'

'Lucie has really been there for me over the past year – she's like a sister to me.' Izzy picked at the gauze taped to the back of her hand, her vein still swollen and the skin around it an inflamed pink. 'I don't want her to think *I* think it's stupid.'

'Well, I'm your *actual* sister. And it is kind of stupid. A womb votive?' I tried to sound light-hearted, teasing, but I'd sailed too close to criticism, and I could sense Izzy closing off to me, her resentment gathering like a monster under the bed.

'Look, I don't ask you to come in every day. But when you do, you could at least bring me what I ask for.' She scratched at the vein in the back of her hand until I felt dizzy. 'And can you please stop being so rude to my friends?'

'I've been rude?'

'You turn on your heel when you see them. Then when you come back it's like you're turfing them out. It's like you're saying, "okay, you can fuck off now. I'm here, bye." You barely spoke to Lucie.'

'That's not fair! I asked her all about your sewing club. And I've been trying to give you space, not . . .'

'You know, you're not the most important person in my life.'

'Oh,' I said, a little gasp of surprise that shamed me. 'I do know that, yeah.'

The rest of the ward seemed unusually quiet, the curtain around Izzy's bed only half-closed. She picked up one of the magazines from her nightstand, scanning the gaudy headlines, leafing through. She kept up the pretence for several pages.

'When's Sasha coming in again?' I asked, but she simply ignored the question, flipped another page. I thought self-righteously about the long flight, tramping up and down the stairs of her building, bagging her dog's droppings each day. 'I'm surprised you want all these well-wishers traipsing in to look at you. I wouldn't.'

'Well, we're different,' she said, though this is exactly where we intersected, in our ram-like stubbornness, our conviction we were being wronged.

'Do you wish you were an only child?' I asked bluntly, shocking her into looking at me.

She took a beat before she answered. 'I was an only child, until I was eleven.'

I'd never thought of it that way around before. My surprise must have shown on my face, because something in Izzy's gaze relented, and she reached a hand towards me, then reconsidered the gesture. In the moment, I wanted to ask her about Mum's other pregnancies, if she remembered them, but the question seemed insensitive in the circumstances. Yet something told me we were thinking about the same thing when Izzy continued. 'You were the lucky one,' she said. 'Always.'

Her phone vibrated on the bed. 'That's Sasha now,' she said, reading her phone. 'He'll be here soon.'

'I should get back to Sunshine.' I got up from the visitor's chair.

Izzy reached out again, this time clasping my hand before I turned away. She eyed my greasy hair, regret tipping into her voice. 'Listen, are you sure you're all right?'

'I—'

'Do you want me to text Lucie and ask if you and Sunshine can stay with her?'

'No. We're fine,' I assured her. 'I'm eating loads of baby carrots so I can see in the dark.'

When I stopped off at the liquor store on my way home, my phone picked up the wifi and I got a friend request from Lucie and an invitation to dinner. She signed off, #powerbuddy #BCstorm #dogmomsunite.

I was vague about my availability.

Womb votive, I typed into the search box and clicked on 'images'. A flood of ancient clay objects, ribbed and corded, some with a tiny face emerging from their stiff clay folds. Kind of womb shaped, I supposed. I read the captions: Anatomical offering, usually moulded from clay. Offered as a request for health, to give thanks after childbirth, in fulfilment of a vow, or to express a desire. Left at healing sanctuaries and religious sites.

Lucie's amethyst geode looked nothing like these anatomical votives, though significantly more like a womb, with its dark, spherical cavity. *She means well*, Izzy had said, but Lucie's gifts made my hackles rise. Izzy didn't believe in any of that stuff – tarot cards, crystals, offerings. Surely she needed a more pragmatic, earth-bound friend to get her through this, not someone who would foist their magical remedies and symbols on her.

When our roles were reversed – when I'd been the ill one and Izzy had come home to Mum and Dad's – she'd walked into my bedroom and opened the window. I was sitting in bed, pushing tangerine segments into my mouth, spitting out the skins. Soft brown bruises pitted my arms and legs, like a week-old apple. I was never diagnosed with anything. 'Let's go for a drive,' she'd said. She drove me out of the city to a forest, where we went on a long, long walk. I was taciturn and awkward, complaining while I sucked on a white square of Kendal Mint Cake Izzy had given me, but she didn't seem to care – we just kept walking. I hadn't worn the right footwear; I had on years-old tennis shoes, white, the soles worn smooth, and they became caked in mud. I fell twice, bruising my hip and managing, somehow, to graze the top of my foot, which took an age to heal. I was miserable and sick with sugar, walking behind her until my legs shook, only half catching anything she said. Izzy walked at full tilt, a pace that made my calves burn. It was a dull and drizzly day, and the wind stung my face.

Afterwards, instead of driving straight home, she drove us into town and parked up near the river, where we sat in the car drinking coffee from paper cups, looking through the windscreen at the muddy Mersey. It was there I noticed something tiny had shifted inside me. Something very small, enough. And when we went again, I talked more, wore the right shoes. It didn't fix anything – my throat still closed over when I tried to eat, and I'd only manage a few morsels at most meals before I had to stop, my body breaking into a sweat, my hands shaking, and my family trying not to look at me. But walking with Izzy gave me a sense of belonging in the world, even as she forged on ahead of me.

I'd been in Vancouver less than two weeks, and everything seemed remote, like the mountains I knew were there, rising in the distance between apartment buildings but eaten up most days by cloud and drizzle. The Scrabble board seemed to be generating its own words, ones I couldn't remember spelling out. Shame, Solo, Little, each of them crossing the other. And my pastel drawings were growing more grotesque and organ-like as I daubed them with my fingers in the dwindling light. I left a trail of red fingerprints on Izzy's bedclothes while I stood at the window wrapped in a duvet, watching people moving on the street below me. To think that all these people had been born. All those strangers, streaked with rain.

That night, I washed my hair in cold water, towelled it dry and went to bed. I dropped the head torch on the nightstand and jumped under the tangled covers, wearing extra layers, sweatpants and tube socks. Outside, someone wailed beneath my window. Shadows seemed to shimmer on the wall.

The wailing came in waves against the glass – guttural, human, incoherent. After a drawn, unrelenting howl, a lone voice called out from a neighbouring window, 'Are you okay?'

'No! The power's out and all my food's spoiled!' Medusa. I recognized her voice, even in its ragged state.

'Everybody's power is out.'

'Yeah, well I'm poor!' she snapped.

And then the crying started again. 'Oh God!' she wailed. 'Oh God!'

It was like the end of days. My phone glowed on one red bar. I swallowed the roaming charges and called the building manager from Izzy's emergency list, but he told me Medusa was 'gaga' and if he tried to intervene she'd tell him to fuck off. He was right, she probably would. But Medusa was really suffering. The building was thirteen storeys – though the lift button said PH, not 13 – and I wondered what floor she lived on, how many flights of stairs she had to climb.

'I don't know. I don't have this shit memorized.' He ended the call.

'Don't go out there,' I said to myself.

'Oh God, oh God,' Medusa cried in the street.

'This is fucking horrendous,' I told Sunshine, curled at my side in Izzy's bed. He sniffed and rolled over, stretching his forelegs into the air.

'Oh, Gaaaawd! Oh, Gaaaawd!'

I closed my eyes. Imagined myself shoving on my boots and going down in the lift. What would I say to her? Could I give her whatever food I could find in the cupboards? Would she be insulted, like when I'd tried to hold the door open? Or mad, like when I'd bumped into her? I couldn't just lie here.

'Oh God!'

When I opened my eyes, a light dinked on in the hallway. The clock on the nightstand flashed its red digits, reset to 12:00 a.m. I leapt out of bed and went to the window, throwing it open to lean out over the street. People were cheering, applauding from their balconies, their windows lit like votives against the sky. Below, Medusa had fallen quiet. She stood in her housecoat, bathed in a pool of fluorescent security lights. Her misery had ended the power cut.

I hurried to the living room and turned on the heating. The radiators crackled to life. 'The lights are back on!' I said out loud to my sister who wasn't there. A surge of disproportionate joy. The ceiling light in the kitchen buzzed and the fridge spilled light and the stench of rot onto my body. I hummed to the voices from the TV as I cleaned out jars of mayonnaise and cartons of milk at the sink and put them in the recycling, bingeing on power as if we might lose it again at any moment.

I threw the decaying organics in with the chicken carcass and rode the lift to the basement. It was freezing down there; out of the corner of my eye I saw the scuttle of a large rodent along the wall. I found the door to the garbage room and disposed of the rubbish as quickly as I could, my footsteps echoing eerily from the bare concrete. By midnight I was scrubbing out the white plastic space of the fridge – the inside as warm as a body.

I thought about taking a hot shower and took off my bandage to reveal the wound between my thumb and forefinger, closed over in a dark scab. My hand throbbed with a dull ache. Instead, I washed my hands and cleaned under my fingernails and then flopped onto the sofa. There were pistachio shells between the couch cushions, but I'd deal with them tomorrow. I couldn't remember eating them, and it was weird for Izzy to have left them. I dug my fingers in and brought out half a joint. This definitely wasn't Izzy's. I wondered if she'd had a party before I arrived. I briefly considered smoking it before flushing it down the toilet, in case she found it in the bin and thought it was mine. I washed my hands again.

'The lights are back on!' I told Sunshine, who'd seemed put out by the sudden flurry of activity. Izzy would be proud of me for scrubbing out her fridge. *Thank fuck*, she'd say, sitting next to me under a blanket on the couch. And then we'd argue about which movie to watch. She'd roll her eyes at anything serious or subtitled. We'd probably end up watching reruns of *Sex and the City*, so that's what I put on. I pulled Sunshine into my lap and huddled under blankets with my absent sister who was still in the hospital, yet I could almost feel her knee pressing against mine, the shape of her filling out the blankets. After that we cycled through Julia Roberts movies until five a.m., when I fell asleep on the sofa in the flickering light from the TV.

10

I must have behaved strangely at the hospital, underdressed for the weather and languid, because Izzy said, 'I think you have a fever, Brooke.' She put her hand to my brow. 'You should go to the drop-in. Did you have dinner with Lucie?'

'No.' My temples throbbed, and my cheeks blared hot. 'You do realize you're the patient, not me?'

'Are you eating properly?'

'Yes.' I'd just eaten the chocolate pudding from Izzy's dinner tray to stop my stomach from growling. 'But don't they say to starve a fever?' We were waiting for someone to sign us out, her bag packed on the white bed. 'Sunshine isn't, though. Eating. He always seems full. He's never hungry.'

'He's probably just fretting for me. Come here.' She rubbed a smear of chocolate from my lip.

That morning, I'd awoken on the sofa to the sound of my own voice, my eyes opening to a bright white light. Swell of sickness in the pit of my stomach. Was I dead? The TV had turned itself off during the few hours of sleep I'd had. I'd been dreaming about the beer hall in Gifu, the rows of bench tables covered with rotting food.

Chicken carcasses and vegetables eaten by mould, fruit pitted with brown festers. Spoiled meat and dairy crawling with fat black flies, lines of ants spilling from the tabletop. Tapered candles flickered, throwing shadows across the roof and drawing me, a sour taste in my mouth, to the bar, where somebody was speaking to me in Japanese, inviting me to the banquet. I followed the voice, though the woman talking was facing the wall, her grey hair tangled down her back; I couldn't stop myself reaching out to touch her shoulder, expecting to see Medusa when she turned. I was trying to speak, but my voice box wouldn't work. I woke up before I saw her face, but I thought I heard the figure say, in English, right into my ear: *I'm your mother now.*

We took a cab back to the apartment. Izzy walked doubled over clutching my hand, her fingers bony and cold. Medusa lingered at the edge of the lobby, near the bronze mailboxes, while we waited for the lift. When we got upstairs, I complained about her to my sister, saying she gave me the creeps. 'Does she always watch you like that?' I asked, but Izzy hadn't even noticed her.

Sunshine was unable to grasp the new rule not to sit in Izzy's lap and had to be restrained from diving on top of her. He'd also grown brave enough to jump on the bed, which was my fault. The dog whimpered at the bedroom door while Izzy slept. I spoke to her from the other room whenever I heard a change in her breathing, signalling that she was awake.

If the empty apartment had felt like a pause, Izzy's return brought the space to life again, reanimating its recesses and pockets, its uses and practicalities. I turned handles and closed latches at her direction, swept sills and opened hinges, was sent looking for things she'd squirrelled away in drawers and boxes and compartments.

We video called often with Mum, but not for long because Izzy found her questions exhausting. 'It's lovely to see you together,' Mum said. 'But you're both so thin! You're disappearing.' They compared hysterectomy notes. 'You still have your cervix, don't you?'

'Does it feel weird you'll never be an auntie?' Izzy asked from bed after one of Mum's calls. She'd been home from the hospital three days; I slept on the pull-out in the living room. She'd been moving gingerly around the apartment, but we hadn't gone outside yet. She tired easily or got the shakes and would have to lie down in the dark. It was odd to see her so depleted.

'I could still be an auntie,' I said finally. Something about how Izzy had phrased the question made me feel as if there was another, truer question behind it. 'Families come in all sizes and shapes. We can have chosen families.'

'But it's different when it's your own –'

'Anyway, I'm Sunshine's auntie, aren't I?' I said, not to Izzy but to the dog, my voice overlapping with hers.

'– sister,' she finished.

Sunshine's tongue lolled from his mouth, and I waved a pair of balled-up socks in his face. 'Do you love your Auntie Brooke?' I said in a stupid baby voice.

I'd done two loads of laundry that morning, brights and darks, using two of the coin-operated top-loader machines in the basement, then one of the complaining dryers, four trips in the lift. In the laundry room, somebody had pinned an errant sock to the noticeboard. A poster composed with marker pen advertised a pair of wicker chairs, only slightly damaged by fire. Someone else was offering two hundred dollars a month for an extra parking space. There were complaints about parcels going missing from the mailbox area, and queries about lost items: *Has anyone seen my daughter's swan costume? Missing since Halloween.* The basement room was cold and foreboding, and the machines made everything about me shake, the walls humming at a high pitch. Still, it was much better than the washing machine I'd had in my apartment in Japan, which was outside on the balcony and chewed holes in all of my clothes.

Now I was folding our clothes away, opening and closing the drawers, putting my holey T-shirts in a stack inside my suitcase and hanging up Izzy's blouses in the wardrobe. I hadn't been able to do any laundry while she was in hospital, and she was annoyed I'd left her blouses to languish at the bottom of the basket, underneath my wet towels. The rasp of the drawers made me think of the little girl next door singing 'Tōryanse', of the swing set creaking in the playground at twilight.

'Do you think you'll ever have kids?' she asked me.

'I'm only twenty-seven,' I said.

'I'm only thirty-eight.'

I folded, smoothed. 'I don't know if I'd like a baby.' The thought gave me an intense feeling of claustrophobia, even disgust. A living thing growing inside you, feeding off your body, then tearing you apart to get out? It was all a bit *Alien*. Then afterwards the feeding would continue, on the outside of your body. I knew I was meant to see this process as beautiful and natural, even powerful, but I couldn't. I just saw everything the baby took from the body, everything I'd be expected to give. I thought I'd make a resistant mother.

'Even if your partner did the pregnancy part?'

'Yeah. I mean . . . I know it's different, but I'd be going through it with her, wouldn't I? It's such a wild transformation. Psychologically, too.' I knew this much from all the mommy horror. 'I'd still have to *become* a mother.'

She nodded. 'You're too selfish.'

'Selfish?' I'd spent the better part of the morning on my hands and knees, scrubbing a thick ring of grime from the bathtub, which had seemed to accumulate out of nowhere. Wasn't this caregiving? Didn't it count?

'Well. You make it clear you're going to do things in your own good time.'

'Is that bad?'

Izzy sighed and shifted gears. 'Whatever happened with that girl you were seeing in Japan?'

'Oh, you know. We were both homesick.' I concentrated on the creases of Izzy's shirt, smoothing the fabric, folding the arms inwards so that the shirt seemed to cradle its elbows. Halving, then halving again. 'I wish you'd met her.' Though they'd never spoken, Izzy had approved of Cecelia on sight. *Oh*, she'd said, when I sent her a picture of the two of us, watching for her reaction on the screen. *She's very feminine, isn't she?* Cecelia and I had made a skit of it. Like if she ordered a strawberry daiquiri I'd say, *oh, she's very feminine*, and then Cee would lean over and bite my arm or something.

'It took you two years to feel homesick?' Izzy asked, sensing an obfuscation.

'Mm,' I said. 'Well, I'd felt it before, of course. Most of us felt it in two waves. When you first arrive, everything is so different, which can be a bit of a shock, but also really exciting. Then after the novelty wears off, everything is so different in a way that becomes hard, at least for a bit, and you have to ride it out. But I didn't experience that second wave of homesickness quite the same as everyone else, because . . .' I swallowed. 'Well, because I was in love for the first time.' I let the sentence linger in the air, feeling the truth of it.

'Why don't you go up to Scotland to see her? When you're home,' Izzy asked.

'We didn't end on good terms.'

'Oh? Mum never mentioned anything.'

'I didn't tell her about it. I just stopped talking about Cee and she never asked about her again.'

Izzy made a face that seemed to offer commiseration. 'I should have come to see you,' she said. 'In Japan. That would have been nice, wouldn't it?'

'I should have come out here before now.' I shrugged, thinking how strange it was for the two of us to be in the same room, having this conversation, bridging so much and leaving so much out. How strange and even lovely it would have been to host my sister in my little apartment in Ogaki, sharing the futon, introducing her to my friends. Walking down the market street together, pouring the fresh, cold well-water into Izzy's cupped hands. Perhaps she'd see me differently, if she'd witnessed something of my life there.

'Do you miss it?'

'Sometimes,' I said. But I was thinking about how this could be my window to ask Izzy about the plans she'd had, how they'd been thwarted, what she felt about it. I was unsure how to go on, feeling that the wrong word would be irrevocable for us. When we were off living our separate lives, separated by distance, by an ocean, by land mass, separated by time zones and the eleven years that cleaved our childhoods into distinct decades – Izzy was born into Thatcher's '80s, while I grew up in a '90s that pivoted at the death of Princess Diana – we were only connected by our mother's calls.

Our childhoods existed separately, hers marked by a kind of inchoate freedom and mine by being held too close.

I knew I'd have to get to the question in increments, letting Izzy lead, waiting for my moment. Even though the stack of babygrows were out of sight, tucked into a corner of the wardrobe, the shape of them haunted the conversation: their butter-yellow gloves and socks made for hemming in baby fingers and toes.

'I thought you seemed happy there, for a time,' Izzy said. 'Will you go back?'

'Maybe. But I don't really know anyone in Ogaki any more – most of my friends were on the program. I should probably try to see another part of the country. I thought I'd travel more – I was full of plans when I arrived, but then I got swept up in things.'

Speaking to my sister, I realized how much my romance with Cecelia had made the rest of my life in Japan feel somehow indistinct, like watching my shadow through paper-panelled shoji. Meanwhile, Cee had been excising my image from her photographs, filtering me out of her memories.

'You would have liked it there, I think,' I told Izzy.

'Yeah?'

'Yeah. In Nara City, there's this temple with a giant golden Buddha, and sacred deer that wander free in the street. You can buy crackers to feed them. They made me think of you, the deer.'

'Because I'm so gentle and spry?' Izzy laughed.

'I had this really strong sense memory, when the deer ate from my hand, of you taking me to the farm when I was little. Did we used to feed the goats or something?'

'Horses, I think. In the paddock.'

'Maybe it stuck with me because I *was* really homesick, during that first wave. Anyway, I imagined you there with me, feeding the deer. Though in reality if you'd come to visit, I probably would have lost you poking around the supermarket.'

'That sounds nice. Now I'm really sorry I didn't come. Did you like the food?' she asked.

'Yes,' I said. 'I do miss that, actually. You can't get decent Japanese food at home.'

'Newsflash: you can here.'

'I tried a place on Davie,' I told her, and described the sushi restaurant with the beat-up booths.

'Pffft. We can do better than that,' Izzy said. 'Once my stomach settles properly, we'll have dinner. Somewhere really nice.'

'I didn't think you liked sushi?'

'It's not my go-to treat, I admit, but I can get us a great recommendation.'

'Okay.' I laughed, pleased – she looked almost excited. 'It's a date.'

I carried on folding the laundry, nodding to a framed weaving that Izzy had hung on the otherwise blank magnolia wall facing the bed.

'Why did you frame that? Why not hang the weaving, so you could touch it?'

'Dust,' she said.

I rolled my eyes. 'What about you, anyway? We all thought you'd come home, eventually, after . . .'

'After Marty ran off with the air hostess?'

'I think they're called flight attendants now.'

'Hmm.'

She was quiet for a bit, watching me fold a succession of the white tank tops I wore underneath everything. 'Do you remember that blue jumper you had, with all the big buttons sewn into it?' she asked.

'Yes, I was obsessed.'

'I'm a bit sad you've washed all these.' She picked up one of the tank tops and refolded until it was a square the size of a handkerchief. 'They smelled like Mum's washing powder when you first came.' She put the white square to her nose, as if to seek out the lost scent. 'When you were little, I used to carry you around everywhere, and try to dress you. Like you were my doll. Mum used to go mad because sometimes I'd disturb you, picking you up when she'd just put you down for a nap, and make you cry.'

Out of the corner of my eye I saw Izzy wipe the back of her hand across her nose. She sniffed, swallowed. I didn't look at her, but reached my hand out and covered hers, the one that was resting, still, on the duvet.

A pipe groaned behind the wall. Izzy slid her hand away, tired perhaps of the gesture, the only one I had. 'Best give this dog his meds,' she said, and started to heave her body out of the bed.

'I can do that—'

'No, I want to.' She steadied her feet on the beige carpet. 'I'm not completely useless, am I, Sun?'

I helped Izzy in and out of the shower. It was difficult for her to step over the side of the bathtub, and she wasn't allowed to stand for too long or get her stitches wet while she cleaned her body. I'm not sure how she accomplished this. I stood on the other side of the plastic shower curtain, feeling inadequate. She had a long list of instructions to abide by.

'Nothing in the vagina for eight weeks!' I'd shout like a drill sergeant if I saw her struggling.

'Oh God, don't make me laugh.'

To create the illusion of privacy, we developed a performance with a towel. It would be whipped off and on behind the curtain and held out for me to hold in the meantime, while the room filled with steam and the poxy extractor fan roared impotently on the ceiling. After climbing out, she'd sit on the edge of the bathtub, and I'd turn my back while she dried herself. She had to pat her incision gently dry. Then I'd help her put on her maxi pad and underwear, and clean drops of her blood from the bathroom floor.

The shower screeched off and I could hear Izzy faffing about with the shower curtain. I reached out and traced the shape of a flattened heart with my finger on the mirror. It dripped down the surface of the steamy glass. Did this count as an anatomical votive? No, I thought. Too ephemeral. The heart was a muscle the size of a fist, but the two curves I'd looped suggested nothing of its dimensions. It was like all the art I'd made.

'Towel, please.'

I held it out to her, facing away. She took it and grabbed my hand while she climbed out of the bath. I was mainly there to act as a ballast, in case Izzy started to feel sick or faint. It crossed my mind that Mum had done something like this for me and now I was doing it for Izzy. I could feel the cut of Mum's wedding ring, how it pressed into my hand as I gripped hers. I felt like a good proxy if I thought of it like that, as a chain of shared experience, a witnessing.

Izzy's bathrobe hung on the back of the bathroom door, a short fluffy one with a pattern of fried eggs. I should have put it on during the power cut and roamed the hallways. I could have followed Medusa back to her apartment and shared my bag of baby carrots and borderline hummus with her, an offering so she wouldn't threaten to eat the dog.

'Look,' Izzy said.

I turned, expecting her to have slipped her nightie on over her head. She was naked, the towel resting in her lap, her shoulders hunched and an arm pressed across her breasts. Thirty-odd stitches stretched in a horizontal line across her lower abdomen. Skin yoked together by thick sutures, her flesh coloured with bruises in variegated, tender-looking blooms, and the swelling beneath her skin uneven and alien-looking. Clumps of dried blood clung to the stitches, an ugly line she wasn't allowed to scrub clean.

I was staring. 'Izzy, your poor stomach,' I said helplessly. I felt sick, and violent, like I wanted to fight someone – she looked like she'd been beaten, and I swallowed an urge to demand to know who'd done it to her. I couldn't get over how rough the stitches were. I'd imagined some sort of surgical precision, but the stitches looked like I could have made them myself with a blunt needle and a spool of thread from Izzy's sewing kit. My own stomach rolled, but Izzy only laughed. 'Your face!'

'It's hot in here,' I said, and opened the door to let out the steam.

The steam seemed to hang in the air, over the day, the radiator rattling and the winter rooms humid as my sister moved painfully between them, growing frustrated with her body.

'Why am I always tired? I'm not doing anything,' she said over the dinner I'd made to her specifications: strawberry jam on burnt toast, two boiled eggs with pepper, no salt, and a banana. We were eating on the sofa in front of the TV, watching some home makeover show Izzy liked.

'You're healing,' I said. 'Your body is working really hard.'

'It must be the sedatives,' she grumbled. 'They make me foggy during the day. But if I don't take them, the pain wakes me up at night.' She pushed some congealed jam around on her plate.

The TV host was describing the TV couple's plans for their outdoor deck. A sunken patio, string lights, fire pit. The host kept using the phrase *forever home*, making it sound as if the couple were rehousing a pet, or buying a cemetery plot.

'Does anyone actually live like this?' I asked, my mind drifting. 'I mean, anyone normal?'

'Normal like us? Are you going to leave those crusts?' She nodded at the plate I'd abandoned on the coffee table. Banana peel and eggshells.

'Yeah, I don't like crusts.' I hugged a pillow in my lap, scritched Sunshine behind his ears.

'You're not a child,' she said.

The couple on TV gushed over something called a butler's pantry.

'Do you think you'll stay here for good?' I asked.

Izzy shifted in her seat and winced, her face grey and her eyes fixed on the TV. 'Why not? This is my home. I've always lived in this apartment.'

'No, I was talking about Can—'

'It's not like I have any reason to move,' she continued. 'Not any more. Anyway, what's wrong with my apartment?'

'Nothing,' I said quickly, though the place gave me a sense of creeping unease. Despite living there for a fortnight, I still found myself taking wrong turns, hatching out on the stairway instead of finding the lift, or blustering into the confined space of the courtyard without thinking. I found its shifting, dingy corridors unreliable, as if the warren made and remade itself in response to the crushing pressure of the concrete exterior, the walls and floors alive with creaks and groans that shuddered through to my bones.

There was something oppressive, too, about the framed article in the lobby, its pride in the provenance of the building's soft, maternal name – Leonora, like a spectre from Poe, or a laundry detergent.

'I'm sorry I said anything, Izzy. Want some apple slices? Tonic water?'

The TV droned on. 'It's hard to find a decent place to live in this city, you know. You'd die if you knew what this place costs me. Do you know anything about rent control? I've been here ten years. I can't afford to move.'

'Izzy, it's nice.' I laughed, trying to lighten the mood; I could tell she had more to say. 'I love your neighbourhood.'

She looked at me, seeming to soften, biting at the cuticle around her thumb. 'I'm not up to talking about the future right now, okay? I can't think that far ahead.'

'All right.'

'Besides, shouldn't you be concentrating on your own living situation? You can't live with Mum and Dad forever. You're nearly thirty. You need to sort your shit out.'

'Things are hard at home, too,' I said. 'I've only been able to find temp work since I got back from Japan. Anyway, Mum and Dad like having me there.'

She hooted. 'They baby you.'

'I know.' I excused myself and went to the bathroom. I stretched my body in front of the mirror and pulled up my shirt. I was definitely due on my period – my stomach and breasts were bloated with a heavy, dull ache. I sucked in my stomach and moved in and out of the light trying to make it look flatter, running my fingertips over my ribcage, counting, taking pictures on my phone. I couldn't get Izzy's alien stomach out of my mind, the wound stretched like a mouth, the coarse stitches, the watermelon cyst that had been cut out of her. I put my phone face-down on the cistern and tapped my wrist with two fingers, the way I'd taught myself during my recovery, repeating affirmations. *You are good*, I told myself. *You are good.*

While I was in the bathroom, Izzy took herself off to bed. I knocked gently on the door with my knuckles. 'Do you need any help?'

'No.' Strained, stubborn. 'I'm good, ta.'

It was only early evening, but I unfolded the couch and made up the bed, smoothing the sheets neatly. If I could be neat and quiet, it might help Izzy. If I could make myself very small, useful and pleasing. Like a bright shiny tool.

In an attempt to untangle these thoughts, I hunted in the kitchen for something more substantial to eat. Sunshine appeared at my side. 'What would Sunshine do?' I asked as I pawed through the contents of the fridge. I threw a piece of steak in the pan and cooked it in parsley and butter, a defiant act of self-care, then plated it up in its little pool of bloody juices and carried it to the sofa, carving a wet slice for the dog and feeding him from my hand.

Izzy had left the TV playing. I browsed through the horror section on the screen, looking for something familiar I might have heard Cecelia talking about. I stopped scrolling at a stylized graphic of a woman clothed in a chador against a bright red background. White shapes marked out her eyes, nose, and forehead, the rest of her face in shadow. A kiss of red lipstick indicated her mouth. *A Girl Walks*

Home Alone at Night, described in the caption as an Iranian vampire spaghetti Western, filmed in crisp black and white. I pressed play.

Sometime later, the eponymous Girl, a vampire, has taken a gorgeous man dressed in a Dracula costume back to her lair and put on a record, a refrain repeating in the music about fear. The song plays almost in its entirety as, slowly, silently, the man approaches the Girl from behind, her neck and collarbone exposed, until she turns towards him. She tilts his head back and he allows her, in total surrender. Her eyes fix on his Adam's apple.

'No way,' I whispered, knife and fork in my hands, blood spilling over my chin. If she wanted to kill him, she could – the moment suspended, mirrorball spinning. I waited for her to sink her teeth into his exposed neck, holding my breath, a piece of meat snagged between my teeth, but instead she presses her ear to his heart, the beat of it surfacing over the music.

A knock came at the door, and I jumped. Sunshine gave a little yap and ran to press his nose to the gap, snuffling. I discarded what remained of the steak on the counter, pulled a cardigan closed across my chest and smoothed a hand over my hair. A text lit up my phone, but I ignored it.

I turned the lock and then the doorknob and stuck my head into the corridor. It was Sasha. 'Hello,' he said. I wondered how he'd charmed his way into the building, the lobby stickered with warnings not to open the door to strangers. Maybe the lock was still broken.

'Hello.'

'I'm here to see Izzy. She knows I'm coming.'

'I'm sorry, she's in bed.'

'I think she has sent you a message.' He looked apologetic, a little embarrassed, a black messenger bag over his shoulder.

My phone was in my hand; I looked down at the screen. *When Sasha gets here just send him in*.

'Oh.' I opened the door.

'Hello, boy,' Sasha said to Sunshine in the same calm tone, as he slipped out of his shoes in the hallway and hung up his coat. He walked directly to the bedroom door, like he'd been there before. The door opened and then closed neatly behind him.

11

Whatever they were doing in there, they did it quietly. Once, I heard a soft laugh. It was feminine, but I thought it didn't sound like Izzy. They must be in bed together. Was he staying the night? The intimacy of it shocked me. Izzy had been cut open and stitched back together; she was sore and irritated and tired. Sasha had come just to be with her. Did he know what she was going through? I felt walled out.

I'd bought a bottle of pinot noir at the liquor store. I bought it as a gift for Izzy, to celebrate her release, but when I was going through the literature at her kitchen table, I realized it was a terrible idea. According to the pamphlets, the alcohol would impair her immune system and slow her recovery, exposing her to infections or even pneumonia. It could thin her blood, stop her scars from healing, and make all of her symptoms worse: brain-fog, nausea, dizziness. Of course it was a stupid idea. I should have emptied the bottle down the sink, but that would have been a waste.

I hunted for the bottle in the pan cupboard, where I'd hidden it. Fuck it, I thought. Sunshine barked at a noise in the corridor, a neighbour jangling keys and talking on the phone. I poured the wine into a mug that said Kiss the Cook and carried it with the bottle into the living room, setting them on the coffee table. Sunshine settled down on my pillow to lick his privates.

Sorry, I texted Izzy.

Almost instantly, three dots.

Don't be silly. Can you turn out the kitchen light?

I got up and flicked the switch. Then I kept going, turning out all the other lights and even lowering the heat, the radiator crackling beneath the window. I snapped off the TV, the Girl's vampiric face blinking out, and I looked through the black window onto the city at the woman having a party across the street. It appeared to be some sort of costume party – figures were dressed in sequins and curled moustaches, and someone had invited two copies of Marilyn Monroe. One guest had gone all out with a monstrous white rabbit costume and was carrying the head underneath their arm, its eyes like silver saucers. I looked from the blank TV screen to the party across the street; it was almost as if the costume party had leapt from inside the TV into the box of light over the road.

I drank from the mug until my head swam, watching the party unfold, the white rabbit sitting on the arm of the sofa talking to someone whose costume I couldn't make out. The Marilyns were joined by Dorothy from *The Wizard of Oz*. I scanned the other partygoers, searching for the girl who lived there, but I couldn't identify her. I wondered why they were having a costume party in November, so soon after Halloween. Was it someone's birthday, an early holiday bash? There were no decorations other than a few sad balloons.

I wanted to be the sort of person who could throw a costume party in my own apartment. In my costume, I would be beloved and able to communicate the whole of my interiority to someone else. I'd be surprising, witty, a catwoman from the moon. I'd toast to Izzy's good health. Quaff champagne with Lucie and Sasha and that mum friend whose name escaped me in the moment. I'd post the photos online and Cecelia would press the small red heart on her phone 4,390 miles away as the crow flies. It looked easy to be a different self in the apartment across the street.

Instead I drank at Izzy's living room window, watching Japanese transit videos on my phone. The screen reflected in the glass, lighting a sliver of my face which hung in the black like a moon. Commuters streamed into subway cars and the train sped away. Another car arrived and poured out.

Eventually I found a recording of somebody walking through the streets of Ogaki. When the filmmaker walked past a bank of shop windows, their body became visible; they carried a video camera swathed in plastic to protect the equipment from a light rainfall, cars sweeping by on the wet road. Everything was the colour of rust or bone, except for the intense green of urban trees, shrill with cicadas, the film's eerie soundtrack. Gaudy streamers hung from the covered walkways, shiny tentacles moving in the breeze. How wet everything felt. Slick green statues of babies. There were only a few people shopping along the high street, quieter than I remembered.

The filmmaker walked me inexorably towards Ogaki Castle, where I knew the cicadas would grow louder, would swallow me. I'd read about a brood of cicadas living underground for seventeen years before they swarmed to breed, and when I first moved to Ogaki I had nightmares about the cicadas infesting my bedclothes, the unfamiliar sound vibrating outside my apartment window. A swarm of desire, the coming brood. The film had been recorded in August and I could feel the humidity even this close to the dark glass, the wintry city beyond it. Pieces of Cecelia came to me in the pitch, her mouth moving soundlessly, her hand reaching out and then pulling away.

I went to the bathroom mirror and smeared red lipstick around my wine-stained mouth, ignoring the clash of it against my hair, then put on a heavy black coat in the hallway, the coat Sasha had hung up. I pulled my boots over my silky pyjama bottoms, tucking in the folds, telling Sunshine to *shhhhhh* as I put on his harness and lead. Then we went out into the corridor together, rode the lift down to the lobby, and stepped out into the night.

I walked Sunshine up and down the street. He was intent on attending to every lamp post and bush, so we walked slowly, sniffing, moving from one scent to another. It felt good to be wearing Sasha's coat. It smelled like cologne, spicy and woody, and there was a reassuring heft to the fabric, the fleece inner lining swaddling my skin.

Outside the opposite building, a small congregation milled about on the scrappy lawn, some of them smoking – plumes of smoke funnelling away in the brisk air – others holding beer bottles and talking in tight circles. A girl with bare, almost-blue legs turned towards us. 'Oh my God, your dog is so cute,' she slurred. Her hair fell in long dark curls studded with daisies, and she wore a peace sign pinned to her coat.

'I'm sorry,' I began, 'he doesn't like—' but Sunshine wagged his tail, pulled me towards the sound of her voice, which grew increasingly high pitched.

'Oh my gosh, aren't you the cutest? Aren't you the cutest bo-oy?' She was down on all fours now.

Not to be outdone, the man next to her knelt in the grass and ran his fingers through Sunshine's woolly coat. He was dressed as some sort of goblin royalty, replete with pointed ears, crown, and blond wig. 'Beautiful animal,' he sang next to Sunshine's ear. Sunshine circled the girl's legs to avoid his attention. 'Aw, I won't hurt you,' he said.

'Wow,' I said to the girl with the peace sign. 'He likes you.'

'You can bring him inside,' she said. 'Just don't let the neighbours see him. Ugh, I've wanted a dog since forever! What's his name?' She pulled me into step with her and we went inside, into the foyer, where everything was quiet. Shiny chrome surfaces distorted our reflections.

'Sunshine.'

'Sunshine! So precious! I'm Elsie.' She leaned towards me, almost pressing me against the wall. 'Whoa. Are you okay?' she said, putting an arm out to steady herself. 'I love your dog. Dogs at parties are my favourite.' Her eyes seemed to grow larger.

'I like your daisies,' I said. She laughed as if I'd told her a joke. I wouldn't be lonely in the city. I wasn't lonely.

The goblin had caught up to us, and we all rode the lift together. He offered to hold my coat so that I could make a grand entrance, pulling it from my shoulders, Elsie taking Sunshine's lead from my hand. He put his arm around me while the girl took photos of Sunshine on her phone. 'You don't mind, do you?' she said.

I was pretty sure I didn't want the goblin's hand on my hip, but I crossed the threshold like that, with his hands on me, confirming that I belonged there. We kicked off our shoes in the hall, and he steered me into the nearest doorway, which opened onto a dark bedroom with a double bed piled with coats. 'Nice pyjamas. What have you come as, anyway?' he asked as he threw Sasha's coat on the bed with the others. Sunshine had followed Elsie into the kitchen at the promise of the word *treat*. 'You need to undo a few more buttons,' the goblin said. 'Show a bit more skin.'

Music thudded the wall from the other room. 'Thanks for the fashion advice.' I was looking at the tangle of coats, their splayed sleeves. Sasha's open arms. Across the street Izzy was closed inside her bedroom with him. 'Don't they look empty?' There was something wrong about the coats being piled together like that, no system. Behind me, the goblin softly closed the door. 'No,' I said. 'Open it.'

He grinned as if I'd caught him doing something slightly mischievous – as if I should find him roguish but charming – and did as I asked, stepping aside as I passed him to go in search of Sunshine and the girl. His grin followed me down the hallway.

'I should probably leave,' I said when I found her, feeding Sunshine from a cereal box on her counter.

'You just got here!'

'I wasn't invited,' I said, a little breathless.

'But I invited you.'

'I think you have me confused with someone else. These are just my pyjamas.'

She laughed, then put a handful of the cereal into her mouth. 'You're funny.' She reached for something with feathers from the kitchen counter and held it out to me. A mask, in peacock colours. 'Here. Put this on, it goes with your hair.'

Elsie's face seemed very close to mine as she slipped the mask loops over my ears and fussed with the peacock feathers. I stumbled away, lowering myself into a bean bag in front of the TV, thinking of the horror film Sasha had interrupted. What happened next to the boy in the Dracula costume? In the scene I'd watched, the Girl had bested her primal hunger for his blood, sublimated it into a desire for his living heart against her face. I wished I'd finished eating the steak.

'You like scary movies?' said the voice of the goblin, and that's when I realized I'd been talking out loud. He was in the orange bean bag opposite mine, and the heel of my right foot was in his hand. People drank at the edges in a dozen costumes, their voices rising to the ceiling in a tangle of gibberish. Nobody danced, though the music played on, nothing I recognized.

'My girlfriend does,' I said.

'Your girlfriend-girlfriend?'

'She's waiting for me,' I added, as if she might be in the room. I wanted to stitch myself to her, to Cecelia, to fade into her. 'Somewhere.' I felt far away behind the peacock mask.

Near the end, in the subway car at night, travelling back from some izakaya together, our reflections sitting across from us in the black window. I smiled at her. We had learned to be vigilant on the packed trains for gropers, but not here in the empty carriage, returning to sleepy Ogaki, with a white man – gaijin – who sat too close, who tried to joke with us in English, who put his hand on Cecelia's breast. She pushed him away, her tote bag falling onto the floor of the subway car and spilling her belongings. She stood and threw a punch, her fist slicing the air, the blow not landing. He laughed and backed away, sneering at her, his hand moving down the front of his pants. I froze, watching the man, feeling Cecelia's rage and surprise pulse through my own body in a hot wave. The man said ugly words and sat on the other side of the car, staring, his hand stroking. I knelt on the floor and scooped Cecelia's things back inside the bag. The train juddered to a stop – not ours, but I took Cee's hand and we got off the train, waiting for the next one silently, still holding hands, at night, in the subway. I didn't ask her if she was okay; the silence throbbed with cicadas.

She came back to my apartment. It was easier to reach than her own, and her bike still leaned outside against the white railing. I offered her a cup of green tea and she said yes. The tension between us grew oppressive, but I felt unable to break it. Finally, she said, 'We should have laughed at him.'

I blinked. 'I was too scared.'

'We should have laughed at him. We gave him too much power, to scare us. We should have laughed at his shrivelled little worm-cock.'

'We were alone, he could have turned violent. He grabbed you!'

'You did nothing,' she spat. 'You were so weak!'

She was right; I'd done nothing, my body coursing with anger, and I couldn't explain why all I could do was kneel on the dirty floor and scoop up her belongings, hold the bag against my body, wait for the station lights to appear through the window, let him speak his disgusting words to Cecelia without protest. I'd always imagined I would fight.

'I'm sorry,' I said, and handed her the mug of tea. 'I didn't know what to do.' She put it on the table next to her and looked at it. We slept on opposite sides of the futon, and in the morning she was gone, the bike no longer leaning against the railing. We never spoke of it again.

'Here, check this out,' the goblin said, his voice reaching me through a discordant wave of synth-pop. He held out his phone, which was playing a pornographic video, the actors dressed like him. 'A preview.' He actually giggled.

I was the girl in peacock feathers, and the girl in peacock feathers laughed. She laughed at men like the goblin.

His hand brushed the silk of my pyjamas. I pushed it away.

'What's your name?' He eyed the letter *A* on my shirt pocket; Izzy's pyjamas also had a letter *A* stitched there. Mum probably hadn't noticed, she was terrible with details.

'Alice.'

'Alice,' he repeated. 'I still think you should undo some buttons.' He leaned over and tried to unfasten me.

I swatted his hand away.

'Come on, quit hiding, I'm not going to hurt you,' he said, and a button came loose over my belly, exposing a small triangle of nacreous flesh, unscarred, only slightly swollen.

My muscles felt heavy, and I was suddenly weary, the room shifting around me, very small and close. 'I can't.' I pulled the mask from my face, pushing it up into my hair. Cecelia's pointy incisors flashed into my mind. 'I'm in a parasocial relationship.'

'A what?' He laughed, reaching once more.

'I *said*—' I grabbed his wrist, channelling Cee's anger, but repeating his words instead: 'I'm not going to hurt you.'

The smile still played on his lips, his pulse juddering beneath my fingers. 'Not even if I ask nicely?'

'Hey,' a voice said, warmly. 'There you are.'

I turned, dropping the goblin's hand. A stranger's arm looped around my waist, lifted me to my feet. 'I've been looking for you,' the stranger said, his lips moving close to my face, hand slipping into mine.

He guided me out onto the balcony, our hands clasped together, the air hitting my face like a wet slap. 'Sorry, I hope I'm not out of line,' he said. 'You looked pretty uncomfortable, and that guy . . .'

'The dog,' I said. 'Where's Sunshine?'

'The dog? It's with Elsie.'

'Do I know you?' There was something familiar about the longish black hair, the uncomplicated beauty of his face.

'Not really. But I've seen you walking up and down Barclay with the dog in all kinds of weather. Here, drink some water.'

'I can't leave Sunshine with a stranger.'

'The dog's fine, I promise. One sip.' He held the brim to my lips.

'No,' I said, because he was a stranger, too, but I took the glass from him to shut him up. I leaned against the railing, and he put his palm on the small of my back, as if to steady me. We were above a small courtyard that would be leafy in summer; a flank of dark windows stared back at us. 'I don't want to fall off this balcony and die.'

'That's good,' he said, in the tone of someone accustomed to humouring drunk girls.

'You're not in costume, either,' I said.

'Wrong. I'm James Dean.' As if to prove it he put an unlit cigarette between his lips

'The resemblance is uncanny.'

He laughed, tucking the cigarette back behind his ear. 'You're not as drunk as I thought. Where are you from?'

'Across the street.'

'Where is your *accent* from? Are you from Scotland or Wales or one of those places?'

'Yeah, one of those places.' I sipped from the water glass in my hand. 'I just haven't eaten properly.'

He took my hand again and led me towards the kitchen. As we passed them, the partygoers turned to look at us, or maybe just at him. Even the white rabbit, whose shabby head sat on the coffee table, whose hair was slick with sweat, tracked us across the room with their eyes. In the kitchen, Elsie was trying to balance a cookie on Sunshine's nose to take a picture, but he kept dropping the cookie on the floor and trying to eat it. She'd snatch it up from the floor and try to balance it again. 'Careful,' I said. 'You'll break his temper.' This was another phrase I'd inherited from Mum.

'Elsie, did we eat all the chips?' James Dean asked. 'You got any crackers?'

I sat cross-legged on the floor next to Sunshine, who immediately curled up on my lap and sighed. 'I know, baby.'

James Dean was opening the kitchen cabinets, and now he turned to me and grinned. 'Shall we balance a treat on your nose?'

Elsie threw a handful of cereal at him before passing the box along the counter. 'Don't be gross, Jamie.'

'Your real name is Jamie?'

'I prefer James, actually. Even more uncanny, right?' Studiously, he tucked a battered cigarette packet into the sleeve of his white T-shirt, then shook some cereal into his hand. 'You want any?'

I shook my head. Elsie was called away to manage a dispute over the music, and James sank down onto the floor next to me. Sunshine emitted a low growl. 'Too close,' I said, and James shuffled away, stretching out one blue-jeaned leg.

'If that guy is such a creep, why is he friends with Elsie?' I asked. 'She seems kind.'

He shrugged. 'Some people think he's funny. He always has weed.'

James had an eye tattooed on his left arm – it looked vaguely Buddhist – and when he noticed me looking at it, rattled off a spiel about spirituality, his anxiety disorder, how he'd turned his back on social media. Everything in the world was connected, every living thing pure energy, and our energies could work together to make something beautiful, if we let them. He really was very pretty; it felt thrilling to be looked at by him.

'Deep,' I said when he'd finished.

'You got any?' he asked, eyeing my ear piercings. 'You look like the sort of girl who has tattoos.'

I shook my head; I'd only got the piercings because of Cee. My eyes were on his Adam's apple. To my horror I found myself leaning in to him, as if for a kiss. I could hear my blood rushing, and the tips of my ears were hot.

He smiled. Pulled his knees to his chest and wrapped his arms around them, like a shy kid. 'How drunk are you?'

'I'm just a little sparkle.'

'A what?'

'A teensy drunk,' I said.

'Can I walk you two home?' He nodded at the dog.

'It's not far.'

'I know,' he said. 'Across the street, right?'

We disentangled Sasha's coat from the others, and I laughed as James pulled on a leather jacket. 'You really committed to the role.'

'What? It's vegan.'

In the middle of the street I stopped, linked my arm through James's arm, and asked him to dance. He seemed amused, wrapped his arms around my back, swayed a little, the dog lead wrapping around our legs as Sunshine circled us. I laughed and pulled away, James tripping over the lead and splashing through a puddle as he caught himself. Someone called out something playful but indecipherable from the assembly on the grass.

James came inside Izzy's building with me; it was in the lift that he brushed his lips against my cheek until I turned my mouth to his. *Why not?* I thought. I expected a playful kiss, a kiss that would barely count, that I'd pull away and laugh, but something twisted in the pit of my stomach and I kissed him with a hunger I was vaguely aware of being embarrassed by even as it was happening. Sunshine pawed at the back of my legs, made an inquisitive little whirring sound, then barked. It was James who pulled away first, a string of spit suspended between our mouths, a smear of red lipstick on his chin. I'd forgotten I was wearing it.

In the corridor he kept his hands off me, to see, maybe, if I could walk in a straight line without his support, a kind of test that I must have passed, because at the door he pulled me against his body and kissed me again. Sunshine whined and scratched at the door, but my feet were off the ground, James Dean's tongue inside my mouth. His hand cupped my jaw, the peacock mask still in my hair and the feathers tickling my neck. I heard cicadas, the sound rising around me.

The door against my back disappeared and James and I stumbled, almost colliding with Sasha, who stood there in the doorway in his underwear. He must have heard Sunshine scratching at the door. Sasha opened his mouth to speak, then closed it again, so that he looked for a few moments like a lost fish. James Dean cradled me in his arms. Finally, Sasha cleared his throat. 'Is that my coat?' he said.

12

In the morning, I woke on the sofa, parched and with an incessant throbbing at my temples. I moved about quietly, drinking two glasses of cold water before dressing in soft clothes. Sunshine must have sneaked into Izzy's bedroom, since he wasn't waiting for me in the kitchen when I made tea. The steak I'd abandoned still sat on the counter and had bled out onto the plate. My stomach heaved – had I really eaten that? Relished cooking it too, a little song in my step as the butter melted, as the pan sizzled. I scraped it into the bin, almost retching, and let the tap run over the plate, meaty juices dripping into the sink.

Across the grey street, the revellers had left the party, leaving a few beer bottles and an empty crisp packet on the lawn that floated about like a windsock. Elsie's apartment looked devoid of people, but I imagined the rabbit crashed out on the sofa, out of sight, the tawdry white head still resting on the coffee table. I wondered if I'd ever see James Dean again, cringing at the memory of the kiss in the lift, the slow-dance in the street. Had I licked his face? I vaguely remembered his stubble against my tongue.

I knocked gently on Izzy's bedroom door. 'Iz. I'm making breakfast.'

No response. Was Sasha still in there?

I put some bread in the toaster and turned on the kitchen radio, low. I just wanted the noise. I wasn't really listening to the programme, which was an unfunny comedy sketch interrupted by laughter in the corridor. A happy bark. The front door opened and Izzy fell inside with Sunshine and Sasha. They all looked bright and fresh. 'You're up early,' Izzy said when she saw me. Sasha was talking to Sunshine, taking off his lead.

'You went outside,' I said.

'Yes, for a walk. Didn't get far.' Her face was flushed, a high rosy colour.

'Do you want toast?'

'No, thanks. Didn't think you'd have an appetite this morning?'

I wasn't sure how much she knew, whether Sasha had told her about James. Izzy teased me about the open wine bottle and I played along, tipping what remained of the wine down the sink and discreetly folding the peacock mask into the rubbish in a clutch of bright feathers. Sasha left quietly, with a minimum of fuss, yet taking something substantial with him from the atmosphere.

'That was nice, but it's taken it out of me.' Izzy sat on the edge of her bed and struggled out of her stretchy pants. I decided she didn't know much about last night. If Sasha had told her about James, she would have quizzed me about it by now.

'So . . .' I manoeuvred around her and pointlessly fluffed the pillows on her neat bed. 'You and Sasha.' There was no sign he'd slept there, not even a rippled sheet or a dent in the pillow. A pink carnation sat in a drinking glass next to the bed. I imagined Sasha packing the flower in his messenger bag and bringing it over.

'He's just a friend.'

I looked at her.

'What? He just stayed over to keep me company. You didn't mind, did you?'

'No. That's fair enough,' I said. She had a leaf tangled in her hair, and I picked it out. 'You just . . . hadn't really mentioned him before I met him at the hospital. I mean, you had, kind of, but I didn't realize you were so close.'

She shrugged. 'It didn't seem that important. It's not like you tell me about all your –' she caught herself, and the next word came out a little quieter '– friends.'

I wanted to ask her directly about Sasha, whether they were serious, serious enough to start a family together. Surely that had been her plan, for after the myomectomy, before everything went wrong. If she'd wanted to try for children, she'd have had to do it soon, in case the fibroids grew back. But she was denying that the two of them were even dating.

'It's completely okay if you're having it off with Sasha,' I insisted, trying to make my voice light, trying to turn it into something we could laugh about together. 'I mean, it's pretty obvious. I saw him in his Y-fronts.'

'Sasha is married,' she said.

'Separated, right?' I corrected.

'Well, yes, but . . .' She sighed and lowered herself down across the bed. 'I shouldn't have invited him over.'

I dropped down next to her, both of us gazing at the ceiling. A cluster of green-black mould had broken out like an ugly rash in one corner of the room. Sunshine grumbled as he curled up on the carpet near our dangling feet.

'He just held me,' she said finally. 'I needed to be with someone, to be held.'

I thought of James's hard body against mine in the doorway, how my feet had left the ground then, too. 'I get it,' I said. 'Does he know about the hysterectomy?'

Her body tensed and she shook her head. 'He knows about the surgery, obviously, but not that it went so wrong.'

'So you weren't planning on having a baby together?'

She turned her head to look at me, wordless, her expression wounded. Something scraped loudly across the floor upstairs, and the pipes creaked and whooshed behind the bedroom wall. The groans and sighs of Izzy's building reminded me of a ship carrying us on some marine voyage – I pictured us rocking under an indigo sky. Sunshine whined as something ticked against the window.

'No,' Izzy said.

I propped my head on my elbow. My sister wore a soft yellow jumper that was very unlike her usual style; I reached out and rubbed its buttery fabric between my forefinger and thumb. 'What about the stuff in the wardrobe?' I asked quietly, surprising myself.

She looked at me, confused. 'What stuff?'

I winced and let go of her sleeve. 'The baby clothes.'

'They're not mine,' she said, her face reddening. 'They're for a friend.'

'It's okay,' I said. 'You can have baby clothes. Do you want to talk about it?'

'They're not mine,' she repeated. 'My friend just had a baby. My friend Talia.'

The carnation at the bedside was already beginning to wilt. 'You're allowed to want things,' I said. 'You're allowed to grieve—'

'They're my things to want!' she snapped. 'I don't have to tell you about them.'

Tick, tick, tick, at the window. I had the disconcerting feeling that somebody else was listening in on us. A fault line of three long cracks in the plaster gave the impression that the ceiling bowed towards us in the middle, as if it was leaning closer to hear us, an interloper in our most intimate conversations.

'I'm just trying to understand—' I started, expecting a form to show itself through the plaster, for a face to press itself through. A rumble of traffic from outside made the walls shiver.

'Don't,' Izzy said firmly. For a moment, I thought she might share my sense that our conversation wasn't private, but one look at her face told me she'd just had enough of my questions.

I pinched the yellow fabric between my fingers as we lay together, our hair splayed around us on the covers. I noticed the fault line cracks had a myriad of hairline cracks branching off them. 'Someone needs to fix that,' I said.

Izzy took a deep breath, then folded her hands above her tummy. 'I nearly killed you when you were a baby.' She said it casually, almost as if she was talking to herself, or maybe to the fractured ceiling.

'You saved my life.' I sat up and perched on the edge of the mattress. I knew the story, me a girl choking on the noodles she'd made me after school, Izzy stuffing her fingers down my throat. 'You've got the story wrong.'

'No, I'm not talking about that. I'm talking about when Mum was carrying you. Before you were born. She was eight months pregnant and I got this idea in my head. I don't know where it came from. She came into the bedroom in the morning, to get me up for school, and I held my breath. I lay still. I let her open the curtains and I locked my eyes on the corner as the light came in. Mum was so big with you, she filled the window.'

She lay serene, spoke evenly, the spaces of my childhood home taking shape in the cadence of her voice. The soft light falling through the window, children playing in the street outside. The big bedroom with its pocked peach walls, which was Izzy's bedroom until she moved out. Perhaps Mum and Dad were already preparing the box bedroom for me – if Mum had been eight months along, they might even have bought a crib. Or with so many disappointments, that may have felt like tempting fate. Maybe the room sat empty. It was strange to think of your own non-existence, a time before you.

'I played dead,' Izzy continued, startling me out of my thoughts. 'I knew Mum hadn't looked at me yet or she would already have reacted. I didn't know what reaction I expected. *Izzy*, she said. *It's ten past seven*. That's how she woke me every day, by reading the clock, except whenever I opened my eyes and looked at the clock, it was always earlier than she said it was. I kept so still, hardly breathing at all even as the moment lengthened. *Time to get up*, she said. *Izzy*. There was this horrible stretch of silence, where I should have said something. I thought about saying something or moving or blinking. I could have pretended I'd been asleep with my eyes open or something. Then she screamed.'

Izzy paused to allow me a reaction. When I was silent, she carried on.

'The scream made me scramble up: I was spluttering, I was saying *sorry I'm sorry*, but her body was already on top of mine, pushing me down, the weight of her pressing me into the mattress, her big belly. She knocked over the glass of water on the bedside table. Then, Dad's voice in the doorway, *what's going on in here?* No clue as to why the two of us were wrestling in the bed. And then Mum's hands grabbing at her belly. *The baby, the baby*, she said, and they got in the car and drove to the hospital. They left me at home, forgot me in the panic. At eleven I could look after myself, of course. Dad never knew the full story because Mum kept my secret; she never told anybody what I'd done. How it almost cost her you.' She paused again, looked at me. 'Maybe that's why this is happening to me. Mum and Dad wanted you so much.'

'You were just a kid,' I said, trying to absorb what she'd told me. 'You couldn't have known . . .'

'No, you don't understand,' Izzy interrupted. 'She thought I was *dead*. She thought I was dead and she just fell apart. She didn't know what to do, it was terrifying. She just left me. She left me to save you.'

The weather had shifted. The apartment would glow around three thirty every day. It would fill with sunlight, the walls lighting up in broad beams. Golden hour, Izzy called it. She'd stayed in bed for most of the day. 'You're not bleeding heavy, are you?' I asked in a quiet voice when I went to check on her, her face sapped of colour. 'We have to go to emergency if you do.'

'I'm fine,' she promised. 'I'm just tired. Can't you draw the curtains?'

We needed groceries. I was trying to feed her things I thought would nourish her – bananas and broth and recipes involving kale. She kept asking for tinned soup and crackers, like Mum made us when we were home from school with stomach bugs.

When I called the lift, the hulk of Medusa stared into the corner, her back to me. I stepped inside, but I kept thinking of a horror movie I'd seen a long time ago, when I was a child surfing cable channels when I should have been in bed asleep. I imagined Medusa's head turning independently of her body, twisting out of joint, the grey hair covering her face. I hummed nervously and felt her shift behind me. The clink of keys. I started to sweat; when the doors opened, I put my head down and marched through the lobby and out into the bright street before the building could alter my path.

Golden light flooded the grounds of the Leonora, reflecting from the windows and blurring its harsh lines. The concrete exterior radiated a rose-coloured glow, its two curved columns glittering like hammered metal. I almost gasped, struck still for a moment, pulled into the building's newly revealed textures and shadows. Poured with sunlight, the Leonora was so beautiful, it seemed to sing. I had only just caught it – a moment later, the sun slipped behind the roof, and the building reverted to its cold blue shadow, the street lined with bare black oaks, leaving me to wonder if I had witnessed the transformation at all.

On the way to the supermarket, it began to rain. I was wearing Izzy's black raincoat. I noticed a woman with a low ponytail carrying an ornate gold mirror under her arm. The mirror was so large that I considered offering her my help, but her head was down and the rain fell in heavy splotches between us, blurring the surface of the glass. I'd stopped at a set of traffic lights and caught myself humming. 'Tōryanse, tōryanse. Koko wa doko no hosomichi ja?' Instead of passing the red shingle church with the arched windows, I went inside.

The interior of the church was panelled with dark wood. It was oppressively dark in there, with large flags bearing saints' crosses hanging from the beams, and little light falling through the stained glass. I walked between the pews towards the altar, which was flanked by two iron racks of votive candles, their flames flickering in a draught. It wasn't my church, but there was something calming about the quiet gathered here in the middle of the city. We'd never been much of a church-going family – christenings, weddings and funerals aside – though I'd once played an angel in the school nativity, a coveted role usually reserved for girls prettier than me. I dropped a coin in the collection box and lit a tealight, holding its wick to the flickering flame of a tapered candle, somebody else's prayer. I didn't know if I was meant to say something, ask for something, give thanks? I just closed my eyes and held an image of the four of us in my mind: Mum, Dad, Izzy, and me, together, safe and well.

When I opened my eyes again and turned away from the altar, I noticed a sign for a labyrinth. The sign looked a bit like the logo on my *Search Me* T-shirt from the library. I took some turns and steps to the rear of the church, expecting to find a hidden maze. But the labyrinth was just a black circle painted onto the floor, like an indoor basketball court. A man silently paced its implied spaces and tunnels. There looked to be no dead-ends. This was less of an adventure than I'd been expecting, but I began walking between the lines and flourishes, trying to contemplate something meaningful, to concentrate on the path I was following. I wondered what the story Izzy had shared meant to her, why she'd told me about it: was it the defining moment of our sisterhood, this thing she'd done before I was even born? My mind held an image of the bright glow of the sun-soaked Leonora, its walls shining like revelation.

I might have asked for answers there in that holy space, but what came to me were the questions from the stupid board game I'd found in Izzy's wardrobe. What would He say is your best quality? Is He a bum or a boob guy? I started to make a list of lonely places in my head. Playground. Internet. A ghost. When I was nearing the centre, another man in a priest's costume cleared his throat. 'You can't wear shoes in here,' he said from the doorway, and pointed to a sign that indeed forbade the wearing of shoes in the labyrinth. 'You're dripping all over the floor.'

'Sorry, Father,' I said, eyeing the feet of the man in the labyrinth. He was wearing trainers and hadn't looked up from his roving meditation. 'I didn't realize.' I stepped out of the labyrinth, crossed the painted lines, and left the church.

When I got back, the Leonora was the same colour as the glowering sky, the neon of the main drag fritzing in the distance. I crept inside the now dim apartment as quietly as I could, setting the groceries down on the carpet. Even Sunshine didn't hear me. The bedroom door was closed, and I slipped out of my shoes and padded silently down the hall. Alert, Sunshine's eyes were fixed on the kitchen and his tail thudded against the living room rug, where the city light pooled in its perpetual green. A spill of kibble rang inside the dog bowl. 'Dinner's ready,' Izzy called from the dark box of the kitchen. 'Come and get it.' I was surprised she was out of bed. She sounded exhausted, hoarse. She'd croaked the words. I reached out and pushed the bedroom door ajar, where Izzy was sitting up in bed, wiping drool from her face with the corner of her sleeve.

'What?' she said.

I turned swiftly, tripping over my own feet and landing face-first on the hall carpet. On my way down I saw it: Medusa gorging herself, bathed in white light from the open fridge, a leftover chicken thigh in one hand and a wing in the other, her mouth dribbling red sauce over her chin. She slurped and gulped and chomped.

Sunshine ran past his dinner bowl to hoover the crumbs at her feet, which were dressed in open-toed sandals, the toenails thick and curled.

'Brooke! Are you okay?' Izzy's voice pitched from the bedroom.

Medusa dropped the meat and it splattered red on the floor. She grunted. I got to my knees, pulling the hair away from my face, taste of blood in my mouth. I'd bitten through my tongue.

Medusa barged through the kitchen doorway, knocking me out of the way. I fell from my knees, my side hitting the concertina door of the coat cupboard. I heard a frightened, guttural sound, but couldn't be sure whether it came from her throat or mine. She toppled the bag of groceries in the hallway, smashing the eggs into the carpet, wrenched the front door open and retreated down the corridor, the wall lights flickering in their sconces as she passed. There was something terrifying about her back, the crawl of her hair, the lumbering pace of her walk.

'Brooke? What's wrong?' Izzy called.

I clambered to my feet and flung myself at the door, turning the lock. Sunshine lapped at the meat on the linoleum, feral with excitement.

'Medusa,' I said, my eye to the peephole. 'She was inside.' Her distorted form turned the corner. I peered into the kitchen, as if I might find someone else, a facsimile of Medusa lingering like a leftover, an echo or a hologram. There was a jar of mayonnaise and a loaf of bread open on the counter, a gooey handprint on the fridge door. I wiped my mouth.

Izzy had thrown back the covers and her legs hung over the side of the bed, a bottle of pills cradled in her hand. 'Are you kidding?'

A spike of adrenaline. 'Should I go after her?' Sunshine pushed his nose into the back of my leg and barked for attention, as if he could sense the thunder in my chest.

'Sunshine, shush!' Izzy snapped. 'What did you say?'

'Medusa.' The peephole felt inverted as I stared at the door, imagining the warren of corridors that lay beyond it. The pipes hummed behind the drywall. 'Do you think she walks up and down the corridors trying doors?'

'She's just an old woman, Brooke.' Izzy had levered herself up, coming to join me in the hallway, swatting at the light switch. 'What's all this mess you've made?'

'I'm going to follow her.'

'Follow who?'

But I was already leaving the apartment. I didn't know where to find her, but I'd seen her so often, lumbering along as if she owned the place, the empurpled housecoat carrying its own peculiar stink.

The sconces flickered as I walked the corridors, casting my shadow on the greasy walls. As I searched for her, I became angrier, and the corridors blurred before my eyes. What was she doing inside our apartment? Had she seen me going out and thought the coast was clear? Who did she think she was?

Medusa's wanderings gave her a superior understanding of the building. She knew the Leonora well, its maze-like passageways and abrupt dead-ends. *The power's out and all my food is spoiled*, she'd cried in the street. Maybe she just needed help. Maybe she would kill us in our sleep. What would I do if I saw her face?

I met myself in the mirror on the wall, my hair messy about my shoulders and blood dripping from my bottom lip. I was still wearing Izzy's black raincoat and smelled a little of frankincense from the damp church. My face was recognizable as my own, but something about it was slightly off, a smudge of light like a migraine aura bending my reflection. When Cecelia cut my hair in the bathroom, she'd leaned into the glass and pushed her tiny nose flat. She was very symmetrical. 'You look nothing like yourself in the mirror,' she told me. 'You'd pass yourself in the street.'

I don't remember taking the lift but must have done so automatically, lost inside my own churning thoughts, because I found myself in the basement. To my right was the door to the laundry room and ahead of me the car park. There was another door to the electrical room which buzzed, the vibrations growing under my feet as I approached it. But there was nothing else down there, no sign of Medusa. Still, I felt a pull. Tony, Tony look around.

The unfinished basement felt more naked than the rest of the building, the insulation exposed, clouding the ceiling like filthy wool. Silver pipes networked up there, too. I looked down at my hands, which were trembling with an outsized rage. Nothing like myself. If I met Medusa down here, alone, in this cramped, underground bunker . . . I shivered. The Leonora suddenly struck me as a kind of monstrous body, crouched in the city but capable of movement – turning its eye on you, rolling onto its scaled belly – the bare walls pocked and a generator rumbling underneath it all, until the day it would finally stop.

Part Two:
Shadowplay

13

When Izzy told Sasha the story of Medusa, it sounded funny: 'What? A snake lady was making a sandwich in your kitchen?' He'd picked up a chain lock and deadbolt from the DIY place after his shift, and now he was fixing them to the door frame.

They were calling the new locks anti-Medusa devices. Sasha was intrigued by the nickname, making a joke about us turning to stone while she raided the fridge. I sat at the kitchen table holding Sunshine, who shivered in my lap, spooked by the intermittent whirr of the electric screwdriver.

Izzy shook her head. They were making a meal of the task in the doorway, my sister offering minute instruction on placement. 'A little more to the left . . . a bit higher, can you line it up with the jamb?'

'She likes everything perpendicular.' I felt the urge to leave them to it, but they were obstructing the door, and I had nowhere to retreat to in the apartment. Not even a room. My bedclothes were folded at the end of the couch.

The screwdriver whined again, and as the sound died away Sasha made another joke about Medusa I didn't catch. Izzy laughed. I felt like I was being locked in and locked out at the same time. 'I don't think it's that funny,' I admonished from the periphery. 'I mean it's technically a home invasion.' I thought about knocking next door and asking if they'd ever caught Medusa eating from their kitchen. 'And how did she even get in?'

'You must have left the door open. She's an old woman. She's got confused and wandered in. If I hadn't been in bed, she would've seen me and realized her mistake.'

'I wouldn't do that. I wouldn't just leave the door open.'

'Well, maybe just unlocked? It can be easy to forget if you're used to living in a house. Anyway, I've reported it. The manager sounded a bit dubious, to be honest. I think he thinks you're making it up. And you know, I didn't even really see her? So it's hard to make a case.'

'You must have seen her.'

'I saw *you*, making a fuss in the hallway, breaking eggs and falling on your face.'

'I locked the door, Izzy.'

'Well, what, you think she broke in just to make herself a sandwich?'

'Stranger things have happened.' Sasha glanced from my sister to me. 'You read about these things all the time, people sneaking in through attic hatches and how do you say it? The space behind the bathroom cabinet? Living in other people's homes.'

'What space behind the bathroom cabinet?' I asked.

'In some old buildings,' he said. 'They were connected. Behind your bathroom cabinet would be your neighbour's bathroom cabinet, and you could see them, sometimes, when you slid open the mirror.'

'He's winding you up,' Izzy said.

'I don't know what you mean, Belle.' He'd kept calling her that, so casual, intimate. I knew she wasn't *Belle* to everyone at work, because of the get-well card, addressed properly, to Izzy. 'It's true.' He smiled at her. 'What apartment does this Méduse live in?'

'Yeah, where does she even live?' I chimed. 'You said she's not on this floor, so why do I always see her up here? I ploughed into her one night. She yelled at the dog.'

'She can be a bit unpleasant,' Izzy told Sasha, then turned to me and shrugged. 'I don't know what number apartment she is, but I usually see her at the mailboxes. I haven't noticed her up here on the seventh floor.'

'Why aren't you more freaked out? The fact she was in here while you were asleep makes it even worse, not better.'

'Oh, Brooke, she's just old. She's harmless.' Izzy laughed, shaking her head with something like fondness. 'What do you want me to do, call the cops on her? We're upgrading security here, okay? You'll be safe, don't worry.' She turned to Sasha. 'My sister's been blessed with a vivid imagination. She used to see an old lady in her bedroom at night.'

'No, I didn't.'

'Yes you did, when you were a kid. You complained about "the lady" watching you. But you were just hanging the latch, you hated going to bed.'

'I don't remem—'

'Hanging the latch?' Sasha asked, confused, tapping the deadbolt.

'Oh – no, it's an expression. It kind of means . . .' My sister looked to me to supply a definition.

'Stalling,' I said.

'Yeah. Like she was pretending there was a ghost so she could stay up later. Now she's seeing old ladies in the kitchen and turning them into the Babadook.'

'I'm not scared for myself—' I started, but trailed off, anticipating the story Izzy might tell about me, some childhood phantom or night terror, that one time I sleepwalked to the front door before Mum discovered me, turning and turning the locked handle. If Izzy wasn't in the room, I could be anyone. I might have reinvented myself, like I did for a time in Japan. But as it was, Izzy was there to remind me of every odd thing I'd said or done as a child.

Now they were talking about something else, something that had happened at the restaurant, and Izzy was smiling at Sasha like they shared some special secret, their bodies on some other frequency altogether. He mirrored her as if to say *mon cœur*.

I lowered the dog to the floor, crossed the room and stepped out onto the balcony. It was dark and the balconies opposite were deserted, Elsie's windows a blank. The neon lights of the main drag rippled pink and green waves into the sky. Spiders had built their webs between Izzy's railings, creating the impression we were living in some sort of nest, metal and concrete held together by threads of silk. Spiders formed clusters for protection, feeding and egg care – they were always mothers in Louise Bourgeois's work, repairing, dominating. I'd heard stories about arachnids laying eggs in people's ears or other body parts, the sacs bursting with scuttling spiderlings one unexpected day. I stood at the railing, my breath turning to fog in the bitter air. I couldn't understand why I was the only one who felt the horror of believing we were home alone only to find out we weren't. Izzy had heard Medusa, too. She must have.

Sunshine tapped the glass, and I slid the door open for him. He jumped over the redbrick sill and sniffed around the dead plants with a too-keen interest, shoving his nose into the remains of Izzy's herb garden – stiff rosemary threaded with creeping oregano, a frostbitten sorrel with a few pale leaves. 'Leave it.' I nudged the dog's head away from the planter, only to find a perfect bird, dead in the soil, one eye staring at us. Its feathers were mussed where Sunshine's muzzle had disturbed it.

A green metal trowel rested among the pots, so I picked it up to poke at the bird. When I flipped it, fat maggots crawled in its flesh. I scooped it up and dropped it over the railing onto the street below. It fell to the spot where Medusa had stood bellowing, floodlit, on the last night of the power cut. There was a figure down there now, staring up at me, then down at the scattered bird, then back up at me.

'Is that you?' The figure moved closer to the building's side exit and the security lights came on. James Dean, dressed in athletic wear. He shielded his eyes, stepped back again into the shadows. 'It is you.'

'It is me,' I called down to the darkness. 'It is.'

The movie theatre James liked was a bus ride away. We gravitated first to the back of the bus and then to the back of the theatre, which was screening a double bill of late-night horror: *Don't Look Now* and *Rosemary's Baby*. I sat in the dark extremely aware of James's body, his thighs spread apart in his black running gear. His hair was pulled back into a low-slung bun. He smelled of bergamot and soap, clean and baby-like in the stale sticky-sweet of the back row.

It was an older theatre, the seats a frayed red velvet and the auditorium shaped like a dark mouth. The scope of the screen was arresting; I'd spent so much time watching things on my phone or Izzy's small television that the cinema screen was imbued with a kind of godforce by its sheer size: a bright, vast image-engine. The soundtrack reverberated through our bodies and the screen pinned us to our seats, carrying us into a dream, the oranges and reds of Venice pulsing as though they might leak out.

James kept his eyes on the movie as he whispered, inclining his head towards me. 'Have you seen this one before? It's a classic.'

'Obviously it's a classic. It says it's a classic on the marquee outside.'

'Old movies are way creepier than the stuff they put out now,' he said. 'Even that weird crackle on the film is creepy. Can you hear it?'

'How old do you think this movie is? It was filmed in the '70s. Crackle.' I scoffed.

He laughed and threw a fistful of popcorn into his mouth. The theatre was largely deserted, a rainy Monday night, just a few couples dotted about the room and something untoward going on in a corner.

'Hard to believe Donald Sutherland was ever not grey,' James said, and shifted lower in his seat.

'These films are both based on books,' I whispered into his ear. 'Well, this one's a short story by Daphne du Maurier. I haven't seen it before, except for the ending.'

'You've only seen the ending? That's the best bit, the twist. How have you managed to only see the ending?' He leaned so close his stubble brushed my cheek.

'It was on one of those clip shows, top 100 scary moments in cinema or something.'

'Well, doesn't that ruin things? I know what happens, but only because I've seen the whole movie before.'

'Sometimes it's good to be prepared for the worst parts.' I waited for the infamous scene to unfold, almost holding my breath, trying to predict how we'd get there: the terrible reveal, the eyes of the cloaked figure, a murderous Red Riding Hood. I could remember the close-up of her face, but not the context.

On the screen, Donald Sutherland and Julie Christie rolled around in bed, their thin white bodies grappling with each other, Sutherland's hands brushing the notches of Christie's arched spine. The scene was intercut with another, of dressing for dinner, so that in one moment Christie was kissing Sutherland's foot and in the next she was jabbing at her eye with a mascara wand.

'Want some?' James tilted the popcorn box towards me, and I took a few pieces.

'I don't even like horror movies, normally,' I confessed. 'This sex scene is very angular, isn't it? Like, it looks painful. Is this the first time they've had sex since their kid drowned?'

'I don't know.' James talked with his mouth full. 'It's married sex, I guess.'

'Yeah, that makes sense. They have sex then they get dressed, over and over again.'

'Why?' he asked.

'Why what?'

'Why don't you like horror movies? Wait – that's not the question. The question is, why are you making yourself watch them if you don't like them?'

'It's an experiment,' I said. Though we'd kept our voices low, somebody turned around several rows ahead and shushed in our general direction. James grinned and squeezed my thigh. A child-sized figure roamed the crooked streets and bridges of Venice in a red cloak. I'd read that for du Maurier, Venice was code for lesbianism. A sexually attractive man was a 'menace'.

Finally, the climax arrived. Christie and Sutherland intercut once more, but separate, searching – for each other, for their dead child, through the Venetian night. Cornered by Sutherland, the figure in red turns, shakes her head. Her expression says: you've misunderstood. She hacks at the man's throat with a knife pulled from her pocket. I found the scene over the top, like most horror climaxes, full of violent excess – it's the excess of emotion that's most disturbing, perhaps. A flood of flashback images, Sutherland convulses on the floor, his shoe peeking out of a gap in the wall, dripping with blood. The film eats itself with too-bright red.

A short intermission between this and *Rosemary's Baby*, but James and I stayed in our seats, tickling each other's hands with our fingertips. 'What happened here?' he asked, stroking his thumb over the scar between my index finger and thumb.

'I sliced my hand with my keys.'

'Ouch.'

I traced the heart line across his palm.

'Can you read the future?' he asked.

'I can't even figure out what's going on now.' I dropped his hand.

'Is it your sister?' On the ride to the cinema, I'd shared my relief to get away from the apartment, looking out of the bus window, the city dripping with night. 'Are you in a fight?'

'We're not fighting exactly. She doesn't really . . . understand something I saw.' It had happened too quickly, perhaps. I needed to blow it up for her, Medusa at the refrigerator, her presence a nightmare the size of the screen.

'When you were kids?'

'No, yesterday. I don't remember her being a kid, she's a lot older than me. *She* remembers *me* in the womb.' I thought of the two of them wrestling in the bed, Mum pressing her pregnant belly into Izzy, her panic and terror. I wasn't really there, of course, an unwitnessing thing in my place, probably the size of a cabbage.

'I have a younger sister.' He squeezed my leg again, more crush than comfort. 'Every conversation we have is a fight about our parents. Even when we're not talking about that, it's really about that. Don't you think we're all just jostling for position? I can't stand that shit. Sometimes it's easier to talk to strangers.'

'You don't feel like a stranger. But yeah, there's less at stake. I mean, your siblings are part of your whole life.'

'I *am* a stranger, though.' He gave me a wry smile, delectable. 'You don't know anything about me.'

'Where do you live?' I asked. 'How close?' I meant to Izzy's apartment, since he'd recognized me from the dog walks, but it came out sounding like a come-on, an urgent request to go home with him. His eyes flicked momentarily to my lap.

'I should tell you something. Something you should know about me.' He paused for effect. 'I'm celibate.'

I held my breath.

'It's voluntary,' he added swiftly, and we broke into laughter. Someone shushed us again, though they were only playing trailers on the screen. 'I just wanted to say it out loud. In case it wasn't clear from . . . the other night. I don't want to send you mixed signals.'

'Oh?'

'I just got really wrapped up in sex,' he explained. 'I wanted it all the time. I didn't like how it controlled me. I did all this reading on testosterone levels and meditation, and I feel better with things as they are.'

'I thought you were coming on to me. At the party.'

'I was a bit. I'm not perfect.'

'And in the elevator?'

'Yeah, that was weird, wasn't it?'

'I felt like this . . .' I fumbled, embarrassed, but he was looking at me now and the screen flickered in blue flashes across his face. 'Hunger. I mean, I'm not often attracted to men.'

'Interesting,' he said, pretending to be coy. It was off-putting, surfacing like that in the middle of our honesty. 'I didn't mean to come to your building tonight. I just found myself there and this dead bird fell in my path. I felt like someone was following me, or watching me, and then I looked up and there you were.'

'Makes me sound pretty creepy.'

'It's like I was saying about energies. People can just be drawn together by something bigger than them, by the universe or whatever. But the energy with you is . . .' He made a gesture with his hand like the curve of a body, or a wave. I wasn't sure what I should take from it. 'And you said you're leaving before the holidays, so maybe this is a test for me on some level, like a test of the id or the ego or something else.'

It amused me that he thought I was in the city for him, somehow. Divine intervention for his libido. 'Now or never.' I brushed the popcorn dust from his T-shirt. 'Let's never.'

There was another, truncated sex scene at the beginning of *Rosemary's Baby*. The couple ate takeout on the floor of their new apartment inside a dark, brooding building near Central Park. Mia Farrow, as Rosemary, suggests they make love, and John Cassavetes, as Guy, turns out the light. They undress separately, on either side of their makeshift table – a broad shelf from the back of a closet Rosemary had uncovered after shifting a heavy dresser. The new knowledge of James's celibacy made the scene more embarrassing to watch while sitting next to him. Their intimacy seems habitual, natural, but Guy spends the rest of the film gaslighting Rosemary, and orchestrates her rape. The building's occupants are prone to slipping into comas or throwing themselves from the roof. 'I know this film is about a demon baby or something but it's giving me real-estate horror,' I whispered. Later, attuned to the desires of the baby she's carrying, Rosemary hungrily consumes raw meat.

'Do you know who Medusa is?' I asked James.

'The myth, you mean?'

'No, in my sister's building. An old lady, with crazy hair. She walks the street sometimes in a dirty old housecoat.'

'Oh. Maybe, I think I've seen her on Barclay before.'

'She was in my sister's apartment. Uninvited.'

'What do you mean, "uninvited"?'

'She was in our kitchen. I caught her, eating our food.'

'What? That's crazy. How did she get in?'

'Well, that's the thing,' I whispered. 'My sister thinks I left the door open and Medusa just wandered in. But I'm sure I locked the door behind me.'

'What did she do when you caught her?'

'She . . . just left. Like it was nothing. Like she'd done it before.'

'Jeez. Are you sure she wasn't just confused? Maybe she has dementia or something? She looks like she's not all there.'

'Yeah, but James: I locked the door.'

'I'm not saying I don't believe you. Maybe it's broken? Or, I don't know, could she even have a key somehow? Maybe she used to know someone who lived in your sister's apartment, and she just got mixed up.'

'No, that wasn't how it—' I started, frustration tipping into my voice. 'I mean, I can't be sure, obviously, but that's not how it *felt*. Her . . . presence.' I pictured the creeping smile Medusa had worn when she'd threatened to eat the dog, and rolled around the word *demented*. Demented by what?

James shrugged. 'Everything looks the same in those big old apartment blocks. That can be scary when you're old, getting lost in your own home, you know? You should call the building manager.' He obviously thought he'd hit upon something with this lay diagnosis, and I didn't feel confident enough to insist on what I saw as Medusa's command of the building – how its serpentine pathways confused me but not her.

'I don't know. Maybe . . .' I started tentatively, gesturing towards the screen, where Rosemary had discovered a connecting doorway inside the closet, one that led into her neighbours' apartment. I thought about what Sasha had said about the bathroom cabinets, their sliding mirrors, and the kabuki stage sets Cecelia loved, with their blinds, walkways, and rotating mechanisms. The little girl's refrain about 'passing through' thrumming against the bedroom wall. 'Maybe there's *something* going on in the building.' I laughed, to make it sound like a joke. But James was watching the screen and lifted his hand to press a finger to his lips. Then he made the same enigmatic gesture again, the curve of a body or a wave, his seeming symbol for some kind of slippery, amorphous energy.

14

We caught the bus back after midnight; James left me at the stop corner with a chaste kiss on the cheek. I walked towards the Leonora alone, the naked oaks dripping into the gutters and a light blinking into the street, washing the tarmac blue, red, blue, red, blue, red. A fire engine. Izzy's building strobed and throbbed.

The Leonora's occupants huddled across the street, some of them holding the hands of small children and others carrying their pets. One woman had a grey parrot on her shoulder, its head bobbing frenetically. A plume of smoke rose from the south side of the building, an acrid smell blowing into the crowd. 'Can you move back please, ma'am?' A firefighter asked, his arm held out in a signal to join the others. *Ma'am?* I thought. Nobody had called me that before.

I scanned the crowd of neighbours in their nightclothes and coats, some of them even in slippers. Medusa wore her housecoat and moved in agitated circles at the edge of the property. When a firefighter asked her to step back across the street, she swore at him loudly and then wandered off, muttering to herself and pulling at her hair. I spotted Sunshine next, crouched at Izzy's heel with his ears flat. Izzy wore her pyjamas and wool coat, her hair mussed. I called her name, jogging over to join her where she stood with her next-door neighbour and the little tōryanse girl.

'Where have you been? I was worried!' My sister wrapped me in a tense hug.

'Nowhere. Just the cinema.' As Izzy pulled away, I exchanged an awkward glance with the next-door neighbour, who held her sleeping daughter in her arms.

'You said you were going for a walk,' Izzy said. 'Didn't you see all my messages?'

'I don't have data on my phone,' I explained, not for the first time. 'Sorry, I thought you'd be okay with Sasha.'

'He didn't stay long after you left.'

'Is it bad?' I asked, fingers of smoke creeping over our heads. Izzy pulled her scarf across her mouth.

'Hi,' the neighbour said, rocking her daughter back and forth. 'I'm Wendy. I think it's just a kitchen fire or something. I checked with the building manager, and he said we can probably go back inside soon.'

'This is my sister, Brooke,' Izzy interjected, lowering her scarf to speak. 'She's visiting from the UK.'

We smiled and bobbed our heads at each other. 'In time for all this excitement,' Wendy joked, half-heartedly. 'Weren't you here for the power cut, too?'

'That's right.' Izzy shivered inside her coat.

'Wasn't it terrible?' Wendy replied, still swaying with the child. 'So many days, up and down all those stairs.'

Izzy grunted her agreement, even though she'd missed the power cut. She rocked with Wendy as if she was holding the child herself. I knelt to pet Sunshine, still whimpering at Izzy's feet.

'My daughter loves your dog. This is Kioko,' Wendy added for my benefit. 'When he barks, she copies him. *I want my bone!* she yells.'

'Oh, I hope he doesn't bother you,' Izzy said. They looked as though they were dancing together, the three of them.

'No, no. Dogs bark, babies cry. These things can't be helped.'

Sunshine sniffed my hand miserably. 'The alarm terrified him,' Izzy said. 'Thank God they've turned it off.'

'I can't believe she's gone back to sleep,' Wendy said. Kioko rested her head on her mother's shoulder peacefully. 'It was so loud in the stairwell.'

'She's so lovely.' Izzy smiled, inclining her head towards Kioko. 'What an angel. Look at her, Brooke.'

When we were allowed back inside, people packed into the lift, and a small crowd gathered outside the manager's office for news. I broke out in a sweat in the lift, pressing myself into the corner, trying to leave space for Kioko's sleeping form, her arm dangling over her mother's. We said goodnight in the corridor and Wendy carried her inside.

'I'm sorry I wasn't here,' I said. 'Did you manage the stairs okay?'

'With Wendy's help,' Izzy said absently. 'Do you want some tea? I don't think I can go back to sleep yet. Sorry for being cross.'

I sat quietly, watching her move around the kitchen. She seemed to be moving all right despite her midnight flit down the stairs.

'What did you see?' she asked suddenly.

'Huh?'

'At the cinema?'

'Oh. Just some scary films. Double feature.'

She frowned, put a cup of chamomile in front of me. 'I thought you didn't like them. Will you eat something? You missed dinner.'

'I stuffed myself with popcorn, thanks.' I blew on the surface of the hot tea. 'Have any creepy things happened in your building?'

She sat and stirred her tea, seeming to consider the question. 'If anything, we've been lucky. There was a stabbing in a building nearby. Just down the block. Some nut went crazy with a knife and started randomly attacking the residents.'

'What? I thought this was a safe neighbourhood.'

'I'm sure it could happen anywhere.'

'Any people jumping off the roof, slipping into comas?'

She looked at me. 'Brooke, I do worry about you sometimes. You haven't seemed yourself these past few days. Do me a favour, don't wander off like that again, okay? Or, at least let me know where you're really going. It's late to be out alone.'

'Okay.' I nodded. 'I didn't mean to freak you out. We didn't decide to go to the movies until—'

'"We"?' Izzy looked at me. 'You don't know anyone here.'

'I went with a friend. Someone I met at the art gallery,' I lied.

'Oh. You should've said. I'm pleased you've made a friend here. There's no need for you to mope around the apartment all day, you know?'

'Well,' I said. 'We only just met. But we saw this movie about a woman with second sight. And another one about this haunted building in Manhattan. I mean, there was some devil worship going on, so not really haunted. It got me thinking about Medusa. Maybe she's cursed or something.'

'Cursed? To what, wander the hallways of the building?'

I shrugged.

'Being old isn't a curse, you know. It happens to all of us, if we're lucky.'

'Being old and forgotten is,' I countered. 'Don't you think she must be lonely?'

Izzy blew on the surface of her tea. 'Maybe she's our protector,' she said. 'Did you ever think of that?'

When Izzy went back to bed, I crept under the covers on the pull-out. As I drifted towards sleep, the sighs and creaks of the building seemed to grow around me, reminding me of the sound I'd heard on the plane as I flew over the Rockies. That half-human caw. Something pulled at my insides, a rhythmic cramping of the muscles, as if I was performing some repetitive motion with my body that made a knot in my stomach, a knot that flared with pain and then ebbed away again.

A sudden jolt shocked me awake, my body tipping as though falling, the mattress no longer beneath me. I stood in the stairwell, my right foot dangling over the precipice. The lights flickered and died away, the stairs descending into black. I shrank away from the edge, flattening myself against the grey concrete wall, my heart racing and the cramp resting heavily in my pelvis. The wall seemed to groan at the touch of my body.

Then the lights cranked back to life, brighter than before, so that I squinted in their glare. I blinked and looked around me, crossing my arms over my chest, my breath fast. I must have walked there in my sleep. The painted concrete was cold and rough beneath my bare feet.

It was Sasha's fault, stirring the memory from childhood, the only episode I knew about. I hurried from the stairwell, back along the vine-patterned carpet to Izzy's green door, vowing to keep the incident to myself.

*

The fire alarm set something in motion with the next-door neighbour: an intimacy struck from the struggle down the stairs, Wendy with her daughter in her arms, Izzy's stitches pulling at her insides, step after step, descending. The next day, while Izzy was sleeping, Wendy tapped at the door to invite us to dinner.

'Nothing fancy. Family style. I've been meaning to make more of an effort since I moved in. Years ago! Just after Kioko was born. Your sister was always so understanding about the baby crying. So many neighbours complained! Can you imagine?'

'I hear her singing sometimes,' I told her. 'I recognize the song. I used to live in Japan.'

'Really?' Wendy smiled, one hand tugging the strap of her handbag over her shoulder. She wore tasselled brogues, the patent leather buffed to a high shine.

'Yes, in Gifu Prefecture. Only for a couple of years. I taught English there.'

'Of course you did,' Wendy said. 'My parents are from Kobe. Is it your first time in Canada? How do you like it?'

'Yeah, it's—'

'You should come visit your sister more often.' She bumped my elbow with her own. 'It can be lonely without family.'

'I know, it's just . . . such a distance to travel, you know?'

Wendy nodded. 'I studied in London. It's not that far, not impossible. I'm sure Izzy would like to see more of her little sister. She was so worried when you went missing last night.'

'I wasn't really missing. I was just at the cinema with a friend.'

Wendy's phone buzzed in her hand and she looked at the screen. 'Oh, I'm so sorry, I'm running late! I hope I see you tonight.' And then she was gone.

When I told Izzy, I thought she'd shrink from such neighbourly intimacy. Instead, she seemed pleased. 'Oh, that's nice of Wendy. But I feel bad about her doing all the cooking. I should make something. Dessert maybe.'

We started pulling ingredients from the kitchen cupboards. 'Would you mind if I didn't go with you?' I stretched for the bag of flour Izzy had pointed to. 'I'd like to invite someone over, if that's okay.'

'Oh, your friend from the art gallery?' she asked brightly.

'Yeah. I mean, it's short notice, but if he's free.' I pretended fascination in a bottle of vanilla extract. 'This is expired.'

'It'll be fine. Wait.' She lifted her eyebrows. 'You made a boy friend?'

'Yes, a boy friend.' I rolled my eyes, bending to grab Izzy's mixing bowl from the corner cupboard.

'You met a boy friend at the art gallery?' she asked sceptically.

'Is that hard to believe?'

'No. No, it's just not . . . what I pictured.'

'What did you picture?'

'You know, like, a little lesbian in socks and loafers,' she teased.

'Brilliant.'

'Is he straight?'

'I never asked directly. You can't tell people's sexuality at a glance, you know,' I chided.

She guffawed. 'You've more than glanced at him. He had you out past midnight.'

'Is this a thing, like, I can't have boys over?'

She laughed. 'Of course you can have boys over, I'm just surprised. So, it's not a date?'

'No,' I said, but there must have been something avoidant about my expression, because she was grinning at me.

'Right,' she said. 'Got it.'

James arrived before Izzy left, so was forced to make excruciating small talk. When he turned his back to hang his jacket, Izzy mouthed 'hot' and fanned her face, a gesture he caught and politely ignored as Izzy pretended to fix her hair.

'Your sister seems nice,' he said after she'd finally left, carrying a plate of fruit pie, tugging Sunshine with her on the lead. Apparently Kioko was excited for an evening with the dog. 'Did you make up?' James asked.

'Kind of. I think she's just sick of me being here all the time. She's doing much better on her own now.'

'Well, I guess that's a good thing. I was surprised to get your message,' he said.

'I'm surprised you came. But I appreciate it. I don't know anyone else in the city.'

'I'd invite you to my place,' he said. 'But I have roommates. We're kind of messy.'

'That's okay. I should probably stay close by anyway, for Izzy. She was a bit worried last night.'

'I keep you out past your curfew?' He grinned.

'Something like that.'

'What did you learn about the movies?' he asked, pulling his jumper off over his head, fleeting stretch of bare torso above his belt buckle. 'You said you were going into research mode.'

'Right. I started reading the books instead. I borrowed Izzy's library card.'

He sunk into the sofa and I sat next to him, poured him wine, held out a plate of smoked salmon bites Izzy had insisted on preparing. 'They're fancy,' he said.

'My sister is very excited for our evening. She promised to text me a four-minute warning and knock three times before she comes in.'

He laughed. 'You want to put a white sock on the door handle or something? Freak her out?'

'Is that what you and your roommates do?' I stuck out my tongue.

We pretended to watch another movie. Not horror, but something rather boring about a bank robbery and stolen identities. My hand went to the nape of James's neck and played with his hair, and he closed his eyes and opened his lips a little. Then he started stroking the pale inside of my arm with his knuckles.

'Your hair's so long,' I said.

'Suits me better. I like your undercut. Are you growing it out?'

'Not by choice. My ex did it for me, before we broke up.'

'There are these people – I think you call them hairdressers,' he joked. He turned towards me and ran his fingers over the regrowth at the back of my skull. We were sitting there holding each other's faces, and the sex scene from *Don't Look Now* came into my mind unbidden.

He accepted the weight of me in his lap as if the gesture had been inevitable, sliding his hands to the back pockets of my jeans. I pushed my hands under his T-shirt, let them drift down over his taut skin until I found his belt buckle. He shook his head and put a hand on mine, so I stopped.

But then he exhaled in a strange, groaning way and put his mouth on mine. The kiss started softly, but soon his hands were on my body. I drew away. 'Wait. We said we'd never.'

'That's right. We did say that.' He unfastened his belt, the leather slithering from the clasp.

'Are you sure?' I asked.

He lifted my shirt over my head and kissed me again. 'We could just make out?' he said.

I smiled at the phrase, my hands moving over his back, pushing under his T-shirt again to grip at his shoulders. He struggled to unhook my bra, and I pretended not to notice, putting my mouth to his neck, trying not to bite. Clean soap smell, like green stems. If I was honest what I really wanted was just to press myself to his skin, into the smell of him, to be held in it. I wanted the feel of his body, the weight of him on top of me.

The catch came undone and he slipped my bra straps down my arms, pushed me away. 'I want to look at you,' he said. My face burned; for a moment I wondered what the hell we were doing. Had I really only met him three days ago? But then his hands were cupping my breasts, which were tender and swollen, and his touch there felt like relief, like being lifted out of myself. I stood up, stepped away, held his hands.

'Come into the bathroom,' I said. 'I'm scared someone will walk in.'

He nodded, followed me inside and closed the door behind us. I turned the lock. 'I swear, I never thought—' he started, but I stopped him with a kiss.

'Shut up,' I mumbled against his lips.

He laughed, and kissed me, pressing me to the wall. I unfastened my jeans, grabbed for his hand. 'Please,' I said, 'touch me.'

'Take these off,' he said. We both wriggled out of our clothes, laughing, uncertain. Then he slipped his hand inside my underwear, took my nipple into his mouth. My breath caught, and I must have moaned loudly because he stopped and said, 'Shhhhh. God, you're so wet.' For a horrible moment I worried I'd started to bleed, and almost told him I might, but the conversation would be worse than the blood, a real mood-killer.

He pulled my underwear off, lifted me up onto the counter. I ran my hands over the expanse of his bare back. I thrummed with a bizarre maternal tenderness towards him, beneficently stroking his skin with my fingertips, cradling him between my legs. I traced feathery motions over his hips, his pubic hair, ran my hand up his inner thigh. He closed his eyes, receptive, then buried his face in my neck. He was hard inside my hand, and I stroked him slowly with my thumb, a tremor in his throat. He moved away, slipping down between my legs, licking the soft hairs on my belly into a swirl. While he was down there, I held his wrists.

'Did you bring a condom?' I asked.

'No. Don't you have one?'

'No.' I laughed. 'I don't usually go for . . .'

'I could pull out,' he said, kissing my inner thigh. 'I'm clean.'

I shook my head, remembering something I'd seen in the recesses of Izzy's bathroom cabinet. A box. I slid from the countertop, my body slapping unerotically against his, and we searched around until we found it.

'You're terrible at celibacy,' I said as he tore the wrapper open. He laughed, rolled the condom on, flipped me to face the bathroom mirror over the sink. I reached out and swatted at the light switch, so that the room went black.

But James turned the light back on again. He gathered my hair into his hands, pushed it over my shoulder to bare my back. 'I like looking at you,' he said.

Standing behind me, he pressed his face to the nape of my neck, traced a few soft kisses there. I felt him pressing against me, and he looked at my face in the mirror. 'Do you really want—'

'Yes, I want it. Hurry.' I was impatient, scared Izzy would come home and this would never happen.

'Will you say "please" again? I liked it.'

'Please.' He pulled my hips towards him, pushing inside, my fingers gripping the edge of the sink. I squeezed my eyes closed tight. He moved slowly, curving his whole body around mine, one of his hands pressed against the mirror, the other still grasping my hip. His breath came in a growl.

'God,' he said. 'Look at me. Open your eyes.' But I didn't want to see, only feel; there was a part of me not even present in the bathroom, a part of me somewhere else, with someone else, a part of me that looked Cecelia in the eyes and spoke her words back to her: *is this what you want?* James's hand moved from my hip to my waist to my breast. He pinched at my nipple, too hard, the way I hated to be touched. My eyes snapped open, and I saw something else in the mirror, something else that wasn't me, my skin flapping loosely in folds from my body, my face spilling a green ooze, a crone-face, wrinkled and contorted in ecstasy.

I screamed and bucked under his body, and I saw it in James's face – his young, beautiful face – in the way he recoiled, pulled out, fell back against the bathtub, tore the shower curtain down on top of him, the clink of the metal hooks. 'What the fuck?' he stammered. He'd seen it, too.

I turned away from the mirror, held out my hands, which were my own hands, my young hands, my stomach rounder than usual but free of pockmarks and folds, my breasts heavier, and down my thigh a thick trail of blood. I turned back to the mirror and the crone had vanished. My own reflection stared back at me.

'Did you—?' I started, but James was slapping the condom at the bathroom floor, pulling up his pants, breathing wildly.

'I don't want this. I don't want any of it, fuck this.' He grabbed the door handle and shook the door as if he was trapped. I reached out and turned the lock and then he was out in the hallway, tripping over his shoes, grabbing his jacket, fleeing, slamming the door behind him.

I opened the lid of the toilet and sat, wiping at the blood with paper, the four tiled walls spinning around me, my heart pulsing. I hadn't imagined it. James had seen it.

I stared at the mint-green bathtub, the limp curtain ripped from its hooks. I replayed the look on James's face as he flinched and sickened, felt his shudder move through my oozing, sore-pitted body. The silver tap began to drip from its wide spout, and something rippled in the distorted reflection there – some dark shape behind me, seeming to grow. I spun around, expecting the hag to loom at my shoulder. But there was only the mirror – reflecting my own face back at me.

15

When I came out of the bathroom, Izzy still hadn't returned. I cleaned things up, brushed my fingers through my hair, fluffed the pillows on the sofa. My grasp on my own body felt tenuous, so I resolved to stay fully conscious, switched on, awake. I knew I wouldn't sleep. I took out the pastels I hadn't touched since Izzy came home from the hospital and tried to capture the face I'd seen in the mirror.

Some of the crayons had broken in half or gone missing, but I worked with what I had. First, I drew the skeleton in a pencil outline, one of those short stubby pencils Izzy had lying around. Then I tried to capture the expression I'd seen, or made, the moment before throwing James off. The woman's eyes rolled back in their sockets with pleasure. A single tooth bit into a wizened bottom lip. The tension in the broad, fleshy jaw. But the essence of it escaped me.

I closed my eyes and drew the contours of my own face from memory without lifting the pencil from the page. It was an exercise I'd read about, an attempt to connect perception and movement, to coordinate the hand and the eye, and something too about empathy.

I was supposed to be looking in the mirror when I did it, but I doubted I'd ever look in a mirror again.

My eyes were in one corner of the page, my lips in another. I closed my eyes again and re-attempted the face I'd seen, my hag face, my future – I wanted to superimpose it over my now-face, to understand how I'd turn from one thing into the other. Two sets of eyes, one lined heavily, drooping, a gangrenous substance clinging to her cheek. On paper she looked like a growth, a mushroom. Hen-of-the-woods. I filled in the gaps between the two faces with flesh colours, and in the bottom corner wrote in pencil: *Thats me.* A Frankenstein draft with a lopsided grin, echoed, twisted, sprawling with desire.

Three knocks came on the door. There was a pause, then the key turned in the lock.

'Only me,' Izzy called before stepping inside. 'Coast clear?'

'He left already.'

She unclipped Sunshine's lead and shuffled out of her shoes, looking up at me brightly. 'Well, how did it go?'

Sunshine nosed my palm; I bent down to kiss him, stroking his ears. How could I tell her? 'We went at it like rabbits. A different sex act in every room.'

'Very funny,' she said, but her eyes lingered on my face longer than I liked.

'Do I look different?'

'You look a bit tired. Around the eyes.'

I felt a shiver of fear. 'I just got my period.'

'Oh.' She laughed in a conspiratorial sort of way. 'Bad timing. I won't miss that.'

*

Only I hadn't got my period. By the next morning, the bleeding had stopped. I was wrong, too, about staying awake. I'd drifted off on the sofa in the early hours, Sunshine curled in a tight ball next to me, and slept like the dead, startling awake and upright at dawn, my shoulder soaked in my own drool. Izzy was already at the kitchen table, drinking coffee and eating a banana. 'It's alive,' she said. 'A bit creepy falling asleep sitting up like that. When I came out here, your eyes were open.'

After I'd been to the bathroom and washed my face, I went back to bed and looked at the screen of my phone. No texts. I tapped out a message to James. *You never have to see me again. Just tell me you saw what I did last night?* Then I opened Cecelia's photo feed: no new updates, only her kohl-winged eyes, three squares of them, looking back at me, and two close-up shots of her bitten pink mouth.

'Hello? Earth to Brooke.'

'Sorry. I feel a bit under the weather.'

'You'll come round. The kettle's not long boiled if you want to make tea. Milk's gone off, though.'

'We just bought it.'

'I know, it's still in date,' she complained. 'It soured overnight. What are all these crazy sketches?'

My papers were still spread across the table. 'Just a face I saw in a dream.'

'Must've been one scary dream.'

'How did last night go?' I asked, to change the subject. 'Did you have a nice time?'

'You know, it *was* nice. It feels silly that we've never done it before. The food was delicious.'

'Did I tell you Wendy told me off for not visiting you more often?'

Izzy laughed. 'No. Did she really?'

'Well. She wasn't really telling me off. She was encouraging me, I suppose. To come back again soon.'

Izzy said nothing, folding the brown-spotted banana skin onto her plate.

'I like that you have such a nice neighbour,' I said. 'I'll feel better knowing that, when I leave.'

'There's no need to worry about me,' Izzy said. 'You know, I think I can get ready by myself this morning.' She carried her cup and plate to the kitchen sink, then kept going into the bathroom. 'I'll shout if I need you.'

I pressed the heels of my palms into my eyes, and when I took them away the room blinked.

'Ummmm, Brooke?' Izzy's voice called, the bathroom door creaking open.

'I'll be right there.'

'No, no . . . don't come in. Did you use these condoms?'

Holy fuck. We left the box out. I cleared my throat. 'Yes.'

Izzy poked her head around the corner, her shoulders bare, a towel knotted at her breast. 'It's just, I'm not sure they're, um . . . I mean, I think they're really old. You slept with him?'

'It's okay. We didn't. I mean, we did, but we didn't, like, finish.' I fixed my gaze on the ceiling, where Izzy's neighbours were moving around, scraping their chairs against the floor.

Izzy came into the room, pulling the towel tighter around her body.

'You look so *thin*,' I said, startled. 'Should you have lost so much weight already?'

'I know.' She adjusted the towel at her middle, giving me a sort of twirl. 'I wouldn't say I look thin, but the swelling has really gone down. Do you want to see?'

'That's okay!' I held up a hand, though I'd seen a flash of pubic hair and a thick purple-red line, the sutures still visible.

She closed the towel neatly, knotting it again between her breasts, then noticed something on the floor and bent to pick it up – James's jumper. She started to fold it, but I reached out and took it from her, rubbing the wool under my thumbs.

Maybe I'd imagined everything, even James's reaction. Or maybe it was my true body he'd been repulsed by, the smear of blood down my leg. Yes, that was probably it. My real, bloody body, responding to his, my grip loosening as I leaked, trembled, and gasped over the sink. Asking him to touch me. How repellent.

Some of these thoughts must have etched themselves on my face because Izzy sat down next to me, spoke softly, brushed the hair from my brow. 'Did he do something to upset you?'

'No. Nothing like that. It was just a bit of a disaster.' I tried to laugh, then pulled the jumper on over my head, hiding my face momentarily, enveloped by the baby smell of James.

'You can't trust a man that pretty. Mr Wonderful, that's what I was calling him next door. I missed his name.' She kissed the top of my head in a swift and angular dart. 'I'm relieved.'

'Relieved about what?'

'Can I tell you a secret?' she asked.

'Yes.'

'Don't tell anyone.'

'That's how secrets work, Izzy.'

'I tampered with those condoms,' she said. 'My heart was in my mouth when I saw you'd used them. So, I mean . . . if he did, even at all . . . we should go and get you a pill or something.'

'Were you trying to get pregnant?'

'Don't tell Sasha. You swore.'

'Izzy!'

'We hardly ever did it.' She brushed away the idea of criticism. 'I was in too much pain most of the time. But, you know, I had plans. For after.'

'After the surgery? I thought so.'

'That's why I have those babygrows.' Her thighs were furred with a soft down. 'I got ahead of myself. I was excited, picturing a little girl with plaits in her hair, blowing raspberries on her belly. I wrote a list of names I liked, and they were all girls' names, that's why I pictured her like that. A real, you know, little person.' A beat of three syllables or more. 'I'm so stupid.'

'Izzy, there are . . . other ways—'

'I know. "Families come in all shapes." I just really wanted to be pregnant.' She tucked her hands under her armpits, holding the towel in place. 'I wanted it more than I've ever wanted anything. It would have all been worth it, to hold my baby in my arms. I know you don't really understand. Maybe when you're older. Maybe not.'

'Are you in love with him? Sasha?'

She shrugged at the question. Her shoulders signalled this was a tangent from the preceding conversation. 'He said it to me once.'

'You didn't say it back?'

'It was a funny moment. The thing with Sasha is, when you're with him, it's like . . . there's a light on you, you're in the sun. But he struggles with object permanence. When he said *I love you*, he wasn't looking at me. He didn't wait for an answer.'

'He's a fuckboy?' That didn't sound right. Plus, he was what, like forty?

'He's a line cook, the job's not great for family life. But you've seen how he shows up for me. And he's not like that, a party guy, he's . . . kind of sensible. But a sexy sensible? Like a really hot dad? Commanding, you know? You should see him unload a dishwasher.' This was the most Izzy thing I'd ever heard, more real and more specific than a declaration of love. 'I think he said the L word by mistake – it was casual, like he was talking to her, his wife. You know, they still have these long phone calls, not even about the kids, but about their marriage, what went wrong. How it might have turned out differently. But when they hang up, he's . . . I don't know. Back in the room.'

'Izzy, he calls her when you're in the room?'

'She calls *him*. He can't just ignore her, she's the mother of his children.'

I asked her if they ever talked about the future, but she answered vaguely, and I wasn't sure whether she was talking about Sasha-and-his-estranged-wife or Sasha-and-Izzy.

'It sounds like you're his secret Vancouver girlfriend? Have you met his kids?'

She shook her head. 'I know, what a mess. But that's my lot now, isn't it? To be with someone who already has a family, or doesn't want one at all? The sick thing is, I can't imagine being with someone who doesn't want kids. What's the point.'

'Those aren't your only choices.'

'I wish you'd stop saying that.' Only my sister could look so stern in terrycloth.

'I just mean . . . there are other options, aren't there? If you want a family. It might be different than you thought, but . . .'

She interrupted me briskly, changing the subject. 'Are you sure Mr Wonderful didn't . . .' A little softness creeping in where she let the sentence hang.

'Come?'

'Hurt you. You look really upset. And you know, if he hurt my baby sister, I'd have to kill him.'

'He didn't do anything wrong,' I said, exing my finger across his jumper. 'Cross my heart.'

16

Since Izzy was making such progress with her recovery, we started taking short walks around the neighbourhood, at least when it was dry. She'd been for her first follow-up appointment and had her stitches removed, which made showering easier – though she still wasn't allowed to scrub the area. She'd seemed buoyed after seeing the doctor, who was enamoured by the surgeon's handiwork, as if Izzy's long incision was a thing of beauty. She'd almost cooed over it, the doctor. *Very nice*, she'd said, rolling Izzy's underwear down, pressing her fingers around the wound.

We rarely made it as far as the park or the seawall, but it felt good to blow away the cobwebs. Izzy would sometimes visit with Wendy next door, though Kioko irritated her at first, vying for her mother's attention, trying to show Izzy her dolls. 'I'm really hungry,' she'd interrupt them. 'I want a cookie.'

'The grownups are talking now,' Wendy would tell her. 'Go draw.' But Kioko drew ghost after ghost. Obake. Some of them were the outlines of figures with holes for eyes and mouths. Some of them had headless bodies or faces where their bellies should be. 'It's my mother,' Wendy said. 'She tells her all these stories. She's too young for them. I've heard them all, too.'

Wendy's company seemed to console my sister in a way mine failed to. Izzy invited me to go with her sometimes, but I liked using the time she spent next door to keep my own art practice alive, attempting to put the crone face to the page, capture her there; if I stopped making things, my hands would pick at the skin around my fingernails, stuff tufts of hair into my mouth, pluck at my eyelashes.

I learned about Kioko's drawings from Izzy, who gossiped on our walks, though never unkindly. I wasn't always sure how to respond to her disclosures, having never met most of the people she talked about, missing context. I offered concern or muttered disapprovingly, lifted my eyebrows or shook my head, trying my best to see things the way I thought she wanted them to be seen.

At the edge of the park, Izzy's street opened onto a rhododendron garden, a squat park building, fenced-in tennis courts, and the denuded golden aspen I'd walked beneath with Sunshine on my first day here. Beyond them, visible through the trees, the seawall curved its way along a stretch of ocean, a distant circle of mountains meeting the blue at the horizon. Large oil tankers sat in the bay; when I'd first seen them, they struck me as aberrant. I'd expected them to be temporary, that they'd leave and unspoil the view. But they were always there, black and red and haunting when shrouded in mist, part of the landscape here where the city spilled into the sea.

'Look up,' Izzy said when we reached the trees. They were barren, dun-coloured, but at the tops they thickened with the structures of large bird's nests, dozens of them. A great blue heron colony had established itself there, though the birds only nested from early spring to late summer, to breed and raise their young.

'I'll send you pictures when the birds are back,' she said. 'This magnolia is gorgeous in the spring, and the birds are so noisy and ungainly, flying overhead.'

'Izzy, you're a birder now?'

'Not really. I did try a birding group, once, but I couldn't get excited about listening for goldfinches or counting mallards.'

'I wonder what I'll be doing next spring,' I said, half expecting an invitation to follow, but she only offered more about the birds.

'I saw an eagle take a heron egg once. He ate it – yolk dripping from his beak, dead-eyed. The sound of the colony in peril is so dramatic! Do you see how the tree trunks have those metal bands? It's to stop raccoons climbing up there to kill the babies and sleep in their nests.'

'Rough. How do you know all this?'

Izzy shrugged. 'It helps me to notice the birds. You know, they shouldn't even be here, it's an odd place for them to nest, in the middle of the city with all this noise. But here they are. They chose this place.'

Clouds scudded over the treetops – the sky felt too close, like we were enclosed beneath it. 'I had to make a call, and I thought I'd feel better either way, once I'd had the operation.' She took a deep, gulping breath. 'I knew there was some risk attached, but I thought that, even if the worst happened, at least it would be decided. No more waiting and wondering.' This was the first time she'd talked openly about what had happened – what she'd lost – since she was in hospital and high on morphine. The air between us throbbed with feeling, her eyes averted. 'You know what Lucie asked me? Did I freeze my eggs. It was the first thing out of her mouth. Like everyone was doing it routinely, how careless of me not to. I won't bore you with the ins and outs of that process – live birth rates in my age bracket.'

She looked at me then and I felt our eleven-year gap flicker between us. We belonged to different brackets, and hers was beyond . . . what? A kind of threshold? It was a bizarre feeling, because Izzy was so young and vital, my big sister going out ahead of me and making everything a bit less scary, so sure of herself.

'Before that, everything was so up in the air . . . trying, you know, in my own ways.' She inclined her head, and I thought of the tampered condoms. 'But the *hope* was hard, trying to trick my way into it, being a mother. My period flash-bombing me even as I was thinking maybe this time . . . My body working at the wrong, useless thing. No babies for you, here's this big lifeless cyst! An interloper! You can have as much of that as you can stomach!'

She wasn't talking to me any more, but to herself, or the sky, or maybe the birds. Her body trembled with a quiet sort of rage, and I was a little afraid – scared to touch her and pierce the moment. She stood there a minute longer, then turned and started walking back to the apartment. 'I want to walk by myself. Please don't say anything.'

'Okay,' I promised, nodding, my throat constricted. 'I'll just walk behind you.'

She never turned around, like on our walks through the forest back home when I was ill. Her body had been so full of vigour and drive, her footing sure and steady. Now she folded in on herself, her back rigid and her shoulders hooked, as if she was holding herself together with physical effort. I was trying not to catch up to her, keeping my promise, though I hoped she could feel me, somehow, that she knew I was still there, honouring the distance between us.

*

By the time we reached the building the clouds had cleared, and a moving truck idled at the kerb, the front door propped open with a cardboard box labelled STUFF. It contained a twisted lampshade, the plug trailing inside on the carpet, as if someone had kicked it. Upstairs, Izzy murmured her greetings into Sunshine's fur, then cupped his face in her hands. 'Mummy's little hero.' His tongue peeped from his mouth as he rolled over for a belly rub. 'Did Mummy leave you behind? I'm sorry.'

'I'll take him out again in a bit,' I said.

She slipped out of her jacket and hung it in the hall cupboard. A bright cold light spilled through the open bedroom door into the hallway. I noticed mildew seeping from the corner of Izzy's bedroom ceiling, creeping in a smeared line towards the bed.

'How long has it been like that?' I'd continued to sleep on the sofa in the living room, but I couldn't imagine the mildew escaping Izzy's notice.

'Yuck.' Her shoulders sank. 'I must have taken my eye off it for too long.' The dog still padded around her ankles, brushing himself against her, a behaviour I associated with cats. 'Oh, Sunshine,' she said fondly. 'He must miss me rolling on the floor with him.' She stroked him with her foot.

'I'll take care of the mildew,' I said, trying to picture my immaculate sister rolling about on the floor with an animal.

Standing on a kitchen chair, I sprayed the corner with mould remover, wearing a mask and rubber gloves that I'd found under the sink. The mould had happened before. There was something wrong with the building after all – it was poorly ventilated. Condensation clung to the glass like a sweating sickness, blurring our view of the street. We opened the sliding door of the balcony and the bedroom window wide. Bitter air filled the rooms. The gesture reminded me of my classrooms in Japan: every morning, whatever the weather or season, the schoolrooms would be aired out, the windows wide to the playground. It became a welcome ritual, a constant no matter which village school I was working in, or which teacher stood on the other side of the room as I slid the windows open in tandem with them – soft white seed heads, birdsong, or flakes of snow drifting in on the air.

I scrubbed at the wall with such force my arm ached. I'd suggested Izzy lie down on the sofa, but instead she kept the dog busy, chucking his favourite stuffed toy across the living room, telling him to fetch. Almost every night, Sunshine would take the lamb into his bed, suck its fabric ears and nose, pump its stuffed belly with his paws, like a puppy feeding from its mother. Now he chased it across the room, clamped it in his jaws, and brought it back so Izzy could throw it again.

'Oops,' I heard, and from my vantage point on the chair saw the lamb sail between the balcony railings, busting through a cobweb. 'Sunshine, *no*.' He'd followed it out there, peered over the edge, his back legs stretching towards the door. He wagged his tail, yapped. Izzy appeared out there too, ushering the dog back inside.

'It's okay,' I called. 'I'll go get it.' I thought the lamb would be simple to find – I'd seen it go over; it couldn't have landed far. When I got downstairs and out into the street, I paced up and down, even looking beneath parked cars and into a nearby rubbish bin. I had to return to the apartment empty-handed, where Izzy distracted the dog with another, less beloved toy. 'Mummy's little hero,' she murmured in his ear, again and again and again.

*

Once we'd finished cleaning, we sat down to talk to Mum, Izzy's phone propped on the coffee table before us, our bodies distorted by the angle. We were all chins, rays of a golden hour uplighting our faces, but Mum kept commenting on how thin Izzy looked. She used the word *gaunt*. 'Are you looking after each other?' she asked. 'I do love seeing you together. Brooke, you look so healthy. It must be the light – you're glowing!'

'I don't think so.' I snorted. But Izzy was looking at me too, as if she was searching for something in my face that she couldn't quite put her finger on.

Mum nodded. 'Look again.'

I took the dog out afterwards, soaking up the last of the golden light, the Leonora basking in the glow. Sunshine stuck his nose into bushes and litter, either peeing on the article of interest or trying to eat it. He snarfled up a discarded french fry, a corner of crumpled tissue, and a cigarette stub before I could stop him. His nose led me back to the edge of the park, where the rhododendrons spread beneath the dormant heron colony.

At the furthest stretch of the lead, Sunshine peed on a patch of rust-coloured snapdragons. I lingered, hesitant to go deeper into the woods, turning over everything Izzy had said that morning. I pictured her standing here through the off-season, waiting for the birds to come back. It seemed like a lonely sort of passion, a pastime belonging to someone unlike the sister I knew. Something haunted me about what she'd said about her body making a lifeless cyst, pouring energy into growing the mass instead of making a baby. Interloper. Did the cyst reproduce or duplicate? Filling with air and fluid, sucking Izzy's blood, capable of movement. I didn't like the idea of some force that could take over your body, kill your only chance at the thing you most wanted, and give you something else in its place.

That night the three of us slept on the pull-out together; the fumes from the mould remover bothered Izzy, making it difficult for her to breathe. The apartment was cold because we'd left the bedroom window open, and a draught crept beneath the door. Sunshine's warm body stretched between us in the middle of the bed.

'Aren't you supposed to be good at finding things? Isn't that why they like you at the library?' Izzy teased once we'd settled down.

'I swear, it wasn't out there.'

'I'll buy him another lamb. But he won't be happy; it won't smell the same.'

'He seems content at the moment,' I said as the dog started to snore.

In the early hours, I was awoken from a bad dream. My half of the bed was damp with sweat, and I felt a terrible thirst. In the dream, I'd been scratching off fragments of wall from Izzy's bedroom and eating them, filling my mouth with plaster, with the taste of saltpetre.

Izzy lay next to me, her breath deep and slow. What kinds of dreams did she have? In the half-awake, the apartment felt porous, like something vital could seep out, or melt through the walls. A tapping at the windowpane made me think of spiders. But after a moment, I interpreted the sound as a rap against the door. Light enough so that Sunshine remained undisturbed.

Gently, I rose from the bed, shrugging out of the blankets, and crept into the hallway, where I could see the door. Somebody tried the doorknob. Hungry and half-dreaming, I watched it turn, the door shaking slightly in its frame, the chain swinging loose because I had forgotten about Medusa. How could I have forgotten about her already?

I walked across the carpet in my socked feet, slowly. Reached out and closed my hand around the gently rattling doorknob. Instantly, it stopped moving. Footsteps pattered on the other side of the door. My heart stabbed wildly against my breastbone as if to the screech of dissonant strings. I pressed my eye to the peephole, lifting myself on tiptoe. Empty corridor, spotlights buzzing over each doorway, sconces rippling light across the walls. I pressed myself closer to the door, trying to outfox the warp of the fish-eye lens. I thought I could see a shadow on the carpet, as if someone was just out of sight around the corner. I strained to see it, until the lights flickered and the shadow shrank away, then vanished altogether.

I cracked open the door. 'Hello?' My voice sounded bodiless, like a returning echo. Corridors of silence. Slow spread of mildew. Nothing in my line of sight.

I padded to the corner where I'd seen the shadow cross the filthy carpet, noticing the scratch of threadbare patches in the pattern beneath my feet. I stretched out a hand to touch the wall, steeling myself before I peered around the corner to the lift landing. Flank of green doors. Nobody there. But the lift chimed and opened as though I had called it.

I hurried back inside the apartment, locked the door and threw the deadbolt, my heart puttering in my chest. I slid on the chain lock and rubbed at a spot between the wall and the doorframe where the plaster was showing. I put my finger in my mouth, but the taste wasn't right. I crept around the apartment, trying different things: paper, which disintegrated in my mouth and stuck to my tongue unpleasantly; brick dust, which I leaned out of the bedroom window to collect from the sill. I thought about the bone I'd taken from Sunshine, the wishbone from the chicken carcass, but the texture was wrong, too greasy, too *organic*. I bolted two glasses of water and tried to forget the urge, and in my sleep I dreamed of a baby made of clay, waking the next morning with both hands resting on my belly.

17

I kept eyeing the doorknob every time I passed through the hallway, expecting to see it turn. Even by the light of the morning, when the night's heavy-footed ghosts seemed to hold less power, I kept a watchful eye on the green door, as if my hypervigilance alone could keep us safe from whatever wanted admittance. I even reached out and turned the knob a few times to test it was secure, locking and unlocking the latch.

Rain hammered down outside, and the window was fogged opaque. I hadn't taken Sunshine out for his morning constitutional yet. I knew what kind of walk it would be – dragging him to a corner of grass, then slinging the green plastic poop bag in the wet rubbish. He would creep along on his belly and hasten to scurry back inside, where I'd have to wipe his paws and rub at his underside with the navy-blue towel set aside for this purpose. I waited for a reprieve from the downpour in my pyjamas while Izzy made herself breakfast.

She sang as she sliced into a grapefruit at the kitchen counter, the smell of it spritzing the air with a bitter tang. Her song relaxed me a little – she had a terrible singing voice, but it was a welcome, normal sound, the sound of someone at home in themselves. I sprawled on my belly on the living room rug with my pencils and paper, trying to draw the old woman out of me again. Was it really a vision of myself? I was desperate to know what James had seen, but he was ignoring my messages.

Sunshine stared down at me with his big glossy eyes and grumbled. He was restless, but I wasn't ready to face the weather, and I worried about leaving Izzy alone in the apartment. I grabbed for something from his pile of toys and threw a rubber ball for him, turning back to the page. He returned it loyally, thrusting his nose under my drawing hand and dropping the ball on the paper with a grunt. He wagged his tail in anticipation. I threw the ball again, and erased the mistake his nose had nudged my hand into making.

'Are you sure you don't want breakfast?' Izzy spooned the last bit of yoghurt from the bottom of her bowl with a horrible metallic scrape.

'I'll have something later,' I said. 'I don't feel like anything yet.'

'Make sure you do,' she said, and locked herself in the bathroom.

Sunshine returned with the ball, and I threw it again. He yapped and ran off happily, his paws thudding across the carpet.

I stared at my rendering of the crone's face on the paper before me. I'd filled the eyes with a deep black, an abyss I might fall into, but they held none of the lust or triumph I'd seen in them in the bathroom mirror. I ripped up the page and screwed it into a ball, then started again, filling in her eyebrows, nose, and mouth, leaving the eyes a blank.

The ball rolled across the paper, across the absent eyes. I lifted it to throw for the dog, but Sunshine wasn't there.

'Sunshine!' I called and waited, but there was no sign of him. He was probably fed up of the game, in need of a walk.

I gathered myself up, going to the coat cupboard for his lead, expecting him to come running as I jangled it. 'Let's go, boy!' I pulled my boots on over my pyjama bottoms, and grabbed Izzy's raincoat. 'Sunshine!' I called again. But he didn't appear.

I kicked off my boots and went into the bedroom, dipping down to check inside his crate. It was devoid of anything but Izzy's old robe, which bore a circular, dog-shaped imprint. A pungent waft of dog met my nose.

I got to my knees and peered under the bed, searching for Sunshine's two brooding eyes looking back at me. There was nothing under there except my suitcase. I walked through the apartment, checking the spot between the sofa and the wall where he'd hide when alarmed, and even out on the balcony, though the door was closed. 'Sunshine,' I repeated, and when Izzy opened the bathroom door, asked, 'Is he in there with you?'

'The dog? No. Can't you find him?'

I shook my head, confused, still holding the dog lead.

She rubbed a towel over her hair. 'Did you look under the bed? Sometimes he crawls under there.'

I went back into the bedroom to check each station, then shook out the quilt as if Sunshine would tumble out. I threw back the pillows, peering into the small gap between the wall and the bed, though I knew he'd never fit down there. 'Sunshine! Is there anywhere he could hide?'

Izzy appeared in the doorway in her egg-patterned robe. 'Under the bed, Brooke, not behind it, for God's—'

'I looked there already!'

At the front door, the deadlock was unfastened, the chain hanging loose. The sight brought me up short; hadn't I been monitoring the door all morning? Had I left it like that? I opened the door hoping to find Sunshine outside, waiting patiently to come in. But there was just a blank spot on the carpet, a flank of green doors. The ping of the lift opening to an empty cab.

I knocked next door, at Wendy's, but there was no answer.

Izzy looked at me expectantly when I returned, her face soft and open.

'He's gone,' I said

A shadow fell across her. 'Brooke,' she said in a calm voice. 'Where have you taken the dog?'

'Izzy, fuck off. He must have slipped out the door. Did you go somewhere, take the rubbish out?'

'When, exactly?' She gestured to her wet hair, exasperated.

'I'll check downstairs,' I said.

I rode the lift down to the lobby in my pyjamas, looking closely into corners, scanning the mailboxes, peeking through the windows of the manager's office. I opened the heavy front door that didn't always latch and poked around the concrete planters in the rain, my hair plastering to my head. Going back inside and looping out through another exit to check the smoker's garden, I found a sheltered spot and let my gaze sift through the dripping November landscape, glancing under the rusted metal bench, toeing a dead hydrangea, stripping off a piece of masonry like bark and testing it between my teeth.

Usually I'd be praying not to see Medusa, but now I wondered where she'd evaporated to, why I hadn't summoned her facing the wall inside the lift. I wound up the stairwell, walked the length of every corridor; if I encountered anyone, I asked them if they'd seen the dog, and, if they lingered long enough, when they'd last seen Medusa. Most people knew who I meant. But they only shook their heads, apologized, averted their gaze or else stared at me, cracked a joke, whispered once my back was turned, giggled, or hoped I'd find him.

'I can't find him,' I told Izzy once I was back at the apartment. She'd emptied the contents of the wardrobe onto the bed, convinced he was hiding inside it. Packing paper, scraps of fabric, the babygrows and hand weights.

'He can't have disappeared.' She waved a red shoe around, her voice shrill. 'He must have got out, followed you somewhere. Did you sneak out to meet that guy?' She pointed the shoe at me.

'While you were in the shower? I don't have to sneak out to meet boys, Izzy. I'm a grown up.'

'Well then, he's somewhere, he's hiding. Do you think he could have got stuck behind something?' She moved her hands over the walls, knocking in various spots, as if there could be some secret compartment that had evaded her in the many years she'd lived there. 'Sunshine! Come here, Sunshine! Treat!'

'Here.' I rifled through the laundry basket. 'If your dog gets lost, you're meant to leave something that smells of you where you last saw him. That way he can follow the scent back.'

'We last saw him in here, Brooke. Honestly! I'm calling the building manager. Someone must've opened the apartment door, and he's got out with them.' She huffed into the other room.

'Did you hear someone open the door?' I asked, following her.

'No, of course not, I was in the shower. But I've come home before to find the apartment unlocked. They're not supposed to, but management lets people inside, to test the fire alarms and fix the plumbing and whatnot. It happens more often than you'd think.'

'I think we would have heard them testing the fire alarms. Besides, wouldn't they knock first?'

'Don't be facetious, Brooke. You were probably daydreaming. Now, whether he'll admit to it is another thing . . .' She slammed the buttons on the phone, relentlessly logical, and waited for the manager to pick up. 'Sunshine must be here somewhere, this can't happen. Dogs don't just disappear!'

Her chest heaved. I didn't tell her about the deadbolt, that I was sure I'd thrown it closed the night before, that I'd checked it was still closed this morning. I was scared she wouldn't believe me, that it would implicate me further, in her mind. 'Ask him if he's seen Medusa,' I told her instead, thinking with some alarm of the night I'd collided with her body, how she'd threatened Sunshine with a kick – threatened to eat the dog. But Izzy only shot me a look that accused me of persecuting the elderly, of hiding something from her. I suppose I was.

We dressed hurriedly and made our way outside together, bumping into Wendy and Kioko in the lobby. 'Have you seen Sunshine?' Izzy asked abruptly. Wendy raised her eyebrows, Kioko tugging at the sleeve of her trenchcoat.

'The dog,' I added.

Wendy's face filled with genuine concern. 'No, oh no, is he lost?'

'Since this morning. He must have got out somehow.'

'Oh, that's too bad! You must be so worried. We can help you look, can't we, honey? Do you want to help our nice neighbours find their doggy?'

'I'm really hungry,' Kioko replied, looking up at Izzy.

Wendy sighed. 'Ignore her please. She's had breakfast; she uses that word for every feeling she has.'

The four of us went out into the street, roving the pavement in a pack. We'd cover more ground if we split up, I thought, but Izzy had fallen into step with Wendy, who was carrying a string bag of groceries, and Kioko had thrown me off guard by putting her small hand in mine. Part of me was touched at the tiny, unthinking gesture, but at the little girl's pace, we fell behind.

'What's your favourite animal?' I asked her. 'Is it a doggy?'

'No,' she said.

'Oh,' I said, remembering her stuffed pig. 'Is it a . . . buta?'

She looked up at me and laughed, her face bright. 'Why?'

'Why what?'

'Why is the doggy lost?'

'I don't know, Kioko. It's like he just disappeared.'

She dropped my hand to lift both of hers in the air, as if miming a vanishing act. 'The dog is all gone?' She frowned.

'Yeah. That's right. Will you tell me if you see him? Can you look for his tail?' I pointed to the trees studding the pavement. 'Remember what it looks like?'

She nodded seriously and took my hand again.

Despite the nickname given to me at the library, I didn't have a good sense of Saint Anthony, whether there was some holy object he'd found, why losers of things prayed for his guidance. I had an inkling it was something to do with retrieving memory, receiving celestial guidance in retracing your steps. Could I have left the door ajar in one of my checks? Had I myself unbolted the lock? Surely not. Had Sunshine followed the ball out into the corridor, or even off the balcony? I shook the thought out of my head. The balcony door was definitely closed, and the ball had rolled its way back to me.

Ahead of us, Izzy and Wendy turned a corner. They were walking so fast we couldn't keep up. Kioko slipped to her knees, and for a moment I thought she might cry, a sharp gasp escaping her mouth. I used my mother's trick, cheering somewhat wildly as I pulled Kioko to her feet – 'Up we go! Hooray!' – and her tears halted before they really began. She gave me a puzzled smile, pleased with herself. I swept the dirt away from her white tights, chattering about whatever rubbish came into my head, trying to make myself less of a stranger to her.

I started to tell her a story about a hunt for mushrooms, and the nature walks I used to take the kids on in Japan, until I was telling her the story of that day in the woods. The boy who'd wandered off in a bright vest. How I'd run through the woods calling his name, looking for the spot of neon between the trees. The panic that had risen in my chest as the forest seemed to expand around me, though I knew the rest of the class was only metres away.

'Daichi!' I'd called, stumbling over tree roots, my knee hitting the mossy earth, my hand almost crushing a golden-coloured mushroom the size of my fist. I looked up, tuning in to the trickling sound of river over rock, and then a splash. 'Daichi!' I pulled myself up and through the trees over the curve of a hill, where I saw the little boy on the bank of a shallow creek, throwing stones.

Almost crying with relief, I took his hand and led him back to the other children. Haruta-sensei thanked me graciously, but I knew I was to blame for his disappearance in the first place; I hadn't watched my charges closely enough. I'd been mulling over a fight I'd had with Cecelia the night before, sulking about it as I trailed behind the group of seven-year-olds.

I faltered, realizing the story might become fodder for Kioko's drawings, the lost boy in the woods. I began to notice posters for missing pets taped to lamp posts, posters I'd seen many times on our walks but that appeared to me now with fresh urgency: reward, lost dog, please call, don't approach, very timid, spot on hind leg, heartbroken, WE NEED HIM NOW MORE THAN EVER.

Izzy and Wendy were far ahead of us when we turned the next corner. 'Can we go faster?' I asked the little girl. 'Shall we catch up with your mummy?'

Instead she drew to a halt. 'I'm really hungry.' Her lip trembled, and she looked at her free hand, a little grubby from her fall, and thrust it towards me.

'It's okay!' I said brightly, but it was too late – she had started to cry. I picked her up, but she was so heavy, her mother far away, the distance between us seeming to stretch the louder Kioko wailed. Her little face grew hot against my cheek. 'It's okay,' I said. Someone slammed a window shut. Kioko leaned back her head and let out a garrulous cry; her feet kicked against my legs. Far in the distance, Wendy turned. Soon, she was coming towards us, her step brisk.

'I'm sorry,' we said to each other, me awkwardly manoeuvring the child out of my arms and into hers. Wendy tried to put her down on the ground, but Kioko lifted her feet, wrapped herself around Wendy's legs, sobbed.

'Mommy's here, it's okay, Mommy's here. Don't *cling*, sweetheart. She's overtired,' Wendy said, turning to me. 'I'd better get her home. I hope you find the dog!'

Despite roaming the neighbourhood until Izzy felt woozy and sick – her frantic energy waning into a ragged grief, her shoulders shaking – we found no sign of Sunshine. Over the following days, I could hear my sister crying through the bathroom door, but she didn't reproach me again. I took the dog lead out for walks, in case I found him, and braced myself for Sunshine's thrash whenever I heard a skateboarder.

I was sure that if he was outside, he would be walking familiar streets, drawn by the scent. It would probably be for the best if he'd been taken in by someone, even the kind of person who'd ignore the number tattooed inside his ear, who'd think instead to keep him for themselves. I worried about coyotes. Sometimes, on my way out, I'd take the stairs, walk along the interior corridors, still convinced he was somewhere inside the building.

Lucie had printed lost dog flyers bearing Sunshine's sweet face at her office. Izzy and I would take sheaves of them out with us – taping them to lamp posts, pinning them onto notice boards inside coffee shops, watching them become obliterated by other signs, being rained upon, blowing away. *Much loved*, the signs declared. *Needs special care*. Lucie wrote the copy herself – Izzy trusted her to find the right language, words of appeal. We flyered the lobby, bumped into neighbours carrying them in the lift, and even knocked on doors in the building.

Sunshine's food and water bowls sat empty in their usual spot; his medications closed inside a Tupperware container. Izzy had tidied all his toys from the rug, but these still sat neatly in a corner, next to the sofa, like the room of an absent child. I missed calling his name, the warmth of it in my mouth.

It was on one of these walks, Sunshine's lead curled in my pocket, that I saw James Dean again. 'It's you,' he said, this time sounding surprised at my appearance before him on the street where my sister lived, as if he hadn't walked me home, as if we were just now bumping into each other in some foreign country.

He wore a shearling jacket and, beneath it, a jumper bearing antlers. It was December. We were at the cusp of evening; Christmas lights had started to appear in windows, wreaths hanging over the doors of the older houses, bulbs glowing red, green and blue over balcony railings in storeys above us. The air smelled like snow but none had fallen. I wasn't sure what to say to him. I gripped the dog lead in my hand inside my pocket and he stood looking back at me blankly, beautiful.

Finally, I put the two thoughts together and spoke. 'You haven't seen my sister's dog, have you? I'm looking for the dog I brought to the party. We've lost him.'

He shook his head. 'I'm sorry.' He scraped his shoe along the ground, stuffed his hands inside his pockets. 'Look, I'm meeting someone, but they're running late. Do you want to grab a quick coffee? There's a place around the corner.'

I knew the place. Most mornings and afternoons it was crowded with people working on laptops, but now that evening had fallen it was quiet. We sat in a red booth, and he unzipped his jacket, showing the rest of the deer. 'Nice sweater.'

'I like the necklace,' he said. I was wearing my black velvet choker, a loose white shirt, and a pair of Izzy's elasticated trousers. My stomach felt knotted and tender; I blamed the stress of the missing dog. 'Can I order something for you? What would you like?'

'I want something . . . chalky,' I said.

'Okay.' He laughed and slid from the booth. I watched him lean against the counter to order the drinks, then scroll through his phone while he waited. He smiled at the screen, then typed out a message. I wondered who he was meeting. The coffee shop windows were decorated with paper snowflakes, tinsel stippled the sills, and they were playing 'Fairytale of New York' over the speakers. Someone whistled as they mopped the floor in the kitchen.

'I got you a matcha,' James said as he placed the drinks on the table. I thanked him, leaning back into the booth, sinking into the pleasant anonymity of the empty coffee shop, a relief from the familial, sorrow-soaked apartment rooms.

'And for the other night,' he said, awkwardly. I wasn't sure what to attach it to: *sorry, thank you*, the cup in front of me. He'd left the sentiment out of the sentence. 'I don't know what happened. I guess I freaked out.'

'You don't know what happened,' I repeated, which came out sounding arch, though I hadn't meant it to.

'I told you I was fucked up about sex.'

'I thought I saw something in the mirror.' A blush burned into my cheeks at the memory of his body curled over mine, his naked arms, but I was determined to press on. 'In the bathroom. Something strange, for a moment.'

He frowned. 'I shouldn't have reacted the way I did.'

'To what?'

He looked pained.

'I'm not being obtuse,' I said. 'I need you to say what you saw.'

'Obtuse,' he repeated. 'Look, it wasn't your fault. It wasn't anything you did. There's nothing wrong with you. You're . . .' His hands grappled with the air in front of him. 'Fine. Better than fine, of course.'

'Did you see an old woman?'

He blinked. 'No. I saw something else.'

'You didn't see me?'

He put his hands flat on the table, as if it would give him strength. 'I saw a weird thing on my face. It was like . . . my face wasn't my real face. I was different.' He looked up at me, weighing his next words. 'My face was blurred out. Not just blurred vision, there was something on my face, making it . . . warped.'

I exhaled, sending tiny cups of foam from my latte across the table. 'I actually feel so much better you saw something. I thought I was maybe losing it.' I put my head in my hands. 'I keep losing things.' The missing crystal and art card and, worst of all, the dog.

'What do you think it means?' he asked.

I ran my fingers over the velvet band at my throat, wondering if I could trust him. 'I think there's something bad in the building.'

His face split into a smile, and then it faded away again. 'You've been watching too many horror movies.' He reached out and folded my hand in his. I noticed that my fingernails were dirty and tried to hide them. 'I think we *experienced* something together. Something closer to, like . . . death. Death of the ego, death of—'

'Yeah,' I broke in. '*Something bad is in the building.*'

'It's not in the building. It's in us.'

I stared at him. 'How is that better?'

'Because we can control it. We can stop ourselves turning into our worst parts . . . into whatever it is you saw, an old woman? Whatever it is I saw, a blank. It was a warning. We can control it; we just have to restrain our . . . are you okay?'

The relief I'd felt at first began to ebb, and something else pulsed in its place. Something hot and sharp. Our worst parts? 'Do you really believe being with me showed you the worst version of yourself?'

'Maybe. Maybe just a . . . non-version. It was like I was losing definition, being erased.' He looked at me, then hurried on, 'But it wasn't about you, or maybe it was, maybe it was a sign for you, too. I don't know. I just know that if I don't change, I'll become that thing. I'll lose my . . . my face.'

'Your looks?'

'Not just on the surface. Inside, too,' he said.

I wanted to ask him what he'd done that was so terrible, why he was so desperate to change; in the intermission at the cinema, he'd told me he'd been driven by sex, that he hadn't liked how it had taken him over – I thought of the cicadas, their desirous swarming to breed. I was trying to frame a question when he spoke again.

'The mirror – it degraded me.' The word sent me over the edge. I couldn't sit there any longer. 'Wait. Don't go! Finish your drink.'

I swigged down the hot matcha, scorching my tongue and throat.

'Brooke, we should part on good terms. Maybe I'm talking shit. It could have been a shared hallucination, or . . .' I picked up my coat and the dog lead fell from the pocket, tangled itself somehow around the table leg. 'Are you leaving?' James continued. 'I thought you'd gone already. Back home, I mean.'

I tugged and tugged at the end of the lead, wanting to exit the conversation, a wave of humiliation threatening to drown me. The man had traced a line down my belly with his tongue. 'Yes. In a few weeks, I'll disappear.' I lifted the table.

James bent and pulled the lead free from the table leg, so that I was briefly tethered to him. I wound the lead back around my wrist, but he didn't let go, only came closer. 'I want us to end on good terms, Brooke. Wish each other well.' He put a hand on my face, ran his thumb across my cheekbone. I hadn't seen him change in the mirror, not a flicker, his face had remained this perfect, this beautiful, while desire had made me wretched, withering, monstrous.

'Have a nice life, James.' I pushed my way out of the coffee shop door, the bell tinkling cheerily overhead.

18

The smell of the dog hung in the apartment; I missed pressing his paw to my nose, his little popcorn feet. When I left to run some errand, I didn't say goodbye to anyone, and when I returned there was no dog to greet me. Long, arduous silences stretched between me and my sister, while the noise of the building became heightened. Wall sounds amplified whenever I was alone; I swore there was something moving around on the other side. I could hear my sister laughing next door with Wendy, only to return to me stone-faced. The silences were arduous for Izzy as well, I suspected. We'd stopped eating together. It had been my sole task to look after the dog, my allowing him to vanish a terrible betrayal of her trust. Without Sunshine I had no legitimate reason to be there; she'd lost the thing she loved most.

While I tried to sleep on my wafer of mattress, my stomach cramping and bilious, the fridge rumbled on in the kitchen and television noise filtered through the walls. It gave me the sense we were hurtling towards something, though I didn't know what. I couldn't pinpoint where the noise was coming from; I'd even stepped out in the small hours, pressing my ear to the doors along the corridor. The pipework telegraphed voices everywhere. I was afraid in case I walked in my sleep again, imagining the stairs cascading endlessly, the building's creaks and groans beckoning me to wander.

The fact that this noise didn't bother Izzy made me feel singled out, as if the building was watching me and knew when to pipe up, at what pitch. I wished Sunshine was still with us – surely he would hear it, too. I imagined the prick of his ears, the flurry of his paws, nose thrust to the gap under the door. His sniff and splutter. The dog ways he had of knowing the building, its people, their paths of motion and habit. After all, dogs could even smell time.

'I must be used to it.' Izzy shrugged when I complained. 'I don't notice any more.' Now and then she'd humour me and make a sour face, but I could tell she wasn't disturbed like I was. Living surrounded by other people made her feel safe.

By then Sunshine had been missing for an entire week. A fake Christmas tree had been erected in the foyer, cheap tinsel and garish lights, empty boxes wrapped in shiny paper underneath. It gave me an ache for home. Just a couple more weeks. I passed the tree each day as I searched the neighbourhood for Sunshine, while Izzy completed her rounds among the neighbours, even persuading the building manager to send out an email to residents.

I hadn't seen Medusa in moons, not since the fire, when I suddenly encountered her on the corner opposite the Leonora. Scarred grey sky, heavy with cloud, yellow clapboard house behind her. She shifted from foot to foot on the pavement, an absent look on her wrinkled face. It was jarring to meet her so abruptly; I'd imagined that when I found her I'd be self-righteous, wag my finger at her and call her a thief. But out in the street, the dog-threatening, home-invading hulk that loomed in my imagination shrank to the dimensions of a lonely old lady. I remembered James's easy empathy at the cinema and Medusa's distress the night of the fire, the way she'd pulled at her own hair, how nobody had approached her, not a single neighbour. Now a couple of crows jumped around her feet. I felt the danger of being like her, coming unstuck from the people around me, losing my place in the wheel of life.

She made no obvious signs of recognition, but I felt her notice me. She turned away – crows flapping and scattering – and moved along the street in her housecoat, then turned again at the intersection, as if wedded to the grid of streets. 'Hey,' I called. 'Hey . . . excuse me?'

I wanted to ask her about the dog. I couldn't shake the idea that she was the key to his disappearance. She knew something, I felt it in my bones. She knew the building better than anyone, its corridors and crevices, its vexing mirrors. How would she react if I confronted her? I was afraid of the fix of her eyes upon me, equally afraid she might dissipate into the air, like smoke.

I followed at a distance as she hobbled towards the park. Maybe she had stolen into the apartment again, taken Sunshine, and was keeping him somewhere. I fell back, waiting to see where she might lead me, compelled to solve the mystery of Medusa as if she were a key on my hoop of library keys: I wanted to know where she fit. But somehow I lost her among the rhododendrons under the herons' nests. She'd moved through a clutch of trees, and when I came out on the other side, I couldn't see her any more. Another vanishing act.

From my pocket, I took a dirty, balled-up T-shirt – my own, not Izzy's, in case she missed it – and wrapped it around a branch in the rhododendron underbrush. I wasn't sure whether I was leaving a scent flag for the dog, or a sign for Medusa: I was here. I'm watching you.

*

That night my sister cooked us both dinner, a hearty soup full of vegetables – squash and broccoli and spinach, zing of ginger. She moved around the kitchen easily, lifting pots from the bottom cupboards and scrabbling around for stock cubes in the top ones, her pants gapping around her waist while mine pinched at my tender belly.

'How's your incision?' I asked.

She looked at me sharply, as if surprised to hear my voice. 'It's fine,' she said, busying herself at the hob. 'I feel more normal with the stitches out. It's still painful, of course. But it's less gruesome to look at.'

'Don't overdo it,' I said, nodding to the open cupboards behind her.

We ate in silence, and after dinner watched TV together – a reality dating show that had been scored exactly like a horror movie. *Tonight!* the voiceover promised.

Somewhere in the building, a dog was howling. A plaintive cry that bled through the walls and had sounded for much of the afternoon. When I'd first heard it, before Izzy came home, I'd stepped out into the corridor and tried to find its origin, but the cry seemed to be coming from everywhere. I'd followed the sound as best as I could, the corridors marine-like and lit with the buzzing wall sconces – it was easy to forget it was still daylight outside. But I kept having to change direction as the howl picked up or died away. I pushed through the doors to the stairwell, hurried down the concrete steps, burst out onto another floor, identical to the previous one, the same leafy swirls in the carpet. I tilted my head to listen, hovering in the space of the doorway. The howl came again, below me. I let the door fall shut as my feet pounded the steps down to another floor, pushing out onto a row of silent green doors with bronze numbers over the peepholes. Again, the doleful wail, but this time it seemed to echo inside my head. Then a strange tapping from below, like a coin bouncing down the stairs. I followed. My quest took me down to the laundry room, where all I could hear was the rumble of the machines, every one of them in use, the howl obscured completely.

I waited for Izzy to notice the howl. She raised the volume on the TV, and I wondered if the cry had finally leaked through to her synapses. I didn't dare to ask. *Do you hear that dog crying?* I rehearsed in my head, imagining the baleful stare that would come back to me. Besides, it didn't sound like Sunshine, not at all – I'd never heard him make a sound like that, dense with mourning.

I could feel Izzy's eyes on me. 'Your hair's grown so long,' she said, ignoring the bigger changes in me, in us.

I rubbed my fingers over the back of my head. 'Would you cut it for me?'

A look of surprise. 'I have scissors, but not clippers. So I'd have to leave the buzzcut. I'm not taking a razor to you, I'm afraid.'

'You can just use the dog clippers. I don't mind.'

She blinked at the mention of the dog, and a howl seemed to drift through the room between us. No reaction. 'We'll do it in the kitchen.' She pressed a button and the TV winked out. 'Go wet your hair. I'll get the clippers.'

At the sink, I pulled my wet hands through the longer strands of hair to dampen them, but left the underneath dry. I sat in a kitchen chair and Izzy draped a towel around my shoulders, tying it at my throat with a pink hair clamp.

'Don't shave it all off in revenge, will you?'

She didn't reply. The clippers buzzed to life and then died away again as she tested them, flicking the switch on and off. I could imagine her face: her lips pressed together in concentration, her eyes focused on the task.

'What comb shall I use?'

'Grade four.'

'These are dog clippers, Brooke.'

'The biggest comb, then.'

She gathered the longer pieces of hair and started to clamp them up in sections. 'Why did you cut it like this in the first place? What possessed you?'

'Cecelia,' I said simply, the name like a shrug, though in truth Izzy tying the towel at my throat had triggered a ripple of association. Cecelia leaning into the mirror, one eye painted with black eyeliner, the other bare and blonde; her silk underskirt with the frayed hem – *oh, she's very feminine*; the thin red bracelet that seemed to sever her wrist; wastebasket full of lipsticked tissues; our bodies squeezed together inside the bathtub, candlelit, cold knees blinking above warm water.

'Did she like your hair short, like this?'

I shrugged. 'I don't know. I just . . . kept trying different things to please her.'

'But you have nice hair,' she protested. 'Nice as it was. So thick.'

'Sometimes,' I said, thinking out loud, 'you just want to change the way someone sees you.'

Izzy ran her fingers over my scalp, quiet. Eventually, she asked, 'Why did you break up?'

'We had a falling out at a party,' I said. 'She made it clear it was the end for us.'

'What do you mean?'

I sighed. 'We threw a party, on the roof. It was a few weeks before the end of term. We had this great view from the roof of our building. It wasn't high up or anything, like yours. But you could see the rice fields in the distance, and we had some garden furniture up there.'

I pictured the string lights against the warm blue sky, the paper umbrellas floating in our drinks. It was after the train incident; I even thought we might have moved on from it. We were all wearing fake flowers in our hair from the 100-yen shop, and Cecelia had fashioned herself a flower-crown worthy of *Midsommar*, her hair twisted gorgeously into elaborate silver-blonde knots.

'Cee was talking to one of our friends about a trip they were planning. They were going to spend the summer travelling around the States, and they were all excited about it. Our friend was from New York, and they were going to stay with her family in Brooklyn at the end of their trip. They'd organized everything. But the trip was news to me – Cecelia had never told me about it, and she didn't even seem to care that I was there, learning about it from this random conversation, my smile falling away. And instead of challenging her . . . I was pathetic. I pretended I *did* know about it, and I kept trying to insert myself into the trip as they were talking. Saying things like, "Oh, I'd love to have cocktails on the roof at the Met." But each time, it was as though I hadn't spoken, as if they couldn't hear my voice. I was standing there with a drink in my hand and a stupid pink magnolia behind my ear.'

I remembered Cee nodding, taking a sip of her beer. I'd laughed, and my laugh came out strangled, exposing a seam of fear underneath. *I bet I sound like a bad tourist*, I'd said, turning to Audrey, self-conscious of my generic little desires. Audrey looked like she was praying the conversation would die off. But Cee had looked as regal as a queen, her hair ablaze with fabric flowers, and it was like I wasn't fit to attend on her any more, let alone receive her favour, her gaze keenly averted. 'I even . . .' I trailed off as I realized Izzy had stopped touching my hair.

'You even what?' She rested her hand on the back of the chair, touching my shoulder.

'I even said, "Oh, my sister lives in Vancouver, we could start there." But Cee didn't even look at me, and our friend . . . she just gave this awkward laugh. It was like Cecelia was ghosting me *to my face*.'

'What happened after that?'

'I didn't want to cry in front of them. I left the party, went home. But I could still hear it going on until the middle of the night, from my apartment. A few days later, she came and collected her things.'

'Did you tell her how you felt? How small she made you feel?'

Please, you don't have to love me, I'll just love you.

'I tried. The thing was, I'd assumed we'd spend the summer together. That maybe, after the program, we'd start another life together. I didn't realize how angry she still was. And as I listened to them talking . . . my summer disappeared, along with the entire relationship. It was humiliating, standing there alone.'

'Why did you let her treat you like that? What did you do to make her so angry?'

I shook my head against the memory: Cecelia's tote bag spilling her belongings across the floor of the subway car, falling to my knees to gather them all up, a man's laughter, my hand grabbing her by the elbow, pulling her away, out of reach. Our bodies in the dark glass of the doors, the high screech of the tracks. Falling to my knees, her tube of lip balm rolling away under a seat. The alarm in Cecelia's voice: *Get. Off. Me.* She'd thrown a punch. I'd picked up her mascara, her diary and coins.

'I'm sorry about Sunshine,' I told Izzy.

'I know you are.' Izzy hesitated, the clippers hovering near the nape of my neck. I think she wanted to ask the question I'd dodged again, but instead she said: 'This isn't some sort of penance, is it? I thought you were growing it out.'

I shrugged. Then she was running the clippers over the back of my head. She was so gentle, like she regretted having to cut it. I didn't care much about my hair. It was the request that mattered. Can you do something for me? I'd asked her, and she hadn't refused. I could feel her concentration through the vibrations of the comb and the steadiness of her hand. She was doing her best for me. We were both doing our best for each other, and falling short of what the other needed, stuck in a pattern neither of us could understand.

Izzy turned off the clippers and blew into the comb, then ran her fingers over my scalp, rubbing away the loose hairs. She took out the clamps one by one and combed my hair, trimming the edges with the hairdressing scissors. 'I did buy those babygrows for Talia,' she said. The scissors *snip-snipped, snip-snipped.* 'But then I couldn't let them go. They were so tiny, and I thought it would be unlucky to give them away before the surgery. I kept hold of them, and now her baby has outgrown them.'

'I shouldn't have been snooping in your wardrobe.' I felt clumsy and juvenile, as if I had held out Cecelia's tote bag like a wound to show Izzy, and Izzy had had to let go of the baby to take it. I couldn't explain the feeling, because I hadn't even told her about what happened on the subway. Only about Cecelia's petty little slight, her revenge. 'It was private,' I said, feeling the tips of my ears blush hot. But I could tell Izzy's mind had fixed upon the growing baby, or perhaps to the wanted child who would never outgrow the clothes Izzy had kept – for luck.

Soon she was pulling the towel away, crossing the room to shake it out on the balcony. Little crescents of reddish hair were scattered all over the linoleum. I got on my knees with the dustpan and brush. This is how I'd make up, I thought, for the lost dog. My bony kneecaps pressed into the floor, my head bowed. I'd make everything in the apartment shine.

19

Izzy told me she'd be out for hours at a hospital appointment; I'd offered to go with her, but she'd laughed and said, 'I think I can manage, thanks all the same.' I went to the supermarket to pick up milk and bread, finding it decked out for the holidays, tinsel and tangerines, packs of dates and seasonal offers on joints of meat.

In the car park they were selling Christmas trees; I lingered in the pine scent long enough to want one desperately. I counted the foreign notes left in my purse and bought a four-foot Norwegian spruce, walking the blocks home with it over my shoulder. Needles littered my clothes and hair when I finally put it down in the hallway, leaving it to lean against the wall, shedding itself.

I went out again to pick up some string lights and baubles from London Drugs, and found a small box of Christmas decorations inside Izzy's wardrobe. I hung these on the tree: silver angels, felt robins, red glitter letters spelling out JOY and PEACE. I snapped photographs and sent them to Mum.

What a nice surprise, Mum messaged me back. *Is she speaking to you yet?*

Izzy must have told her about the dog. I'll admit this annoyed me, because I'd been keeping the rift out of my messages home, not wanting to worry Mum and Dad. But of course Izzy would need to talk about the dog to someone, since she was pointedly not talking to me about it, and it made sense that she'd lean on Mum in her grief. Besides, the apartment was filled with the light of a golden hour – I knew that even the stark concrete exterior of the Leonora would be bathed in a rose-coloured glow – and it felt so like a gift I remained undaunted.

We're good, I texted back, hoping to manifest a secure attachment between us.

That dog, Mum commiserated. I watched the three dots, waiting for the end of the sentence. *It's a real wrench for her. First the hysterectomy, now this.*

After I'd decorated the tree and vacuumed the pine needles, I dusted the candles on the bookshelf ready for lighting, using a torn piece of fabric. I expected Izzy home at any moment and wanted everything to be perfect. In my haste, I knocked over the framed photograph of Izzy and Mum, which fell on its face with a disconcerting thwack. I cringed. This was the only photograph on display in Izzy's home. Righting the frame and checking for damage, I noticed a thumbprint over Mum's belly. The sun flooded the room, casting my own shadow over the image.

I'm not sure what compelled me to turn the frame over in my hands, unclip the metal clasps. As I pulled the backing away, a fold in the photograph sprang out. Dad. He had been in the photograph after all, not just his disembodied hand resting on the baby bump. I pulled the photo away from the frame and smoothed out the crease, the better to see it: our family. Izzy, Mum, Dad, and in Dad's lap, an arm wrapped around it, a baby with a round, chubby face and a shock of copper hair.

The air sang with something. I stared at my own infant face for a long moment. *I nearly killed you when you were a baby*, she'd said. Outside, the sun was sinking behind the horizon and the streets below were holding dusk, the black outlines of the oaks making a latticework of the sky. I carefully put the photo back inside the frame, closing the clasps. I rubbed the glass until it gleamed, my adult face caught in the last of the reflected light from the window.

I knew if I confronted Izzy about the photo, she'd find a way to laugh it off. It wasn't so much that she'd folded me out of the frame that bothered me – it had stung, sure, seeing that baby version of myself, an open smile on my face, how I'd been hidden away – but it was more the lie Izzy had told, giving me a story about Mum carrying me, how the dates aligned. I'd felt close to her when she'd told me that, surrounded by family, Dad's hand holding all of us together. But she'd turned me and Dad to the wall, hadn't wanted to see us.

Dad. As I waited in the dusk, putting away dishes, mopping the linoleum, I thought about that split down the centre of the photo. The fold made a weathered line between the four of us, Izzy and Mum on one side, me and Dad on the other. Surely that couldn't be how Izzy felt about our family? I'd known nothing else, but she had been old enough to remember a time before Dad, a time before me – years of history shared between them before I was born. It was for Izzy that he'd become a father; I knew how much they loved each other. Maybe the weathered line was temporal for her, a kind of before and after? But no, there was Mum's pregnant belly to account for, rupturing Izzy's doctored image. Perhaps it only served to emphasize Mum's mumness, like a goddess to be worshipped.

The apartment was gleaming by the time I heard the front door. 'Can I smell pine?' Izzy called as she slipped out of her shoes.

I stood to greet her when she came into the room, knowing these were the moments she missed Sunshine the most. 'Surprise!' I sang. But it was me who was surprised – she looked completely different, her lips painted red and her hair bleached a honeyed blonde.

'Wow,' I said, bringing my hands to cover my mouth. 'Your hair.'

She raised her hand to frame her face. 'Not too drastic?'

It was such a big change from the purple box-dye she'd used since she was a teenager, always colouring it at home, and I told her as much.

'It wasn't *purple*,' she said. 'It was burgundy.'

'I thought you had a hospital appointment today?'

'No, that's next week. I said hair appointment, didn't I? Sorry it took so long, it was quite the procedure.' She dropped her shopping bags onto the floor. 'It's very festive in here! I don't think we're actually allowed real trees in the building. Did anyone see you?' She wound her scarf from her throat. 'Not sure how I'll get it out, once it's gone all dead and stiff.'

I hadn't thought of that. 'It's just – we normally have Christmas at home, together, except for last year. And the year before.' She shrugged off her coat while I was talking and went to hang it in the hall cupboard. 'I thought we could do an early one, you and me, before I go back.'

'Right. My friends used to call me Saint Izzy for travelling back every year. But it just got too hard to get the time off work. You know, people with young families, they deserve the time together.'

She was back in the room now, facing me with her bombshell hair. 'Christmas is for kids.'

'Well, Mum approves of the tree. I sent her a photo.'

'I hope she'll feel the same about my hair,' Izzy joked. 'Dreading that call.'

I suggested we take a photograph together, in front of the tree, send it to Mum and Dad. 'It's been ages since we had a picture togeth—'

She cut me off, sitting on the sofa and rubbing the arch of her right foot. 'I think this red lip would push her over the edge. Maybe another day. I need to get used to it myself. The tree looks great, Brooke. Well done.'

For dinner, Izzy grilled aubergine to have with the leftover soup; I toasted a couple of Pop Tarts. Her back stiffened when I pressed the toaster lever down with a clunk, and she shook her head as I chewed on a corner of pastry at the table. In the glow of the fairy lights, she tucked a frond of freshly blonde hair behind her ear. 'You know, I was thinking about what you said earlier, about hosting an early Christmas.'

'Yeah?' I was pretty sure I hadn't uttered the word *hosting*.

'I might have some people over this weekend, for a games night. Not the whole crowd, just a few. We could do a holiday spread. I know you think my games nights are a bit sad, or middle-aged, or whatever. But would you mind?'

I shrugged; I was disappointed and wanted her to know it. 'It's your apartment.'

'Do you want to join us?'

'Of course.'

'You can invite that lad if you like.' She took a sip from her water glass, made googly eyes at me. 'Mr Wonderful.'

'James. No, thanks.' Although she was technically speaking to me – trying, even, to be nice – there was a distance there, an affected nonchalance, and the makeover felt like just another layer of mask.

'I thought you said nothing bad happened between you? If you don't invite him, you won't know anyone.'

'I'll know you. And Sasha. Besides, it would just be awkward, after . . . you know.'

'Well, I've noticed you still wear his jumper.'

I shrugged, and something in her seemed to relent.

'About Sasha,' she said. 'I might sleep over at his place tonight. He said he'd text me when he gets off work. Will you be okay here by yourself?'

'He's not coming here? Why not?'

'To be honest, I could do with a change of scene – cabin fever's setting in a bit. And, actually, I was thinking of telling him. About the hysterectomy. So it will be better if we're alone.'

'Oh,' I said. 'Well, that's good. I think it's good for you to talk about it.'

She nodded. 'But you can't say anything at the party. I mean, about me and Sasha, to the others. He doesn't like people to know. I mean, they know, my friends, not all of them, of course, but he can't *know* they know. He appreciates discretion, restraint. He kind of knows they know, but not that they know everything.'

'I literally wouldn't know what to say about it.' Something about the mystery of Sasha reminded me of the photo, our spliced family, neatly compartmentalized.

I couldn't explain why I felt so wounded. Only that I'd been thinking of the two of us, repairing something there, and she was inviting all these other people in. But I knew how much she loved to play host. Maybe the party was her way of bringing *me* in, though I couldn't convince myself of that, not with the photograph so freshly discovered, and the lost dog like an open wound throbbing between us.

I hunted around for something nice to say. 'That aubergine thing smells good.'

'Have some.' She held a forkful out for me to taste, which I did, swallowing something that managed to be both rubbery and slimy. 'I can plate some up for you if you want?'

I refused the offer but made the right noises, trying not to gag. 'Remember I used to eat the things you didn't like from your plate? So that you'd spend time with me?'

'No.' She frowned. 'I don't remember that. Why are you eating Pop Tarts for dinner?' So much of what she'd said to me over the last few days had an implied *for God's sake* after it.

'I had a big lunch. I'm still full.' I nibbled the last morsel of pastry and washed it down my throat with water.

'What lunch? What did you have?' Izzy asked, narrowing her eyes.

I got up from the table and went to scrape the crumbs from my plate.

'Brooke, what lunch?' she repeated, but I turned on the tap and clattered the dishes in the sink, pretending not to hear her.

After a text message had summoned Izzy to Sasha's place, I sat up late in the empty apartment, listening to the building sigh and moan provocatively. As a distraction I put on *Seven*, but all the gore made me lightheaded, almost faint. I turned it off and ran myself a bath. As the water ran, I undressed in front of the mirror, counting my sins and leaving my clothes in a pile on the floor, running my hands over the shorn part of my scalp. I unscrewed the studs from my triple helix, examined the punctured cartilage underneath. Three tiny holes at the top of my ear. Behind me, the room throbbed with layers of memory: Cecelia changing out the jewellery in her own piercings, dabbing at the holes with a saline solution and laughing at my reflection, how I winced in sympathy. *Hey, why don't you get yours done, too?* James's ragged breath at my ear, the shower curtain torn out of its clips, the trail of dark red blood, thick and clotted down my thigh. What had I really seen? Was the face in the mirror my fate, my karma, as James believed, or had something else stolen into the moment? Something animal behind the walls.

I stared at my reflection for so long that my vision blurred, and I saw myself in double, my breasts low, heavy and tender, my stomach twice as swollen. I blinked the sight away and noticed a smudge on the glass. I reached out to rub it away, but it wouldn't budge.

Looking down, I realized the mark was on my body. A green-black smear in the centre of my abdomen, stretching between my breasts and my bellybutton. I touched it; it reminded me of the mildew on the ceiling. I scrubbed at whatever the growth was with my nails until it flaked away, raking red lines across my skin.

In the bathtub I felt closer to the pipes as they whirred behind the drywall. I soaped the marks on my belly, imagined leaving the taps to run until the room filled with water and sealed me inside as I exfoliated my whole body, sloughing off the dead cells. When I got out, my skin glowing and pink, I cleaned the bath with something like fury, finding a strange satisfaction in the shining tile and the heavy chemical scent of the cleaning products, which reminded me of a foaming spray I'd used in my little bathroom in Japan. I scooped my clothes up for the laundry basket and slipped into the egg-patterned bathrobe hanging on the back of the door.

As I tied the robe closed, I caught a flash of myself in the mirror and a scream tore from my throat. My naked body – eaten away, pitted with the pink slime of oozing sores, a green fungus clinging to my cheek. The spectre dropped its head back in hideous abandon and reached to embrace me in its wrinkled, sagging arms.

The room lurched. I grabbed for the nearest object, a scented candle in a weighty jar, and launched it at the glass. Instantly, a crack splintered the rotting body like a spider's web. I covered my face with my hands and cowered in the doorway, hiding from my own reflection. I searched my body, shrugging out of the bathrobe and lifting my arms, touching my breasts and thighs. I was clean, my skin unblemished – no oozing sores or pitted flesh. I took several deep breaths, waited for my heartbeat to slow, and confronted my image again: I was just a girl, my face cleaved into fragments by the crack in the glass.

Could I have imagined it, worrying the sex with James so much I'd brought the crone back to life? I blinked and touched my body again, cupped my hands around my distended belly. What was happening to me?

I wasn't sure how I'd explain the broken mirror to Izzy – another accident, another ruined thing in my wake. My mind began to fracture; I became afraid that the smashed mirror would let something in, whatever it was that had been living behind the walls, that had cracked and bowed the bedroom ceiling, that rattled and slithered around behind the plaster.

I shivered, reaching to dislodge a shard of mirror, cutting my fingers on the glass as I tore at it with my fingernails. Fat drops of blood in the sink. I was always bleeding in this place, the Leonora a rusty blade pricking and slitting my skin. My efforts had revealed a pale sliver of wall in the centre of the broken mirror, like a blank eye. I tapped there; the sound was hollow but firm – I'd half-expected the surface to tear like white paper shoji. On the other side of the wall was Izzy's walk-in wardrobe.

I caught myself talking to the dog for comfort. 'Where are you hiding, Sun? My good boy, where are you?' I took to knocking on the other walls, the way Izzy had when he'd first vanished. Perhaps the walls had swallowed Sunshine. I pressed my face to the living room wall, my lips moving against the plaster. 'Do you miss us?' I called. 'We miss you.' I crawled on my knees to his pile of belongings beside the sofa, looking first for the lamb with its ruined face, forgetting that had been lost, too. Why couldn't I find him? If this was a library, where would I look?

I toured the library stacks with my ring of keys, all the lock mechanisms in the building invisible behind their keyholes. I thought of Sunshine's belly, the pink spot on his chest, the thrum of his heartbeat underneath thin, soft wisps of fur. I picked up one of his other toys and took it to bed with me, but it was no substitute for the breathing body of the dog – immobile, weightless, dead.

My stomach churned until I fell into a series of anxiety dreams, one bleeding into another. James tapped at the living room window. I wasn't sure how he'd climbed his way up there, but when I slid open the balcony door and stepped outside, I saw that a green kudzu vine had taken over the side of the building, sprouting purple arrow-shaped flowers. James seemed to hover on the other side of the balcony railing, and when I said his name, he smiled. In my hand was a shard of glass from the mirror, and I held it up for him so he could see his reflection in the moonlight. But he screamed and covered his eyes, letting go of the railing and falling backwards to the street below. I tried to shout his name but it wouldn't leave my mouth – no sound emerging but a ratcheting groan, sharp and grinding beneath my ribs. I braced myself against the railing, leaning over to see where his body had smashed into the street. But he wasn't there. No trace of him remained.

'Brooke,' Izzy said, and I turned and saw her silhouette inside the dark apartment, her eyes glowing like twin orbs. I woke barefoot on the concrete floor of the balcony, the railing in my hands and the night breeze tugging at my nightdress.

20

Everyone arrived at Izzy's Christmas party with a comment about the dog. First Wendy and Kioko, an hour earlier than invited, ostensibly to help with any setup. I'd been reading *Jane Eyre* and facing the wall, rain dripping outside the windows. Kioko pointed to me and said, 'Dog?'

'Not yet,' I said, shaking my head at her sadly. 'No Sunshine.'

Izzy ushered me off the couch and into the kitchen, to manage the pots bubbling on the stove, while Wendy set out Kioko's colouring pens on the coffee table.

Lucie embraced my sister in the hallway, her chin tucked neatly against Izzy's shoulder. 'It's so different here without Sunshine.' She carried a large pink gift bag and a fruit basket, leaving Izzy to cradle the basket as she pulled away. 'How are you coping? I'd be inconsolable if I lost Cosmos.' Next, she popped her head into the galley kitchen. 'Good to see you, Brooke!' She enunciated each syllable with special care. She'd swept sparkly blue eyeshadow over her lids and wore her hair in two knots on top of her head. 'We never did have that dinner, did we?' I eyed the gift bag, wondering if there was another womb-shaped object inside.

Izzy's friend Talia arrived toting a large-eyed infant and a bearded man in a cardigan. 'Your hair looks amazing! Fuck, who even are you? Sorry again.' Talia pressed a hand to her own stomach. 'It's so hard to get a sitter when they're this young.' It made me wonder who else knew about the hysterectomy, apart from me, Sasha, and Lucie. The baby seemed enormous, its head bulbous in the crook of Talia's arm. Everyone cooed and gathered around it; the baby held the centre of things.

Stirring the pots, adjusting the heat, I was grateful for a task that kept me out of the small talk. I didn't know how to act like a normal person since my body had started searching for oblivion while I slept.

Perhaps Talia didn't know about Izzy's hysterectomy, I thought, or else the kid would be a bit much. On the surface Izzy seemed composed, but who could guess at the knot in her stomach? She reached out and squeezed one baby foot. 'Oh, Tally,' she said. 'I could eat him.'

'And who's this?' Talia said, smiling widely and invading the space of the kitchen, infant in arms.

'Tally!' Izzy laughed. 'It's my sister, Brooke. You met at the hospital.'

'Oh my gosh, I'm so sorry! Mommy brain, am I right?' She seemed to expect a response to this, lingering there, looking at me. 'Well, I'll just go give him a feed,' Talia said, not to me or Izzy but to the cardigan man unloading bags in the hallway. I'd caught the name *Todd*, but I wasn't sure whether it belonged to the man or the baby, or maybe both of them.

'Fingers crossed he'll sleep afterwards.' Talia carried the baby into Izzy's bedroom, closing the door behind her. I hoped Izzy hadn't left anything private out. Big Todd carted several of the bags into the living room, supplies I supposed they needed to keep the baby alive.

I heard Lucie say, 'What in the world happened to your mirror?'

'Don't ask,' Izzy said. She'd scolded me for the cracked mirror, slamming the bedroom door behind her. I tapped on it from the other side, promising to pay for the damage.

A splat of pulped carrot burped onto my shirt. 'Shit.' I dropped the spoon and pulled the fabric away from my skin. It was one of Izzy's shirts, a floaty, oversized affair she'd loaned me for the occasion, along with a green amulet necklace, which I'd paired with her elasticated trousers. I'd attempted to squeeze into my smart jeans, but the zipper wouldn't close. I'd shown them to Izzy in dismay, the denim pulled tight across my hips.

'They probably shrunk in the wash,' she said, though I thought I registered alarm on her face. 'Those washers downstairs are pretty rough.'

I'd forgotten Talia was in the bedroom and walked in on the feeding. She sat on the other side of the bed, cradling the baby, facing the wall, her dress pulled down to reveal one shoulder, the child's small head and swirl of soft dark hair visible. A suckling sound, the baby breathing. A yeasty sort of smell.

'Oh! Sorry!'

But Talia was reading her phone and didn't react, her thumb roaming the screen. I stepped inside the wardrobe, stripping off the shirt, hunting for another on Izzy's rail, then giving up and pulling one of my own tees out of the laundry basket. My clothes were mostly still in the suitcase under the bed, and this was one of my looser-fitting T-shirts, Breton-striped, free of slogans. I kept the amulet because it reminded me of something the tour guide at the VAG would wear.

When I stepped out of the wardrobe, Talia was buttoning her

dress, the baby stretched out on the bed, noiselessly kicking its feet. She'd seen me changing in there, and now she smiled and asked, 'How far along are you?'

I stared at her, uncomprehending. 'Oh, shit.' Her hand went to her heart. 'I'm so sorry, my bad. All I see and think about now is babies.'

I stammered something diminishing and left the room, pulling at the hem of my T-shirt, and resumed my post in the kitchen. I reached out to turn on the radio, only it had gone from its usual spot. Izzy must have tidied it away.

'How about some music?' I called, swallowing a feeling of panic, but the women were busy with each other in the sitting area, Lucie unpacking the pink bag in a crinkle of paper and ribbon, trying to involve Kioko.

'Oh, this one is wine, that's just for the mommies! Hey, where's Sasha?' asked Lucie.

'He's always late, you know what it's like at the restaurant.' Izzy stood, lifted her glass and brought it with her into the kitchen. 'Damn, has this burner gone out?'

She'd been cagey about Sasha since she'd spent the night with him. When I asked her how it had gone – how he'd reacted to her news – she said he'd reassured her that nothing had changed between them. 'Is that a good thing?' I'd asked. But she'd only shrugged and told me to eat something.

She took over at the stove – click, click, click of the ignition – leaving me purposeless and hovering behind her, while Wendy asked polite questions about the baby in the other room: how many months, whether he was teething, how well he slept through the night. Talia had joined them and handed the baby off to Todd, who sat affably in the armchair, receiving their offspring without comment.

'Can you grab that plate?' Izzy said. 'Use the tongs, no, the glass bowl for the salad, where's the radio gone?'

'I thought you moved it,' I said.

'We'll look for it later. Must have a narcoleptic in the family.'

'Narcoleptics can't stay awake. I think you mean kleptomaniac.'

'That, too.'

'Are you saying I took it? Where would I take it?'

'I'm not saying anything. Here, take those out, they're ready.'

We arranged the dishes on the table, stack of black paper napkins, tower of plates, tray of silverware. Food slick and shiny under the lights. 'Help yourselves!' Izzy shepherded the women around the table, motioning with an imaginary spoon. 'Dig in.'

'You know, with your half-sister here I really notice your accent.' Lucie laughed. 'You sound totally different. Doesn't she, Tally?'

'So Irish,' Talia said.

'But we're not Irish,' I said.

'I mean, *here* you are,' Talia said enigmatically.

'Noone is an Irish name,' Izzy said. 'But don't say half-sister, I hate that word. She's my sister.'

I felt a swell of good feeling, leaning against the wall with an empty plate against my stomach. Izzy put her hand on the small of my back, pushed me gently forward. The space felt crowded with six adults and two children, despite the two Todds remaining in the corner by the window. Lucie forked a mouthful of salad into her mouth, a crouton falling to the linoleum, and Izzy bent to pick it up. The little girl pulled at Wendy's skirt, then sneezed across the table. 'You want to try some ham, sweetie?' The ham dangling and slippery on the end of the fork, something wet dripping onto the tablecloth. My stomach rolled, but I ate a cherry and spat out the stone into one of the black napkin squares.

'Izzy, I'm so *sad* about your dog,' Talia said. 'No sign of him, still? I wonder how he got out?'

'Someone must have him, don't you think?' Lucie rejoined. My ears pricked up. 'It makes no sense for him to get out of the apartment *and* out of the building. It's not like he called the elevator. Did you flyer the lobby?'

'Of course. Didn't you see them when you came in?' Izzy asked.

'No, there was nothing.' Lucie shook her head. 'I was a bit surprised. I've printed off more for you, they're in the gift bag, somewhere.'

'We blitzed it again this morning. Are you sure? The building manager keeps taking them down.'

'Maybe whoever took the dog is taking them down,' I ventured, and Lucie caught my eye.

'I suppose I can't believe a neighbour would be so awful,' Izzy said. 'It would be such an evil thing to do.'

'Hmm, I wouldn't be so sure.' Wendy stroked Kioko's hair tenderly. 'Plenty of strangers, people moving in, moving out.'

The little girl wore a pale pink leotard and ballerina tutu with black leggings – a last-minute concession to get her out the door, Wendy explained. She brushed a My Little Pony with a pink plastic comb, now and then pausing to take something from her plate and push it into her mouth, humming to herself, a cheerful tune I didn't recognize. Kioko tugged on Wendy's arm to get her attention, then whispered into her ear. 'I'll ask later,' Wendy said, and wiped at her chin.

'Dogs wander off all the time,' Todd announced from the corner. Everyone turned to stare at him. The baby was slack in his arms like a doll, its pale, skinny legs sticking out at an uncomfortable angle, its neck crooked. 'Well, they do.'

'Honey, support the head,' Talia said.

'I *am*.' He shifted his elbow, adjusting the baby.

'Besides,' Izzy said. 'I've knocked on practically every door in the building.'

'Knock again,' Lucie urged. 'It couldn't hurt. Send Brooke. You'd do that for her, wouldn't you?'

'Of course,' I said. 'As soon as we realized, I—'

'See? You can't give up on him. You'll get him back, I know it,' Lucie said earnestly.

In the circle around the table, the smell of the buffet was ripe and vegetal, rimed with animal fat. 'Are you swimming again, yet?' Talia asked Izzy. 'I really miss my Mommy-to-be class.'

Izzy shook her head, picked at a crumb on her plate. 'I think it'll be a while before I'm up for it.'

'I can't wait to get the baby into the pool,' Talia said dreamily, her eyes widening in a mirror of her progeny. 'We could be going to classes already. You know you can start them at, like, four months old? But you have to be *so* careful they don't get cold in the water, like thirty minutes, absolute max. By the time you get ready and get in, it's not worth it. I hardly have the energy to shave my legs, let alone . . .'

Izzy stepped into the kitchen, ducked to open and close the oven door, picked something up from the counter and put it back down again. She opened one of the high cabinets so that it blocked her face from view, tiptoed as if to peer into it, then turned her body towards the front door, away from us. I thought I saw her blot her eyes with a tea towel. 'I think I hear something,' she said, and in a few steps, she crossed the kitchen and hallway, opened the front door, went out into the corridor, and closed the door behind her.

'Me, I wanted a water birth, but Todd wouldn't hear of it,' Talia was saying. 'A little water baby, that's what I wanted.'

'How was the birth?' Wendy asked.

'A bloodbath! Todd almost passed out.'

'But so worth it when you hold them in your arms, right?'

'Mmm.' Talia seemed to be somewhere else, reliving something specific. She opened her mouth to speak again, only Lucie leaned in and mouthed the word *surgery*. Talia brought her hand to her collarbone in a gesture of apology.

I slid my plate onto the kitchen counter, making to follow Izzy, but she opened the front door and stepped back inside. 'Need any help?' I asked.

'I thought I heard Sasha out there on the phone,' she said plausibly, busying herself at the sink, insisting she was fine. If the others hadn't been so close, I might have said something like, *the baby, it must be so hard*. But she was trying to hold herself together and a soft word would be like a knife to the heart.

I moved away from her friends gathered around the table and dropped down on the sofa. This party had been a terrible idea, I should have pushed back on it. Had I made all this happen with the Christmas tree, my attempts at festivity setting a chain of events in motion that ended with a baby inside the apartment? I knew Izzy had met the baby before, had visited Talia after the birth, but now her whole world was different.

'Hey.' Todd lumbered to his feet. 'If you're done eating, would you mind holding the little one?' He was already lowering it into my arms, which had betrayed me by looking open and receptive. 'There you go, you got the head.'

I held the sleeping baby, held my breath. I'd thought all babies were chubby and wriggly, jiggling their legs and sucking their fists, but maybe this one had outgrown that phase because it was lanky and stiff, the bare legs stretched out over my knees. Its head felt heavy and solid as a bowling ball. I had an irrational fear that I would drop the baby and lose it, that it would roll away and disappear into the ether.

'Uhhh?' I swallowed the word *help*, looking for Izzy as I adjusted the baby's woollen blanket, trying to cover its stubborn limbs.

How come Talia was allowed to flaunt her new baby, and Lucie could offer a clumsy response like *did you freeze your eggs?* and not be subject to Izzy's death stare, her freezing out? *I just have to hold it*, I told myself, *it's not even awake*. But somehow that was worse, the sleeping child at once unaware, but with a frown on his face like my own dark monologue had troubled him. Suddenly, in my arms and despite its heft, the baby seemed very fragile and precious, like something I could fracture with one intrusive thought.

I sat frozen like that while they all ate and chattered, Todd downing three cauliflower cheese rolls in succession, refilling his glass, stretching his arms above his head until his belly sagged over his belt buckle. 'Honey,' Talia admonished, then rolled her eyes in my direction.

I seized the moment. 'Is there somewhere we can put him down, maybe?' I lifted the baby in her general direction. 'I'm not really great with—'

'What? Oh. He'll wake if we put him down.' She bent to take the baby from me. 'It's okay. Just let go. I got him.'

'I'll hold him,' said Izzy abruptly. 'I haven't had any cuddles yet. I'll just go wash my hands.'

'Are you sure? He's heavier than he looks,' Talia called after her. We exchanged cryptic glances; *Talia must know, after all*, I thought. When Izzy came back wiggling her fingers, Talia handed the baby over, his rosebud lips quivering and parting with a sigh. Izzy gazed down into his face and cooed, though he remained asleep. 'He's perfect,' she whispered, cupping his foot.

'Does he need the blanket?' I held it out to her.

'No, it's warm in here,' Talia said, fanning her face.

'All these bodies,' I commiserated.

'I can hold the baby now?' Kioko whined to Wendy.

'No, sweetheart, the baby's still sleeping. Why don't you go colour?'

Kioko huffed and wandered over to play with the tree ornaments, giving voices first to the silver angels and then the felt robins. 'Ba, ba, ba, ba, ba,' she sang as she stripped a branch of its green needles, opening her hand and letting them fall to the carpet. The kid had imagination; I liked her.

'Eat something,' Izzy whispered to me, bumping my elbow with her own as she rocked the baby. 'Look how small, Brooke.'

'Are there cheese and pickle toothpicks?'

'No. Have some hummus. It's Christmas.' She nodded to the tree, symbol of the season. 'Lucie's been admiring your handiwork.' Her voice was still hushed although the room was filling with chatter and noise, as if she and the baby and I stood inside our own, separate sphere. 'I think you two could be friends, you know? If you made a little effort?'

I was surprised Izzy was making small talk, her face alight and her body swaying happily. I looked at her as if she was holding a bomb. She babbled something in a low, animal murmur, her nose touching the baby's fine hair.

'Isn't he a bit heavy for you? Want me to take him back?'

'No, don't take him.' She stared down at the child's face, pursing her lips as if to copy its expression. 'It's okay, you know,' she said. 'I'm okay.'

'I'm sorry about the mirror,' I said.

'It doesn't matter. The mirror can be replaced.' She stroked the back of the baby's head tentatively. 'You can take the seven years' bad luck, though. I'm too old for that.'

The landline rang, puncturing the moment. I moved to answer it before it woke the baby, but Izzy hugged him to her body and picked up the receiver. 'Oh hi,' she said quietly into the phone. 'Glad you made it. Come on up.' She pressed the buzzer and slipped the phone back in its cradle, seeming to regard me anew, still rocking from foot to foot. 'Why aren't you wearing the shirt I picked out?'

Izzy herself wore a patterned wrap dress with a complicated print of puzzling ropes, checks, and red florals. She reached out and pulled at the hem of my T-shirt. 'This looks creased. Go and put something else on.'

'It's fine. I'm comfortable.' Did I embarrass her in front of Sasha and her friends? I nearly asked her if I looked pregnant.

The baby whined and stirred in her arms. She shushed and bobbed, but the baby wriggled, kicking one little foot, and started to cry. He rubbed his eyes with his two tiny fists.

'Here,' Lucie said, appearing at Izzy's side. 'It's my turn. You shouldn't be lifting yet, should you?' She shot me a look, her eyes a double tsk tsk.

'They say nothing heavier than your baby,' Izzy murmured.

'What? Izzy, that's for a C-section.' Lucie reached into Izzy's arms, and as she lifted him the baby broke into fresh wailing. 'Oh dear,' Lucie said, turning away at the apex of the baby's howl. 'Let's find Mama.'

'Are you sure you're okay?' I asked Izzy, whose gaze had followed the crying baby.

When she looked back at me she seemed lost for a moment, but then frowned and asked why I was so pale. She lifted my hand to tut at my torn cuticles. 'You look tired. And witchy.' A rap on the door. 'Too late now.' She fluffed my hair, trying to cover the part she'd shaved.

'I have a black hat somewhere,' I joked. 'It's nice and pointy.'

She ignored me, turning me to face the hallway. 'Why don't you answer the door?'

21

When I swung open the door, the spotlights in the corridor buzzed overhead, framing James in a ridiculous halo. He'd grown a thatch of thick stubble and wore a pair of sunglasses, which he pulled from his face when I answered. 'Why are you wearing sunglasses indoors, at night?'

'The lights are bothering me,' he said. 'I've been having these headaches.'

'Oh.' I pushed him out into the corridor, closed the door behind me. 'What are you doing here?'

'You invited me.'

'I what?'

He pulled his phone out of his pocket and showed me the text.

'This isn't me,' I said, handing him back the phone. 'I'm sorry – I think this is a stunt by my sister. She wanted me to invite you, but I . . .'

'Now you're just trying to hurt my feelings.' He leaned in and kissed me on the cheek, his stubble rough against my skin. I remembered the growl in his throat, his hand on my hip, the string of spit between us that first night in the lift. 'I thought you wanted to make things right between us before you left.'

I stared at him. He did look a little more rugged than usual. 'Did you not find a party invitation via text a bit breezy, considering our last conversation? Why are you so stuck on ending things well?'

He shrugged, raised his eyebrows in appeal. 'I'm making up for past wrongs?'

'Well, that's a red flag.' I looked at him for a long moment. 'I can't believe you'd even come back here. The mirror creeps me out every time I go to the bathroom.'

'I had to come back,' he said, licking his lips. 'I keep having these migraines. The ones that blur your vision. I see this bright light, and then I know it's coming, and I have to take painkillers and lie down in a dark room until it passes. I need your—'

The door opened behind me. 'James, what are you doing out here? Come in.' Izzy reached for his arm, pulling him over the threshold.

'Izzy—' I started, but she was in full host mode.

'Take off your shoes, grab some food. Brooke will introduce you to everyone.' She ushered us inside.

I took James into the living room and rushed a round of introductions, escaping to fetch him a drink. When I returned, Lucie was asking what James did for a living and Todd wanted to know how much he paid in rent.

Talia interrupted her husband, tapping her lip with one finger. 'You remind me of someone . . .' she told James. 'It's on the tip of my tongue.'

James answered the questions put his way in short fashion, confirming that he lived with two roommates, was twenty-five, had never done any modelling, was a rideshare member, worked long hours in animation for a gaming company, and was saving for a trip to Europe.

'I didn't know you worked in animation,' I said. It seemed like something that should have come up.

'See? We are strangers,' he said. I hadn't even known he was only twenty-five, younger than me. He seemed older, somehow, or ageless in the way of an actor remembered for a single performance.

The presence of the others had opened Izzy up – she moved like a breeze through the room, seemingly without pain, a bottle in her hand, refilling glasses. She gave people tasks: Wendy could you just . . . ? James would you mind . . . ? There was a sheen of sweat on her forehead and her cheeks were pink.

Sasha arrived, shaking his jacket out in the hallway and stamping his feet. 'Sorry, everybody, I got held up.' He joined us in the sitting area, his glasses clouding with the heat of the room. He took them off to wipe them on his shirt. 'It's snowing.'

'Let me get you a plate,' Izzy said.

'Great,' Sasha said. 'I'm starving.'

'Don't say "starve".' Izzy shook a napkin into his lap. 'You're not *starving*.'

'Starve and stare have the same root,' I said. 'To starve could mean to freeze or turn to stone. You could "starve in ice" – it meant "be rigid".'

'Thank you for that,' Izzy said.

'I thought it was topical, with the snow,' I replied.

'You teach English, yes?' Sasha raised a forkful of carrot and turnip, which I thought of as my dish even though I'd only stirred it while it was on the hob.

'I did it for a couple of years, a work abroad thing. It wasn't proper teaching. I'm just interested in the roots of things. Words, I mean.'

Izzy coughed into her fist and shot me a look, which I interpreted as a signal for me to mind my manners. 'Sasha, you remember James,' I offered. 'You've briefly met before. He's twenty-five and works in animation. James, this is Sasha. He's a married man who works with my sister.'

The baby woke with a gurgle that morphed into a red-faced roar and continued despite a nappy change, the smell causing Sasha to put aside his plate. First Talia and then Todd rocked the baby, pacing the apartment from room to room, the baby screaming at the top of his lungs, the nappy in a plastic bag on the rug. Nobody had washed their hands.

'Oh no,' Sasha said. 'Oh no, what's happened to you? May I?' He held his arms out to Todd for the baby, bobbed up and down with him, shush shushing. 'What terrible tragedy has befallen you? Oh no, oh dear, oh dear.'

Quieting, the baby reached out and pulled the glasses from Sasha's face. Izzy stood at Sasha's elbow, peering over his shoulder. I thought she was about to touch Sasha's arm and coo at the baby, grab his tiny bunched hand, but instead she turned her face away and looked at the carpet. There was something tender about the motion, as if she might find the lost dog at her feet.

'Oh, that's right, they look better on you,' Sasha murmured. 'Want to come see the snow?' He carried the baby over to the balcony door. I slid it open for them, lifting the curtains to one side and letting in a raft of cold air.

'Ah, there now, look.' Sasha cupped the baby's head with a fatherly hand. The baby only looked with wonder into Sasha's face, squeezing the glasses in his fist. Talia unclenched his little fingers, prompting a fresh wail. 'No, no, no, it's okay,' said Sasha.

'It's okay, little man. Aw, here's Mama.' He handed the baby over to Talia.

James leaned closer to me, held out a joint. 'Is it okay if I smoke this in here?'

I pushed him towards the balcony door, steering him out of Izzy's view. We stepped over the sill, slid the door closed behind us.

It was quieter out there, the baby's cries muffled, the snow banking on branches and falling in flurries under the glow of the streetlights. No vine growing up the side of the building, no nightdress flapping in the breeze, nothing like my nightmare. James cupped his hands around his mouth, lit the joint, then slipped the lighter into the back pocket of his jeans. 'We should've brought our jackets,' I said, the cold puckering my bare arms into gooseflesh. 'Want me to get them?'

He let out a stream of smoke. 'No, come here.' He put his arms around me. 'I'll keep you warm.' He smelled like spirits.

'Are you drunk?'

He shook his head.

'You are,' I said.

'I had a drink before I came over. Dutch courage. I'm not drunk, though. That room was enough to sober me up.' He offered me the joint, holding it to my lips. I shook my head. 'You feel soft and warm,' he said.

'What were you going to tell me before?' I asked. His body curved around mine, but I was afraid of what had happened between us, afraid of premonitions.

The door slid open before he could answer; the baby howled. 'There you are,' Izzy said. James coughed, pulling away. Izzy slid the door closed behind her, hiding a smile. 'God, it's hot in there. Can I have a drag on that?'

'You smoke?' I asked.

'Only at parties, when it's there.' She took the joint.

'So it was yours,' I said. 'I found a stub in the couch cushions. When you were in hospital.'

She frowned, flicked her eyes to James. 'Um, I wouldn't have left that there. I'm not an animal.'

'Then whose was it?' I asked.

She shrugged, then read my mind. 'Don't start. You think Medusa comes over, makes a sandwich, watches TV and gets high on my sofa?' She passed the smoke back to James.

'What if it's true?' he said.

'There were pistachio shells, too,' I added, though I knew it wouldn't help convince her.

'I'm sorry to hear about your dog,' James offered.

Kioko's face appeared at the glass – she'd slipped under the curtains. The little girl pressed her nose against the window, leaving a circle of breath there. She banged her fists against the pane. 'Home, home, home, home!' Wendy's hand appeared, then disappeared, pulling her away.

'Thanks. Better go back inside. Don't stay too long out here.' Izzy rubbed my arm. 'You'll catch your death.' When she went inside, she pulled the curtains open wide, though I doubted they could see us through the glass, not with the room lit up like that.

'You know, we did this already,' James said when she'd gone. My mouth opened to speak but he nodded in the direction of Elsie's apartment across the street. 'Over there. We could make this our thing.'

'I go home in a week and a bit.' It was funny to watch Izzy with her friends inside the apartment, folding herself under Sasha's arm, holding a glass of something out to Lucie, laughing at a joke Wendy must have made. Sasha reached up absently and tugged a lock of Izzy's newly blonde hair. Behind them, Talia and Todd rocked and shushed the baby, the three of them in a sort of embrace. Those were her people, I thought, James and me on the other side of the glass. When I left, all the parts of my sister's life would carry on without me, unchanged by my absence.

'Do you ever feel lonely?' I asked James, my eyes still on my sister.

'All the time,' he said casually, as if I'd asked him if he ever felt cold.

I turned to look at him. Snowflakes in his dark hair. 'Why did you come here tonight?' I asked. 'I thought I was making you degenerate or something. That was your theory, wasn't it? Like some Dorian Gray curse.'

'Dorian what?' He took another drag, smoke billowing from his mouth and dissipating into the black night. His mouth was partially obscured by his hand holding the joint and then the cloud of smoke, but his lips were still beautiful and sort of inviting. 'I need to ask you something,' he said. 'You're the only person who can help me.'

'Go on.' I reached for his free hand and traced my thumb along his fingertips, then lifted the back of his hand to my mouth and lightly kissed his knuckles.

He watched me do this for a long moment. 'You look different.'

'It's my hair, Izzy cut it.'

'No, it's something else.'

I shrugged and dropped his hand, but a shiver of panic ran through my veins. It *was* something else. I'd noticed it even though I'd been avoiding looking at myself for too long in the mirror. I looked softer, somehow, my face kind of pillowy.

He leaned back against the balcony railing before he spoke again.

I edged forward, tense – he seemed far too blithe about the drop, his limbs loose. 'When you pushed me off you, in the bathroom . . .' Here came the concern, blooming gently in his voice. 'I thought at first I'd done something wrong, that I'd hurt you?' He met my eyes. 'Then I saw the thing on my face. I didn't know you'd seen something else. I thought you pushed me away because you'd seen me. The real me, underneath. It all changed so quickly from something that felt good to . . .'

I nodded, still nervous. 'I thought you saw *me*.'

'Then the headaches started and . . . the way you left the coffee shop. I started to think maybe I did do something bad, after all. Did I hurt you?'

'Hurt me . . . like, when we were together? No,' I said, and shivered. 'Is that what you needed to ask me?'

He shook his head no, his eyes shining in the snow light. 'I can't stop looking at my face. I'm scared in case it disappears.' He grasped my hand. 'Nobody else is ever going to believe me.'

'James—'

'I keep thinking, what if it happens again? Has it happened to you again?'

He'd pulled me close to the railing and his eyes were pleading. I wanted to lift myself up on tiptoe and kiss his neck; I wanted to lie, to make him feel better. 'I saw *something*,' I said.

He exhaled, his breath hot on my skin.

'But it wasn't the same. I wasn't . . . it didn't happen during sex, or anything like that. I had this weird mark on my body, and . . .' My other hand gripped his collar, as if to pull him back from the edge. Snow drifted between us, accumulating in Izzy's dead and dormant herb garden, and the joint still burned away in James's free hand.

'My reflection changed again,' I told him, 'in the mirror. It was only a moment, but I saw it. Her. The old woman. Then I broke the mirror and it was gone.'

'You broke the mirror?' he whispered.

'Yes,' I said, and then, more firmly than I truly believed, 'it was in the mirror, James. It's not inside you.' I wanted to release him from the grip of the spectre.

My hand was still in his and he squeezed it. 'But what about my headaches?'

Izzy rapped on the window, breaking the spell.

'You better put that out,' I said, stepping out of our strange embrace. 'Let's go inside. Maybe we could slip out later. Talk properly?'

He seemed dazed and flicked ash into the air, turning around to face the street. 'I'll be another minute.'

Inside, Talia and Todd were packing up, apologizing for bailing before the game. I'd forgotten we were meant to play one. As they gathered their things, which had spread across the entire apartment, Izzy boxed up food for them to take home, and Sasha helped to dress the baby for outside and settle him into his carrier. The child had calmed the moment he'd sensed they were leaving. Izzy followed them to the door, still fussing over the boy.

'You're very natural with him,' Wendy said to Sasha. 'Do you have kids?'

'Yes.' He sat opposite her, his long legs stretched across the rug. 'Two boys.'

'Where are they tonight?' In Wendy's lap, Kioko dozed, her satin-slippered feet on the coffee table, one of the silver angels closed in her hand.

'With their mother. They live in Montreal.'

'Oh! And you're all the way here. You must miss them terribly.'

'We visit,' Sasha replied. Izzy had told me the kids had bunkbeds in Sasha's apartment, inside a windowless den. That once she'd woken up alone and found him lying in there, under musty Spider-Man sheets.

'What brought you here?'

'Oh, it's a long story.' He smiled in place of a real answer.

'How long have you two been together?' Wendy prodded.

'My wife and I?'

'Oh,' Wendy said, her hand floating to her mouth. 'I'm sorry, I meant you and Izzy.'

I was listening closely to their exchange while trying to appear uninterested, when Lucie thrust a sheaf of lost-dog flyers at me. 'You could start now. Before it gets too late.' She seemed to have cast me as an ally in her dognap theory, which, I supposed, I sort of was.

'– my good friend,' I thought I heard Sasha say.

'What's this?' James stepped back inside, dropping next to me on the carpet.

'I'm saying, they should go another round, to find the dog. Izzy's dog Sunshine has been missing for days,' Lucie said. 'She's putting on a brave face, but she's distraught. Your sister is too stoic for her own good,' she told me, as if I didn't know this about her.

I heard the words *sorry* and *assume* from Wendy.

'Brooke's already searched the neighbourhood for him,' James said, sounding a little defensive on my behalf. 'She was doing that the last time I saw her.'

Sparks, I heard, then a note of denial.

'But don't you think he's probably in the building somewhere?' Lucie shivered. 'Such a weather-beaten old place.'

I returned my attention to the lost dog. Though I knew the sound wasn't Sunshine – no Sunshine I recognized – the eerie dog howl echoed inside my head. My tongue remembered the gristle and splinter of the chicken bone; how he'd bitten my hand as a last recourse.

'I do,' I said. 'But I only suspect one person. I don't know what apartment she lives in.'

Lucie nodded. 'Izzy told me about your theory. But you can't just keep walking the neighbourhood crying for hours.' My face must have looked stricken, because here she reached out to grab my wrist, saying in a confidential tone, though within earshot of everyone else, 'She told me. Besides' – Lucie released her grip, her voice lifting – 'won't you find out where "Medusa" lives if you canvass the whole building?'

James reached out and took the sheaf of flyers from Lucie's hand, halved it and handed half back to her. 'Why don't we all go?' he said.

22

Somehow this search party for the dog became the game we'd gathered to play. 'You know, when I invited you all over, it wasn't for this,' Izzy said after Talia and Todd had departed with the baby. She sprawled next to Sasha on the rug. 'It's late to be calling on neighbours. There's still dessert.'

'I could do with a break between courses.' Lucie hamstered her cheeks with air, tossed her half of the stack of lost dog flyers on the coffee table. 'I'm stuffed.'

'It's not so late,' said Sasha.

'Maybe we can find the dog together,' James whispered in my ear. 'Would that help?'

'I wasn't crying,' I whispered back. 'I don't know why she told Lucie that.'

'You were crying when I met you in the street.' He blinked, his hand moving to cup my elbow. 'That's why I invited you for coffee, I thought you were crying over me. It's okay if you were – it's best to confront these things. I cry all the time.'

'Shall we do it, yes?' Sasha was saying, leafing through Lucie's pile of photocopies. 'Better than Pictionary. Whoever knocks on the most doors wins?'

'It isn't a game,' Izzy said.

'Come on.' He placed a comforting hand on her arm. 'Let us help. Maybe we'll really find him.'

'Or a clue,' Lucie said, sounding almost excited at the prospect. 'Let's split into pairs. Plus kiddo, of course.'

'Oh, I think we'll call it a night,' Wendy said, Kioko drowsing in her lap. 'I'm sorry, she's worn out.'

'Without Wendy, the numbers are uneven,' Lucie said, forlorn, a little frown on her face.

'I'll go solo,' I said. I wanted to be alone with James, but I was wary of conjuring the crone again in some creepy corner of the building. What had drawn her out? The desire that crackled between us? Did my crone-double want James, too?

'You shouldn't go by yourself,' Izzy said.

'It's okay,' I told her. 'I know what I'm looking for. I'll float between you.' I avoided James's eye.

'I can help you on this floor,' Wendy offered. 'I just have to put her to bed first. Come with me.'

Amid the murmuring and dividing, putting on shoes in the narrow hallway, Lucie pulled me aside once more, into the kitchen. 'You're a champ. I think this will be good for your sister. Taking action. Her energy is a bit up and down tonight, don't you think? I mean she's usually so . . .' She held her palm out flat. 'And the hair? *Blonde* Izzy? Her aura is troubling. I wonder if she should come and stay with me.'

'I think she's coping better than most people would,' I said, inexplicably offended on Izzy's behalf. 'She's the strongest person I know. You could always bring her another crystal, if it makes you feel better.' I would have liked to walk away after this, but Sasha and

Izzy were still lingering in the doorway, Sasha's thumb stroking Izzy's chin.

Lucie looked a little stunned at my remark, her mouth puckering. 'You don't believe in sympathetic magic? I'm surprised.'

I wasn't familiar with the phrase, but I didn't want her to know it. 'Why would you be surprised?'

'Well, Izzy tells me you're an artist,' Lucie explained.

'Izzy said that?' A little bolt of pleasure.

'And that you're more, uh . . . *sensitive* than her. Artists are usually more open to living alongside the magical, to walking in both worlds. The crystal is a conduit.'

I rolled my eyes. 'Come on.'

'Yes, well. It may sound silly to you. But rituals gather people together, often around potent objects. They can make life worth living when you're in pain.' She cast her eyes to the floor, and I felt suddenly wretched. She'd been there for my sister when I wasn't, after all. But I really wasn't up for a lecture on crystals. Lucie continued: 'Giving our pain to another vessel can—'

Izzy stuck her head around the corner, a smile breaking across her face when she saw the two of us, our heads together. 'What are you two gossiping about? Can you hurry up? Wendy is waiting, Brooke.'

I knew where the little girl slept, since she'd serenaded me to sleep most nights while Izzy was in the hospital. The layout of Wendy's apartment mirrored Izzy's, the bedrooms pressed together. Kioko – whose sleepiness had deserted her now she was going to bed – demanded I come with them into the bedroom, ordering me to lie down on the floor while Wendy read to us from a storybook.

Mother and daughter shared the room, with a double bed in one corner and Kioko on a child-sized bed pushed against the shared wall. There were two suitcases next to the wardrobe, and a tumble of clothes on top of them.

'Excuse the mess,' Wendy said. 'We're going to stay with family for Christmas.'

'Oh, in Japan?'

'No.' She laughed. 'They're just a few hours' drive away, but kids need a lot of stuff.'

'Oh,' I said, embarrassed by my mistake. 'Do you get any mould in here? We've had a terrible problem with it recently.'

Wendy shook her head and tucked Kioko under the covers, then hunted for something underneath the bed. 'Here it is,' she said, pulling out a portable nightlight. 'How did that get under there?'

Kioko giggled.

'Did you hide this from Mommy?' Wendy laughed. She turned the nightlight over in her hands, pressed a switch on its underside, and set it down on Kioko's bedside table. It played soft music and spun horses and stars onto the ceiling, cast the shadows of unfamiliar objects across the room.

In the glow, Wendy read from the book, a placid story about princesses and toads. But it wasn't long before Kioko started to mouth her special song to the soft twinkle of the nightlight, picking it up near the end. 'Iki wa yoi yoi, kaeri wa kowai.' I recognized the last word – *scary*. Wendy put the book to one side. I opened my mouth and the song burbled out of it, my pronunciation wavering away from Kioko's, wavering into the wrong key.

Wendy looked surprised; the little girl stopped and laughed.

'Sorry,' I said. 'My Japanese is pretty fuzzy. But the kids at my school used to sing it.'

'Ah,' Wendy said after a beat. 'That's right. I forgot that you lived there.' She sang the line again for me. 'It means something like . . . going is good . . . or maybe safe, but returning will be scary.'

'Mommy, just sing the song,' whined Kioko.

Wendy started the song from the beginning while I lay supine on the floor, squeezing one of Kioko's cloth dolls in my arms. The little girl sang another line to the burble of the nightlight, and a constellation of horses danced across the ceiling. Wendy had pinned Kioko's drawings to the wall, but there were none of her scary monsters, her shapeshifting obake. Only windowed houses with chimneys and gardens, stick-figure families holding hands, the flattened Ms of a sky streaked with birds. Still, there was something about the drawings, a surreal quality to Kioko's combinations: a kitten under a black rainbow, a dolly with button-eyes inside an egg, a hatching pattern that could be a meadow or prison-wall scratch. Black spirals crowned a tree, clothed a stick figure, glowered in the space where a sun might shine.

Kioko's voice was breathy and slower than the true melody. 'Ofuda wo osame ni mairimasu.' I recognized *ofuda* – they were charms or offerings that could be bought at shrines and temples, sometimes simple objects made of paper or cloth, other times more elaborately wrought.

When they reached the end of the song, Wendy leaned over to tickle Kioko's tummy. 'Good job, everyone.' She clapped her hands quietly. 'Now it's time for nice, good dreams.'

'Again,' whined Kioko.

Wendy kissed her forehead. 'Just you this time. We want to hear your pretty voice.'

Kioko only made it through a few lines before she drifted off. The song seemed to comfort her – to make the bedroom feel safe enough for her to fall asleep as the nightlight spun its stars and moons across the ceiling, the little illuminated horses.

I was caught by the latticework of the nursery rhyme, its mysterious exchange that I couldn't follow, only catching odd words and phrases – you may enter, please let me through, the narrow path. A journey that might be difficult to return from. Hearing them sing it here in the space of the bedroom felt much different than hearing its tinny incantation on the darkening streets of Ogaki – waiting for something to respond to my feeble konbanwa, anticipating the grip of some spectre at the crossing. The song seemed to hold a kind of talismanic power, but I didn't understand if it was leading us into or out of danger.

The light coming through the open door dipped away and then came back again with an incandescent buzz, momentarily elongating the shadows on the wall, so that they loomed closer to us, then sprung back into the corners of the room.

Wendy and I watched the hall light flicker from our stations around Kioko's bed. 'I hope it doesn't—' Wendy began, as the light shivered, then winked out, the nightlight still mercifully spinning, holding us in a warm, soft bubble.

We waited for the power to return, listening to Kioko's breath deepen and stretch. The silence felt oppressive, and I found myself staring at a groove in Wendy's forehead. 'She's nice like this,' Wendy said at last, her voice a whisper. 'Sometimes I forget, then every night, a surprise, the quiet.'

'It looks hard,' I said, and she nodded but said no more. 'What's the hardest thing about it?' I pressed.

Wendy's eyes seemed to be evaluating me, whether she could be truthful. 'Breastfeeding,' she said. She must have registered my confusion, because she laughed. 'Oh, I don't do it any more. But the shock of it, the little mouth clamping . . . I can still feel it. I even felt it when that baby cried.' She bobbed her head towards the wall between her bedroom and ours.

I shuddered. 'What does it feel like?'

'It's like . . . falling into a black hole. They feed so often at first, it feels like it's all you're doing. I was a prisoner to it, on the sofa hour after hour through day and night. Your day doesn't end, you know? It's continuous. Thank God for my mother. She practically moved in.'

I remembered Talia's thumb roving across the screen of her phone, the sucking noises. I even thought I'd heard a contented baby sigh. And through the phone, all those other mothers with their network of suckling babies. Thousands of mouths to feed.

'I got out before her teeth came.' Wendy folded her hands neatly in her lap and closed her eyes. 'Just a few more minutes, to make sure she's asleep.'

We lapsed into silence again. I thought myself back onto the bullet train with Cecelia, the way she'd taken selfies in the light from the window, how she'd yawned like a beautiful cat, then fallen asleep across two seats.

We'd taken the bullet train to Kyoto first, and then to Tokyo, planning our excursions over beers and bowls of salty edamame at the izakaya, windchimes jangling as we pointed at the map. That summer Cecelia had started to dress all in white – she said it was cooler, that it didn't absorb the sun. She looked ethereal and somehow affluent in her cool cottons and linens, while I sweated behind her in my cut-off jeans and running shoes. In Kyoto I couldn't stop lingering in doorways, taking photographs of the patterned awnings flapping in the breeze, bright neon buzzing over the traditional curved roof tiles. We ate steaming okonomiyaki and pottered around junk shops and flea markets, browsing stacks of tiny plates, bamboo cake-stands, ikebana vases, and ceramic cats. Cecelia chatted easily with the market vendors in Japanese, complimenting them on their designs and asking about the smells of different incense sticks. From one vendor, we bought floral-printed tenugui towels as gifts for our mothers – all her foreign customers liked these as souvenirs, she advised us.

'You shouldn't rely on me so much,' Cecelia told me as she tried on an embroidered jacket, her bags hanging from my arms. 'You'll never learn.'

What I remembered most about our trip to Tokyo were the zebra-striped scramble crossings, studded with crowds of intersecting strangers. To cross successfully, you had to move at the pace of the person in front of you and be aware of the trajectories of those around you. I was quite good at navigating them, but I preferred it when we stopped for tea with an elevated view of the scramble so I could observe the crossing from a safe distance. Cecelia grew bored of this very quickly; it was out of keeping with her new diaphanous persona, and anyway, we were running late for the gallery. We still had to figure out how to get from Shibuya to the Teien Art Museum and had to ask for help from the couple sitting at the next table. Cecelia wanted to see a retrospective of Toshiko Okanoue's photo collages – made from cutups of American magazines left by the Allied occupation, copies of *Life* and *Vogue* the artist had picked up in secondhand bookshops. Cee got hooked on the surrealists after watching some Japanese horror movie from the 1920s, and a friend had recommended the exhibition to her, scoffing at a description she'd read of Okanoue as an 'accidental' surrealist.

When we arrived, the gallery rooms were crowded with men who had their jackets folded over their arms; students in clusters of three or four, brightly dressed and spilling with chatter, taking pictures on their phones; and older women in pairs, clutching at each other's arms, scarves in their hair or knotted at their throats. Cecelia floated through the rooms in a stiff mid-length skirt the colour of sacking material bleached by the sun and a white cheesecloth blouse, her face devoid of makeup – she gave that up in the white phase, too. She looked a bit indefinite and desiccated, like a dead moth, as she stared up at a collage of a splayed coat with flowers bursting from its lapels, a dog that had swallowed a clock.

Headless women echoed through the collages on the gallery walls, the heads switched out for accessories or animals – a consequence of Okanoue's fashion studies, the decapitated shadow of the dressmaker's dummy. In *Incubation*, a woman lounges awkwardly across rolling fields, her head replaced with a butterfly, two eggs balanced in her lap. The wall labels described the collages as dreamlike, but to me they felt nightmarish, like a kind of collapse, all glamour and terror. Standing in front of *The Miracle of Silence* had lurched me to the precipice of nausea, with its line of headless women sweeping in a clearing, its five black dogs in the grass. But Cecelia had been drawn to the horror of it, gazing up at the image, her fingers touching her own neck, the red thread still circling her wrist.

The battery-powered nightlight splashed its scenes across the bedroom ceiling, illuminating Kioko's pinned-up drawings. Wendy had bought it during the last, days-long power cut to help Kioko sleep; she'd also acquired a battery-powered lantern, which she carried with us out into the corridor.

I scrambled around in Izzy's catch-all basket until I found my trusty head torch. 'You still want to do this?' I asked.

'It's fine,' Wendy said. 'I can check on the neighbours while we're at it; I worry about the older ones when the power goes out.'

'Do you think it's because of the snow?' I asked.

'Who knows? Sometimes I think they're letting this building rot, waiting for a developer to take it over. They never fix anything. It feels so much older than it should. At least they can't put the rent up if they don't make improvements. I'm not sure where else we'd go. This city is so expensive.'

'Do you ever hear—?' I stopped. I'd been about to say voices, but that wasn't what I meant. What I wanted to ask was: do you ever feel like the building is talking to you, taunting you? Not with voices – or not only with voices – but with sounds that seemed to be directed, somehow, at you? Sounds that ripple beneath the walls. That whisper to you, telling you to step this way, or that? That transport you in your sleep? Do you ever hear . . . ghosts?

Wendy rescued me from having to finish this sentence. 'I don't mean to pry, but . . .' she started.

'Go ahead.'

'I'm worried I might have offended your sister's friend.'

'Sasha.'

She nodded. 'I hear him coming and going at odd hours. The walls, you know, they're not thick. I mean, he calls her *Belle*. He is her boyfriend, right? I didn't put my foot in it?'

I zipped my mouth shut and swallowed the key.

'Oh, it's like that, eh?' She laughed. 'Your one is very handsome.'

I opened my mouth to protest, but realized I'd sound just like Sasha. For now James would be *my one*.

We started at the end of the corridor and worked our way past our own front doors. Wendy was good at talking to the neighbours, warming them up before holding out the flyers. She seemed at one with the social world. We shone our lights on Sunshine's Xeroxed face, standing in doorways asking if they'd seen any sign of him over the last few days. His disappearance had been mysterious, we explained – he'd gone missing from a locked apartment. I couldn't imagine Izzy being this categorical, but to me it was important.

'Things go missing here all the time,' one neighbour complained. 'Even my tea towels, and my ginger cookies. Try to get someone to take you seriously about a stolen tea towel. They say I leave them in the laundry machine. I don't leave them. Can I flyer about my cookies? No.' She closed the door in our faces.

Another elderly neighbour was convinced he'd solved our mystery, pointing at the flyer with a declarative finger. He described a strange girl he'd seen taking the dog for walks. 'Something off about her.' He narrowed his eyes at me without a flicker of recognition. 'The dog woman, coming and going at all hours, hiding her face. I'd look into that one.'

Another neighbour shoved dog treats into our hands, leftover from her dearly departed pet, who'd suffered into old age, his eyes cloudy with cataracts, his back legs ceasing to function. 'People don't realize how hard it is to lose a dog,' she told us. 'Of course, you've still the hope yours will come back to you.' She scratched the mole on her chin with a curved, flame-painted acrylic. 'Unless the coyotes have got him. They're in touch with another force, you know, dogs. They're like angels. They come into your life exactly when you need them.'

'I think we should put her down as a question mark,' Wendy said once the woman had closed the door, blowing kisses at Sunshine's pixelated face. 'People are weird about their dogs, huh?'

When we'd exhausted the doors along the corridor, Wendy made her apologies and returned to her daughter, asking me where I'd go next.

'I'll check in with the others.' I thanked her. 'Domo arigatou gozaimasu.'

'Hai!' she said, and smiled. 'Oyasumi.' She stepped inside and closed the door, taking the blue glow of the lantern with her.

23

But the others weren't in my plans at all. I wanted to search the only place left: the basement. Laundry room, garbage room and cavernous car park. Everything slipped sideways as I moved along the corridor in the white beam of the head torch. The lights flickered overhead, as if struggling to come back to life, and the pipework sighed and rushed, telegraphing human voices. I couldn't decipher any of the words, the sounds repeating and murmuring in a preverbal babble.

At the mirror I saw only a bright light approaching, the suggestion of my body beneath it. I climbed down the stairs, expecting to bump into the others searching for Sunshine, or at least another occupant caught in the power cut. But I walked the blue-grey stairs alone, meeting not a single soul until I finally stepped out into the unfinished basement.

It felt even more cell-like down there in the dark, my light creating a tunnel before me, shadows crowding my body. I *felt* the dark, heavy and malodorous, like a pelted creature breathing at my back. I heard a drip, drip, drip, the damp creeping under my clothes. Again, that strange pull tugged at my limbs, drawing me deeper into the basement, my light revealing its concrete walls, alive and porous-looking with green-black mould.

In the laundry room I leaned around the bulky machines, even creaking open their metal doors, fearful of what I might find inside. Something mangled and bloody? My light shone on a few abandoned articles of clothing slumped in the corner like an effigy. In the garbage room, residents had sorted their effluvia into organics and recyclables, flattened their cardboard boxes, tied their rubbish bags, but the smell of rotting food still threatened to overwhelm me. 'Sunshine!' I backed away from the dumpster, overflowing with shiny rubbish bags. If he was in there, I didn't want to know.

The car park stretched like a dark bunker, my footsteps echoing – it was too big, too easy to get lost in there, and the cars all looked the same, their headlights reflecting the glow of my torch like glassy eyes. All the while I held my breath, expecting to meet somebody, to encounter something crouched between the vehicles. The space palpitated with a kind of presence, a feeling that throbbed at my ears. I was sure that at any moment I'd collide into another body, sprinting at me in the dark and knocking me off my feet.

I yelled the dog's name a few times and then slipped back inside the atrium, where I found the only remaining door to be opened. I rolled the phrase *dog woman* over in my mind, picturing the neighbour pointing his finger at the flyer and looking up at me. *Something off about her*, he'd said. I almost laughed to myself, but stopped with a shudder when I realized why *dog woman* sounded so familiar to me. It was the title of a series of Paula Rego's pastel canvases, based on a Portuguese fairy tale: an old woman convinced by the voice of a child to eat her pets one by one.

I expected the door to the electrical room to be locked, but it swung open to a bank of humming machines. I wasn't sure what was making them hum, since the power had gone out. Were they cooling themselves down, running on some reserve of energy? I doubted it was safe to be in here for long. Wouldn't the residual electrical currents disrupt something at a cellular level?

Behind the machines was an anteroom full of equipment: metal buckets, sacks of salt, and an enormous, gleaming snow shovel. I leaned on a wall and it seemed to give way. I pushed again, this time with both my hands. Now I was in another room, the hum alive in my ears. The Leonora was surely still feeding on something. Bare walls, exposed piping, the ceiling dripping with insulation. The damp intensified, the air clogged with the stagnant smell of something organic – mouldering leaves or brackish water.

Ahead of me there was a sunken space and that sunken space was lined with tall stacks of newspaper, like a nest. Could it have once been a swimming pool? That didn't make sense, down here in the basement, and it was too small. Yet there were steps going down into the nest, and a dim glow emanated from inside it. It seemed to be a well.

I hesitated, trying to figure out what I was seeing, hearing Cecelia's voice in the pitch, her affectionate mocking. *You're one of those girls that always goes down into the basement. Follow the strange noise in the dead of night.* Her mouth sucking at the spoon, face lit up by the laptop. Mommy horror. The women on the screen burrowing through underground caverns in the glow of a red flare, their hands slipping over the cave walls. Disturbing something ancient and hungry.

The beam from my head torch lit my way down the steps; as I descended, I was reminded of the bathtub, the feeling of being close to the pipes, pressed in, held by water. The walls of the well were made from something older than the concrete of the rest of the basement – thick stone, slick with mildew. The dank seeped into my bones, and when I reached the bottom the ground yielded beneath my feet like bare earth.

The nest was full of stuff. A hair scrunchie. A bottle of bath salts. Our kitchen radio, dangling mutely from an orange extension cord. A bed of loose blankets, a station for preparing food – coffee jug, sugar cubes, dog treats. The ocular glint of an amethyst geode.

Under the blankets, movement. Not under the blankets – atop them, the mauve housecoat melding with the blankets and the shadows, the wiry hair on end, two eyes, watching me. Medusa. She blinked, then opened her mouth as if to scream.

But instead of screaming, a loud, high bark. My eyes adjusted to the gloom, and I saw the space more clearly, lit by a candle burning inside a lamp next to the bed. Sunshine had been curled up in a pile with Medusa, and now he was straining to meet me, the old woman holding onto him, pressing him close, and making her own bleating sounds of distress.

'Let him go!' A swell of panic rippled through my voice, alien and hollow in the pit. Sunshine squirmed with movement, his eyes caught in the light of my torch, two shining green orbs. 'Let him come to me!'

She let go and the dog yapped and bounded over to me, jumped at my knees. I bent to pick him up, the weight of him wriggling in my arms. I wanted to turn and flee, but I was afraid to turn my back to Medusa – afraid of her body hulking towards me and pulling me down, dragging me deeper into the well, suffocating me in the damp earth.

'He wanted to come with me,' she snapped.

'I know.' My voice trembled. 'He likes you, I can tell.' The atmosphere filled my lungs, damp and dripping with mildew. The walls looked soft with it. 'But he needs his medicine. He's not well.'

She pointed a gnarled finger at me. 'How did *you* get down here?'

I stammered something incoherent.

Medusa pulled herself from her slumped position half-kneeling on the makeshift bed. She lifted the lamp, flame wavering, holding it before her as she stumbled towards me, her free hand outstretched to thwart the beam of my own bright light. I shrank away, hoisted Sunshine under my arm and slid the torch from my head, clutching it in my hand so that Medusa and I could look each other in the face. My heart hammered against my breastbone, a singing in my ears. How would we get out of her pit, her nest, her well? Would Medusa and I have to strike some bargain for me to leave with the dog?

'This is my building,' she started, her shielding hand reaching for my face. But then she stopped, her eyes fixed on mine and milky in the strange light. I swallowed, heaved the dog above my hip. 'I see you in there,' she screeched, suddenly gripping my chin, squeezing my face in her fingers. 'Leave the girl alone!'

I cried out. 'Please. I won't tell anyone.'

'I see you!' Rage thrilled her voice. 'Get out!'

Sunshine began to growl.

'Get out!' Medusa screamed, the flame guttering inside the lamp. 'Get out of there!'

I cast my eyes around the well, backing into the steps, her hand still pushing at my face. 'Please,' I begged, wrenching myself from her grasp. 'Don't hurt us.'

She stopped, her face seeming to crack. She started to laugh. Her laugh echoed horribly from the walls. She lifted the lamp right up to my face – I felt the heat of the candle – her features distorted on the other side of the flame, her mouth wrinkling into a tight, warped o.

She blew the candle out.

The flame extinguished with a tearing sound. I sucked in a wave of smoke, her putrid breath. My foot searched for the rung of the ladder and I climbed backwards, somehow, out of the well, squeezing the dog. My torch flashed around Medusa's pit as she started to mutter to herself, pacing the enclosed space, knocking over the stacks of newspaper, pulling at her hair.

I turned and ran with the dog in my arms, trying to find the way out, my small beam of light scattering across the walls until I found the opening. I thrust myself through it, rushing towards the bank of humming machines, but somehow turned myself around in the little anteroom.

The ceiling began to glow. The power had been restored, the buzz from the machines changing in pitch. In front of me was the wall I'd put my weight against to enter Medusa's lair, charged now with its own kind of intensity. It looked ordinary and solid apart from some pockmarks in the concrete. I ran my hand over the rough texture of the wall and a small chip of concrete dislodged and fell to my feet, leaving a tiny hole behind a breath of dust. Sunshine whined in my arms, his dog heart beating against me. *Don't cry.* Poised to run, I put a trembling hand against the concrete and pushed. But this time, nothing happened. The wall wouldn't give way to me.

As I travelled up in the lift, something washed over me. I should have been hysterical, but the further I got from the basement, the more I was able to disassociate from what had happened down there.

The lift buttons glowed before me, beautiful in their orderliness. I counted the floors as we rose up to Izzy's apartment, wiping tears from my cheeks and stepping out with the dog in tow.

The door to the apartment was open, and strangers spilled into the corridor, unlacing their shoes. Music filtered through the bodies and pulsed gently against the walls. Sunshine ran ahead of me, past the boots discarded in the hallway. Shrieks of surprise. The others had returned.

'Where did you find him?' Izzy squealed over the music, in a heap on the floor with the dog, who lunged excitedly to lick her face. 'He's filthy.' Her hands were deep in his fur, and she rolled onto her back and lifted him in the air. Sunshine's tongue lolled from his mouth and a glob of drool dripped onto Izzy's shoulder. She laughed and kissed his muzzle. 'Has he been in the rubbish?'

'Yes. That's where I found him.' I knew I'd sound hysterical if I told her about the terrifying crone in the basement, how she lived parasitically off the power supply. The search party formed a circle around the coffee table – James sat with his arms wrapped around his knees, catching my eye and transmitting a desire to be rescued – but strangers crowded the room. Some I recognized vaguely as neighbours, others I'd never seen before. I imagined the way they would all look at me if I opened my mouth and started talking about Medusa.

'Poor thing, he must have been scavenging,' Lucie said.

Izzy had lowered the dog onto her chest, and he was lapping at her cheeks, her chin and neck. 'Oh, never leave me again,' she murmured, cupping his head in her hands and kissing his ears. 'Naughty boy. Let's get you something to eat. Yes, you're home!' She disentangled herself from the dog and climbed to her feet. Sunshine followed Izzy into the kitchen, huffing with pleasure, his nose pressed to her calf. I followed behind, pushing my way through the unknown guests.

'Why are all these people here?' I almost had to shout. On the counter, music pumped from a speaker I'd never seen before, hooked up to somebody's phone.

'The more the merrier!' Izzy opened the fridge to strip the chicken for the dog. 'Your face is dirty,' she said, ripping the cling away from the bird and attacking it with a fork. 'Were you scrabbling around in the trash? My God.' She looked up at the ceiling, her face ecstatic and washed with light, and dropped her hand with the fork.

'I didn't really find . . .' I started. 'I mean, he wasn't . . .' I couldn't find the necessary words. I imagined leading the crowd down to the basement, trying to push my way through the wall again. *It was here*, I'd swear. *A doorway*.

'I cannot believe you found him! I hope he's not traumatized.' Izzy knelt on the floor and made cooing sounds at the dog's muzzle. 'How did you get down there, hey? You stinky boy. Actually, let's make everyone leave and get him in the bath.'

But nobody did leave. I stepped into the bathroom for a moment alone, locking the door, and stared at my reflection in the shattered mirror, trying to process what was happening around me. The mark of Medusa's fingers smudged my jaw, my features kaleidoscoped by the glass. I pictured Medusa's face in the moment before she blew the candle out, a look sweeping across it like triumph. Her milky eyes. There was something familiar about the look, but I couldn't place it, like a word trapped on the tip of my tongue.

There were more questions in the living room, after I'd scrubbed Medusa's mark from my skin and joined them around the coffee table – Izzy, James, Lucie, Sasha, and the others I didn't recognize. Sunshine ate scraps of chicken from Izzy's hands, licking her fingers clean, while I spun a story about hearing him whine through the dark. How he'd seemed scared and crawled to me on his belly.

'What made you go down there?' Lucie wanted to know. 'In the dark! So creepy.'

'So brave,' Izzy said, kneeling before the dog. She sucked the tips of her fingers. Sunshine's tail thudded against the carpet.

'Funny, you did say you knew what you were looking for,' Lucie went on. 'But your theory was wrong. About the old woman.'

'Maybe,' I said cautiously, my nerves spiking. 'Who knows where he's been all this time? *Someone's* been looking after him.' I could have said, *the old woman had him. I got him back*. But they would want details. *You see, there's a well under this place . . .*

Was Medusa dangerous? And would Izzy be in danger if I couldn't convince her? It was impossible to think straight with all these strangers. Izzy and I could talk later. Perhaps I would take her down to the basement, risk cementing her disbelief at the wall.

I locked eyes with James across the table. He was watching me steadily, as if he knew something was wrong. James would believe me, I thought, after what happened to us. James I could tell.

'Even luckier that you found him by yourself,' Lucie said.

'No, you don't understand.' Izzy's dress had slipped to reveal a shoulder. 'She's famous for finding things. What's it they call you at the library? Saint Anthony.'

'Tony-Tony look-around,' I mumbled. When Lucie laughed, I leaned towards her across the table. 'It's a kind of um . . . sympathetic magic,' I chanced.

Lucie blinked. 'That's not—' she stopped herself, seeming to consider it. The glitter eyeshadow had mostly flaked off, but spots of it glinted at the tip of her nose and chin.

Izzy clapped her hands. 'Dessert!'

'Well done,' Sasha said when Izzy left the coffee table with Sunshine at her heels. 'You've made your sister very happy.'

'Why are all these people here?' I asked. 'Did she invite them?'

'Your sister is a good sport,' Sasha said, drinking a shot of red liquid from an egg cup, and pouring one for me.

'Here we go.' Izzy lowered a platter of desserts before us: frosted cupcakes, dense brownies, little cups of chocolate ooze. My teeth hurt just to look at them. She pushed the platter under my nose. 'Returning hero has first dibs.'

'Oh!' I said, the thick treacly smell of the display overpowering me. 'They all look delicious, I can't choose. Let someone else go first.' I waved my hands, waved the plate away. 'Lucie should—'

'No, you go,' Izzy slurred. She'd been drinking, unwise on her diet of pills. Or had she stopped taking them? 'Pick your favourite.'

'They look so yummy.' I made a buzzing sound in my throat, my hand hovering over the cakes, trying to pick one. If I chose first, I'd have to eat it. My insides clenched.

'Stop being so polite.' Izzy thrust the platter closer to my face. 'Take the big one, with the chocolate sprinkles. It's your favourite.'

'It's not my favourite.' A laugh died on my lips, and I looked around for an ally. 'James, want to split with me?'

James leaned towards me and opened his mouth to speak.

'There's plenty to go round,' Izzy almost snapped, seeming to forget the dozens of people she'd invited back to the apartment. 'Come on, which one do you want?'

'Belle, ça a l'air délicieux,' Sasha interjected. 'You've spoilt us.'

'Diet starts tomorrow,' Lucie sang.

'Let Sasha choose first,' I insisted. 'He's our guest. I've already eaten so much.' My stomach felt tight as a drum. The people in the room seemed to be moving in all directions, like the pedestrians on the scramble crossings in Tokyo.

'Nonsense. You've hardly touched a thing. You're not going to get out of it.'

I reached for one of the lemon meringue cups, the smallest thing on the platter, but Izzy jolted it backwards, made a sucking sound with her teeth. I picked up the dense cake she indicated, holding it like something charged with power. I pushed the slab into my mouth, feeling it crumble at the corners, my fingertips gloopy with chocolate.

'Mmmmm.' The sponge clagged my tongue. 'Good.' But something tasted undeniably sour; I gagged. By some reflex, James put his hand to my mouth, and I spat the cake into it. 'I'm sorry!' Mortification cemented every bone in my body. I pressed a square of black paper napkin to my lips and wiped it over my tongue. 'Something's wrong with it.'

'What are you talking about?' Izzy lifted a piece of cake to her nose and sniffed it. Then she nibbled the edge. 'It's fine.' She frowned. 'A bit tough.' Her tongue licked at the frosting. 'Shit, it's turned.' She picked up the cake knife and cut into it. There were spots of mould in the sponge.

I got up from the table and ran into the kitchen, retching into the sink. A ring of people recoiled, making sounds of disgust and carrying their drinks away from me. I rinsed my mouth underneath the tap, letting the water crawl down my neck and soak my T-shirt. The speaker emptied dance beats into the room, and the light overhead shone bright enough to blur my vision. A hand on my shoulder. 'Are you okay?' James.

'Maybe we should give up on trying to end things well.' I wiped my mouth, clung to the countertop. 'I just spat in your hand.' The ceiling light burned into the back of my neck. I was shouting so he could hear me over the music.

'I've had worse.' He rolled his sleeves to the elbow and washed his hands calmly at the sink. Was this intimacy? 'Maybe we're not meant to end things at all,' he said, but then winced and squeezed his eyes shut.

'Are you all right?' I asked.

He opened his eyes again, then reached over to lower the volume on the speaker. 'My head is pounding. I'll give it to you, this building is bad vibes. It's like nobody here has ever been to a real party. I don't know why I don't just leave.'

'Why are all these people here?' I asked him.

He shrugged, drying his hands. 'They were here when I got back with the glitter lady.' He meant Lucie. 'Your sister seems a bit manic? Why did she push you like that?' He leaned in close so he could lower his voice, his mouth next to my ear. 'To eat the cake.'

I shook my head.

The bathroom door stood open on its hinges just steps across the hallway, as if inviting us inside. James's chest rose and fell, his fingers stroking my arm, tentative. If I told him about Medusa in the basement, would I be pulling him into something bad? A world where walls moved and mirrors contained warnings? He was so afraid of disappearing.

'I broke the mirror,' I reminded him, and his eyes flicked to the open door. 'You should see someone about the headaches.' I pressed my hand to his cheek, then whispered in his ear. 'You've been kind.'

I turned away before he could respond, my elbow slipping from his fingers. I went back into the living room and opened the balcony door, but two or three strangers amassed out there, so I left it open to the night sky and sat on the sofa with Sunshine. Someone had switched out the dance track for a festive playlist. Izzy wandered around the fluctuating groups of people, inventing travel plans on the spot. I heard the word *Barcelona* drift from wherever she stood, and once, to Lucie, a high, exasperated, *She does it to make me feel sorry for her!* They seemed to be arguing, Izzy tugging her hand out of Lucie's reach.

I rubbed Sunshine behind the ears and watched the snow falling through the open window. In the kitchen, Elvis drawled about being home for Christmas. I was desperate for the party to end.

'Did you know Elvis recorded "Are You Lonesome Tonight?" in the dark?' I asked the man sitting next to me, mistaking him for James. It was quieter out here than in the kitchen, no need to scream. The stranger looked at me with kind brown eyes, only a little surprised, so I continued. 'There's a whole section of that song where he's talking, not really singing. Just talking into the dark. His twin died at birth. Elvis survived him.'

A few blank beats. 'Are you the dog woman?' he said.

'What?'

He nodded to Sunshine in my lap. 'I keep hearing about a dog woman at this party. Is it you?'

I got up, looking into the faces of the people milling across the beige carpet, searching for James, but I couldn't find him. *Because I've all but stopped eating*, I could have answered to the question he'd posed at the sink. Or, *Because every time I try to eat, my throat constricts. My body rejects it. Because I sweat my way through tiny morsels of food and pretend it's not happening.*

Over the music the words *dog woman* kept surfacing, but I must have been imagining it – neighbours grouped in twos and threes to talk about the dog woman who roamed the halls, cast her eyes to the floor and avoided saying hello.

Because my body is swelling and bulging beyond my control. Here I could have grabbed a great fistful of my own flesh, tangible evidence, something demonstrable. *While my sister only gets stronger! Because she wants me to admit to it, the not-eating, the nausea.*

Dog woman who they'd seen roaming the streets with a leash and no dog. Dog woman who dressed poorly and smelled a bit odd, a bit, well, doggy. Dog woman who, if you thought about it, moved a bit like a dog. Postured like a dog, bared her teeth and gnashed and sank to all fours.

Because she thinks I'm doing it on purpose. That I'm playing tricks on her, the way she tricked our mother. But it isn't me, it's not me!

Dog woman passed into the stuff of legend as they drank, as I searched for James, until finally all of the strangers poured one by one from the apartment into the corridor, Sasha hanging back behind the others to tap the chain lock on his way out. 'Don't forget to keep the snake lady out.' He winked, leaving me alone with my sister, who sat on the floor cradling the dog's head in her lap, and finally the night was over.

Part Three:
Quickenings

24

I watched Sunshine closely for any signs of harm, mindful of the medications he'd missed. He slipped easily back into his old routines, begging for Milk-Bones after dinner and humping his stuffed giraffe before bed. He was sleeping on the sofa with me when I felt the first movement. It wasn't anything significant, like a kick or a poke, but a small, undeniable flutter. Sunshine rested his head on my belly, and in the moment the flutter came, he lifted his head and looked at my belly, too, one ear flicked back to show the seashell pink inside.

Since the party, and even before, I'd been doing my best to ignore the swelling, blaming it on eating the wrong things. I read unscientific articles about mass and weight, cut out certain foods, restricted my diet in ways familiar to me from Izzy's teen years. During my own years of disordered eating – a paradox of a term, so neat and incapable of summoning the experience – my throat had simply closed over, my stomach refusing to accept certain foods until there was hardly anything left. I'd had no control over it, not even the illusion of control.

The flutter in my belly was something I couldn't ignore, like a twitch in my eyelid. The first thing I did was look up my symptoms online, where I read the word *quickening* over and over again. Quick: archaic for living, as in *the quick and the dead*. Quicken: to hasten, animate, or excite. The first motions of foetal life.

I knew what I was reading was impossible, going to Izzy's wall calendar despite myself, counting back the weeks. The months between Cecelia and James had been an abyss for sex of any kind, though Izzy had scribbled a red question mark in the middle of August. I had one week left of my trip; unlike my arrival, my return flight hadn't made it onto Izzy's calendar.

I went to the pharmacy and bought a pregnancy test for my own peace of mind. I took both tests included in the box, sitting on the toilet watching for the appearance of two thin lines, both tests coming back negative. This was enough to reassure me for a few hours, but then I felt the flutter again, more intensely, while I was washing dishes, pain like a knot in the small of my back, something beating in my belly.

I told no one. I spent my nights sleepless, my calves cramping and my face bathed in the glow of my screen. I'd found message boards for cryptic pregnancies, which ran the gamut from people with no idea they were pregnant until the moment they went into labour, to the inverse: people who knew they were pregnant, but no one believed them. Not until they'd given birth in some dramatic fashion – on the kitchen tile, in the back of a taxi, on a packed commuter train.

Some of the people posting on the boards fiercely believed they were in the grip of a cryptic pregnancy. Negative urine and blood tests, inconclusive ultrasounds, and doubting partners marked these stories. *I (23f) was NINE months pregnant but my husband (34m)*

REFUSED to believe me, one comment replied to a cryptic thread. *You are probably pregnant, too! Tests and scans can't show EVERYTHING. Maybe you have a tilted uterus? The twins were behind my RIBS!*

I couldn't deny there was some truth to the comment. I already knew there were limits to what an ultrasound could detect; that's how Izzy had lost everything, the future she'd carefully planned retracting out of focus.

One woman who posted frequently on the boards was convinced she was in her eleventh month of pregnancy, that her gestation period was simply longer than the medical profession allowed. As much as I trawled the boards, I couldn't find the opposite phenomenon: a pregnancy with an accelerated gestation period.

Then there were phantom pregnancies, in which someone could present with all of the symptoms, even raised pregnancy hormones and positive tests, everything but the baby and the birth. These cases of pseudocyesis were usually in response to some sort of trauma – a lost child, a terrible family accident, a deep bonewish for a baby – the body communicating its pain, the brain believing in the existence of a baby that wasn't there. A cruel kind of conjuring.

I thought about posting on the message boards, but the other responses were about as helpful as shaking a Magic 8 Ball. Even the straightforward pregnancy stories I read about on the internet were riddled with thwarted expectations and medical mysteries, with sudden pools of blood and disbelief. I drafted a post anyway, listing all of my symptoms, my lack of desire for a child.

Maybe it was the latter that stopped me from clicking submit – it cancelled me out of most of the categories. *Not Izzy, though*, I thought, and stroked Sunshine's head.

All of this internet activity had infected my algorithm. Now every time I went online I was bombarded by advertisements for everything from baby thermometers to nipple-soothing pads. A pop-up tried to sell me a body suit designed to imitate the shape and heft of the second trimester. This was how I found the Doppler, an ultrasound kit which could be conducted at home and delivered with priority overnight shipping.

I realized, of course, that I could have something completely different wrong with me. A tumour or a parasite. I might have ingested some spiny creature that set up camp in my abdomen, that shot tentacles of pain all over my body, that made me swell and vomit and sweat. Or perhaps it was something gynaecological – my period still hadn't materialized. The culprit for that absence alone could be anything from weight change, hormonal irregularity, early menopause, thyroid issues, and a raft of chronic conditions.

Sunshine sat in my lap on the pull-out, his eyelashes fluttering as if he was fighting to stay awake, as if he was there to keep me safe. I would go to the walk-in clinic, pay the money, I resolved. I would go the very next day. But in the morning a parcel had arrived for me, the Doppler kit, and I decided it wouldn't hurt to try it out.

Headphones in, screen hidden, I viewed a few Doppler tutorials online, feeling ridiculous as I watched the women lube their abdomens. They'd bare an expanse of flesh to the camera, belly-first, some jiggly and soft, some taut and with a dark line creeping from the navel, bifurcating their middles.

I waited until I was alone, complaining of feeling ill and staying in bed while Izzy went for her second follow-up with the doctor. Her final one, hopefully. She didn't want me there, anyway. I drank two glasses of water, pulled down the waistband of my pyjamas and underwear, squeezed the ultrasound gel across my belly, somehow managing to get it everywhere: the edge of my hand, my hair, the sofa cushions.

I put the microphone on top of the gel before pressing the button on the machine, pushing the gel around in small, circular motions. Whooshing noises, gurgles and blips, then a rhythmic pulse, a heart rate registering numerically on the screen. I'd been prepared for this by the videos I'd watched – not to mistake the din of my own insides for a foetal heartbeat. Still, I dropped the microphone in fright, the machine crackling with static until I recovered it and pressed it again to the dome of my belly, a hard and frightening thing in itself.

The beating was only my own pulse, the blood rushing through my arteries. I exhaled in relief, relaxing back onto the splayed sofa cushions, my legs still tangled in the sheets. Only the shift seemed to push my heart rate up on the monitor until it thudded at a gallop, the little heart icon pulsating on the screen. I sat up, pressing the microphone deeper into my flesh, but lost the sound.

I became so engrossed in hunting for the beat that I failed to hear the door opening. 'What are you doing?' Izzy said, and I dropped the microphone to another wave of static. I fumbled to turn off the machine.

'I thought I found a heartbeat,' I said.

She stared at me, horrified. 'What?'

'My period's late,' I wailed, feeling the contradiction of what I was saying. That wasn't how pregnancy worked.

'Your belly looks like mine.' She was frozen in place at the threshold between rooms. 'Like it used to look. Exactly like it used to look.'

'I'm sorry.'

Izzy sat next to me on the pull-out, squeezing a pillow in her lap, her face fraught and pale.

'How was your appointment?' I asked in a small voice.

She looked at me gravely, ignoring the question. 'I *knew* you'd find a way to make this about you.'

'What? Izzy—'

'You need to go to a doctor. You can't be pregnant. It doesn't make sense.' Some of the gel had transferred to her hands, and she rubbed them together as if to wipe them clean.

'I know,' I said. But she was staring at the Doppler.

'If you're doing this on purpose, it's very cruel. It's very cruel, Brooke.'

'How do you think I'm doing *this* on purpose?' I gestured to the exposed bump that had taken over my body, the weight of it pressing me into the sofa cushions. I felt like a snake that had swallowed an egg.

She paused for a minute, thunderstruck. 'You could have some sort of cyst. They can be hereditary, problems like that. Or it could be environmental.' She picked up the Doppler, turned it over in her hands. 'I can't fucking believe you bought this rather than go to a doctor.'

'It just seemed easier.' My eyes filled with tears. 'I wanted to understand it before I went in. I've had other symptoms, too. And look at me.'

Her eyes went to the mound of my belly. Hesitantly, she pressed a hand there, a soft, breathy *oh* escaping from her lips. Then she drew her hand away again. 'You really thought you heard something?'

'I don't know. I thought so.'

'Let's just make sure,' she said. 'So we know what to tell the doctor.'

I squeezed more of the gel onto my belly and handed her the microphone, turning on the machine once she'd tentatively pressed it to the bump. She pushed the wand over my skin and I shuddered. 'Okay?' she said.

'It's cold.' The machine whooshed and pulsed. 'That's just my own stuff, those noises.'

'You can explain ultrasounds to me after you've had the one they insert.'

'A foetal heart rate is very fast, like a—'

Thump-thump, thump-thump, thump-thump. A rhythmic sound, like hoofbeats. We both heard it, our eyes locking. But the numbers on the Doppler screen remained low.

'Maybe we're not doing it right.' She pressed the microphone until it dimpled my flesh. The galloping grew more distinct, but still the numbers next to the pulsing heart icon were low. Whatever my sister and I could both hear, it did not register as a foetal heartbeat on the Doppler. I turned up the volume until we were surrounded by an electronic thump. 'You were a miracle baby,' Izzy said. Mir-acle, mir-acle, mir-acle, went the strange thump. 'Realistically, you shouldn't have been born.'

Izzy came with me to the walk-in clinic, paid the fee, and waited in the seating area while I went inside and explained my symptoms to a man in his mid-sixties with white hair. 'You must be very excited,' he said at first, inattentive. My voice faltered as I told him about my late period, the negative test, the Doppler kit – he looked up from his notes to peer at me – the hoofbeats. 'Are you sexually active?' he asked. 'Do you practise safe sex?' I made up a story about a split condom, explaining it had happened only weeks ago. He pulled up my shirt and examined my swollen stomach, digging his fingers deep into my flesh. His face was unperturbed. 'It's not your appendix,' he said, his inflection rising as if asking a question.

'No.' I told him again about the Doppler, the beat we'd heard. 'Not just me. My sister heard it, too.'

He frowned. 'Those home devices are really not advisable. They can be misleading, with potentially tragic results. Besides which, we can't detect a foetal heartbeat on approved devices until at least the second trimester. It was likely your own heartbeat you heard.'

Feeling chastised, I wrapped my hands around my protruding belly. 'I'm not imagining *this*,' I insisted.

'I see.' The doctor looked at me over his glasses, then held up a gloved finger. He disappeared from the room for what felt like eons. Eventually, a nurse entered, greeting me cheerfully. She wore a blue uniform and carried a more medical-looking version of the Doppler I'd ordered.

I lay flat on the examination table with my shirt under my ribs as she waved the wand over my belly, pressing it into my skin near my bellybutton. The radio static of my insides rumbled on, filling the room.

The nurse peered into my face, her expression kind. 'See, dear?' she said. 'Nothing there to worry about.' Her voice was patient but firm, as if I was a child and she had shone a torch under the bed to reveal there was no monster hiding underneath. 'Doctor would like some samples.' She wiped the cold gel from my abdomen with a rough paper towel and sent me to the washroom with a receptacle the size of a test tube to pee in.

When I went back out to the waiting room, Izzy sat with her handbag curled in her lap, her eyes fixed on the spot where I'd reappeared. 'I'm not pregnant,' I told her under my breath as I collected my things from the chair next to hers. 'He wants me to see my family doctor as soon as I get home.'

We walked out into the street together, drifting in the opposite direction to home, away from the busy thoroughfare. Izzy kept peering at my face, but I mostly watched the pavement under my feet. 'Does he think it could be a cyst?' she asked.

'He wouldn't speculate. He said my doctor will probably refer me for an ultrasound. A proper one.'

'Can't we do that here?'

'It would take time to get an appointment. He gave me a requisition for a blood test, but he said I could wait for that, too. I'd have to pay for it here. He said it was non-urgent.'

She nodded, but her eyes were fixed now on the lump under my jacket. Ahead of us, the street met Beach Avenue, opening onto a promenade of trees, the ocean flashing like an iridescent fish scale. 'Did you tell him about your family history? Mum's miscarriages?'

I nodded.

'What about the heartbeat we heard?' she asked, almost breathless.

'I don't know, Izzy, they checked. Our machine must be glitching.'

'Maybe it's something else. Could it be anything to do with your old trouble?' She meant the disordered eating, the dizzying anxiety that had confined me to the bedroom.

I shrugged.

Izzy grew exasperated. 'Brooke, did you ask him any questions?'

'He says my doctor will refer me for *help*. He seemed to think I was making it all up. Look, I've done what you asked. I've been to the clinic. Can we drop this now? I'm really embarrassed.'

'Embarrassed?' she repeated, her eyebrows aloft. 'Well, don't think I haven't noticed you haven't been eating properly. I thought you were sulking at first. You were eating so beautifully when you arrived.'

'Nothing like this happened before,' I said in a small voice. The disordered eating had messed up my periods, but not with such an alarming result. When they came back I'd felt a kind of elation, like I'd reached a milestone in my recovery. It had taken so much to get better, to learn how to live inside my body. The thought of starting again was exhausting.

If we turned right and kept walking, the avenue would lead us to the herons' nests. I wasn't ready for the flood of those associations, so I sat down on a bench overlooking the seawall, facing the water. Seagulls competed for the overspill from a rubbish bin, but that was okay, the gulls meant nothing to me. Izzy was still talking.

'This could be the start of a long road for you.' She sat next to me and folded the handbag in her lap again. She sat exactly like our mother did whenever she rode the bus. 'You should think seriously about whether you want children or not and make some plans. I'm not telling you this because of your . . . choices.'

'Choices.' I plucked the word from her mouth. What did she mean? My stalled life? My art, my queerness? Maybe just my solitude. My way of being was so alien to her.

'I waited too long. Maybe if I'd tried earlier, I would have got pregnant. Maybe I still would've gone through all this shit, but I could have already had my baby. I'll never know. I wasted those early years with Marty, taking the pill – tricking my body into thinking it was already pregnant, that's what it does – waiting for him to be ready. And then, I don't know, I didn't meet anyone else, I was working, I lived in a tiny apartment, all my money going to rent, flying back and forth to see everyone. I thought I had time, and then I started bleeding. I was scared it was early menopause at first – it reminded me of what Mum went through. I had a window of opportunity with Sasha, but even then, I didn't realize . . . it was my last chance. Don't be like me, don't wait. You need to take control of your life.'

'But I don't want a baby! I truly don't. Maybe I'll change my mind one day and maybe it will be too late, but I can't have one *just in case*. You're so sure. I've never been sure like that about anything.' I crossed my arms, hugging the fabric of my hoodie, squirrelling my hands inside the sleeves. I was thinking of the phrase she'd used, tricking the body. Was I being tricked by something inside, some hormonal response to the place or the predicament I'd found myself in?

'You're twenty-seven,' Izzy said. 'I wasn't always sure. How do you know you don't want one?'

'How do you know you do? What if you've just been conditioned to want one? That could be a trick, too.'

She exhaled sharply. All the air seemed to have left her body, as if I'd punched her. She shook her head. 'I can't explain the feeling to you. It's like . . . I know my baby is waiting for me. Not like she's a soul floating around waiting for me to, I don't know, fulfil some biological destiny. I don't believe any of that shit, you know I don't. But like . . . she's this . . .' Her voice wavered, then came back with a heartbreaking emphasis. '*Beautiful possibility*.' She paused for a few beats, gathering herself, a finger shaking at her lips. Everything about her seemed watery in that moment, fluid. She brimmed with the idea of the baby. It almost seemed real – a round, soft form bundled between us. 'I guess I can't accept her impossibility. I literally don't have a womb any more.'

We sat looking out at the ocean, waves lapping at the rocks, the birds scavenging from the rubbish. Despite our division, despite her anguish, Izzy's presence calmed me, knowing that whatever it was, she was there, next to me. 'I'm sorry I'm doing this to you,' I said, and then, because I couldn't wait for an answer any longer, 'Why did you fold me and Dad out of the photograph?'

She knew what I was talking about. She didn't pretend otherwise.

'Do you resent me for being born?' I asked.

She frowned, wiping at her eyes and cheeks. The beautiful possibility of the baby still lingered between us. She felt caught by my question – not like I'd discovered some trespass she had to answer for, but that it hooked her momentarily out of something she felt so deeply, a guttural longing, my question pulling her roughly out of its fever and into relationship with me, her sister. 'I only folded it because it's a sad picture, otherwise. If Mum's pregnant with you in it, that's a nicer story. I don't want to look at it and think of that time, all those miscarriages. Or for anyone to ask me about it. Besides, *I* know you're in it. And Dad.'

The truth of it hit me. 'I never thought about it like that.'

'Don't tell Mum. I don't want her to feel like her other pregnancies didn't matter. That one especially.'

'I wanted to ask if you remembered them, but it always felt too private, like we shouldn't talk about it. Like it just belongs to Mum. And Dad, I suppose.' The wind had picked up and the waves rolled in, shushing around the rocks beyond the seawall, making little eddies and vortexes. 'Why that one especially? Because she got so far along?'

'No. I can't really explain it. It's just that when I did hear her talk about the miscarriages, sometimes she talked as if . . . as if they were all *you*. Attempts at having you. But she got pregnant again after you were born. So that one was different. Maybe it's wrong of me to say that.' She shook her head. 'I'm sure they all felt individual to her. I was only a kid, I couldn't wrap my head around it. I was glad when you were born.'

I felt such a rush of relief, of love, I rested my head on her shoulder. She was glad I was born. The seagulls were fighting over a few loose french fries, and a woman walked by with a Dalmatian at the end of a lead.

'I like that picture of me and Mum, the two of us with our plaits. I'm the double of her.' She pushed my wayward curls out of her face. 'Honestly, sometimes it's like you don't know me at all. I don't think you've understood anything that's happened to me. What you still have a chance at.'

'A baby, you mean? I've already told you—'

'Not just a baby. It's more than that. There's an . . . ongoingness. A part of you that lives on outside your body, like how Mum's part of us. Would you really give that up? The chance to be a mother, to create life?'

'An ongoingness?'

'The way mothers are, I don't know, part of the river of time.'

Part of the river of time? 'And we're not?' This kind of talk made me feel like an insect specimen flattened inside a display case, a pin shoved through my thorax. It made me never want to let anything inside my body again – nil by mouth, zero penetration. 'I've never heard you say anything like that before. Did you hear that from Lucie?'

'*I'm* just going to turn forty and then fifty and no one will care. What else is there?' Izzy looked down at her folded hands.

'What else . . . ?' I was stunned. Did she really think my life was meaningless? That her own life would be meaningless without the act of giving birth? Didn't we love each other, and didn't that mean something? 'Everything else.'

But Izzy didn't seem to hear me. My *everything else* was flimsy and ephemeral to her, it blew away on the breeze.

'I've got so much love for a baby.' Izzy's voice carried the ache of her longing. 'I think it would crack me open, in a good way. I've seen it happen to other people.' She turned to me, her handbag in her lap, her body still echoing our mother's body. 'Let's entertain the possibility, for a moment, that you're pregnant—' She stopped my protests with a raised hand. 'You didn't do this by yourself. Maybe James has fucking He-Man sperm, I don't know. Is there not some tiny part of you that would be happy? Wouldn't you feel complete?'

She looked so hopeful, like her belief in miracles rested on my answer, but I only felt claustrophobic. I couldn't think of what to say.

25

My symptoms persisted, even increased. The flutters in my stomach became rolling and turning, like a crashing surf. My insides stretched and twisted as I moved around the apartment, closing myself away from prying eyes until it was time to fly home. I'd packed most of my things already. I'd been hoping, somehow, that the knotted thing inside me would resolve itself before I had to explain anything to Mum and Dad, or to anyone. I could still hide the bump with the right clothes. Part of me believed I just had to wait it out, like the first wave of homesickness that had threatened to overwhelm me in Japan.

My hopes for a tidy resolution were dashed once I noticed the pattern, how the movements responded to light and darkness, to sound, to sugar. I drifted to other sorts of message boards, ones that were pure fantasy, explicitly speculative in nature: stories of immaculate conception, alien implantation, satanic broods, and epic romance. These romances generally involved an unreachable husband, lost at war or sea. The longed-for and lost haunted the forums, asking *what if?*

Women waited, brave and stubborn, for some return, the vigil stretching the pregnancy over a slippery expanse of time, the message-board posts spanning years. I traced entire simulated families, their histories poorly slapped together: birth orders confused, or children with birthdays celebrated in May and again in October. The message board's code of conduct encouraged readers to suspend their disbelief; everyone who came there had a particular need to fulfil.

I fought impulses to sing to the bump, to stroke the thing sucking and growing inside me. The knot had infiltrated my brain, my behaviours. When Izzy wasn't looking – I didn't want to upset her, to flaunt my abundant body – I rubbed my belly with lotion in front of the bathroom mirror, and found myself talking to it out loud, simultaneously repelled and grimly attracted. There were wisps of new hair sprouting along my hairline, coarser and more tightly curled.

'I think we should go to a hospital,' Izzy said, joining me in the glow on the sofa one night, interrupting my message-board reading. 'We should have gone straight there in the first place.'

I refused. I'd hated the hospital when she'd been there, the dismissive way my sister had been spoken to, denying her full personhood. The language of the place: *fresh hysterectomy*. The doctor at the walk-in, too, his doubting gaze over his glasses, the admonishing trick he'd pulled – it had felt like a trick – by sending the nurse in with the Doppler. My passport and documents were neatly arranged on the coffee table. 'I'll just rest. I'll rest until it's time to go home. It might go away.' I closed my eyes as if to perform the restorative power of sleep.

'Your flight is the day after tomorrow.' She leaned over and switched on the table lamp.

'I know, but . . .' I looked at her, her lifted brow. 'It's this place,'

I said. 'I think it's something about this place, that's why this is happening to me. Once I'm home, maybe . . .' I gripped my swollen belly.

Izzy looked at me doubtfully. 'I don't think it's just going to vanish of its own accord, Brooke.'

'But you said it could be environmental.' I could hear the whine in my voice, how irrational I sounded.

'There's something going on inside you,' she insisted, gesturing to my abdomen. 'You can't travel home like this. What if something happens? We need to sort this out, get you . . . some help.' She chewed her lip. 'Why don't we give the Doppler thing another shot? You're bigger now.'

I turned over, pulling up my shirt, my sweatpants rolled beneath the bulge of my belly. 'You don't need the Doppler,' I admitted. 'You can feel it moving.'

'What?' Her face broke open. It was a joy she struggled to suppress. 'Really?'

'Here.' I dragged her hand across my belly. 'Just wait a while.' But the thing knotted inside me had already started to swim.

Izzy made an astonished *oh* sound, instinctively pulling her hand away, then moved her whole body closer to the swimming, swirling movement, placing her ear on my stomach. I stroked the bleached hair away from her other ear, held her still. I knew there was no heartbeat, no baby, but still I heard something, pulsing in my ears, rising over the music of Izzy's enchanted face, filling the room.

'It's not real,' I said to her. 'You know it can't be real.' But she looked right through me, as if to something far away.

*

Izzy called the airline, gave them some story, cancelled my flight. We told Mum and Dad I was staying for Christmas, that I felt bad leaving Izzy to cope alone. Mum was cross with us for the late decision – she'd bought gifts, treats, stripped and remade my bed, everything ready to receive her youngest daughter. When Izzy talked about what a good nurse I'd made, Mum softened, but only a little. 'So, I'm to have no daughters this Christmas,' she said. Izzy made a weak promise to come home next year. Mum didn't seem convinced.

I found myself swaying wherever I stood, as if rocking a baby inside me, an involuntary motion. I thought of the knot in my belly as my little parasite, and this name became soft and loving in my mouth, a term of endearment. 'My little parasite needs a lot of rest,' I might joke, starting from a nap on the sofa in the middle of the day. I dug out the babygrows from Izzy's wardrobe and draped them over my belly. 'My little parasite needs a cute new outfit.' Izzy beamed and pressed the super-soft stuffed bunny to her cheek.

'You look gorgeous,' she said, which wasn't true. 'You're glowing.' My eyes were sunken and puffy, my complexion sapped of colour.

'My little parasite needs all my energy – it's sucking my lifeforce.' We laughed.

Each of us allowed for a shift in the arrangement so that now it was Izzy bringing me food, tucking me in, massaging my calves. My limbs cramped and spasmed, my stomach muscles gapping and bulging, deforming the shape of my belly. Izzy stroked my forehead and scrubbed and stretched, while I lay in bed and grew more swollen, heavier.

My body had reached the end of something; a churning began, a kind of accounting. I felt my stomach register every missed meal, every retch into the toilet I'd put it through in the past. I was hungry –

voraciously hungry. I'd felt before like I could sleep for a week, and that's how I felt about eating; my body needed me to fill a hole.

But I had no appetite for food, only hunger. I wanted to chew bits of metal, grind plaster between my teeth, mouth charcoal into a paste, line my stomach. I ate instead whatever Izzy gave me, every crumb: I consumed packets of crisps and ran a wet finger over the silver paper to gather crystals of salt. I ate apples down to the core, then swallowed the core itself, spitting out the tiny red pips lest a tree grow from my stomach. 'That's good,' Izzy would say. 'We have to keep your strength up.'

How she loved me now.

Izzy was doting and kind as she moved me into the bedroom, changed the sheets, folding and smoothing, stroking my brow with lullaby hands. 'Let's tuck you in nice and tight.' She took away my phone. 'No scary movies, no bad dreams.' Her voice soothed and her hair fell in blonde tresses, unfamiliar to me still, as if she was someone else's sister.

Everything else seemed to retract – there were no more mentions of Lucie or Wendy or even Sasha. I accepted all of this. It was somehow wrong to bring an outside party into the equation. Other people would upset the balance, I thought, my insides sloshing around as I waddled from bedroom to bathroom to empty my bladder, Izzy glowing maternally as she loomed at the front door, a threshold I'd promised not to cross. Why had I promised this? Nobody could see me, Izzy said, what might happen to our little parasite? She cubed fruit, roasted squash, mushed bananas, feeding them to me in bed from a tray.

She spooned yoghurt into my mouth, made little encouraging noises, lifted a handful of pomegranate seeds, let me eat from her palm like a bird, wiped my chin with a clean white linen, and told me I was good. 'I'll do that for you,' she said of any small task, 'leave it to me,' and I, exhausted, complied, dozing off and waking with the bedclothes in my mouth, my desire to consume blooming even in my sleep.

In the middle of the night, I woke with a pit of longing in my stomach. Bottomlessly hungry, I dragged my body to the refrigerator and ate whatever I could find, cutting mould away from blocks of cheese and spitting out rotten spots of fruit. Mould bloomed, too, across the wall behind the bed, until all we could do was laugh like girls, like sisters, and pull the bed away from the wall into the centre of the room, so that I floated there like a passenger in a boat.

Izzy wasn't always with me, watching. She still had to walk Sunshine, and I'd hear the front door closing softly behind them, the jangle of the lead. If I could manage it then, I would heave myself up and move around the empty apartment, bleary-eyed, pulling open the balcony door to feel the cold air on my face, surprised to find myself still . . . what? Still pregnant? Couldn't be. My little parasite wasn't a real baby. It was only a figment, a shadow hand on the wall.

Sometimes Izzy sat outside the bedroom door on a chair. I could see her shadow moving under the gap in the door, such a large gap, anything might crawl in. I asked her what she was doing out there and she showed me: my favourite shirt, mended. My jeans and T-shirts, their holes patched. She was sewing, letting out waistbands, closing up tears, leaving the stitches visible, showing her work. Her mending was beautiful, like works of art. But why was she guarding the door?

I slept through long stretches of the day, waking up in light and dark, searching for the glowing numbers of the clock, 5:12 p.m.

blinking into 3:33 a.m. Sometimes I woke up with my thumb in my mouth, sucking on it, and slick between my legs. My mind played out all kinds of lurid fantasies I'd never entertained before – would a true pregnancy be this animal? I came once, in my sleep, and a stabbing pain ripped through the middle of me, so that I was terrified to touch myself despite any ungovernable urge I might have.

When I was conscious, I sang quietly to the little parasite – Kioko's tōryanse song, the language coming back to me in a flood of association. A sense memory not just of getting lost in the narrow streets at twilight, but of the old stone of the Ogaki fortress, the cold shock of the well water dripping from the ladle, and the shrine we'd visited in Kyoto with its curved roof and latticed walls. A red gate, my body vibrating with the press of cicadas, Cecelia, the two of us cycling through country roads to her little apartment, tick of the wheels as we lifted our feet from the pedals, our skin salty with sweat in the summer heat. It was kinder to maroon myself there, in the past, before things changed between us, before she saw me, the faults in me, my weakness.

Fatigue flooded my body, knocking me off my feet. Our little parasite was bleeding me dry, clawing its way deep into my uterus, leaving the husk of me stretched out beneath Izzy's duvet. I observed my body assenting to chew and swallow, letting things in from the external world: ham rolls, mustard, orange rind, sweet potato, avocado, corn on the cob. Some of these foods out of season, hard and tasteless, with threads that snagged between my teeth. When I dreamed, I dreamed of forests, black skies, pine needles, a woman swimming through a red ocean under moonlight, her face covered by an animal mask, sometimes a wolf or a bear. In these dreams there was a cave I needed to reach, and something living inside it that was slippery and cold.

Some of the food Izzy brought me was dusted with an off-white powder. 'Are you drugging me?' I asked, licking the spoon.

'It's just folic acid,' she said. 'And a prenatal vitamin. For you, and for the baby. They reduce the risk of birth defects. I thought you might resist the idea, but I can give you the caplets instead, if you like?'

For the baby? *Birth* defects? No, no. That all sounded real.

'It can't hurt,' she added, rubbing my shoulder.

'They're giving me headaches,' I stammered. Events were running away from me. Birth? I couldn't *give birth* to this thing. 'And my stomach is off.'

'That's probably the iron. I'll give you a lower dose for now.' She carried the empty dishes out on a tray, her blonde hair neat and smooth.

One night while I raided the fridge – my hunger seemed to peak after dark – Sunshine padded in to vacuum the crumbs around my feet. A jar of dead chrysanthemums sat next to the sink in murky water, waiting to be tipped. I sat on the linoleum, feeding the dog from my fingers, breaking off pieces of beef stick and dried duck liver for him to beg, asking for his paw. I'd found my phone hidden in the treat drawer, and I switched it on, slipping it under my thigh to muffle any sound. As I drank from a glass of Clamato, I noticed a tarot card pressed beneath a magnet on the fridge: seven of swords. I hadn't seen this gift from Lucie since the hospital – I hadn't even realized that Izzy had brought the deck home with her. My sister slept on in the living room, accustomed to my midnight binges.

I burped and wiped my mouth with the back of my hand. Izzy hadn't been able to convince me to drink Clamato at the beginning of my visit. She'd tried to tempt me with a cocktail called a Caesar but I just looked at her, disgust naked on my face. 'Clam and tomato? *Clam* and tomato?'

'It doesn't taste like fish, I swear,' she'd promised. But it kind of did; my mouth brimmed with the tang of brine and salt as I sat on Izzy's kitchen floor with my enormous belly protruding from beneath my T-shirt.

I wondered if Izzy ever dreamed of the herons' nests she'd taken me to, or of the herons themselves, soaring massive overhead. My phone spewed several alert banners – for true crime episodes, Cecelia's online activity, my sudden drop-off in screen time. It was the twenty-fourth of December, 1:04 a.m. Jesus. I'd received a long missive from James via text, but I didn't have the focus to read beyond the first and last lines: a *Wow that was weird* opener brought to a *think of me fondly* close. I hadn't heard from him since the party; maybe he'd felt safer sending a message once he believed I'd left the country. So this was his final goodbye, his last attempt to end things well.

Above the body of his message was a profile picture of his face, a burnt-orange beanie pulled over his long hair, kissable Adam's apple. He looked like an autumn boyfriend you might order from a catalogue. *Fondly*. I remembered his pulse jumping beneath my fingers, his wrists crossed in my hands as he bowed between my legs. If I'd bothered to craft a romance for the fantasy fertility boards, James Dean would have made such a good phantom husband.

Zero notifications from my mother. That was a surprise. But when I clicked on 'Mum' in my message app, an entire conversation full of good cheer and forgiveness unfolded. Izzy had taken my place, typing out reassuring, bland responses that sounded nothing like me, littered with festive emojis. I was being taken over. Even in my present state, I was hurt Mum couldn't tell the difference. She must have thought us happy.

A string of messages from Lucie pulsed in my hand.

YESTERDAY:

Hi are you still in Vancouver??? Sunshine OK?

Is Izzy still mad at me?

TODAY:

Hey sorry to bug you but nobody's seen Izzy. I'm worried.

I'm coming over with pizza OK? No answer from Iz.

Can you buzz me in? Just ringing out. I see lights on.

Today? I started to type out a response, but I was afraid Izzy would read it. I didn't want her to know I'd discovered her hiding place, in case . . . in case I needed what? To call for help? Instead, I looked up the tarot card Izzy had pinned to the fridge. I scrolled through pages of results to the briefest, most distilled meaning I could find: If someone won't give you what you want, you'll have to take it.

I looked at the sharp blades on the tarot card, picturing Izzy's tidy hair, her neat trays of food, her mouth saying *open wide*, and her chef's knives, very sharp. A baby? The phone rested on my melon belly, huge and undeniable, my skin painfully stretched.

My blood pulsed in my ears. I knew the power lay not in the cards themselves, but in the meaning the querent made from them. Querent: the one who seeks. I tried to picture Izzy shuffling the deck, closing her eyes and asking the cards a question. It was hard to imagine the sister I knew doing something like that in earnest, and all I could muster was a memory of her in the hospital bed, her face ashen beneath her purple hair, the cards fanned out before her. I felt her scratch at the swollen vein in the back of her seeking hand, saw her surrounded by monstrous lilac-petalled chrysanthemum heads, bowing under their own weight.

I powered down and returned the phone to the drawer before I retreated to my pit, creeping past the opening to the living room where Izzy slumbered. The bedroom had a bitter sort of smell now, and water trickled behind the wall, reminding me of Medusa's lair.

I threw the bedroom curtains back and cracked the window open, quietly, so quietly, the chilly air prickling my bare arms and belly. I filled the window, my hands against the glass. Despite the hour, many of the windows were lit across the street and beyond, high in the glass towers – warm squares of yellow light rising into the black sky. Here and there a figure moved about inside their little box of light.

If someone won't give you what you want, you'll have to take it. The question you asked the tarot was more revealing than the card itself, the burning desire it uncovered. What was it Izzy had wanted to know, and why had she needed to tack this ominous answer – theft, betrayal, deception – to the fridge she fed me from? Was she screwing her courage to the sticking place?

I left the curtain wide, climbed into bed and pulled the duvet under my nose, exhausted, a gnawing hunger returning already to my belly. There were too many questions, too many potent images – they overcame me with a seasick feeling, like the flashing, blood-soaked scenes at the end of a horror movie. I concentrated on the dripping sound behind the wall and scratched at the spot on my abdomen where the mildew had clung – the strange, sticky growth I had scraped away with my fingers, scoring red lines on my skin. Had that substance been some trace of this parasitic invasion? Had the same green-black mould that infested the walls somehow seeped inside me?

Mildew proliferated across the wall and my hair grew faster than Izzy could cut it, splitting at the ends. She'd taken to trimming them with nail clippers, as if she didn't trust me near the scissors. My head was haloed by my fraying hair and my cheeks were stippled with spider veins. When I asked her how long I'd been in the room, she told me it had only been five days. 'That can't be right,' I said, though it chimed with the time stamps on my text messages. 'I'm enormous. And what about the clock?' The way it seemed to jump through hoops in time, carrying me forward by half-days whenever I looked at it. Izzy lay on the bed next to me, rolling me over, tucking herself into me, her knees against the pits of my knees, her arms around my swollen belly. She only meant to hold me but her arms were bony and vice-like.

'It's Christmas Eve,' she said softly. 'You slept all week.'

When Izzy cradled me on the bed, my body felt knotted with hers – the unseemly black stitches that had once stretched across her lower abdomen the inverse of my own expanding belly. Something precious and strange had been given to me, and wrapped inside my sister's arms, I felt how much she wanted it. 'It's all right,' she cooed. 'It's all right.' But her wanting came over me in waves. She was in the grip of something.

'I'm sinking,' I told her, but she had no knack for metaphor, and when I repeated myself she asked only what I meant. Whatever it was that knotted inside me rippled beneath her touch. I tried to twist away from her but her arms tightened.

‘I borrowed this from the little girl,’ she said, her arm briefly releasing me before snaking back around my belly. I heard the twinkle of the nightlight before the horses span across the ceiling, the moons and the stars. She must have gone next door while I was asleep. Dimly, I remembered Wendy saying they were going away for Christmas, the suitcases by the wardrobe. Had Izzy stolen it?

Under this strange equine galaxy, the mildew-pitted walls glowing and pulsing around us, I thought about the mystery of origins – was something actually growing inside me? Was it separate from me, or just a part of my body, like a limb or a fingernail? And if it came from my body, if I grew it, somehow, where would it go? Would it be absorbed, once more, inside me? Or would it tear a way out? Where did it end and where did I begin? Was I carrying a baby? Or some small evil?

Izzy’s hand was warm, and her wrist pulsed with something like love. I thought for a moment she might whisper in my ear, *thank you*, but instead she said in a small clear voice like a bell, ‘Mine.’

26

After that I vowed to stop eating real food. I left my Christmas dinner untouched – a festive improvisation of loaded nachos, skewered chicken, green and red peppers, potatoes mashed with butter. I sat unsteadily at the kitchen table with Izzy, watching her watch me not-eat. It was the first time we'd sat at the table together since we'd cancelled my return home. The kitchen behind her was messy, the counters piled with dirty dishes, crusts and rinds. 'Everything spoils so quickly,' she said apologetically.

I looked at the food on my plate, imagined how it would fester inside my quickening body. What a waste; Mum'd kill us if she knew. I recollected, dimly, being ill and not eating and Mum bringing me flowers, bringing me champagne, explaining calmly to me that I was just existing. 'Where's Mum?' I asked Izzy, though I'd meant to ask for my phone. 'Can we call to wish her Merry Christmas? She'll be upset if we don't.'

'Will you eat something for me?' Izzy replied. 'I'll make you anything. We'll call Mum once you've eaten something.'

I requested pancakes, blueberries, Oreos, candied lemons. Feeding me must have been costing Izzy a fortune.

'Candied lemons?'

'That's what I want.'

But when she brought them to me in bed, I couldn't push them past my lips. I knew she was lying about calling Mum. How could she let her see me like this? I'd tried to call home already – dead of night, refrigerator glow, slow rasp of the treat drawer – but Izzy had changed her hiding place for the phone. I'd stood looking at the front door, the deadbolt thrown and the chain lock slotted into place, Izzy snoring softly on the pull-out with the dog.

The building's corridors stretched endlessly on the other side of the door. I'd reached out my hand and touched the doorknob, remembered the night I'd seen it turn. By itself? The walls thrummed. I'd imagined myself unlocking the door and stepping out onto the psychedelic carpet, into corridors that seemed to shift and move, that delivered you to the basement or threw a mirror in your path, halting you with your own reflection. If I made it outside, where would I go? Who would help me? I'd wander alone in the black night, stagger through rhododendrons and woods, wade into the waiting blue inlet, belly-first.

Perhaps it was a good thing that Izzy wouldn't let me call Mum. If she didn't see me soon, she would know we were in trouble. She would know and she would get on a plane and come and pierce whatever spell we were living under, charge into the lobby with a shield and sword.

I shook my head. The lemon slices Izzy proffered were sticky, the pulp translucent and glass-like.

'Eat something, Brooke,' she said. 'You have to eat.'

'Sorry, Izzy.' I put my hands over the stretch of my stomach. 'My eyes are bigger than my belly.' I laughed until she left the bedroom, then realized my bladder felt viciously full.

Sunshine followed me into the bathroom. I tickled his chin as I peed, my underwear at my ankles. 'Silly dog. I suppose she is your master. But I rescued you, too. Remember?' He turned and sat on my foot with a sigh, as if affording me some dignity.

Finally, my sister brought me something I wanted, unbidden – my pastel crayons. I chewed on one, then swallowed it down, the colour staining my lips and tongue. Izzy watched while I drank a glass of water, then wiped at my face and neck with a flannel. 'I'm sorry there are no Christmas presents.' She shook her head, dabbing my brow with the flannel, dampening my hair. 'When you're giving me something so precious. Anything of mine you want you can have.' She squeezed my hand, my fingers curling around the wet flannel. 'Anything.'

'I don't want anything from you.'

When she left me, sighing, I took the other pastels from the packet and climbed out of bed. My skin felt clammy where Izzy had washed me, and rank in the places she'd ignored, the places underneath my clothes. I took down Izzy's framed weaving from the non-swamp wall and pushed the pastels over the magnolia paint, smudged repeating yonic shapes with my fingers and hands, figuring the old woman I'd seen in the mirror, looping her face in serpentine letters, *noone, noone, noone*, our very name shaped like a tunnel.

Moving my hands like this was the only thing that made me feel like myself again, better than tapping on my wrist, *you are good, you are good*. My hands were still my own, my fingers on the walls that held me, walls that breathed and sighed with their own inner life.

While I was drawing, the telephone rang. 'I'll come down,' I heard Izzy say when she answered. 'No. *Because*, Sasha.' A sigh. 'Okay. Okay! Five minutes. I'll buzz you in.'

The bedroom door opened. I pictured myself as Izzy might see me, standing with my pastel crayon to the wall, my clothes and hair dusted with colour. 'Let's get you in the shower,' she said. 'Quick.' She led me there like an elderly child, both of her hands holding mine, stepping backwards into the bathroom. A rap came on the front door, Sunshine rushing to yap and yelp. Izzy turned on the shower. 'Undress,' she prompted. 'Don't come out.'

I did undress, and baptized myself under the spray, water trickling over my melon belly in rivulets, drenching my hair. Sasha was inside the apartment, I thought numbly. Surely he'd notice how we'd come unstuck, even without entering the bedroom. I turned off the water, watched the droplets bead and slip down my skin. In the other room, raised voices.

I climbed out of the tub and scoured my nails at the sink, brushed my hair in front of the fractured mirror, and brushed my teeth until my gums bled. I felt pure, like a relic, and pretty. I spat blood into the sink. My breasts were threaded with thick blue veins, and my nipples were huge, tender and pink. *Good for feeding*, an involuntary thought that made me shudder with nausea. I wrapped my body in a big white towel, then reached out and opened the bathroom door with a crack.

The apartment needed a good clean; a waft of putrid air met my nose from the rubbish gathered under the kitchen sink. The voices died away with the crack of the door, and I padded along the soiled carpet to the living room, where Sasha sat on the sofa with his elbows on his knees. Seeing me, he sat up, his mouth opening as if to say something but no sound coming out. He adjusted his glasses.

There were takeout containers from the restaurant on the coffee table, but they were untouched. One of them leaked gravy onto the surface of the table. A raft of pine needles piled beneath the unlit tree, and Sasha hadn't taken off his shoes. I didn't look at Izzy, but heard her say calmly, 'Brooke, you're not decent. Didn't you realize Sasha was here?'

'Yes,' I replied, my arms around the big white towel.

'Goodnight, Brooke,' she said softly.

'Goodnight, Isobel.'

I crawled back into Izzy's bed, naked and alone, as an argument raged in the living room. I was too exhausted to get dressed. My limbs felt so heavy, my belly tender against the mattress. Sasha's voice pulsed through the dark. 'What the hell's been going on here? The girl looks tranqued. Have you completely lost your mind, Belle?' A string of accusations in French, in which I caught only the expletives. Izzy's responses were quieter, subdued, so that it was difficult to make out how she explained our situation, if she offered explanation at all. After a while, the front door slammed. I heard a few low sobs before everything fell quiet again.

When Izzy creaked open the bedroom door, I closed my eyes. *Tranqued*, I thought. *Yes*. My body was scoured and alien on the outside, ringing on the inside with panic and a sickly confusion. Whatever was inside me felt hard, knotted, and sharp. Izzy turned on the nightlight, put a hand in my still-wet curls and kissed my forehead. I opened my eyes. 'What did you tell him?' I asked drowsily. 'What did you say?'

'I told him we're having a baby,' she whispered. Then she sat with her back to me, watching the stars and horses traverse my wall drawings, my cave art.

Anchored by my belly, the endings of all the horror movies I'd managed to sit through for their entirety with Cecelia flashed through my mind. *And Little Red Cap returned home happily, and no one harmed her.* If this was a horror movie, what would happen at the end? I wondered. In *The Descent*, there were two possible endings, obvious from the very beginning: she rises, or she sinks further, into madness. Soaked in blood, circle of flame, hallucinating a dead daughter. What would happen to me, to the thing growing inside me? A baby? It couldn't be. If I didn't give birth to something, how would any of us be redeemed?

It was around this time I started to sense another presence in the room. Perhaps it had been there all along. My eyes were beginning to clear – the room had lost its soft focus, the edges coming back bright. My perception was shifting, as though my solitude was capable of tuning me into another plane of being, a heightened sense of reality.

At first I thought the presence was the woman I'd drawn into the wall, looking back at me. But her face had been crowded out by swirls and folds, leaving only the impression of a face – a drooping eye, a look not of lust or passion but of detached curiosity. I started to wonder if the presence was the knot inside me, whether it had transformed from some*thing* into some*one*. But the presence came only at night, pressing, it seemed, against the walls. If not friendly, the presence became familiar to me, came with a smell of outside, of dead leaves.

I needed to know what it was.

'Who's there?' My voice cracked. The nightlight rippled its cosmos across the wall, and in the centre, a dark shape. 'Who's there?' I asked, more sharply, speaking to shadows.

A breath. Under the twinkling bells of the nightlight's tune, I heard a laboured sort of breathing, and then a quiet hum that increased in volume to a low rumble.

My eyes adjusted until the dark shape was the silhouette of a stooped, broad figure, the nightlight picking out the mauve housecoat. Medusa was standing at the foot of the bed, her breath heavy, her voice coming to me in a throaty growl.

'I can't hear you.' Shrill note of panic in my voice, my hands clutching the bedclothes.

Medusa placed one knee on the bed. Then a hand, her arm reaching towards me. She climbed up, crawling over my body, her soft breasts, her thick middle pressing against the dome of my belly, the knot I was carrying. Finally, her face was over mine, and her mouth was moving, her eyes wide.

It must be a dream. One of those dreams where you try and try to scream, and then you wake up calling for someone. I squeezed my eyes shut, opened them again, but Medusa's face was still there, her nose inches from my nose. She was whispering, her words thrumming densely like a press of bees nesting behind the wall, the weight of her body painful against my belly. Her hand moved up the inside of my leg, creeping under my nightdress, her fingertips rough and her bitten-down fingernails snagging my skin.

Her hand stopped at the swell of my stomach. Something inside me clenched and rolled. I gasped. 'Please.' I was crying, my cheeks wet, my hand snaking between us to grab at her hand. 'No, please. What are you doing?' I squeezed my eyes closed again, turned my head away from Medusa's foul breath, whimpering.

The bed seemed to shift beneath me, to lift and crash back to the floor. My eyes snapped open and I pushed myself up on my elbows, a scream burbling in my throat. There was no body on top of mine. Medusa sat on the floor in the corner. She lifted a finger and pressed it to her lips. *Shhhhhh.*

After a few soft beats, Medusa rose from the corner and turned the nightlight off. The Leonora emitted the quiet hum that signalled most of its occupants were asleep. She dragged my body into a sitting position, and I felt her dress me in warm items from my suitcase under the bed – a baggy hoodie lined with fleece, mismatched tube socks. She tugged the hoodie over my head, and I lifted my arms into the sleeves like a small child might, her hands fleeting at my elbows. She did this wordlessly, my foot on her thigh as she knelt before me, pushing my trainer onto my foot. She heaved me up and settled me upright, my body swaying with the effort, the bulk of the knot so heavy now. My movements felt sluggish and unwieldy, but her grip was steady and sure, almost practised, almost tender.

I couldn't be sure where my sister was, why the dog didn't bother us, neither of them seeming to sense us moving around like this, sneaking out of the bedroom and along the hallway, Medusa's hobble rocking me into the lift. Deep night, no noises in the pipes, only the whoosh and chime of the lift doors opening onto the lobby.

She led me outside and along the lamplit streets. The streets were largely deserted, but I heard the occasional whistle, a scrape, the wheels of a supermarket trolley, a man's voice talking to himself in a swift staccato. Medusa walked me to the edge of the woods, near the herons' nests and dark shadows of the rhododendrons. 'I can't go any further,' she said, the first discernible words she'd spoken to me. I remembered the day I'd followed her through the streets after Sunshine went missing, how I'd tied the scent-flag here in the underbrush, to mark the spot where I had lost her, to let her know: I was here.

'The world peters out at the treeline,' she said.

Whatever she meant by this, whatever limit she was trying to describe, she sat me down in the damp grass, and we watched the sky between the crown of trees above us while she ate pistachios from a reserve of them in her housecoat pocket. After a while I realized that the thing in my belly had grown perfectly still, had not moved or pinched or thumped. Odd – it was usually more active than ever at night, my nocturnal knot-baby. I felt no peculiar sensation, though my belly was bloated as ever, my ankles swollen and sore.

In the inky darkness of the clearing, I started talking. I told her everything in a disjointed rush – the details of Izzy's surgery and Cecelia on the train and how I'd known all along that Medusa had taken the dog. Medusa only stared at me, her fingers working at the pistachio shells, her mouth chewing. I repeated Izzy's story of how she'd nearly killed me when I was inside my mother's womb. I didn't know why I was sharing these intimacies with Medusa, of all people; I needed to get the story out of my head, to string the facts together, to try to make sense of where I was, why I was sitting in a clearing with a living ghost that haunted my sister's building.

I told her that something was growing inside me, and how I felt weak, so weak, to be allowing this situation to continue and too weak to do anything about it. I told her about the sickness weighing down my limbs and curling inside my belly. How I felt that if my brain was strong enough it would simply let go of the symptoms that were taking hold of my body and the knot would go away, I could kill it with a wish, with a decision, I could simply decide to swallow, to nurture myself, to be well.

I told her how I couldn't eat, how I only wanted things that were bad for me, inorganic things, the stuff the building was made from.

Medusa grunted and chewed. She reached out her hand, offering me some of her pistachios. I held out my palm to receive them.

A breeze whispered through the firs. 'I caught you eating in our kitchen,' I said, shelling a pistachio. 'Do you remember?'

'Nothing's wrong with my memory,' she spat.

'Had you been inside the apartment before?' I was thinking of James's suggestion, that Medusa had known a previous occupant, and of the pistachio shells I'd found between the sofa cushions. I crushed one between my teeth.

A ripple of amusement crossed her face. 'One of my favourites.' Her cheeks were sunken and crinkled, her eyes bright. 'Early riser, good strong patterns, out in the world all day, all day.' She was talking about my sister. 'I hope she never leaves. I like feeding the dog.' Her eyes narrowed. 'Your comings and goings were harder to figure out.'

'Mine . . . ?'

'A few close calls.' She leaned her whole body towards me. 'Some spots sigh or heave when you step on them; you have to know the spots to avoid the creaks.'

I thought of the odd smell lingering in the apartment rooms sometimes, the sudden ring of scum inside the bathtub, the eerie sense of recent occupation when I'd return from a hospital visit. How Sunshine, who hated strangers and alerted at every creak in the corridor, had abided Medusa to eat from our kitchen, perhaps even loved her.

I had to work hard to marry this Medusa, her fingers busy shelling pistachios, with the basement-dwelling crone who blew out the candle to frighten me. Had she stolen me from the bedroom for company, like the dog? Was I her pet now?

'How do you do it?' I asked.

'Do what?'

'The way you move through walls.'

She snorted. 'I've lived there a long time. The walls know me.'

'What about the little girl next door, Kioko? Is it you who's scaring her?'

Medusa snapped her eyes to mine. 'I try to avoid the little ones. But they see everything.'

She reached out a veined hand and patted my belly, sprinkling pistachio shells from her sleeve. I flinched at the sudden gesture, but nothing stirred inside me this time – nothing like the swimming that responded to Izzy's hand there. Medusa chuckled grimly.

'What's funny?' I demanded.

'I knew it had crawled its way in here . . .' Her knuckles flexed, purple and wizened, as she tapped a finger to the side of her head. 'But there?' She gripped her own middle through the rotten housecoat and barked with laughter.

'What do you mean? What crawled inside? Oh, God. Is it something bad?'

'You know what it is,' she insisted, dropping her voice to a ragged whisper. 'The little parasite.'

I flinched and clutched at my belly. Had I told her, in my rambling, of our special name for my growing bump? 'How did you—?'

But Medusa had dragged herself to her feet and turned away from me.

'Don't leave me here. Please, I'm scared to go back by myself.'

She stopped. I waited for her to give me her hand, but she simply hovered there on the periphery, the shape of her echoing the silhouette of the rhododendron bush.

I scrambled to my feet, brushing Medusa's pistachio shells from my pyjamas, tottering, losing my balance. She righted me, guiding me through the puzzle of surfaced tree roots. Our trudging wound us through the empty streets and back to the building, which loomed against the slate sky with a sinister, animate dark. A waiting dark. Should we even go inside? I gripped Medusa's arm, a little well of panic rising, but she walked on unfazed, her pace brisk. She returned me to Izzy's front door like a parcel, then staggered back down the corridor without another word, turning the corner and disappearing from view.

Nervously, I pressed the door open, hoping to creep back into bed before Izzy discovered I was missing. I wasn't sure what she would do, but I knew it would hurt her, the not knowing where I was – or, rather, where I had taken the knot baby. *Mine*, she had said, her hands around my belly. *Mine*.

What was she waiting for? How long would she wait? I held my breath as I moved along the hallway, finding Izzy and Sunshine still slumbering on in the living room, the dog having wormed his way into bed, her limbs splayed out from underneath the covers. A pale arm in the green neon light.

27

When I woke, sunlight burnished the bedroom curtains, a yellow glow in the mouldering room. It was past noon already. I pushed myself up from the mattress, swung my legs over the side, and planted my swollen feet before levering my body to stand, straining under the dome of my belly, the fattening parasite. I pressed a hand to my stomach. The thing I carried throbbed and shifted beneath the surface of my stretched skin.

In the kitchen I turned on the tap, hearing voices in the corridor. I went to the peephole and peered through. Izzy's neighbours were making their way to the lift – a middle-aged woman chatting with the elderly man who'd called me 'dog woman'. Maybe a daughter? She brushed something from the shoulder of his jacket as they walked. I touched the doorknob unconsciously, a little leap of yearning at the retreating figures.

'What are you doing out of bed?'

I jumped, turning to see Izzy standing at the kitchen sink. 'Christ,' I said. 'You scared me.' She wore a stained T-shirt tucked into jeans that sagged around her middle. The weight had fallen off her.

I'd left the tap running, and she reached out and turned off the water. 'Are you thirsty?' she asked, pulling a glass from the cabinet.

I nodded, and she filled the glass and gave it to me.

'Do you want to take your vitamins now?' Izzy asked casually, pulling a Ziploc full of little round pills from a drawer. 'You shouldn't skip any more days, really, not this far gone.'

I hesitated, then held out my hand for one. She looked at my palm and then placed a small white pill in the centre. I put the pill in my mouth, took a sip of water.

'Will you look at the state we're in?' she muttered, turning away. 'Sink's blocked.' She took a knife from the draining board and stabbed at a glut of vegetable peelings caught in the plughole, while I stood holding the water glass. Discreetly, I slipped the pill from under my tongue, spat it into my hand. Izzy rinsed the sink and wiped her hands on a dirty gingham tea towel.

Something about the curl of her hands inside the towel reminded me of that moment I'd shared with James at the sink. How he'd washed his hands right there, such lovely hands, well groomed. My decision to protect him from the knowledge of Medusa's lair. Why had I felt that need? A crone living in the basement seemed the least of my worries now. Knowing she was down there and might visit me in the bedroom felt almost like comfort.

'What are you staring at?' Izzy asked. I'd been looking at her hands, thinking. There had been something else about the party, something James had said. *I don't know why I don't just leave.* As if there was some attachment, some membrane holding him here. As if his release required permission. It reminded me of how easily I'd left with Medusa the night before, when now I couldn't so much as touch the doorknob without summoning my sister.

'Nothing,' I said to Izzy, trying to make my face appear bright. 'Where did you walk Sunshine this morning?'

She opened the fridge and mimed browsing the shelves, so that she was obscured from my view. 'He's with Lucie.'

'Lucie was here?' My voice too high, tipping into desperation. 'I didn't hear—'

'No, I took him to meet her this morning. You were dead to the world. She's keeping him for a little while.'

'Why?'

Izzy poked her head around the door to look at me. 'I didn't like to leave you,' she said.

I swallowed. 'Not even to walk the dog?'

She reached out and put her hand on my shoulder. 'Not with how big you are. How fast everything is moving. I can't keep anything fresh.' She gestured to the interior of the fridge, opening the door wide for me to see. A few sticks of butter, a carton of milk, wilted salad leaves, a red string bag of wrinkled mandarins, half an onion turning brown on the shelf.

'Don't worry, I'm expecting a delivery. We have to get you eating well again. We've done it before, haven't we?' She tossed a wizened mandarin in the air and caught it. 'Want one?'

'What did you tell her?'

'Hmm?' She pulled at the string bag and threw it on the counter, mandarins spilling across the linoleum. She kicked one away.

'Lucie.'

'Oh. I told her we were going to the island for New Year. She agrees a little trip would do us good – she had some things to say at the party, about my behaviour. She thought I was being . . . harsh, I think. To you.' She paused, scratched at her neck, her collarbone jutting against her pallid skin. I wondered what Lucie had thought when she saw my sister like this, unkempt and rail-thin. 'So she can't know we're here in the apartment. I don't want her to think I'm some sort of liar. Drink up.' Izzy touched the bottom of my glass and tilted it towards my mouth.

I drank, a bead of water slipping down my chin.

'Let's get you settled again, shall we? Did you want to use the bathroom first?'

I closed myself in there, racking my brain for some way to make sense of what was happening to us. The apartment felt ominous without the friendly presence of the dog, and it reminded me of that stretch of days, more than a week, when he'd been missing. I flushed the pill down the toilet.

Back in the bedroom, Izzy sat hunched on the edge of the bed looking at my cave art with a puzzled expression on her face. 'I don't think this can be good for the baby. They make a lot of dust, those crayons.' Neither of us had opened the curtains.

'It would have been nice to see Lucie,' I said, lowering myself to sit next to Izzy. 'I'm sorry about when Sasha was here. You could have invited her over, you know. Just because I'm like this, you can't stop living your life.'

'It's no sacrifice,' Izzy said, crossing her arms. She looked so angular and severe, her jaw sharp. 'Why, what do you want to talk to Lucie about?'

'I . . . I thought she was interesting, at the party. We were talking about art. About those womb votive thingies. Sympathetic magic, I think she called it? Maybe that could be part of what's going on here.'

'What do you mean?' Izzy frowned.

'I mean, I don't know,' I started. 'Maybe you've given me . . . or I've taken on . . . some of your symptoms from before.'

Izzy stared at me. 'Is this one of your little stories from the message boards you told me about?'

Noone, noone, noone, our name scrawled on the wall.

'How is your scar healing up?' I asked, trying a different tack. 'It's been, what? Six weeks now.'

'Longer,' Izzy said. 'It itches a lot, actually.'

'Itches?'

'Yes, it really itches, but like, *under* the skin. So you can't scratch it, obviously. And if I move in a certain way, it pulls. No one talked to me about *adhesions* at the hospital – I had to read about them in a pamphlet. One of the pamphlets you brought home, actually. So, thanks, I guess.'

'Adhesions?'

'Yeah. It's when the scar tissue binds your internal bits and pieces together. Your tissues and organs.' She looked at my face. 'Gross, isn't it? Normally they slip off each other so you can move around easily, but the scar tissue turns it all into a thick cord.' She curled her hands as if twisting a length of rope. 'Talia said she'd hook me up with her physio – she's doing pelvic floor – but it's expensive. The incision has healed over nicely, though. The doctor was happy with it, anyway. Would you like to see?'

'Yes, please, I would.'

She undid the gold button and zipper of her jeans, and let herself fall back onto the mattress. The jeans pushed down easily over her hips, and she hooked her thumbs in her underwear to reveal a thick red line above her pubic hair. Her belly sagged in loose folds and her ribs poked at her skin. 'It feels kind of knobbly,' she said, lifting her head to look at the scar. 'You can touch it if you like.'

The room still held that gauzy yellow glow, the light burning at the window. I was afraid, my fingers remembering the bumpy ridge that shifted beneath my fingers the last time Izzy had invited me to touch her, the night before her surgery to remove the uterine cyst. But this was the closest I'd felt to the real Izzy for a long time, and though my own body had transformed so completely since that night, it was almost as if the bump wasn't there any more, between us – at least for the moment. I wanted that moment to stretch out, to hold us for a while.

I traced a finger gently along Izzy's scar, stretched almost from hip to hip. It was raised and firm, puckering the surrounding skin like a rough seam. I pushed against it a little, feeling a fibrous sort of cord, and she drew in a breath.

'Sorry, it's sensitive there,' she said. 'At that end especially. You can feel where they tied it, how it's thicker, more swollen? Talia – her friend had a C-section – said it's because of where the surgeon is when they make the incision. Like, they're leaning over your body to cut into you, so they tug harder on one side. Something like that.' Her voice was so steady, matter of fact.

'I didn't realize you were still in so much pain, Izzy. I'm sorry.'

She shrugged. 'It's better than how it was before, with the cyst in there. Well, less painful, I mean. Things are worse than before, obviously.'

A truck rumbled by on the street outside, making the building vibrate, the lampshade wobbling ever so slightly on the nightstand, and whatever Izzy said next was drowned out by a sudden cry from my own mouth. A painful thud against my ribcage, a kick in my gut that snatched my breath. I doubled over, sucking air through my teeth.

'Brooke?' Izzy bolted upright, her arms at my shoulders.

'It's kicking me.' I gasped. 'I mean, a real powerful *kick*.'

Izzy's hands scrambled to my belly, pressing into my skin. Her jeans were still undone and her own belly pouched through the opening, her face expectant in the yellow light from the window. The kick didn't come again, but she laughed anyway. 'See? This is why I can't leave you alone. I can't miss out on moments like this.'

'I don't like it, Izzy.' My breath came in strange little gulps and my shoulders shook. 'It feels strong.' But she misheard me.

'It's not wrong,' Izzy said. 'It's not wrong, Brooke, it's beautiful.'

'Izzy, whatever's happening here, it's not normal.'

'Remember "our little parasite"?' she prompted, giving my arms a cheerful jiggle. 'Hm? Remember, how you sang to it? Things were better then, I think. You seemed better in yourself.' She rubbed my arm.

'But it's kicking me now!' I cried.

'Come on,' she cooed, pushing herself off the bed and kneeling before me. She ran her hands down my limp arms and threaded her fingers through mine. 'It's going to be okay, Brooke. I promise.'

I couldn't answer her, a choking sob overtaking my body.

'Oh, come on.' She gave a gentle laugh. 'It's okay – it's just your hormones.' She let go of my hands and pushed my shirt up. Stretchmarks bloomed across my lower belly in angry red welts, as if the skin had been torn at by something clawed – as if it might rupture and split.

I froze at the sight of it, terrified that the kick would come again, so strong I might see the outline of a foot. Izzy wrapped her arms around my middle, her lips close to my scarred skin. 'I won't let anything bad happen to you,' she murmured, and rested her head there, her cheek pressed to the taut curve of my belly, the tremors underneath.

When Medusa came again, she walked me to the clearing, hunkered down, looked towards the treeline. Past the herons' nests, the park spilled into ocean, and the sun had long set behind the blue mountains ringing the bay. 'Can't you take me somewhere else? I mean . . . can we go anywhere else?' I asked, thinking of what she'd said last time, about the world petering out, and about her movements through the same gridded streets, like something caged.

I didn't think she was going to answer, but then her voice started up as if a switch had been flicked, her eyes on a fixed point in the distance. 'Sometimes I can get on a bus out to the cemetery and back. Mountain View. There and back only. No detours.'

Her answers always seemed to provoke more questions. My eyes took in the dark surroundings, the curled black leaves, the tower blocks behind us. 'What do you do out there, at the cemetery?'

'Make my visits. Take them things.'

'You have people buried there? Family?'

'Yes,' she said tersely, as if I'd asked the question in disbelief, as if I doubted she'd ever had a mother or a grandfather. 'It's a kind of exchange we make. You wouldn't know about it. Don't ask.' A streetlight hummed beyond the thicket. 'Why are you stuck –' she leaned forward and prodded my belly '– like this?'

I put my hand over the place she'd prodded, stroked the bump. Often when I did this whatever was inside me would slither or stir, but now it was still, though it felt unquiet. Like someone listening, a kind of attentiveness. 'I don't know what it is,' I insisted. 'I don't know what's happening to me. How long I've been there, in the room. I tried to track the patterns.' I showed her my shoelace, in which I'd tied several knots. 'But I lost count.'

'Patterns are important.' She folded her arms across her middle so that she looked, almost, to be cradling her breasts. 'They should be observed.'

What could be happening inside my body, unseen? I'd read about the stages of pregnancy, the foetus growing from the size of a strawberry to an apple, kicking, punching around with little fists, even hiccupping, forming ears to listen and covered in a fine down of hair, then turning into a pomegranate. But what was happening to me had happened all at once: the stages were muddled, and made no sense. The knot's existence was a kind of annihilation – of time, of the natural order of things, of the person I was before.

'How did you know something was wrong with me? I mean before, in the basement. You grabbed my face. You said, "get out". Who were you talking to?'

A look passed across her face that reminded me of the look she'd given me when I'd held the door open all those weeks ago. Indignant, angry, threatened. 'Not who,' she said slowly, elongating the 'o' sound so that her mouth hung pursed and wrinkled. 'What.'

'What?' I whispered, afraid to conjure the creature from behind the walls, afraid it was already swallowing me whole.

'I saw it in you, the little parasite. But I felt it in me, first.' She leaned in again, but she didn't prod me this time, only gestured to where my hands rested. 'There's a craving worm in my belly. It wants things. Not just the small offerings any more, *big* things. Like the radio. I knew I wouldn't get away with that one, so careless! But the worm wanted it. The worm can take whatever it wants to take. And the dog!' She laughed, stroked one hand over the back of the other, as if remembering Sunshine's soft fur. 'I knew it was over, then. I've been so careful, for so long. Kept myself hidden, holed up, taking the small, leftover things no one wanted.'

Small, leftover things. How long had she been down there?

'Then you came, kept my secret. I waited for them all to come, to discover my hole. But you didn't tell, did you?'

I hadn't told. But not out of kindness – out of fear, or maybe denial. Is that why she was helping me?

We sat there a while longer in silence. I didn't want to hear any more, I didn't want the knot to hear. I didn't want to be bound up in Medusa's logic, to be trapped inside her sunken well with a parasite that had made its home inside both of us: my knot baby, her craving worm.

'Why shouldn't I have the radio?' she muttered, then turned to me. 'I didn't always live down there. You should leave now.'

'But it's dark,' I said stupidly. 'I'm by myself. I don't have keys.'

'You should've brought them. You should always carry a key.' Medusa took her own key out of her pocket. It looked different to mine, ancient and dull, with no physical correlation to the locks in the building. I had an eye for such things after my key work at the library. She slipped it away again. 'You'll find your way inside. We left the apartment unlocked. Besides, it's not so dark any more. But you should leave now. While you can.'

I stumbled away from the wooded edge of the city and walked back along the night-drenched streets. I walked with my hands wrapped around my belly, as if I was carrying it in my arms. Whenever I heard footsteps or saw the shape of someone ahead, I crossed over to the other side of the street. But by the time I reached the building, panting with fatigue, I was desperate to see someone, a neighbour going in or coming out, someone who'd let me inside, who'd speak to me about something normal, like the weather. I needn't have worried; the latch was stuck and the door to the building sat slightly ajar. I simply wrenched it open, rode the lift up, and turned the handle into Izzy's apartment.

28

From the shadow of her body and a contented hum, I knew Izzy sat on the other side of the bedroom door, altering my clothes. I passed her to empty my bladder – opening the bedroom door, waiting as she moved her chair with a cheerfully detached, 'Morning, lazy bones,' her sewing box at her feet. She was holding two long spiked needles dangling a yellow web, and as she stood a ball of yellow wool unspooled its way along the hall towards the bathroom. She held up one tiny woollen foot to show me. 'I'm making booties. Aren't they cute?'

Are you fucking serious? I wanted to scream. 'Izzy,' I said, my voice coming out strained and breathless. It *was* getting harder to breathe, as if something was pressing on my lungs, my expanding belly pushing my organs out of place. 'Please.'

'Oh, you'll like them when they're finished,' she said, tucking the bootie away again, waving a hand. 'Don't look now.'

I stole a sidelong glance into the kitchen – the calendar hung on the opposite wall, difficult to read, but Izzy had marked the days in a glut of thick red crosses. December twenty-eighth? Twenty-ninth? A new year seemed impossible.

I performed a cursory wash at the sink, moving my hands over my swollen body, a different lifeform in the mirror than the girl who'd felt desired. My face was ribboned into shards by the broken glass, and my skin felt stretched and tender, my lower belly covered in purple marks that reached upwards like tongues of flame. My bellybutton gaped grotesquely. It wasn't the pink slime and gangrene of my vision, but it was close. How could Izzy see me like this and pretend everything was normal and good?

I couldn't imagine James touching me, not like this, though I craved his baby-soft skin beneath my fingers, imagined him lying naked among the bedclothes in the foetal position. I'd rub his feet and brush his hair and sing to him, breathe in his green-stem scent, be the big spoon. *If Cecelia could see me now*, I thought. She'd stare and shudder, fascinated, the way she'd looked at Okanoue's headless women.

I trembled with revulsion as the knot wriggled, sharp inside my uterus; my knees bent to the linoleum, hands grabbing for the rim of the toilet bowl, stomach rolling and bile burning my throat. I gagged and choked. Maybe I could expel the knot this way – maybe I would vomit a stream of green-black mould and my belly would flatten and my body would be returned to me. But as I sank feebly between the toilet bowl and the sink, I knew it wasn't possible to rid myself of the knot this way. The sickness was just another sign of its infestation. I balled my fists over my belly, grunting with frustration, crying without tears.

Afterwards, I spat into the sink, washed my face and hands in cold water. I felt as if I'd been abducted by aliens and probed, sent back wrong. I opened the bathroom cabinet and groped around until I found a slim stick of black eyeliner and a soft brown eyebrow pencil, tipping them into my pocket.

'Feel better?' Izzy beamed as I passed her in the chair again. Her smile was impersonal – she required no answer, her head bent back to her knitting. She was making clothes for the baby she expected me to birth, the knot I wanted to beat out of my body.

I wrapped a hand around Izzy's wrist. She startled, the needles falling from her grasp, her mouth dropping open. I was squeezing harder than I'd meant to. 'Help me,' I said to her through gritted teeth.

'Brooke, you're hurting my wrist,' she said in alarm.

'Help me!' I seethed.

'I *am* helping you, Brooke.'

'You were right, we should go to the hospital, there must be something *really* wrong—'

'The hospital?' She tried to tug her hand from my grip, but I held on. She shook her head, her eyes filling with pity, an artificial sort of solicitousness entering her voice. 'They won't believe you. Remember how that doctor kept sending you away when you couldn't eat?'

I stared at her, a sharp pain forming in my chest. 'Please, Izzy. We have to get rid of it.'

She blinked, her face twisting in disbelief. 'Get rid of it?' She looked appalled, taking my words and repeating them back to me as if they were inscrutable, unconscionable. 'I don't think that's really what you want, not now you've felt it kick, surely?'

I held her gaze, and she leaned forward, speaking in a quieter voice.

'How will it look? You can't walk into an emergency room so far gone, asking them to get rid of it. There'll be torches and pitchforks. No, I'm keeping you safe here. You and the baby.'

I imagined the baying crowd she'd conjured for me, could hear them amassing in the street below the window, calling for blood. 'But I'm not *far gone*,' I enunciated slowly. 'And I can't have a baby, Izzy. I don't know how.'

She laughed, but there was a dark sound underneath it, a brewing vexation. 'Your body knows how, silly. Look.' She gestured to my belly, and when I looked down she took a pin from her sewing box and stuck it in my hand.

I gasped and wrenched my hand back, drew out the pin by its round pink head.

'Someone got out of the wrong side of the bed today,' Izzy said coolly, and turned back to her knitting.

Back in the bedroom, I changed my clothes inside Izzy's wardrobe, taking the eyeliner and brow pencil out of my pocket with a shaky hand. I pulled out a wad of packing paper, layering the pages on the bed so they wouldn't tear. Wet drops marred the pages as I gathered them, and I wiped my face with my sleeve. I slipped a large board underneath the paper, an old painted shelf from the wardrobe that had been propped against an interior wall. I moved slowly, quietly, swallowing my sobs; I didn't want Izzy to stop her knitting, interrupt me, insist I lie down or try to feed me some earthy substance, prick me all over with pins.

I opened the nightstand, where I'd secreted the remaining pastel crayons. I wished I had the rest of my art supplies from my room at Mum and Dad's – my stash of Conté pencils, gesso, fixative, masking tape, hard and soft pastel sticks in a brilliant array of pigments. I wanted more.

My body coursed with agitation, the kind of agitation I'd seen in Medusa, that wouldn't allow her stillness. A craving worm in the belly, world petering out at the edges, her basement dwelling. Would these be the contours of my life, too?

Now I took up the eyeliner and brow pencil to outline the figures on the page, my hands calming and my breath evening as I drew. Two sisters leaning against one another, conjoined, almost, at the middle. They took form in rough strokes before my eyes. One of them, her back to the viewer, dressed herself in folds of black crinoline. She was very alive, her joints seeming to move and stretch like a dancer's, her neck twisting to look over her shoulder as I sketched in her face. When her body shifted, she crackled.

The oil pastels were thick, sticky, and semi-fluid, allowing me to build up and scratch through layers of colour, while the soft pastels were chalky and dense with pigment. I pursed my lips to blow on the makeshift canvas, dispersing excess powder like spent skin: inky black, peach fuzz, kid pink. The colours looked tactile, like swatches of fabric. My belly kept getting in the way, forcing me into new positions, new perspectives. I drew with my eyes unfocused, seeing beyond the surface of the paper, my fingers walking through areas of light and shadow. The shadows created possibility, waiting to be fed.

I continued to shade in the black crinoline until I was all thunder and crackle. Yes, that was me – the shadow sister, her head shaved, her features large and wounded. The figure in the foreground was Izzy. I'd captured something of her without trying very hard. I was especially pleased with the mouth. There was no curl to the lip, but you could feel it, absolutely, underneath. Vibrating the surface of the image. She could be about to howl.

I sketched in every flaw of her skin: a faint pink birthmark, the wrinkles beginning around her eyes. I even gave her some of mine: freckles, the weird patch of hair on my cheek. Her face was patchworked and beautiful. I gave her Mum's perfectly arched eyebrows. I don't know why, but the more I drew these other things in, details belonging to other women in the family, the more Izzy she became, almost breathing from the page, her skin glowing and porous. She was looking at me, even, her eyes like the swim of a fish.

I filled in her body with a smear of fleshy crayon. I was drawing a nude portrait, I realized, without making the decision to, shading in her belly, the way I'd seen it, after her hysterectomy, the stitches twined and threaded through her in a ruthless limb. And here again another dimension, beneath the layer of bruised skin, the ghost of the uterine cyst that had been cut out of her seemed to remain underneath. A present absence.

It wasn't very technically accomplished, the proportions off-kilter, but I'd never drawn anything like this before. I'd never seen, felt another body so clearly, and my hands did not pause and needed no instruction. They knew exactly what to do.

But the patchwork sister looked too naked – there was something missing. I used a violet crayon to chalk in a long necklace of fraying feathers that brushed over her breasts to tickle her stomach, the puckered scar. The feathers belonged there; now she had something to preen.

When I was finished the bed was prismatic with colour, like holding a crystal up to the light. I hid the drawing under the bed, and manoeuvred the heavy board back into the wardrobe, revealing a rectangle of white sheet, an unspoilt field.

I rested for a moment against the swamp wall, my lungs heaving, brushing my knuckles over the spored, sponge-like surface. Smell of mushrooms, of rhododendron mulch, of nighttime in the park. The air inside the room was dank, like stale breath. I thought of

Wendy and Kioko, singing to one another on the other side of the wall, the kid's drawings pinned to it. I missed their familiar sounds and movements, even the rasp of the drawers. Their nightlight sat on top of Izzy's nightstand. 'Tōryanse, tōryanse.' The song scratched from my throat in a near-whisper, but I stalled out, waiting for a response from a little girl that never came. The song didn't belong to me, either.

I shook the dusty sheets in the air, crayon flakes of colour falling all around me, settling on my skin.

The third time Medusa came to me, I had no will to move. I didn't want to go outside any more, to risk discovery, only to traipse back unchanged. I'd been watching a spider scuttle back and forth across the threshold, in the too-large gap under the door, and the spider had somehow shifted, elongated, transformed, like a dream that deposits you in a new location or exchanges your father for a lover you once had, the thread of the dream unbroken.

Where the spider scuttled, I watched Cecelia leave the room over and over – *you're weak, you're weak, you're weak* – not for the final time, of course, but the time before that, the time I ran after her. She'd hesitated, and this is the moment I returned to, to comfort myself in my bedship. Her eyes sweeping the floor, for a second, almost turning around.

'Cecelia,' I whispered aloud. 'What if the longing just keeps growing, what if it's always there, like a pulse?'

Did I mean longing, or regret? I was thinking of the baby Izzy had always wanted. How was she ever supposed to let it go, that bone-deep wish, so lonely, shared by no one? Where does it go, the orphaned desire? Can you give it to someone else?

Maybe if I hadn't gone after Cecelia, debased myself, she would have come back to me. Maybe I'd held on too tight. If I'd let her go, that thing on the bed might never have happened.

This was no revelation. I'd had these thoughts hundreds of times before, on three different continents. Tony, Tony look around; I'd thought that by running the memory over and over in my mind, I could change something about what had happened, or at least discover some new dimension. Like Izzy's curled lip in the drawing I'd made of us – not really there, but possible, discernible, the ghost growth throbbing beneath the wicked scar. I thought I could reconstruct the scene and walk around it, look at it from some new angle. Find Cecelia's flicker of hesitation rippling through her subsequent actions, locate a soft part to press against. But the elements were always the same, the result fixed. I begged, pathetic, and she left, repulsed.

The spider stirred again in the corner. I inched the camera of my memory to the scene on the futon, once Cecelia had come back inside, after I'd started to undress in the street. The way she'd thrown me to the mattress. *What the fuck is wrong with you*. It wasn't a question.

Afterwards, how still and how silently we'd lain next to each other, back-to-back, not touching. Her final departure I'd only heard, not seen, in the gentle morning light, the street waking up beyond the window. Door closing behind her with a soft click.

Maybe she was ashamed of what she'd done. Hand pressed tight across my mouth, the heel of her hand hot and fleshy, her fingers scraping painfully inside me. The moment charged with anger, like a smack. My hands struggled to respond, clutching at her back, pushing at her shoulders. Nothing like it usually was between us.

The idea rang like a struck pot. Is that why she'd left Japan? So she didn't have to see me again, in the aftermath?

'I know they call me Medusa,' the old woman said from the shadows. I didn't startle at the intrusion; I'd already felt her there. 'But I have names for them, too.'

I wished she'd go away, leave me with Cecelia, with the gap under the door, the shadowy possibility I'd lurched into: the notion of Cecelia's shame. Despite my frustration, I still had so many questions for Medusa. I felt she held the key to everything, that we were tentacles of the same beast, the three of us. Me, Izzy, and Medusa. Maiden, mother, crone.

'What's your real name?' I asked.

'It's better no one knows. It's better if they can't find you. If they can find you, they can put you somewhere. Like this.'

I asked her what I should do. She thought about my question for a long time. 'If they hold a door open for you, you can't step through it. Never be in their debt. That's how they get past you.'

'You held a door open for me,' I protested, but she was steadfast, adamant.

'You won't get anything past me. There's no point trying. You can keep those thoughts to yourself.'

I felt her slipping away and reached out to grab her, caught both her hands in my own. Why come and interrupt me only to vanish again? I put her hands over the knot twisting my insides, my shirt moving up my belly with the effort, so that her rough palms pressed against my bare skin.

The taut mound of my belly was even more swollen than the last time I'd dared to look; it had swallowed my pelvis and bore a dark line down the centre. *Linea nigra*, it was called, that line. I'd looked it up when I watched the Doppler videos, when I saw the mommy bloggers proudly displaying them. They were a track on the body to guide the baby to the breast, where they might feed. But my line was thicker than the ones I'd seen on the women – a thick smear marked me, sooty like mildew, tender like a bruise, a mark I could no longer scratch away.

I felt the panic well up in me. 'Please,' I begged, 'can't you just take it?'

'I don't want it,' she said with distaste. 'I've got no use for a baby. Insides spilling out.'

I cried, 'Is it a baby?' I couldn't imagine it, whatever this thing was, living outside me in some human form.

'I don't want it!' Medusa seethed. 'Not like I wanted the dog, which you took away from me. My friend!' Her face rippled horribly, from righteous anger into a covetous grin. 'Not like I wanted the boy.'

She was taunting me, but with what? 'What boy?'

'The boy. The boy in the mirror, behind you.' She made an obscene gesture with her hands, her body rocking in a way that felt sickeningly familiar. 'Fucking.'

I stared at her, feeling her body like a skin over my own, clinging to me like an ooze, the mauve robe seeming to crawl with life.

She began to laugh, then faltered. 'That was me. I was with you, in the mirror. Didn't you recognize me?'

Medusa. Medusa was the thing that had stepped into my body, made it shrivel and sag.

'I was only looking at you,' she said defensively. 'And the boy. Both of you, together. And I felt something soft and pushed in. I've never done it before.'

There was a rushing sound in my ears, as though I was falling.

'I didn't feel it, then,' she said, grabbing for my belly. 'This thing crawling inside you. All I felt was . . .' She grasped at her own body, bit her bottom lip, lascivious. 'Ah. Gave him a scare, didn't I?'

I stared at her in horror. 'He didn't see you like I did. His face . . . he said his face . . .' But I couldn't explain what had happened to James. 'What did you do to him?'

'Nothing.' She shifted into anger again, exploding: 'It's your own fault! There's something soft in you, a way in, a tender spot. You have to close it off, like I have. Build a Medusa. I'll show you.'

I heard the keening, but at first I didn't know it was coming from me. From deep inside me, erupting into a Laura Palmer scream. Medusa screwed her eyes shut and let the swamp wall swallow her. I pulled myself onto my knees on the bed, curling my body tight around the knot. The door burst open. I kept keening, unable to stop the sound spilling from my mouth. Izzy's hands on my back. 'What's happening?' Her voice escalated in fear.

'Make it go away.' I sobbed. 'Make it go away.'

'Come on.' She wrapped herself around me, holding me, rocking me. 'Come on, you're strong, I know you're strong. You can get through this.' My limbs vibrated with something electric, with energy, and I could still hear the roar in my ears even though I was no longer making it.

I grappled with my sister, the weight of my belly pressing her into the mattress. I crawled from the tangle of sheets, crushing her body beneath mine, and pulled my suitcase from under the bed – the drawing I'd made of us creasing under the wheels. I turned on the ceiling light, wanting her to see me, wanting her to see everything, to understand.

'Look at this mark.' I pulled up my shirt to reveal the thick, inky line staining my abdomen. 'Look at it.' The way she'd invited me to look at her stitches, showing them to me without warning. 'This is my body,' I told her, knowing the knot was listening, sensing Medusa behind the wall. 'It's mine!'

'I know, I know, hush now.' Izzy spoke in the quiet voice she used to soothe me. 'Brooke, you're not making sense. Lie down.'

I balled my fists, staring her in the eye, rage coursing through my veins. I punched hard into my tender, swollen abdomen, into the fleshy knot that rippled and swam beneath my skin – beneath my thudding fists – a parasite that pulsed with air and fluid and drank my blood. Could it scream? I hit and hit and hit, grunting with the effort.

Izzy gasped and lunged towards me, grabbing my hands, shoving me against the wall with the full force of her body. 'No! Brooke! Stop it!'

'This isn't you,' I rasped, her face above mine, her hands locking my wrists at my sides.

'Stop struggling!'

'You wouldn't keep me holed up like this.' My words turned into sobs, the fight going out of my body. Would I carry this knotted thing around with me until I died? Would I be forced to tear it out?

'I thought you came here to help me,' Izzy said, her eyes unblinking. 'Not the other way around. This would help. Why can't you do it for me?'

The sudden coldness in her voice sent a shudder through me.

'Do what?' I sobbed.

'It's what you've wanted, isn't it? For me to ask for your help. Well, now I'm asking. Otherwise, what are you here for?'

'What if it kills me? What if it replaces me? Maybe you'll come in carrying a tray one day, and I won't be here any more.'

'Now you're just being dramatic.' It was as if she didn't know we were trapped inside a horror movie. 'People give birth every day, thousands of them.' Her voice smoothed and reasoned. She let go of my wrists and rubbed my arms. 'Now, we'll stop this nonsense, thank you.'

'Whatever *it* is will be left in my place. What then?' I saw it cross her face, the bafflement, the sly, unguarded thought: *So what?*

She rolled her sleeves to the elbow.

I pushed past her and flung the suitcase closed, abandoning the detritus of my other belongings. 'So what?!'

'Brooke, it might be your body, but it's *my* baby, the one I've been waiting for. It's not even like I asked you to carry it,' she said, crossing her arms. 'It's not even like we had to go through some sort of medical surrogacy. It's just been given to you, and *you don't want it.*' She was very still, despite the passion behind her words, her eyes imploring mine. 'How can you be so selfish? If I could switch places with you, I would.'

I believed it. I turned from her, pulling the suitcase behind me, my movements clumsy and strained under the weight of my belly, the knot jabbing painfully under my skin, all elbows. The wheels of the suitcase trundled over the threshold, rolled down the carpeted hallway, then bumped into the corridor – Sunshine barking in consternation, Izzy at my heels. 'Wait,' she was saying, following me out of the apartment, 'please, your body can do this. The baby can be ours. I want—' Her voice cracked.

'We don't even know what this is,' I shrieked, staggering away from her. 'I wish we could switch places, too! But we can't!'

'I'll love it for you. *Please*. Don't leave me.' Her hands reaching, grabbing at my clothes.

'I can't let this happen to me. I can't. I don't want it.'

The lift doors scraped open. I hadn't called for it, it had simply arrived. 'Brooke,' Izzy said, though she didn't follow me inside. 'You're my *sister*.'

I held out my hand for her. This was a madness; it couldn't be happening. 'Come with me. Izzy, it's not safe here, there's something bad in the building. It hates us.' Something seethed between my teeth. 'It's pitting us against each other.' There had to be something bad in the building. It couldn't be us; we couldn't have made this happen ourselves.

The doors began to slide shut. Izzy slammed her hand against the metal, jammed her foot across the threshold. 'Brooke.' The doors groaned open. 'Come back inside. I promise I'll listen to you, we'll work this out. Where are you even going? Are you going to the hospital? Are you going to him?'

It took me several beats to realize she was talking about James. It hadn't occurred to me to turn to him for help. I didn't even know where he lived. Izzy could see I was unmoved, determined. I knew exactly where to go – I'd give Medusa all my belongings, everything I had to offer. If she could step inside my body, surely she could take the knot out.

'I'll make it go away,' Izzy said quickly.

I shook my head. 'How could you?'

'I've an idea, something . . . something we could try. A remedy. I can make you something to drink. I think it will work.'

I frowned. I hadn't meant the mechanics of it, how the disappearance might be accomplished. I meant her abandoning the beautiful possibility of a baby, what she saw as her chance at motherhood. 'You wouldn't . . .' I started, then a thought struck me. 'You wouldn't give me anything . . . bad, would you?'

She shook her head, her eyes wide, a tear spilling down her cheek. 'It helped me. It used to help me, with the pain. It's a herbal remedy, gentle.'

I was shaking my head now. 'No, Izzy, that won't do anything—'

'No,' she cut in. 'No, listen. When you're pregnant, there are certain ingredients you . . . shouldn't have, aren't there? Herbs that can make your uterus contract or relax. You must have read about them, in your research?'

I did recall something like that. Even chamomile tea was restricted during pregnancy.

'I'd stir it into warm milk,' Izzy continued. 'And the pain would stop, for a little while. It gave me some relief. You're right, Brooke, this isn't the way.'

'It won't kill it?' I don't know why I put it like that. I wanted whatever was growing inside me to simply evaporate, to migrate out of my body, like an exhalation. But the thought of it coming to any harm also terrified me – when I'd beat my fists against my belly, I'd terrified myself. Izzy had moved her foot, and the lift doors shuddered to close again. I held the button to keep them open.

'It's harmless. We'll just . . . dull it, like a pain. That's how we should treat it. That's what I had to do, for so long. We'll make it go away.' She took my hand in both of hers. 'If it doesn't work, I'll take you to the hospital myself. I can explain it all, don't worry about that. Come on. I'm sorry.' She was crying, tears streaking her face. I'd never seen her this open before, this vulnerable.

I stepped out of the lift. She brought my hand to her lips, rubbed it, kissed it. 'Thank you,' she said. I let her lead me down the corridor, passing all the neighbours' closed doors. Had none of them heard my scream? I watched Izzy swing the green door open, cross over onto the carpet in the hallway. She closed the door behind me, her face still wet, a crescent of mascara smudged beneath one eye. 'You sit down now. I'll warm the milk.'

29

I floated in the ocean, salt on my eyes and tongue, churn in my stomach. I wanted to be sick. There was no sun, only the body of a sea creature above me. I knew I was dreaming; I was trying to logic my way out of the dream by identifying the creature. Long, branch-like tentacles, barbed with hooks, and a pulsing centre shaped like a star. I tried to swim to avoid the embrace of its branching arms, but I couldn't move; I was sinking up towards the throbbing star, and I was trying to shout – that's why my mouth was full of salt.

I snapped awake, recognizing the pattern of mildew on the ceiling as something submarine. The sheets were soaked. Why was I back in Izzy's bed? I'd just been drinking the warm milk at the table, which Izzy had poured into a clear, tempered glass patterned with red hearts. There was a chip in the rim, and I drank around it, the milk clouding the glass. Izzy stood in the kitchen unpacking apples, removing stickers from each one. 'There's a chip in this glass,' I said. That's all I could remember.

Now, in the bed, there was something stuffed inside my mouth. I sucked air in through my nose in a rising panic. Something wrapped itself around my face, tightening my jaw. The sea creature was trying to suffocate me. I tried to scream again, like in the dream, only I was awake, and I could make a noise now, a muffled cry. I wanted to rip the creature off my face, but my hands wouldn't move and my arms were dull with a heavy ache. I pulled and pulled at my hands, grabbing at rope, the tentacles of the sea creature restraining my wrists. No, I was right the first time. Rope, tying me to the bedposts, its edge frayed, coarse against my skin. Where had the rope come from? The door opened and Cecelia came in – she stepped straight through from our time in Japan, wearing the white clothes, her hair still silvery and dressed with the stiff fabric flowers. A ghost I couldn't stop conjuring. 'See?' she said, the word dripping with disgust. 'Look at you, just lying there.'

What did Cecelia want from me, to tear my own sister's eyes out? Even if I could, if my limbs weren't weighing me down, I wouldn't do it.

You shouldn't have done that to me. Though unable to speak, I knew ghost Cecelia could hear my words. *You shouldn't have treated me like that. I didn't deserve it.*

'You'll be a little confused,' Izzy said. 'Don't worry, it'll pass.' She knelt at the foot of the bed, looping rope around my ankle, tautening my limbs until I was spread-eagled on the bed. She looked at the tender mound of my stomach, which was still there, which hadn't gone away. I thought she might touch it, but a tremor of revulsion moved through her body. Some mother she'd make, I thought cruelly. 'Are you in pain?'

I tugged feebly at the ropes. How else could I answer her?

'I'm sorry you're not comfortable. I'll think of something else. You made me panic, I'm sorry. I didn't know what else to do. I can't let you hurt the baby. Will you forgive me?' She came and sat next to me on the bed. I tried to shrink away from her, but my limbs weren't my own. She hadn't wiped her face, and two dark halfmoons were raked under her eyes. This alone was disconcerting, how messy her face was, my immaculate sister whose skin was always scoured clean. 'I don't think it will be long now.' She stroked my forehead. 'You'll forgive me, when it's over, won't you? It will all be worth it. When the baby's here.'

Izzy stayed with me for a long time, shushing me, stroking my hair. I swam in and out of consciousness, her face looming above me, rippling into existence whenever I opened my eyes. In the marshy depths, I could hold on to the idea this was only a nightmare, that I'd wake and find my older sister getting ready for work, judging my laziness. My sister before they cut away her womb, grabbing my hand and pushing it into her belly, saying, 'Feel it.' The way the growth moved beneath my touch. 'Whatever happens, I'll be glad to be rid of this.'

That sister would never do this to me. Had the parasite crawled inside her, too? But these thoughts were fleeting, slippery, and I couldn't follow them over the bilious rise and fall of the tainted milk.

Half-awake, I fell again and again, my limbs tumbling over themselves, the weight of my belly pulling me down like an anchor, to the green-black depths of the ocean. Or stepping out of the window, the pavement rushing to meet me, a flood of images from all the horror movies I'd ever seen drowning my synapses, cloaked figures in red. Then blinking my eyes open to Izzy's face, the halo of her blonde hair, my arms and legs bound and my mouth stuffed with a rag.

'Maybe we should pray?' she said. 'We should pray, for the baby.'

There is no baby. It's a mass. An interloping cyst covered in dead grey skin, it wants to stay alive, keep growing. It's going to grow until it eats me.

'Shush, shush,' she said, as if she could hear my thoughts. I must have been mouthing the gag.

It's a big lifeless cyst! It fled you and hid inside me.

'Stop! Stop it. You won't like what happens if you make noise,' she chided, raising her eyebrows.

I blinked, quieted by the threat. My sister was threatening me. I looked at her face in a kind of dark wonder. I couldn't feel what she felt, that need for a baby. But I didn't believe that her desire alone, no matter how primal, how deeply felt, would drive her to act this way, make a monster of her. She pushed a thread of honey-blonde hair behind her ear, smoothed her clothes. She looked sickly and haggard. I saw her suffering.

'There, now. If we want a miracle, we should pray, shouldn't we? You don't want to stay like this, do you? When the baby comes, we both get what we want.'

And she did start to pray, then. She closed her eyes and squeezed my arm, murmuring fervently under her breath. I'd never heard her pray before. I watched her, hoping for a pause, a break in the spell. Soon, I closed my eyes, Izzy's prayers like susurrations, her singular voice, febrile and lonely.

I don't think I prayed for anything as the darkness came to claim me, only: *Mum*.

After that I killed my sister in my sleep and left her body out in the open for scavengers. I was too scared to admit what I'd done, but I sensed our mother suspected, and as I slept Mum hovered in my doorway in her dressing gown, like she needed to check on me through the night because I was such a danger to the family. I'd open my eyes in the dream and Mum would be there looming, watching me closely. I'd taken something precious from her and she knew it, even though the body still hadn't been discovered. I don't know how they'd missed it – maybe something had already eaten my sister. I'd hidden some clue inside the bedside lamp and was terrified of switching it on lest my secret be revealed. Cicadas hammered at the bedroom window, their bodies splattering against the glass. As a family we drove out to the airport to pick Izzy up from her flight, and I tried to hide my panic, waiting in the multistorey instead of going in to meet her at the gate – what would I say to Mum and Dad when she didn't appear? But she did appear and came back to the car chatting happily with Mum. I'd imagined the murder. It was all in my head. But when I woke for real, I could remember every detail, my sister's body out there somewhere, slowly turning to rot.

There were no cicadas beating against the window. Instead, music thumped the inside of my skull. Izzy had left me alone in the room, left the music playing, to drown out any noise I might make despite the gag. She didn't want any neighbours interfering. But wouldn't they find it odd? The endless loop, the operatic notes of the balladeer repeating *stay stay stay*.

It was dark in the room, but I had little idea what time it was. I waited for Medusa to come back, to free me. The last time I saw her, I'd keened. She'd stepped inside my body, through the mirror. She'd wanted James. I had no way to tell if it was even my own desire I'd felt, or hers. If Medusa stepped into my body again, would she feel the thing growing inside me? Did she know what was happening now, my wrists rubbed raw, my throat scraped dry? The room stunk of urine.

My brain looped dreams of falling through air, past the blank eyes of windows, picking up speed, quickening towards the pavement. Instead of waking when my body hit the ground, I found myself in an operating theatre, my sister's face obscured behind a surgical mask. A light shone in my face, and Medusa stood between my legs, thrusting an ungloved hand inside me. Globs of white goo. 'Save the baby.' Izzy's voice came from every direction, vibrating through the walls of the room, which I saw now were the damp walls of Medusa's well. Izzy's face didn't seem to move behind her mask; it was a lifesize doll of Izzy, her blue eyes large and unblinking, like the hand-me-down dolls we'd had as children, first belonging to her, then to me. 'Save the baby, let her die.' I woke up before any sort of birth, sweating through my nightie, through the sheets of Izzy's bed.

I prayed for another power cut. If the power went out, the music would stop and I could find some way to make noise. I'd lost all feeling in my hands, and my belly cramped and rumbled loudly – the knot baby nudging and thumping at my uterus, as if spurring me to action.

Under the music, something shifted on the other side of the swamp wall. My heart somersaulted. Was it Medusa coming to my rescue, stepping again from the shadows to dress me and take me outside?

Drawers rasped and scraped, and a door banged shut. Wendy, unpacking? Or the little girl, jumping around inside the bedroom they shared. Were they home? I sucked in as much breath as I could and tried to push the rag from my mouth, making a sad strangled cry. It was useless; I'd never be heard above the din of the music.

I wasn't thinking only of myself. Izzy needed help. I knew this wasn't her; it had to be something else, something making her act this way, driving her onwards. *The craving worm*, Medusa had called the thing that made her take other people's belongings, take bigger and bigger risks, put herself in danger. The craving worm in her belly. Had the craving worm made her step inside my body? Had the craving worm wanted James?

And what about Kioko? She had spoken of obake so naturally, as if she wasn't afraid, only curious. Had she seen Medusa walking through walls? Some trace evidence of whatever it was that lived behind and between, spreading like the green-black mould on my sister's bedroom ceiling? Is that what she was drawing – those stick figures with their black spiral dresses, the prison scratch at the corners of the pages? Perhaps the drawings were for protection, like the nightlight – like my own attempts to capture the face I'd seen in the mirror, and my cave art on the wall.

A knocking sound interrupted my thoughts. Knock, knock, knock, over my head. I twisted in the bed as much as I could, straining my neck, as if I'd be able to see the hand rapping on the wall behind me, the bed sailing still in the middle of the room. A woman's voice, the words indistinct. Wendy? Knock, knock, knock. As if to say, *I can hear you*, or maybe, *turn it down*.

My skin felt wet and cold, slippery with sweat. I pulled at the ropes, burning my wrists, bending my fingers, straining, straining, almost crying with the pain. I'd never be able to free myself, to reach the wall. Instead, I made a fist.

Tap, tap, tap against the bedpost. The sound was so light, so soft – I tried to wrest my hand free again, but the rope would only give so much. Tap, tap, tap. I kept it up, hoping somehow she'd hear the pattern. Why hadn't Wendy come to the door to complain? Perhaps she had complained, and Izzy ignored her, or made some excuse. Now the pipes rushed and clanged, obscuring my feeble little beats against the post. But I could still hear the voice, and then, coming from the other side of the wall, three knocks.

I tapped out a response, matching the rhythm as closely as I could. Tap, tap, tap.

Louder, more deliberate, a reply: knock, knock, knock.

The bedroom door swung open, and Izzy snapped off the music, cutting the singer's voice dead. 'You're awake,' she murmured, and she came over and fussed with the bedclothes, tucking them more tightly around me. I held myself stiff, waiting for the knocks to come through the wall again and give me away.

Instead, a thunder of knocks against the front door. Izzy cried out and clamped her hands over my mouth, over the gag. I couldn't speak, but I could still beg. I pulled at the ropes with my hands and feet; I pleaded with her, tried to telegraph love.

Izzy twisted the gag tighter, her nails scratching my skin. She looked very sorry, like she had no choice. She even kissed my face. Another round of raps at the door. 'Izzy?' I heard Wendy call. My sister stood up, wiped her nose and smoothed her hair, then left the room to answer the door.

All I could hear was a warble of *my daughter is trying to sleep*. I strained and strained against the ropes, contorting my body, tapping my knuckles against the bedpost. The noise was so feeble, so futile, Wendy would never hear me in the doorway. I squeezed my eyes closed and slammed my head against the headboard, my heels digging into the mattress. Once, twice, three times, my groans muffled, buzzing in my ears. Even if she couldn't hear me, surely Wendy would see something was wrong, hatch some sort of intervention. My sister looked possessed.

I heard the front door close quietly. Normally. Beaten and dizzy, the room tilting on its axis, I pictured Wendy the way I'd seen her last, proffering the blue lantern, slipping out of sight. Oyasumi.

My head ached so much I could hardly breathe, and something was tightening and stretching in my belly, cramping my pelvis and ligaments. I tried to focus on outside sounds – car horns, people yelling, now and then a siren's blare, the world going on around me – but the twist of pain made me frantic.

A kind of annihilation. The stages of pregnancy. Where was I now, on the scale? What fruit was I carrying that made me blossom this way, so dark? Whatever was taking shape inside my body, my sister believed it was a baby. Her baby. She didn't care how it got here, only that it arrived unscathed. It was only natural for her to feel this way. Maternal instinct.

Could I make her believe I wanted this, too? Was it cruel to go along with her fantasy, or was make-believing a baby the key that would release me? Superstition rioted through my blood at the prospect. I was terrified that if I pretended, I would have to endure a birth – as if I could imagine a real baby into existence.

When Izzy came back with the milk glass in her hand, she carried it across the room and set it down on the nightstand. Her hands were trembling, and the milk spilled in a filmy white splash. 'That wasn't very clever, was it? I need you to drink the milk again.' Her voice was shaking, too. She pressed her hand to my belly now, the first time, as far as I was aware, that she'd touched it since she'd tied me to the bed.

'I've decided it's a girl.' She smiled, tears in her eyes, and sat next to me. Then, in a near-whisper, as if she was confessing something: 'I've chosen a name.'

I didn't want to know. There were no more knocks, but I thought Wendy or Kioko could still be there, just on the other side of the wall. Izzy's face blurred and warped before my eyes.

'Ah, no, I can't tell you. It's unlucky. But don't worry, it's a family name, you'll like it.' She winked. Her tone shifted as she put her hands around my throat. 'I'm going to take this off now,' she said. 'I expect you to be quiet.'

She pulled at the gag as if unribboning a parcel, a smile still playing across her face. 'I can't wait to meet my daughter. Can you?' She unstuffed my mouth. I coughed, almost choking as she drew out the rag.

'Water,' I said. 'Please.'

'Just the milk for now.' She put the glass to my lips and I drank it, my throat dry and rough, my body responding before I had a chance to stop myself. 'There, now,' she said. 'Good girl.'

'What's in it?' I rasped.

'Just a sedative. Don't worry, it won't hurt the baby.'

I don't care if it hurts the baby. 'Everything hurts,' I said. 'I'm in pain.'

'We all have to make sacrifices. Nobody said having a baby would be easy.'

I looked into her face. 'Where are you?' I cried. 'Are you still in there?'

'Shush, you'll disturb the neighbours.'

'*Izzy.*' I tried to yell, my throat so raw it sounded like a croak.

'I can see you still need this,' she said sternly, bringing the rag to my face.

'No,' I said, panic tipping me over the edge. 'No, listen – I shouldn't be lying like this. I'm too big.'

'You'll survive.'

'No. Listen, Izzy, please, it's bad for the baby! There's a vein that carries blood to it . . . to her. And if I lie on my back, the vein compresses. It cuts the supply off. It's called the *vena cava*.'

'How would you know about something like that?' She narrowed her eyes.

'I read about it. When I ordered the Doppler. I was reading all these forums . . . Please.'

Izzy only looked at me. I cut my eyes away from hers, addressing my belly in a tentative voice. 'You don't like it, do you, sweetheart?' I'd sung to the bump in front of Izzy before, but these were the first words I'd spoken to it aloud in her presence. Something rippled beneath my skin.

'You miss me rocking you, don't you?' Tethered to the bed frame, I swayed my body like a lilting boat, humming softly, my spine radiating pain through my pelvis and shoulders. I felt a slither of movement, something pulsing inside my belly.

I hoped this acknowledgement of a baby would appease Izzy. But alarm spread across her face and she clutched the rag to her chest, as if to soothe a crying child. *Oh*, I thought, *I've seeded something*.

'Yes,' I said in the same hushing tone, rocking grotesquely at the limits of what the weight of my belly and the restraints would allow, gripping the rope in my hands. 'It's bad for the baby.' The parasite rolled and thrashed. Did it feel pleasure? 'My little one.'

Izzy flinched. I wasn't sure which had unsettled her – the idea that her own actions might harm the baby, or that I'd called it sweetheart, called it mine.

'What's wrong with you?' Izzy whispered, her face wild with grief. She stuffed the rag inside my mouth and forced it down my throat, clamping her hand over my chin until I thought I might pass out. I had no time to prepare myself, and choked painfully on the suffocating rag as she tied the cloth behind my neck. 'Good night,' she said when her work was finished, leaving the room, closing the door.

30

I'm not sure whether the sedative took effect very quickly, or if I really did pass out, because there's a stretch of time that I remember as nothing but darkness, a nothing that impressed a sense of duration upon me, that suspended me, unmoving, in the pitch. It was like staring at a blank wall for hours, without any thoughts in my head except for a wish to see the sky. Later, I wondered if the sedative had seeped through my system into the knot baby, made it sleep, stopped it infecting my dreams. Or if some other metamorphosis was happening in my absent slumber. The next thing I remember beyond this formlessness is a repetition: Izzy with a glass of milk in her hand, standing over me, then leaning down to place the glass carefully on the nightstand.

I let my body soften, unfocusing my eyes, tilting my gaze beyond my sister into the shadows above the door. I remembered every detail of the story she'd told me, how she'd almost killed me simply by playing dead.

'Time for your milk,' Izzy said. 'Are you going to drink it all down for me?'

My body sank limply into the mattress. I did not stir or breathe.

'Brooke. Do you promise to be quiet?'

Even the knot inside me was still.

'Brooke.' Izzy snapped on the bedside lamp. I didn't blink, I couldn't see her face. The quick and the dead. The quick and the dead.

She did not scream but swallowed a surprised sob. 'Brooke?' She fell on me, lifted my shoulders to meet hers, her body shuddering. I let myself be shaken limp, my head lolling and my eyes fixed. She cradled my head, her fingers scrabbling to unfasten the gag. A loud, guttural wail escaped her. But as she pressed her hand over my mouth, I choked on the vile rag. I coughed, helpless to stop the contractions of my throat, and she knew then, of course, that I was breathing, that I was playing a trick.

She stopped unfastening, but the bindings had loosened, making it easier for me to breathe. Instead of being angry with me, she collapsed.

My sister wrapped herself around the bump. 'Please come out,' she cried into my skin, pulling up my shirt so that I could feel her mouth moving against my belly. 'Please, I can't wait any longer. Please, Brooke, can't you help it to come?'

I shook my head. *I'm sorry*. Ever the late-blooming latecomer.

She heaved a sigh. 'I need you to drink the milk.'

I shook my head, more slowly, spill of tears wetting my earlobes.

'Please, just let me keep you safe until the baby comes. Things don't have to be nasty. No more playing dead.'

I cried, curling my body against her as I squirmed on the bed. This couldn't be my sister. The knot inside me had started to respond, whether to her touch or my struggle, I couldn't tell, but I felt something buckle and kick.

'Please,' she said, her eyes wild and pink rimmed. 'I'm scared. I don't know what I might do.'

I froze, then. What violence was my sister capable of? I thought of the knife block in the kitchen, those chef's knives, so sharp. The twining scar on her own belly, the way it marked out where she might cut into mine.

'If you're good, I'll untie you,' she said. 'I'll roll you onto your side.'

My throat was raw, my head lurched and spun, and something sharp butted painfully against my ribs. I nodded. *I'll behave.*

She untied the gag and pulled the cloth from my mouth. I sucked in air. With her hand behind my head, lifting me, she put the glass to my lips. I'd forgotten about the chip and felt the rough edge of the glass slit my lip as I drank – greedily, sloppily, the taste of my own blood on my tongue, the milk slipping down my neck, wetting my collar. 'Oh dear.' Izzy blotted my lip with the rag. 'I hope that didn't hurt. Are you going to be good?'

I nodded, and she leaned over and switched on the nightlight.

'Why do you have that?' I asked in ragged whisper, thinking again of the mother and daughter on the other side of Izzy's bedroom wall. 'Did you steal it?'

'Of course not,' she said, as if this was the worst accusation I could level. 'Kioko gave it to me before they left. She said you needed it. I wasn't going to accept it, but she was so insistent. She said it would keep the ghosts away. Don't worry, I'll give it back.'

'When?' I asked. 'When will you give it back? After what? What's going to happen, Izzy?'

The knife loomed large in my imagination. If there was no birth, would there be a gutting? Could she really do that to me? And what would she find inside me?

'I'll untie you once you fall asleep,' she promised.

My sister hummed quietly to the nightlight's melody, almost beneath her breath, while she waited for the drug to take effect. I hummed along with her until my eyes grew heavy. I didn't have the energy to yell, but as I drifted away, I fixed my eyes on the drawing I'd made of the two of us, rolled up against the door of the wardrobe. 'It's for you,' I whispered before the room went black, 'I made it for you.'

When I woke in the dark, I had no idea how much time had passed. The moon beamed through the window, curtains drawn back, my hands beneath my curled body. They tingled with pins and needles. I coughed, realized the gag was gone, the rope no longer binding my wrists and ankles. Izzy sat facing away from me, her hands caressing the bump that protruded from my middle. The sheets were bright white, crisp and clean. Somehow, I'd been bathed. A silver bowl full of water sat on the floor, a towel folded next to it. I didn't like how it felt, weirdly ceremonial.

Feeling me stir, Izzy turned. Her face was clean. I opened my mouth, about to protest, to plead. But she spoke, interrupting the sound. 'She's been moving in there. She's alive.'

On the floor, the drawing I'd made was half-spread across the carpet, weighted down with something, crimped at the edges. The coil of the paper manipulated the sisters, so they seemed to regard each other, the shadow sister in her crinoline black looking over her shoulder. The perspective had shifted. The patchwork sister held her gaze – tranquil, fragmented, the two of them equals.

'Don't worry,' Izzy said, wiping at her eyes. 'I'm just saying goodbye.' I didn't like that either. Too ambiguous.

'Please.' The word tore my throat, the room filled with a chill sense of possibility. The moonlight made the sister's pastel face look somehow immortal, like she'd been sculpted from marble. I'd used all the colours in it, given her back the purple hair.

'It's good,' she said, nodding to the portrait. 'You're good.'

'Thank you. I'm proud of it.'

'I shouldn't have . . .' She placed her hand on my belly again. 'She moved so much while you were sleeping. Now she's quiet.'

'Must be its turn to sleep.'

Her eyes met mine. 'You do have a feeling for her, then? I thought you were taunting me before, waggling your belly at me like that, calling her yours.'

'I wasn't taunting you.'

She wiped her nose on her sleeve. 'I didn't know about the *vena cava*.'

'I'm sorry. I didn't mean to be cruel. I just wanted you to—'

'Why did you stop singing to her?' she interrupted.

'Izzy, I don't want it inside me.'

'I thought you loved her.' A tear slid down her face. 'Do you have to fight it? What if you . . . ?'

'Give in? Give you what you want? What do you think could be growing this fast?' I tried to appeal to her senses. Whatever parasite was growing inside me, it couldn't be anything good. Whether with intent or by instinct, the way it blossomed beneath my skin had made me wretched and helpless, warping my body inside out. 'It's not a . . . normal baby.'

Her face lit up with something like appeal, her eyebrows lifted, her cheeks wet. 'Nobody knows what kind of baby they'll get.'

I felt like I was staring at that blank wall again, an abyss before me.

'What about me?' I asked. 'Do you even care what happens to me? What if you lose me?'

'Of course I do. I bathed you. I fed you.' She shook her head. 'I don't know what alternative you think you have. I'm giving you a way out. What's the thing Mum says? "What's done cannot be undone"?'

'That's Lady Macbeth. Mum says, "A done bun can't be undone".'

'Oh, that's right.'

Somehow the mention of our mother, her words in the room, pierced through to something else, some other layer between us. A reminder of our relation to one another outside the confines of the room, before the knot inside me had reconfigured everything. Mum was our touchstone, bringing us back into ourselves. She'd birthed us both.

Izzy reached for my hand, flinching at the raw pink of my chafed wrist.

'My hands have gone dead,' I said. 'I must have slept on them.'

She took both my hands in hers, rubbing them back to feeling. 'I can't pretend I don't want this baby. *My daughter*. The chance to be a mother?' Her lip quivered. 'You said you made her for me.'

A wave ripped through me, then. My breath caught in my throat. I gripped Izzy's hands in mine.

'Oh my God,' she cried. 'Is she coming?'

I shook my head. *No, no.* I could feel the knot twisting in my belly, like somebody was pulling it tighter, tighter. 'No,' I moaned. I pulled myself to my feet, shoving Izzy out of my way with a strength that surprised the both of us. No time left.

I slipped on something in the doorway as I manoeuvred around the chair set there – some slippery material underfoot, Izzy's pile of mending.

'Brooke! Come back – you made her for me!'

I gripped the doorframe. Pain shuddered through me, arching my back like an animal. *Everything must be emptied out.* On my way out of the apartment, I stuffed my feet into my boots, grabbed for a coat, keys, swatting my sister's protests away. She followed me down the hallway, put her hands on my lower back. 'Breathe,' she said.

I reached an arm into the kitchen, feeling for the knife block on the countertop. I pulled out the largest blade, knocking the rest of them to the floor, and turned towards her. She staggered back, her face frozen into the uncanny mask she'd been wearing in the dreams of my delivery. She raised her hands, wild-eyed, and finally let me go.

When I reached the basement, I went directly to the electrical room and pushed my way to the wall of Medusa's chamber. I thought it would open to me this time – with the accumulated power of the knife, of the premonition that had torn through me, making me drink the milk: *Cut it out.*

I could feel Medusa under my skin now, the way she had been when I saw her in the mirror when I was with James. There was a larger exchange going on, bigger than the knot in my belly. But the wall would not let me pass.

'I know you're in there!' I banged my fists against the wall. 'I know you're in there, come back!' I banged my fists again and again until I cracked the pocked concrete. The roar of the pain had grown so loud I carried it inside every fibre of my body.

I scrabbled my hands over the rough surface until I found the tiny hole that had appeared on my last encounter with the wall. With my fingernails, I scratched and dug around the hole. Shards of concrete flaked away, and a spume of grey dust poured out like sand, collecting at my feet. The wall crumbled as I widened the hole with my hands, uncovering a bunker of earth on the other side. I knew this couldn't be right – this wasn't like before, but I scooped out handfuls of earth and pushed my way inside the small dark space until I was on my hands and knees crawling through dirt, mouthfeel of dirt, my belly dragging in the muck, my hands caked.

A weight cramped the middle of me. Ache in the belly, thighs, a sharp twist burrowing through my gut and down my spine. I thought of the words *buried alive*, but pushed the thought ahead as the tunnel lightened to a slate in which I could see my fingernails rimed with earth. I knew what I wanted: to taste the heart of the place, to give the knot back to whatever had given it to me, or else sink my teeth into the throbbing centre and feel the blood ooze out. I bored my way out of the other side, my arm finding air, then pushed my head and shoulders into the open – I was in the well with Medusa.

I crawled out and spat a wad of earth on the ground. 'You're bleeding,' she said, though there was no visible sign of blood anywhere on me, not on the outside. I slipped my fingers under my waistband and they came away trailing strings of jelly, a bright red mucus gumming my hand, a show of blood. 'It's almost your time.'

31

Medusa put her hands on my naked belly. Stretched out on her makeshift bed, I put my hands over hers. How long had it been since she'd been touched by someone, for real? Her palms were calloused and rough against my skin, my belly halved by the inky line. 'You want it to go away,' she said. 'Even if it is a baby? A real, live child?'

It's my baby, the one I've been waiting for, Izzy had said. *You made her for me*. Pain worked through my body like a turning screw, tearing me inside out. I gasped, then fished the knife from my coat pocket and handed it to Medusa with a trembling hand.

'Stupid girl.' Medusa shook her head. 'I won't need this.' She threw the knife at a pile of belongings – vase of wooden spoons, moth-eaten textiles, large yellow sponge, steel bucket, what appeared in the gloom to be the severed wing of a swan. The blade struck the wall flatly.

'You won't?' I blinked, my shirt gathered underneath my chin. Izzy had patched a tear under the right armpit with a silken material, leaving the stitches visible, evidence of her mending.

'Of course not! A knife. Ha!' She held up a wizened finger. 'But it's a strong answer to what I asked you.'

'No, wait,' I said, afraid she would begin. The pain had spread to my back and shoulders, the base of my skull. 'Please. Do you know where it came from? The knot. What is it?' I asked her, because Medusa seemed to possess some otherworldly knowledge. Or underworldly. My unlikely midwife.

'It's hard to sleep down here,' she answered. 'Sometimes, I imagine a dark spot in the middle of the universe, like a pupil, and I pour myself into that spot until I'm gone.'

A pupil in the centre of the earth. A womby eye. The mystery of origins would persist.

'The knot,' she repeated reflectively. 'The knot. Yes, that's what it feels like.'

'So you can feel it!' I cried. 'Why didn't you come back? To the room. Couldn't you feel what was happening to us up there?'

'That part was between you and your sister,' Medusa said. 'Do you think I owe you something?'

The knot. Would whatever was happening to us tie my sister to this place, in some unholy bond? What kind of creature could grow so quickly, make my body bend to its will? I thought of Izzy, her bone-deep wish for a baby like a lit flame inside her, how she'd healed the family photograph with a story and a crease, her knack for feeding the people around her. How she'd taken my hand and pressed it to her belly, the cyst she'd carried crawling under my skin.

'I think we're connected,' I said.

Medusa snorted. 'Are we now?'

'How else do you explain it?' I asked. 'All this muddling up. You stepping into my body when I was . . . with James.' My hips were on fire; my very bones seemed to have organized themselves against me.

'The boy,' said Medusa, her face flaring. 'I don't explain it.

Something crawled inside you; the craving worm. It takes what you want and it turns it against you, gives it back wrong, gives you something . . .' She paused. 'Not quite right.'

The streets of Venice swam before my eyes, their smoky reds and oranges. I imagined Izzy stumbling over bridges, treading dark water into a dark church, searching for the lost daughter in her red hood, but finding something evil, something that flashed a knife at her throat.

Something not quite right. 'What did you want?' I asked her.

Medusa flinched, then cast her eyes around her well. 'It wasn't this.'

The pain peaked, creasing me in half. I panted and wheezed, and she brushed at my brow with the sleeve of her housecoat, purplish with filth.

'Maybe you do owe me something.' I breathed. 'Maybe we all owe each other something.'

'You wanted him,' Medusa retorted. 'We both did. That body, so hard-smooth, and the eyes, like moons, like a doe! So young. And trying so hard to be good. Are you sure you didn't want *this*?' She prodded my belly as I squeezed my eyes shut.

'*I* don't want it. My sister does. Some –' a pain ripped through the middle of me '– violent confusion in the family . . . You, you, you . . .' But I had lost the thread, and as the pain receded, I stared around the well, not quite comprehending what I was doing there.

'Easy,' Medusa said firmly, as if to calm me.

'Why did you come back?' I asked in a pleading sort of voice. 'The second time, in the mirror? I saw you.'

She frowned. 'Not me.' Her hands went into her hair and she scratched at her scalp. 'Must have been *it*. I only wanted the boy . . .'

'It?'

'The *thing* behind the walls. The parasite.'

'You're lying,' I spat, pulling in short rasping breaths between my teeth. My skin itched at the thought of that same mushrooming organism – a parasite that ratcheted the pipework and shifted walls – burrowing beneath my flesh. Is that what I had seen in the mirror, the creature showing itself as a withered hag, flesh pitted with oozing sores, reaching to enfold me? 'No. You came back, I saw you. I broke the mirror. My face turned into your face, my body – we were the same.'

She looked at me blankly, then leaned in to me, her finger waggling in the dank basement air. 'We're not the same. And I don't have all day to chitter chatter.' She paused, her hands floating above my skin. 'What's your verdict?'

You made her for me. The family photograph, the baby folded out to make a kinder story. The baby who was me. The way Izzy had looked at herself, my patchworked version of her, in the drawing, of two sisters with their eyes full of each other. Their deep and complete regard. All my mother's trying stood behind my shoulder. The knot inside me was trespassing in my body; I couldn't let it swallow me whole. Whatever was growing inside me, it was a stranger.

I nodded, a curl sticking to my forehead with sweat. I didn't know to what spell, what magic or medicine I was consenting. But I wanted it to stop, this rough transformation of the body I'd never cared for, and which seemed suddenly precious, life-giving. *My* life. I trusted Medusa's hands, her thievery, the way she walked through walls.

I spoke the words with no shame and all of the love I could summon. 'Make it go away.'

*

Leaving together was easy. The doors of the building opened for Medusa like magic. Outside, a sift of snow had powdered the streets overnight, and the sky thrummed with falling. Two sets of footprints led down the block towards the park, one human, one hound. A dog walker.

The cold felt like relief against the ache of my body, slick with sweat and clotted with mud, my limbs burdened with groaning expectation. Medusa's walk was a hobbled float. She muttered and howled about the cold – how it would creep into the basement, a glistening skin on the old stone walls – all the way down the block. I didn't want her to have to go back down there, the mildewed walls of the Leonora holding her hostage, feeding off her sorrow, her loneliness.

'Where are we going?' I whined. 'I thought you were going to help me.'

'We're going to visit the graves.'

'What? What are you talking about? I can't keep walking—' A tremor in the pit of me. 'Please.'

'We're not going to *walk* there,' she chided, patting her pockets, which were stuffed with trinkets. 'It's a kind of exchange we make.'

I felt stunned into hopelessness. I'd asked for Medusa's help and now she had me following her around in a mindless loop, a madwoman myself. The ground rumbled beneath my feet and the knot began to pull and contract. 'Why is the ground shaking?' I panted.

Across the street, a man scraped a snow shovel along the pavement. The road was deserted. It seemed unlikely the bus would come, and I reached out a hand and placed it on Medusa's arm, carefully, the way I'd touch an animal I was afraid to spook, an animal with a powerful jaw and sharp teeth. 'Let's turn back.'

'You want to go back?' she asked, prodding my belly with a finger. 'Lock your*self* in that room and wait for whatever comes?'

'I thought you were going to help me. You're not going to help me, are you?'

'You've yet to do *your* part.' She pointed the finger in my face. 'It still has to slither its way out of you.'

'What?'

Her face, with its fleshy jowls and hollow, wrinkled cheeks, seemed to kaleidoscope, so that I saw three of her. Six dark eyes. 'It has no other way out.'

'No . . .' I heaved, my hands going to my belly. 'No, I can't go through this! You were meant to take it—'

'Do what you like, stay or come.' Medusa dismissed me. 'But if it slithers out of you in that room . . .' She stopped talking, turning to look down the street. She held her arm out.

'If it comes when I'm back there, what?'

'I can't help you, then. Nobody can. You'll be in the grip of it.'

The bus rumbled towards us in a hiss of tyres and a crunch of snow, and the doors levered open like a gasp.

We were the only passengers, the windows fogged with condensation and the heaters blowing sticky air. Medusa sighed and crossed her arms in the seat beside me, closed her eyes. 'We'll be there soon,' she said, and promptly fell asleep.

The bus dropped us at the cemetery gates. A large white void in the middle of the city, enclosed by tall hedges. Perhaps there was a mountain view, but they were invisible today, swallowed by a hooded, bulging sky.

Medusa pulled items from her pockets as she drifted across the frozen grass, which was stippled with mismatched headstones like broken teeth. We trundled past utilitarian buildings, a few elaborate monuments and mausoleums among the smaller gravestones. I followed in Medusa's wake, a riot inside me, my head spinning. My entire body trembled with the cold, or perhaps the pain; I carried something sharp inside me that stabbed at my belly, grinding against the cradle of my pelvis while I sucked cold gasps of air. Time began to dilate – I felt as if I'd slipped through some temporal crack, suspended between contractions. The streetlamps were haloed and the snow veiled the landscape in absence. The snow soothed me, like standing in front of an Agnes Martin.

An avenue of trees led to a covered structure ornamented with disused fountains and large stone urns, the doorway a gaping mouth. Inside, the roof tilted upwards and the black and white tiled pathways were lined with recessed shelves and slots, like a dovecote. Inside each niche, mourners had placed trinkets: tealights, yellow flowers, rocks, bird statues, framed photographs.

Medusa was suddenly at my side. 'I have to keep one eye out for the groundskeeper,' she said. 'He chases me off the cemetery lawns, like a stray dog. I don't think he appreciates my offerings. I saw him putting up signs about *litter*.' She eyeballed me, as if to make sure I understood the implicit hostility of the signs. 'I like the columbarium best. I'd prefer to be above ground, after.' She took something from her pocket and bent to place it on a shelf, then blustered back outside.

A columbarium. All these objects indicating visitation, love. I found myself looking for anything womb-shaped among the offerings as I followed the pathways and moved deeper into the cavern, though

Medusa remained outside, performing her own rituals. I thought about the amethyst geode glistening in the dark of Medusa's well, that thing Lucie had said about giving your pain to another vessel: an anatomical votive, a surrogate womb.

The cemetery was a holy place of inscription; I ran my fingers over the epitaphs carved in the stone of each columbaria: con te partirò, waiting to be woken, born asleep, only light. Mother, mother, mother, mother. Repetition like lamentation. A sign read: Cemetery staff will dispose of items that are weathered, unsightly, excessive, or otherwise do not comply.

It was warmer inside the columbarium, a relief from the bitter cold, but as I catalogued the ephemera I became disoriented; every corner I turned seemed to offer no way out, only more tributes to the dead, a maze of other people's memories, a library of their ancestors, stretched to eternity. I started to hum the little girl's tōryanse song: you may pass, you may enter, we've come to dedicate our offerings. 'Koko wa doko no hosomichi ja?'

A rectangle of daylight appeared ahead. Outside, I turned on the spot, but didn't have long to search: Medusa's silhouette was indelible against the snow, and I hurried to catch up with her, something clinging to me from the mournful atmosphere inside the columbarium.

At a particular grave Medusa stopped, swept her foot across the ground to reveal letters etched in stone. She began to go through her pockets, the items emerging and then disappearing again into the folds of her housecoat. Pink bed socks, a clay pipe, the ace of hearts with a finger smudge, a yellow bobbin, a torn page from a map. I realized these were items she'd stolen from people in the building; the small objects seemed to vibrate with other lives.

Eventually she drew a novelty salt-shaker out of her pocket and placed it on the grave with something like reverence. Medusa closed her eyes. I closed mine too, beside her, and crossed my hands over my belly. When I opened my eyes, she was already weaving between the headstones to another grave, leaving a channel in the snow that I staggered through after her.

Beloved wife and daughter, the name obscured by a spray of Christmas flowers, wilting and dripping under the snow. 'Did you know her?' I asked.

Medusa plucked one still-blooming rose from the display and placed a small plastic children's toy among the stones, an animal figurine, maybe a fox. 'She used to live in the building,' she said, frowning at me for interrupting her remembrance. 'With her family. They're all gone now.'

So this was her ritual, her offering. What did it mean to her? What pathway – an exchange, she'd called it – did she believe she was making between the living and the dead with these humble objects?

With the rose tucked somewhere underneath her housecoat – I wondered briefly about its thorns, if she felt the scratch of them against her skin, whether they drew blood – Medusa moved on to another grave, but I stopped following her. The falling snow was dizzying, and my fingertips were numb.

I pulled the lapels of my coat around my throat, realizing that it wasn't mine at all, but Izzy's good wool coat. It was longer on me than on her and trailed in the snow, the hem ruined. I felt strangely sorry for it. My boots sunk to the ankles in the snow drift as I made my own staggering path away from the grave to one of the statues to rest.

A gothic-looking angel, with plumy sleeves and wings, hands clasped beneath her middle, a Latin phrase carved beneath. She had a stout figure, ample belly, and a ruffle that snaked down the front of her dress like a barbed scar. Her head brimmed with elaborate stone curls, her hefty brow and eyes contorted as though in the grip of some agony. More gargoyle than angel: her mouth was open and emerging from it was a pointed stone tongue. Snow drifted and melted from the carved face, fingers, the tips of her wings. For an instant the cold drip took me back to Medusa's well.

At the foot of the statue, the snow began to bloom with red flowers. *Flood*, I thought, Sasha mopping the kitchen tile in the restaurant after Izzy, the red petals creeping outwards in the snow, rich and velveteen. I blinked, the snow beneath my feet turning to crimson, deepening. The flowers blooming there were spots of blood.

I pressed my hand to my face and it came away slick with red. My nose was bleeding, and blood bubbled in my throat. I leaned forward, resting my head against the stone, and pinched the bridge of my nose. *Don't swallow*, I told myself, my face gushing with blood and snot and saliva, dripping from my chin, the taste of pennies in my mouth. But the blood poured and coursed down my throat, thickening until I spat up a fat clot of dark red, gagging and retching, dripping pearls of blood from my mouth onto the crystalline ground.

Underneath the coat's wool, my thighs were wet and sticky, the front of my sweatpants suddenly soaked. A cry ripped from my constricted throat when I saw the clot, when I felt something else throb and contract inside me, as if trying to claw its way deeper. I held on, gripping the wings of the gargoyle, the screw turning again and again, rending my insides until I thought I'd split in two. A hand pressed against my lower back, and I felt Medusa there, behind me.

'Almost there,' she said. 'Almost time.' There was no other noise but the roar tearing from my throat, no heart beating but our two hearts.

My incomprehensible fate had rushed to meet me. My hands were empty, my bare limbs splayed. I kept reaching for Medusa, grasping air; I wanted her to squeeze my hands, to give me leverage, but she pressed her two hands to my belly, her face looking down between my legs. Her hair crawled with something living. *I am unmoored*, I thought, my body spread on the ground, the woollen coat a wet pelt between me and the snow. I groped wildly for something to fasten my mind to, my hand finding the sleeve of my sister's coat. Had I made her a promise? I was not religious but I prayed *oh God, oh God, oh God*. Something turned over inside me. The roar that tore from me seemed like another creature, a thing being birthed from my throat. I lay down half-naked to die.

The gargoyle loomed over me, her face mirroring my pain with her jutting stone tongue, her eyes a mask of terror. *I am dying, my own body expelling me.* A smell invaded my nose, something animal. My belly rose before me, a dome of flesh, and now it was writhing, too, a shape protruding from the skin like . . . like what? An elbow, or a knee. The abattoir smell. I thought: *I have never heard a scream like this before.* Something clamped and cinched my middle, pulling my insides tighter and tighter. Medusa's face bathed in sweat, my whole body a shudder, a dark red shadow. My eyes locked on Medusa's downturned face, her eyelids, the tip of her nose. Was it a trick? I thought: *she is eviscerating me.*

The pain dark red. A rip in the flesh, a pulsing womb overtaking my body. I kicked at Medusa's shoulder, tried to free myself from the hand tightening its grip inside me. *I die slow.* My mouth filled with copper, with earth, my tongue knotted. I was lowing now, like an animal, harbouring an urge to crawl on all fours. In my agony a voice came to me, telling me to bear down. *It is Medusa*, I thought, and her voice attached itself to her mouth, her eyes on mine. She looked at me through a veil of snow. An ache like a barbed scar snaked along my body. Something gripped and tore; I squeezed my eyes closed and called for my own mother. As I gnashed my teeth, the snow took on the colour of Izzy's perpetual green light and a presence crept behind the bedroom wall marked with my cave art, eyes peering through the loops and tunnels I'd made there. No, no. Was I back in the room?

My hands stung with cold, my fingertips sticky and pink with blood. The pain was raw and spiked. *Bear down*, Medusa said, and I obeyed. Why wasn't she telling me to push? Why was she telling me to bear? My back arched. I was leaking scarlet ribbons. I was unravelling. I was at the red gates in Kyoto, Cecelia at my side, dressed in white. I sank through the snow, Izzy's coat wrapping its arms around me. The pain bolted through me like kudzu vines; I sank down, down, grappling for the surface. I sucked in air as if about to slip underwater, and before my next gasp, the earth rolled: *I am far away, I have disappeared, I am the snow falling on Medusa, I am back inside the well.* Pain bloomed from my throat and burrowed down my spine. Spasm of light, my own mewling cry. *Drip, drip, drip.* My hands were still empty. They grappled along the glistening stone walls, searching for an opening, for a way to be born.

32

I am chest-deep in a pool of something thicker than blood, something vile-smelling and vivid crimson. I slosh through it, the sound strangely smothered, my arms lifted out of the gore. Above me, the walls of Medusa's well stretch higher than before, and in a crescent of white light at its top the face of the gargoyle looms, her pointed tongue and rippled brow fixed in twisted sorrow. It must still be going on up there. The birthing.

'Hello?' I call, my voice echoing around me. *Hello, hello, hello*. A bitter taste floods my mouth, and I wipe my tongue on the back of my hand, trying to rid myself of it. As I push through the grisly substance, the pool undulates around me, lapping at my arms and breasts. My body shivers, my big belly submerged in blood, my balance off-kilter. My hands scratch at the stone walls, searching for a hook or crevice, a way to lever myself from the silt.

A soft, wet thing glances against my bare skin under the surface. I drop my hands into the red pool, stirring something that fans and flares around my body like seaweed or animal gut, slick tendrils clinging to my fingers. An invisible finger traces against my cheekbone, a touch like a membrane frill. Something fleshy suckers itself onto my thigh; another licks the small of my back. Whatever the things are, they are capable of movement, of attachment. I grab at my legs, at my back, and rip at the feelers, flailing in the viscera. A scream scrapes from my throat, an ache burrowing into my lungs.

If it slithers out of you in that room, Medusa had said, *you'll be in the grip of it.*

Panic bristles through my veins. I cradle my belly, eyeing the frothing surface of the pool as I wade backwards into the wall, seeking shelter. I remember the ladder, but looking into the white light above me, I can't see it. No way out.

I turn, press my body to the curved wall, the stone sooty with green-black mould, its joins seeping a sticky red substance. My foot searches for a gap and I drag my body up and out of the pool – my big belly weighty and cumbersome, my ligaments stretching to snap. I climb until my hips clear the surface, but my hand slips and I crash back down into liquid, among the living, sucking things. The swell carries me towards the centre of the pool, where the blood is somehow deeper, where I have to tread my limbs to stay afloat.

My breath heaves in my chest; its labour means I must still be alive. Something sharp butts against my belly and when I dash against it, it lifts high out of the water and I see a white, smooth flank, like bone. Kicking, I propel my body backwards, hit my head on the jutting rock wall. I cling there, try to press myself away from whatever it is that floats underneath – a creature gathering itself in a sticky red mass around me, forming like scar tissue.

I squeeze my eyes closed. The pain waits for me on the other side of the wall. It throbs, palpitating under my hands now. A sound comes to me in the dark, a faint mewling like the cry I made when I sank underground. There is so much pain to go through. Is my sister still upstairs, sitting in the dark bedroom, waiting for a baby to be born? There is no baby here. Only something bad. Something trying to trick me, to kill me. To damage all of us.

The mewling sound amplifies around me, growing into a warped trill. There *must* be a way out. I know there's a ladder. I climbed it before.

Something bony and ridged rubs against my left forearm, my right shoulder. An impossible hunger mouths my body, and across my round belly a soft-sharp rake of fingernails.

I shriek and reel away, the pool writhing violently with movement. My head slips under and a thick ooze fills my nose. Red behind my eyes. Amniotic sounds. As I sink into the red dark, I struggle for breath and a fist of gore shoves itself inside my mouth.

I choke and gag on the bloody fist. A heartbeat pulses hot and fast in my ears. What does it want with my body? What more can it want me to endure? Will it devour me?

My body jerks in the red cavern as I force myself through liquid like a vessel, ripping at the fleshy substance with my teeth. I push myself out of the ooze. My mouth pulls and tears, spits out a wad of blood, roars. A corresponding wail, inhuman, echoes from the stone walls. The feelers withdraw and Medusa's voice cuts through the cacophony, shouting, 'Bear down! Bear down!'

I kick, half swim the short distance to the other side of the well, reaching a ledge where I can place my feet, sucking in dank air. A sickly feeling overcomes me and I retch into the pool, shuddering. The stone walls ripple with life, a ratcheting sound.

Under the surface, something hot and rank prickles my palm. Corded and grisly between my fingers, the way I imagined Izzy's cyst felt under her skin. I lift it out of the blood. As I raise it in my trembling hand, the bloody liquid streams away and the gore oozes down my arms, flowing back into the pool.

'Bear down!' Medusa rasps, and I know then what to do. I pull in a breath, close my eyes, and plunge under the surface, kicking as I go – kicking all the way down.

33

I surfaced into a grim silence. My body wrecked and riven, I trembled at the base of the statue, the wool coat spread beneath me. The statue's face was locked in horror overhead, watching me as she had watched over me in the well. The snow had stopped falling and the white sky stretched above us like a cataract. Its filminess brought the cemetery fields into sharp focus – a rush of tombstones, crosses, hands closed in prayer – a seamless snow-lit blue.

I had made it, somehow, out of the well.

'We should bury it,' Medusa said, after a pause, her cheek and the tip of her nose smeared with red.

'What?' I said, shocked at the idea of a mass, a real thing that had been born. But there was nothing left to bury. Only a mess of blood between my legs, a stain creeping silently across the wool coat like a shadow.

My hands almost numb, I dragged myself up onto my knees, leaving the bloodied wool coat – the only evidence of my labour, nothing waiting in its folds – at the statue's feet. Perhaps she was a kind of angel, after all, her face contorted in protest, a gargoyle to keep us safe. 'I don't even believe,' I said. I scooped a fresh handful of snow and rubbed it over my face, let it drip inside my mouth.

'You don't have to believe,' Medusa said. 'You just have to make your offering. Not to this fixed lady, here, with her stone wings. To the earth. The underneath. The earth will take us all back.'

Medusa gathered the wool coat, scooping up snow, muck and gore. No baby. No bad thing. She muttered something that could have been prayer, or a spell. I shook my head, repelling her incantations: they made me think of my sister, pleading for her own miracle. My body shuddered with a heavy aftershock as Medusa cradled the coat. Was this my offering or hers? My thoughts were slippery – the *her* in my mind could have been Izzy or Medusa, or both of them at once.

Breathless and sore, my legs shaking, I struggled back into the rest of my wet clothes and boots, the blood-soaked sweatpants clinging to my skin. Medusa held the bundled coat out to me like a sling between her two hands. 'Here,' she said. 'I'll find a shovel.'

I took the coat from her, staring at the curious wet weight in my arms. All that remained of my struggle in the well, of my sister's longing, her lit flame.

'You did well,' Medusa said. 'You survived.'

Barbaric, I thought, as the blade struck the wet earth, its vibration travelling through me. The ground beneath the cemetery lawn was somehow, miraculously, forgiving. Surely Medusa was punishing me, making me dig the hole, my body sweating in cold sheets? *A buried life I couldn't access any more.* They were my own words, about something else, another stretch of time, the girl I used to be distant, forgotten. Now I only turned the earth. Maybe Medusa would lay me down in an open grave. Pile on soil, shovel after shovel, the groundskeeper absent, nobody to bother her. I felt at peace with the idea; now I was the creature burrowing its way in. A subterranean thing. I was the sing of the blade.

Dizzy, I leaned on the shovel, which slipped from under me, crashing to the snow. I slumped to the ground at the edge of the hole, my knees wet. Next to the maw of the grave, my sister's wool coat. I reached out to rub the fabric between my fingers, finding a dry, soft part of the sleeve and pressing it to my face. I knew there was no baby, had never been, but still. I kissed it. 'I couldn't do it, you know that Izzy, don't you? I could never make it real.'

My vision waned and clouded at the edges. Chiaroscuro, a dark red shadow creeping in, staining the snow. I watched the coat disappear, pinkish circles soaking through the fabric, and held onto the sleeve for as long as I could.

That's the last thing I could remember, the sleeve in my hand, the white world slipping away in a whistling blizzard, until I woke up wrapped in Medusa's mauve housecoat. The woman herself had vanished. I was alone.

The horror of birth can't be captured. I'd heard mothers say they forget the pain of childbirth once they hold their babies in their arms. My own mother would disagree with this, firm in her refusal, but she wouldn't go on; she wouldn't admit any more than this.

When I came to, the ground beneath me was checkered, and shelves of unfamiliar belongings lined the walls. A draught howled through the narrow cavern where I found myself lodged. Under the gaze of family portraits, their faces blurred and strange – I thought of Dad's hand on Mum's belly, a sister folded out – I realized I was inside the columbarium.

Shadows played inside the recesses: small patterned vases, dominoes, a pocket mirror. Candles had been lit along the pathway in their dirty glass votives, and the air seeping in through an entrance made their pale flames dip and flicker. Something scuttled away when I moved, but there was nobody else with me in there – no one living. No Medusa.

I was alone, in a way I hadn't been for weeks. No stirrings inside my belly, no little parasite.

I dragged myself up from the floor, my limbs frozen and stiff. I rubbed and rubbed at my hands, tugged Medusa's housecoat more tightly around me, the overripe scent of her a strange comfort. The elbows were worn and patchy with mildew, and clumps of matted grey hair clung to the material.

I found myself staring, suddenly, at the stolen film still – in the candlelight, Sherman's blonde grasped for a book of horror and averted her gaze. I plucked the card away and slipped it inside Medusa's pocket. *It's a kind of exchange we make*, she'd said.

Outside the arched doorway: the drip of snowmelt and an inky sky, thick fog drifting across the lawns. I must have been out cold for the entire day. How many hours had I lain there, alone? I felt delirious, forsaken. Statues rose eerily from the fog, but I couldn't find a human figure among them. In the distance, a large dog sniffed around one of the headstones. I made my way towards it through the dazzling snow and haze.

When I reached the headstone there were only animal prints in the snow, but they made me feel better somehow. I must have seen a dog. I slumped to rest against the grave, its surface covered with gritty ice. The cold seeped into the bruised core of me, and I allowed myself to think of the wool coat. The sleeve pressed to my cheek as the wool bloomed red. Medusa would surely have completed the burial – it was her insistence that we bury it, her belief in offerings. Dust to dust. What if I went and dug the coat up? What would I find? The fog whispered to me about transformation, as if what we'd planted could have been a seed.

I opened my mouth to call her name. But the only word I had was the myth that had become attached to her, a name chosen to further estrange her. *It's better no one knows*, she'd said, when I'd asked for her real one. *It's better if they can't find you*. 'Medusa,' I rasped, hoping my voice would carry across the open fields. This was the emptiest space I'd experienced in the city, yet I knew it was full of bodies, underneath. 'Med-usa!' A chill broke through my bones – I had the sense that she was out there, frozen in place like one of the statues, starved in ice, unresponsive and shrouded by mist.

I felt myself being pulled into sleep, slumped against a stranger's headstone. *I'll just close my eyes*, I thought, my limbs screaming. *I'm so tired. I can't make it back*. But as I drifted into half-dream, a sound pierced the murk. A strange bleating, and then a high, sharp bark that sounded almost like a scream.

I peered around the headstone in the direction of the bark. What I saw was the mouth of the cemetery – two stone pillars – and in the space between them, the shape of a deer. A pair of eyes glowed in the dark: *tapetum lucidum*, eyeshine. What light they were reflecting I couldn't tell, but they were looking directly at me. I hadn't been abandoned: I was wearing Medusa's robe. She had protected me, after all.

In another moment, the deer had turned away its gaze and sunk lithely into shadow. Outside the cemetery gates, across the street, a bus pulled into the stop.

Despite the horror of my appearance, no one flinched as I boarded the too-bright bus. Wearing the robe was like being inside a different body. I'd made a Medusa of myself in the mauve housecoat, dripping coins from her pocket into the machine until the driver waved me on. I sat under the glare of the interior lights, trying to look through the window but mainly encountering my own pale reflection, dirt streaked across my face. I wondered what I smelt like to the other riders, shadowy presences I could feel but dared not look at.

Blood had dried into thick scales between my thighs; under the housecoat, my skin felt raw and cracked, my body irrevocably altered. I blinked back tears and pulled at a thread in the worn fabric of Medusa's housecoat, which seemed to give off its own heat, like something alive. My solitary face in the black bus window reminded me with a pang of that first journey on the SkyTrain with Izzy, how companionable we'd looked in the dark glass, how like sisters, our faces overlapping.

Inside, I still carried the ache of the birthing. Now and then, a tremor of pain shot through me. *Afterpain*, I thought, a word which made no sense because the pain was ongoing even as I named it. But when I got up from the seat at my stop, there was at least no smear of blood beneath me.

I made my way back to Izzy's building – my thighs chafing painfully, the blood there a thick dark crust – nursing a primal longing to be inside, to be swaddled and enfolded, as if the apartment might serve as a kind of cocoon. I knew my body had given something, had let something go. That something else needed to be restored.

The pavements were flecked with dirty blue salt, the oaks smothered with snow. At the intersection I paused to look up, to find Izzy's balcony, the square of yellow light suggesting she was home. All that had happened in the bedroom was beginning to seem shrouded and unreal, though I could still conjure the taste of the gag in my mouth, and my wrists were scrubbed pink, a tender place at the cuffs of Medusa's housecoat where the icy air bit into my skin.

I pulled Medusa's key from her pocket. It felt weighty and smooth in the palm of my hand, like something from another century. I eyed the modern glass door uncertainly, but the key slid into the lock without issue. Slowly, as if something might shatter, I turned the key and let myself inside. There was an eerie emptiness in the lobby, and the palm-printed wallpaper and psychedelic carpets looked banal and regular, like any liminal space. The glass-fronted manager's office was empty, too, and the screens along the west wall inside it displayed ordinary black and white footage of the car park and courtyard garden. No phantoms, no ghosts. Not even another occupant.

I wondered what state Medusa's well would be in if I rode the lift down to the basement. Whether the wall would let me past. What might be lurking underneath.

I called the lift and met my reflection again as the doors opened, seeing myself more clearly now in the overhead lights – the dark, bloody smears across my face, the mauve of Medusa's rotting robe hanging oddly from my shoulders, my bloodied sweatpants. I opened the housecoat and lifted my shirt, traced my fingers across my alien belly, still swollen, and the dark smudge of the *linea nigra*.

I lingered outside Izzy's front door, my hand raised to knock.

Lingered too long, because soon there came sniffing and scratching at the door, and a moment later it swung open and Izzy stood in front of me – Sunshine somehow at her feet – her face melting instantly into hot terror.

She said my name, *Brooke* – how odd it sounded – and pulled my soiled body against hers, gripping my shoulders and pressing herself so tightly against my belly it hurt. Her embrace was agony, her heart thudding against my chest. She took my hand and pulled me over the threshold, the dog nosing my legs, pushing his muzzle into my other, dropped hand.

Behind Izzy, the door to the bedroom was open, and the walls had been scrubbed to a sullied magnolia, free of the creeping mildew and my fecund cave art but still bearing their shadows. The place hung with a heavy disinfectant smell, and the carpet was clean. In the living room the tree had been taken down – there were no pine needles on any surface. I looked at Izzy's hand in mine and saw her skin was chapped and scraped raw with the labour of her purging.

'You're freezing,' she said, blowing onto my hands. 'Is that . . . blood? Are you hurt?'

'It's dirt.' I couldn't find any more words. I held on to my sister, giving in sweetly to a sudden weakness, grateful as I rested my body against hers.

'Let me run you a hot bath. I'm so sorry, Brooke. Where did you go?' She pushed my filthy hair away from my face. 'What about the baby?'

The baby, the baby, an endless echo. 'It's gone,' I said, not having the fight to explain about the cemetery, the bloodstained coat, Medusa's well. Izzy looked at me in a new way, her red-raw hands going to her throat, a sound escaping from her mouth.

She let out a strange animal cry, her face suddenly sodden and terrible, and sank to the floor, where I joined her, exhausted, her body shuddering against my own.

In the still dark, we woke. I lay there for a while, sprawled on the living room floor with my sister, our limbs tangled and the dog breathing between us. When Sunshine noticed me stirring, his tail thumped against the carpet. It was a comfort to see him there, and I reached out to tousle his ears.

The building made its usual nocturnal noises, but they seemed benign and unremarkable, and there was a strange peace in the room with us. I couldn't feel Medusa's presence behind the walls, nor the intrusive thrum that had tormented me. Something had loosened its grip. I wondered if Kioko had registered the difference, whether her haunted drawings would stop. I would have to thank her for the gift of the nightlight, return it to its rightful place at her bedside. I hoped she wouldn't need it any more, that our ritual had banished the shapeshifting ghosts from the walls, that the parasite had lost its chokehold on the Leonora.

I turned to my sister and saw her outline in the ever-present glow from the window, the city beyond it, her eyelashes blinking open and closed, her breath steady. In the low light, her silhouetted face looked so much like our mother's.

'How are you feeling?' I whispered. 'Did you sleep?'

'Not much,' she said, looking at the ceiling. 'You slept like the dead.' She turned towards me. 'You were snoring.'

'I dreamed we were far away from here,' I said. 'In the future. We were happy.'

'Why?' she asked.

'I can't remember.' Sunshine rolled beneath my hand so I was stroking the soft folds of his neck. 'When did you get the dog back?'

'I called Lucie when you left. She helped me clean the place. I wanted to try to find you, but . . . I didn't know where to start. With any of it. And I thought maybe . . . you were safer. Without me.' Izzy sighed and lay on her back again. 'I feel restless. I've been lying here all night thinking about what happened. What I . . . what I did to you.'

'You weren't yourself,' I said.

'What if I was?' she said. 'What if that's who I am?'

'I know you've lost something here.' I watched her eyelashes flicker; she reached out to brush me with the back of her hand, tentative, as if afraid to feel the absence under my skin.

'So have you,' she said. 'What will we tell Mum?'

The question surprised me. I hadn't thought of telling anybody anything – I wanted to shut it away. Perhaps that's what Izzy was testing. Whether I would tell on her. The idea felt almost deliciously small and incongruous.

'We'll tell her we're sorry for missing Christmas,' I said. 'We'll tell her . . . we went away somewhere and we couldn't call her. We'll tell her we tried to call her, but we just couldn't, and we're sorry for being such terrible daughters.'

'I'm not sure that will cut it,' Izzy said. 'We can tell her . . . tell her that I had some crisis.'

I almost laughed at this vague euphemism. 'We can't do that. She'll want details.'

'*I* want details,' Izzy said, suddenly desperate. 'I need to know what happened. I need to know *why*. What made me . . . It was so scary.'

'I know.' My fingers were toying with the frayed sleeves of Medusa's housecoat, which I still wore over my shattered body. I slipped my hand inside the pocket and fished out the film still I'd reclaimed from the columbarium. With Izzy's eyes on me, I heaved my body up from the floor, shambled over to the bookshelf, and reached to place the art card. There, outside its frame and propped against Izzy's books, was our family photograph. Izzy and Mum with their matching plaits, Dad's hand resting on Mum's pregnant belly, so tender. Me as a baby, sitting in Dad's lap with my shock of copper hair. The crease in the centre bent the image slightly, so that we all folded towards each other. I ran my finger along the crease and, almost as an afterthought, traced a circle around my smiling infant face.

'If Mum was here in this room with us,' I said, 'and you didn't have to hide or explain anything to her, if she just knew by looking at us, the way she does sometimes – what would you want to say?'

Izzy chewed her bottom lip, then pulled herself up to sit with her legs crossed. In concentration, her face took on the contours of our mother's again – in the strange city light that fell across her cheekbone, in the cosmic dust of our existence. When she opened her mouth, part of me expected her to echo one of Mum's sayings.

'Please let me come through this,' she said.

The sentence was disarmingly simple. 'Please . . .' I began, but my voice faltered, suddenly thick with grief, and I sank back to the floor. My limbs ached not just from the birth but from being tied down to the bed by my sister. My God.

I took a deep breath, exhaled. 'Please let me come through this,' I said. 'Yeah, it's good.' I recognized something, hearing the lyric wavering through the wall in a child's voice. *Even in my fear, let me pass.*

'Please let me come through this,' Izzy said, blinking tears that spilled down her cheeks. I knew she wasn't talking about what had happened in the bedroom. She meant the hysterectomy, the years of pain, the trying, the betrayal of her body. She was asking our mother to save her, to get her to the other side.

I moved to sit opposite Izzy and put my hands on her knees. She looked at me and her face was fervent, it was wreckage; I felt trapped and frightened by her longing, but I couldn't turn away from my sister, I would never be able to turn away from her again.

We murmured the words together, our voices overlapping, our fingers threaded. 'Please let me come through this.' I was talking about the bloody wool coat, the graveyard dirt on my knees. The bad thing that had tried to gather its parts together in the well. To birth itself through me.

Even though the nightlight was not playing, was not even in the room with us, the room span with horses and stars. I touched Izzy's wet face with the back of my hand, and she leaned forward and folded me in her arms. 'Please let me come through this,' she cried, burying her face in my shoulder, and when she said it again the words were indecipherable because she was speaking into the curve of my neck, but of course I understood her anyway, through my body, to my bones.

We washed and dressed in the January dark, sharing the bathroom, ignoring the shattered glass of the mirror, seeing ourselves in each other instead. Izzy's hands were familiar and practised as she leaned over the side of the bathtub to sponge the blood from my face and wash my hair, her fingers raking my scalp. I took the sponge from her to bathe the caked blood from between my thighs, to soak my bloated belly, while she did me the kindness of looking away. My abdomen was distended and painful, but I couldn't feel the pressure of the knot moving underneath. My skin, though swollen and tender, still streaked by scars, no longer felt ready to split.

Izzy had gathered the blonde hair at the nape of her neck, her face austere in its cleanliness. With fondness I thought of the purple line that used to stain her earlobes and neck whenever she used the box-dye. Her body no longer seemed to pain her, and her fluidity suggested a sense of belonging, of being in the place she was supposed to be. But her shoulders still folded inwards, as if she needed to protect herself from something – from me, perhaps, or the grief of the lost baby, the future she'd almost had.

Izzy looked alarmed as the bath water turned pink, but only caught my eye and swallowed whatever it was she'd been about to say. I stared back at her, defiant.

'Do you want to sleep some more?' she asked, scrunching my hair dry with a towel.

'No. I want to keep walking.' The pain was worse when my body was still, but in truth I was a little afraid of the bedroom, being confined there, scared of my sister and how little my life had meant to her. My suitcase was still in the basement.

Izzy nodded, as if she knew all that.

Medusa's warning throbbed beneath my skin: *If it slithers its way out of you in that room . . . you'll be in the grip of it.* A curl of blood stained the bathwater, a red bloom. I felt again the suck and pull of the feelers wrap around my leg, the ridged mouth against my shoulder. I shivered, splashed the water so that the blood dissipated, and climbed out of the bath, my reflection cleaved by the broken mirror.

If I'd been tied to the bed when the pains began, that turning screw, would something have been born in that room? To me? To Izzy? Would the knotted thing have swallowed me in the well, eviscerated me? A tremor of fear and revulsion ran through me.

We put the dog on the lead and took him out into the snow – the streets soft, dripping and abandoned. He led us towards the park, leaving a trail of prints behind us, the dog alert and happy, his nose to the ground. On the walk, Izzy watched my movements, pensive, waiting for me to speak, to offer explanation for something that couldn't be explained. Her cheeks were rosy and when we reached the herons' nests she stuffed her hands under her armpits. The tension strung taut between us like a cord.

The ground was sheltered here, the air warmed by the earth, and Sunshine sniffed around in the exposed roots of the firs, a puzzle between our feet. 'I wonder what he likes about this place.' Aching from my core, I tilted my head to look at the sky; there were no stars, and snow had begun to fall in soft wisps. Come spring the nests above us would brim with life again, the great blues returning to mate, to incubate and fledge, and my sister would stand beneath them in wonder, without me, without the child she'd almost willed into being.

Izzy shook her head. 'Where . . .' she asked, following my gaze to look at the outline of the tree canopy against the sky, 'where did it go?'

In the clearing, the world seemed small and quiet. The rhododendrons grew around us in a huddle, their shapes and shadows reminding me of Medusa, the dark green tendrils glistening with ice. Where had she gone? Was she safe? Had she been released? I thought of the mauve housecoat I'd discarded on the bathroom floor, an item of clothing that Izzy had studiously ignored. When I got home, I'd fold it lovingly, press it to my cheek, begin to catalogue the traces of Medusa.

Soon the sun would rise over the other side of the city, its light sweeping the ocean before us, seeping into blue, and by noon fissures would melt in the snow. The bright, golden aspen had lost all its leaves, and what remained of them was buried, rotting beneath ice. But the memory of them still burned against the changing sky.

'I had to bury it,' I said. I owed it to her to tell her something of the truth.

'What?' Izzy's eyes snapped to the swollen outline of my belly, comprehending something – perhaps for the first time – of what had moved through me. 'What did you bury?' She was closer to me now, her hands gripping my elbows.

'It was nothing,' I told her, breathless, the phrase ringing falsely in the gap between us. My body remembered the way the gore had fallen apart in my hands, returning to the pool, sliding out of my arms. Was it *nothing*? I didn't know. But I knew what my sister would picture, the baby her heart wanted, and whatever had moved through me, it wasn't that. 'I bled out into your wool coat, and then I buried it. I'm sorry.' I opened my jacket, lifted the clean shirt to bare my belly, flakes of snow landing to melt on my skin. It was difficult to see the inkblot markings in the dim, the dark smudge that still crept down the middle of me, the *linea nigra*. Would it mark me forever?

'No,' she said, her face threatening collapse.

I put her hand on my belly so she could feel the difference – how still, how quiet underneath. 'There was no baby, Izzy.'

Her eyes left the markings stretched across my belly to meet mine. I cupped her face with my other hand, so she wouldn't turn away. A feeling moved between us, something beyond definition, and she made a small sound of grief and clutched her own body. I recognized the feeling passing between us as akin to the strange kind of love I'd felt for the knot baby, our little parasite, a love tipped all over with fear.

We held each other like that as the snow fell in a shiver. I rested my forehead against hers, something about the cloud of our mingled breath, our creased bellies, and the falling snow making a way for intimacy. I put my hands over her scar, the place they'd cut the growth out, the part of her they'd taken away, as if I might feel a kick.

Author's Note

Thank you to Sarah J. Sloat and Sarabande Books for allowing me to quote from *Hotel Almighty*, a book-length erasure poem of Stephen King's *Misery*. The authoritative line from Sloat's text reads 'you could hardly have missed the *Thousands of impossible flowers known in the technical jargon as* laughing'. The line Brooke admires is from the version of this poem published online in *Escape into Life:* 'you could hardly have missed the *Thousands of impossible flowers* trying to be born'. I'm very pleased to be able to include it in my novel.

Acknowledgements

It gives me such pleasure to thank everyone who made this book possible: the teams at HarperCollins and Borough Press, especially my three brilliant editors, Suzie Dooré, Jennifer Lambert, and Liz Velez. This novel transformed more than once thanks to your wise and generous readings, and I'm grateful for the creative alchemy you brought to it. I feel very lucky. Thank you to my agents, Evan Brown and Amanda Orozco, for your dedication, your kindness, and your belief in the book.

I wrote the first draft while studying for an MFA in Creative Writing at the University of British Columbia, and give my enduring thanks to Alix Ohlin, whose sharp insights, timely questions, and boundless encouragement were essential in bringing this novel to life. Thank you to Sheryda Warrener for teaching me to see new possibilities in language and art, on the page and in the world beyond it. My heartfelt thanks to Hiromi Goto for our conversations about mommy horror and her invaluable notes on the novel. My work on this project was also made possible by a SSHRC Canada Graduate Scholarship and the support of the British Columbia Arts Council, for which I am very grateful.

This novel is, in part, my small tribute to feminist horror in cinema, literature, and visual art. I'm grateful for the work that has gone before, for the stories that continue to enrich and transform the genre, and to the readers and audiences who seek them out.

I wrote this story with my whole, terrified heart, and I'm deeply grateful for my friends and family who supported me through the writing process in countless ways. Thank you to my sisters and nieces, and especially to my big sister for getting on a plane when my daughter was born. Thanks always to my mum and dad, who once ripped a Stephen King novel in half because the other couldn't wait to start reading it. Thanks to Albie for being the original mashed potato.

To Shane – for the gift of your kindness, humour, and love, and for everything we've made together. And to Saoirse, the love of our lives, for all the joy you bring us.